VANGUARD

What Reviewers Say About Gun Brooke's Work

Ice Queen

"I'm a sucker for a story about a single mother and in this case, it really adds depth to Susanna's character. The conflict that threatens Susanna and Aislin's future isn't a convoluted series of events. It's the insecurities they each bring into the relationship that they're forced to acknowledge and deal with. To me this felt authentic. The book is a quick read with plenty of spice..."—*Lesbian Review*

Treason

"The adventure was edge-of-your-seat levels of gripping and exciting. ...I really enjoyed this final addition to the Exodus series and particularly liked the ending. As always it was a very well written book."—Melina Bickard, Librarian, Waterloo Library (UK)

Insult to Injury

"This novel tugged at my heart all the way, much the same way as *Coffee Sonata*. It's a story of new beginnings, of rediscovering oneself, of trusting again (both others and oneself)."—*Jude in the Stars*

"If you love a good, slow-burn romantic novel, then grab this book."—*Rainbow Reflections*

"[A] light romance that left me with just the right amount of 'aw shucks' at the end."—*C-Spot Reviews*

"I was glad to see a disabled lead for a change, and I enjoyed the author's style—the book was written in the first person alternating between the main characters and I felt that gave me more insight into each character and their motivations."—Melina Bickard, Librarian, Waterloo Library (UK)

Wayworn Lovers

"*Wayworn Lovers* is a super dramatic, angsty read, very much in line with Brooke's other contemporary romances. …I'm definitely in the 'love them' camp."—*Lesbian Review*

Thorns of the Past

"What I really liked from the offset is that Brooke steered clear of the typical butch PI with femme damsel in distress trope. Both main characters are what I would call ordinary women—they both wear suits for work, they both dress down in sweatpants and sweatshirts in the evening. As a result, I instantly found it a lot easier to relate, and connect with both. Each of their pasts hold dreadful memories and pain, and the passages where they opened up to each other about those events were very moving."—*Rainbow Reviews*

"I loved the romance between Darcy and Sabrina and the story really carried it well, with each of them learning that they have a safe haven with the other."—*Lesbian Review*

Escape: Exodus Book Three

"I've been a keen follower of the Exodus series for a while now and I was looking forward to the latest installment. It didn't disappoint. The action was edge-of-your-seat thrilling, especially towards the end, with several threats facing the Exodus mission. Some very intriguing subplots were introduced, and I look forward to reading more about these in the next book."—Melina Bickard, Librarian, Waterloo Library, London (UK)

Pathfinder

"I found the characters very likable and the plot compelling. I loved watching their relationship grow. From their first meeting, they're impressed and intrigued by each other. This matures into an easy friendship, and from there into dancing, kisses, and more. …I'm looking forward to seeing the rest of the series!"—*All Our Worlds: Diverse Fantastic Fiction*

Soul Unique

"This is the first book that Gun Brooke has written in a first person perspective, and that was 100% the correct choice. She avoids the pitfalls of trying to tell a story about living with an autism spectrum disorder that she's never experienced, instead making it the story of someone who falls in love with a person living with Asperger's. …*Soul Unique* is her best. It was an ambitious project that turned out beautifully. I highly recommend it."—*Lesbian Review*

"Yet another success from Gun Brooke. The premise is interesting, the leads are likeable and the supporting characters are well-developed. The first person narrative works well, and I really enjoyed reading about a character with Asperger's."—Melina Bickard, Librarian, Waterloo Library (London)

Advance: Exodus Book One

"*Advance* is an exciting space adventure, hopeful even through times of darkness. The romance and action are balanced perfectly, interesting the audience as much in the fleet's mission as in Dael and Spinner's romance. I'm looking forward to the next book in the series!"—*All Our Worlds: Diverse Fantastic Fiction*

The Blush Factor

"Gun Brooke captures very well the two different 'worlds' the two main characters live in and folds this setting neatly into the story. So, if you are looking for a well-edited, multi-layered romance with engaging characters this is a great read and maybe a re-read for those days when comfort food is a must."—*Lesbians on the Loose*

The Supreme Constellations Series

"[*Protector of the Realm*] is first and foremost a romance, and whilst it has action and adventure, it is the romance that drives it. The book moves along at a cracking pace, and there is much happening throughout to make it a good page-turner. The action sequences are very well done, and make for an adrenaline rush."
—*Lesbian Review*

"Brooke is an amazing author. Never have I read a book where I started at the top of the page and don't know what will happen two paragraphs later. She keeps the excitement going, and the pages turning."—*Family and Friends Magazine*

Fierce Overture

"Gun Brooke creates memorable characters, and Noelle and Helena are no exception. Each woman is 'more than meets the eye' as each exhibits depth, fears, and longings. And the sexual tension between them is real, hot, and raw."—*Just About Write*

September Canvas

"In this character-driven story, trust is earned and secrets are uncovered. Deanna and Faythe are fully fleshed out and prove to the reader each has much depth, talent, wit and problem-solving abilities. *September Canvas* is a good read with a thoroughly satisfying conclusion."—*Just About Write*

Sheridan's Fate—*Lambda Literary Award Finalist*

"Sheridan's fire and Lark's warm embers are enough to make this book sizzle. Brooke, however, has gone beyond the wonderful emotional explorations of these characters to tell the story of those who, for various reasons, become differently-abled. Whether it is a bullet, an illness, or a problem at birth, many women and men find themselves in Sheridan's situation. Her courage and Lark's gentleness and determination send this romance into a 'must read.'"—*Just About Write*

Coffee Sonata

"In *Coffee Sonata*, the lives of these four women become intertwined. In forming friendships and love, closets and disabilities are discussed, along with differences in age and backgrounds. Love and friendship are areas filled with complexity and nuances. Brooke takes her time to savor the complexities while her main characters savor their excellent cups of coffee. If you enjoy a good love story, a great setting, and wonderful characters, look for Coffee Sonata at your favorite gay and lesbian bookstore." —*Family & Friends Magazine*

Course of Action

"Brooke's words capture the intensity of their growing relationship. Her prose throughout the book is breathtaking and heart-stopping. Where have you been hiding, Gun Brooke? I, for one, would like to see more romances from this author."—*Independent Gay Writer*

Visit us at www.boldstrokesbooks.com

By the Author

Romances
Course of Action
Coffee Sonata
Sheridan's Fate
September Canvas
Fierce Overture
Speed Demons
The Blush Factor
Soul Unique
A Reluctant Enterprise
Piece of Cake
Thorns of the Past
Wayworn Lovers
Insult to Injury
Ice Queen
Limelight
Her Boss's Wife
Scarlet Love

Science Fiction

Supreme Constellations Series
Protector of the Realm
Rebel's Quest
Warrior's Valor
Pirate's Fortune

Exodus Series
Advance
Pathfinder
Escape
Arrival
Treason

The Dennamore Scrolls
Yearning
Velocity
Homeworld

Freedom Series
Skyscraper
Vanguard

Lunar Eclipse
Renegade's War
The Amaranthine Law

Novella Anthology
Change Horizons

VANGUARD

by

Gun Brooke

2025

VANGUARD
© 2025 By Gun Brooke. All Rights Reserved.

ISBN 13: 978-1-63679-818-9

This Trade Paperback Original Is Published By
Bold Strokes Books, Inc.
P.O. Box 249
Valley Falls, NY 12185

First Edition: August 2025

Credits
Editor: Shelley Thrasher
Production Design: Susan Ramundo
Cover Design By Gun Brooke
Photos From www.pexels.com

Acknowledgments

Writing this series is so rewarding and challenging in the best of ways, I'm ready to thank whatever deity made me focus my mind enough to dive into it. The characters are so vivid to me, and I see the world my mind envisions so clearly—in the year 2502.

Working on a series is wrestling with a beast of your own making. It sometimes happens that my wonderful readers remember details even better than I do, and I try to be as meticulous as I can—but unsurprisingly, I usually end up with a discrepancy or two. What still makes all that extra work worth it is the amazing relationship I develop with my characters, as I get to know them intimately and down to their molecules. Sometimes a reader will feel they get really attached to one or more of the characters too, and we end up having interesting conversations about them and the story.

I want you, my reader, to know that I am humbled and happy that you chose to buy my book. I am grateful that you take time out of your busy life and allow me to entertain you for a while. I hope you will continue to like this series.

I owe my editor, Dr. Shelley Thrasher, so much, as usual. Shelley, you are such a big part of what makes writing fun for me. I'm so glad to be working with you on my manuscripts.

I want to thank Bold Strokes Books, and that means everyone from Radclyffe, Sandra, Cindy, Stacia, Toni, Ruth, and those I don't always know the name of, who work tirelessly to make BSB a wonderful home for writers.

My first readers, Annika, Eden, Gin, Mayra, and Sam, thank you for all the hours you have put into beta reading and encouraging me. It's a lot of fun to read your comments and educational to see what you pick up in the first draft.

On a very personal note, I want to tell my precious family, especially my children, Malin and Henrik, that I really appreciate that you take pride in what I do. So do the older among my grandchildren, and one of them, William, together with Henrik, was part of brainstorming ideas about a futuristic society where some people live in skyscrapers and others live in tunnels and sewers. That was especially fun for me!

My group of painter friends, my brother and sister-in-law, my two neighbors who are also my very good friends, mean so much to me, and you help me in so many other ways which in turn helps me gather my energy to keep writing.

My fanfiction friends—without you, there would not be any books at all. That's where it all began, and it's still such an amazingly rewarding and fun place to hang out online. I appreciate all of you!

And lastly, on the sappiest of notes, I want to give a shoutout to my dogs. They care for me unconditionally, when everyone else is busy doing something else.

Dedication

For Malin and Henrik
Always

Chapter One

Beth pushed herself out of her seat of the SkyBird, the sleek, cigar-shaped vessel she and her friends had used to escape the corrupt authorities of ESC, Eastern Seaboard City. Having flown from the secret area installed above the 926th floor in the skyscraper they had just evacuated from, they had been in the air for more than two hours with the other 449 vessels. Their random flight paths helped confuse the ESC forces unavoidably launched to pursue them.

"How's everyone?" Kaelyn Dark called out. As the leader of the group of resistance fighters Beth belonged to, she always made sure her team was all right. She had frequented the tunnels and other underground areas far beneath the skyscrapers that lined most of the former US East Coast and never hesitated to take the initiative, if required. A tall, sinewy woman with short, dark hair, she was already on her feet, going from person to person in the eight-seater SkyBird belonging to the Garcia family.

"I'm good, Kae. Where are we?" Beth walked over to the hatch. From there, she could see that her other comrade in arms, Foster, a grizzly bear of a man, was all right and standing up.

"No clue. Have to check with those who know how to interpret the navigational system." Kae bent over Dr. Rayne Garcia, who had just endured emergency surgery. "Rayne?"

"I'm a bit jostled, but I'm all right. Thirsty, though." Rayne, the Celestial doctor, born and bred in luxury in the skyscrapers, had risked her life more than once to help the disenfranchised Subterranean people in the tunnels. After being shot by a high-yield energy weapon, she had undergone surgery well, but she looked pale.

"Here." Kae pulled a bottle of water from Rayne's armrest. "Drink." She caressed Rayne's cheek quickly before moving on to the next former patient. An eight-year-old boy, Wes, sat behind Rayne across the aisle from his sister, Tania, who had already checked on him. Wes's eyes were huge in his small face, but he seemed okay, as far as Beth could see.

Rayne's parents, Madelon and Rocque Garcia, appeared from the front. "That went better than I feared," Madelon, stylish and calm even now, said. "Judging from the instruments, we are where our leadership programmed us to be. Approximately."

Rocque, Rayne's father, wrapped an arm around his wife and regarded Rayne intently. "Nothing came undone when we went through the turbulence earlier?"

"I'm all right, Father." Rayne looked back at Wes. "I should examine you, young man."

"Not a chance. Not yet." Kae placed a hand on her shoulder. "We need to check where the others have landed first. Some are probably close and others spread out within certain parameters."

"Most likely," Madelon said. "The dissident leadership has weekly used a complex algorithm to alter the flight plans slightly over the years in case we were infiltrated. Delmonte's SkyBird makes it possible for her to remain in contact with the larger vessel that holds our computer core. Any last-minute alterations would have been instantaneous."

"I still say we need to open this damn hatch," Beth said, growing impatient. She hadn't breathed unfiltered air since she left her home in the tunnels a week ago. "Come on."

"Beth's right. While Madelon and Rocque contact their leadership, we need to establish a perimeter and make sure those we might spot from here are all right."

Beth looked expectantly at the Garcias and indicated the hatch. "Well?"

Madelon appeared close to rolling her eyes but stepped over and pressed her face into an indentation that resembled a mask made from glass. "There. Now, all of you can open and close it via voice command. But—" She held up a hand when Beth opened her mouth. "Before you leave, we all need to put on a tactical suit and a GemLink."

"A what?" Kae maneuvered past Rayne.

"The GemLink? It's a wristband that will help us communicate. Later I'll help you install all the features, or at least the ones you're comfortable using. But for now, proximity alert, communication, and general alerts are default settings. The band will read your biosignature, but it will only broadcast that information to someone else if you allow it."

Rocque had pulled a flat box from a storage compartment next to the hatch and now opened it. Beth craned her neck to see. Ten items that resembled bracelets sat in marked indentations in the box. The two at the top contained symbols Beth couldn't decipher and a milky stone.

"Is that the gem part of the GemLink?" Beth asked and studied Rocque as he placed the item against his left wrist.

"You're not wrong, Beth," he said. "Put one on your non-dominant hand. It'll attach and self-adjust."

"Not sure about this," Foster said. "But I suppose." He accepted a GemLink from Madelon and looked surprised when it circled his wrist and attached itself without a problem, despite his muscular frame.

Beth put hers on and handed one to each Tania and Wes. Madelon gave the last one marked by a symbol to Rayne, who slowly put it on.

When they were all outfitted, Madelon stood where everyone could see her. "It is voice controlled, but if you prefer stealth, you can tap the gem and then operate the hovering screen that appears above it."

Beth thought of the massive screen she'd seen disappear into thin air in Rayne's apartment in the skyscraper they had just fled from. She tapped the gem and flinched when a screen seemed to shoot out from her wrist. There she could read what looked like her vital signs, and small dots appeared to indicate the individuals standing around her.

"All right. We'll have to learn on the fly," Kae said.

"The suits you talked about?" Beth said. "I'm not joking. I need to get out of this can."

Kae patted her shoulder. "Soon. Just breathe."

Rocque opened a narrow cabinet and pulled it out. "They're self-adjusting. Here. Helmets. Same goes for them. They'll save you from a blast to the head. The suits will absorb energy blasts from most known weapons. Just put them on top of what you're wearing."

"Will you help Rayne into hers?" Kae asked, and Beth looked over at the woman who had fallen asleep again in her seat.

"We'll help her and the children." Madelon gripped Kae's shoulders. "You have my word."

Beth was already in her suit and found that when she fastened the metal clasps, the suit molded itself to the shape of her body. It even fit around her boots. She tugged on the helmet and found it held all kinds of technology at the front. "This thing might just trip me up if it slides stuff in front of my face." She shook her head at Foster, who looked hesitatingly at the helmet that appeared too small. "Oh, please. Just tug it on. Your brain's not that big." She grinned at him, and for a moment she forgot about her claustrophobia.

Foster grimaced but pulled the helmet on and then chuckled when it expanded to fit him. "I'll be damned."

"The helmet has all the usual technology. Night-vision, visor, mapping, etcetera. I would imagine night-vision is the most important for you." Madelon looked them over. "You're all set."

"We need to arm ourselves before we exit," Beth said.

"Of course. No problem." Rocque opened a larger cabinet. "Nova blasters and shadow pulses. You know how the blasters work, and you've already used the shadow pulses. All of them are fully loaded, with extra energy pods available in their bodies."

"Excellent." Foster grabbed a Nova blaster. Kae and Beth followed suit, and Beth felt infinitely safer when she knew she could defend herself and her friends.

"Keep in touch via the GemLink," Madelon said and pulled a computer console onto her lap, where she sat next to her daughter. "In the meantime, I'm going to try to reach our leadership."

Beth looked sternly at the sensors sitting around the hatch's frame. "Hatch open." Would being direct work? At first, she didn't think so, but then she heard a soft hiss, accompanied by a whirring sound, and the hatch opened and slid up along the ceiling bulkhead.

"It's rather intimidating, stepping out into nature." Kae moved past Beth, giving her a crooked smile. She stepped outside with her Nova blaster ready and made a familiar gesture for Beth and Foster to follow.

Beth's blaster was set to stun, but she also made sure she knew where the sensor for set-to-kill was located. This state-of-the-art version of her remodeled old weapon from her life in the tunnels seemed familiar, but its capabilities appeared endless. It was however reassuringly similar, and she moved into formation behind Kae, with Foster at her side.

"I see shapes up ahead," Kae said in a low voice and checked her GemLink. "According to this thing, they're friendlies."

"Let's hope they think we are as well." Beth spoke under her breath. She was getting used to the settling dusk, and the faint moonlight from above the clouds created enough light for her to make out the closest forms. She had seen enough trees to figure out what they were. The ground was uneven, which she was used to, but she hadn't felt the high grass around her feet before now. She had to raise her feet higher than usual, which felt weird.

"We're going to have to split up but stay within sensor range. I won't be happy if I lose track of either of you in the wilderness. All right?" Kae glanced sternly at Foster and Beth.

"Got it," Beth said. "I'll head toward the height over there." She pointed and then checked her GemLink. "Eh, southwest of us."

"I'll head toward the grove over there." Foster pointed southeast. "I've always wanted to see real-life wild trees."

"You're ridiculous." Kae snorted and checked her device. "That means I'll go toward the contacts due north. I expect you to report in every half hour."

"Aye." Foster raised his fist and then disappeared in his chosen direction.

Beth bumped Kae's shoulder with her fist. "You stay safe, too, Kae. This is uncharted territory for us. And it's getting darker."

"Remember the features built in the helmet. Use them."

"All right. Do I just order them like with the hatch?"

"Night-vision on," Kae said, and when Beth saw a faint red glow around the edge of her visor, she repeated the command.

"Now that's more like it. Foster? Did you hear that?" She looked after him and could clearly see his outline.

"Yeah, already got that going. After they showed me how to inflate food in their skyscrapers, I made it a point to become tech-savvy." Foster raised his hand in the air. "Later. Let's find some more people."

"Strength in numbers," Kae said. "As the man said, later, Beth."

Beth started walking toward the ridge to the southwest. She checked her GemLink and did her best to keep a straight line through the shrubbery before her. Scanning the ground, she made sure she saw no signs of disturbed soil, which could mean someone had put down landmines. They had been subjected to that danger in the tunnels, and looking for traps was second nature for her and her comrades.

It was strange to imagine how her life had changed since Kae had decided to take young Wes to a skyscraper medical clinic. It had been only a little more than a week ago, and here they were, having helped create the situation where the Celestial dissidents, who had resided in the skyscrapers in secret for decades, were now on the run. Beth thought of her own people, who lived in hardship in the tunnels, and what might be happening there now.

Had all of the Celestial forces gone after the dissidents, or had the authorities sent them into the tunnels as well? Her stomach clenched at the thought of the men, women, and children who tried to stay alive down below, and how much she would like to be back there to help keep them safe.

After half an hour, Foster managed to start a joint communication channel with Beth and Kae. Neither of them had anything to report, but Kae said she was closing in on two other SkyBirds and that she saw movement on her GemLink.

Beth kept walking, and within ten minutes, she stood in front of some dense shrubbery that seemed impenetrable. She would have to go around it. Just to be sure she didn't miss anything, she raised her blaster and aimed among the bushes. Her visor appeared to realize what she was doing and increased its night-vision capabilities. As Beth slowly circled what looked like a small forest, she was certain no one would be able to walk through it without making a lot of noise.

Ready to continue, Beth was just about to turn to the right and continue circling the grove, when something shiny flashed enough to hurt her eyes. Throwing herself to the ground, Beth raised her GemLink to her lips. "Beth to Kae."

"Kae here."

"I've spotted something in that small forest before the ridge. It's shiny, and, damn, the visor nearly blinded me before it readjusted. I'm going in to investigate."

"Hey, be careful. Keep me on an open link. Remember that Foster is also on this channel in case we need to join you," Kae said quickly. "Use caution, Beth. Remember. Backup will take a while to reach you."

"Got it. I'm moving in." Relieved that her visor had readjusted itself, Beth pushed branches aside and made her way into the shrubs.

The smooth surface of the suit was a blessing, as some of the branches had evil thorns. She was wearing gloves, of sorts, but the damn things still caught her a few times just below her GemLink. Cursing, she used the blaster to push the branches and twigs aside. If this was what nature had to offer, she wondered why people romanticized it. A lot of Kae's old-fashioned paper books from the time when humanity resided all over the planet spoke of returning to nature, of living with it and respecting it. "How about if nature gives a little respect in return," she mumbled. "Ow. Fuck."

"You okay, kid?" Foster asked over his link.

"Just thorns. Nasty little suckers." Beth bent and crawled under a particularly vicious-looking branch, and when she stood, she found herself staring at a demolished SkyBird. "We have a crashed SkyBird here. I don't see any signs of life. The hatch is closed." She moved slowly around the bird.

"Can they have already left it and moved out?" Kae asked. "I'm five minutes from three SkyBirds, and they seem to have landed all right. As soon as I make contact, I'll move to your position. The people over here might be able to help."

"Same here. I see two SkyBirds about five or six minutes from my location. I'll return to you, Beth, when I've made contact. Be careful now. Don't hurt yourself." Foster sounded concerned.

"I'll be fine." Beth had been able to search only half the ship from the outside. She saw some smoke from beneath it, but no open flames. She walked back around it. The hatch seemed reasonably undamaged. She approached it, and, removing her gloves, she ran her fingertips around the edges. The metal was cool, which would suggest there wasn't a fire inside. If the nose of the SkyBird hadn't pointed forty-five degrees off the ground toward the sky, she might have been able to look through its only windows.

"Open hatch." She guessed the command wouldn't work, but it was worth a try. Glancing at her GemLink, she had an idea. "Beth to Madelon Garcia."

"Madelon here. Go on."

"I'm in a bit of a jam. I just found a crashed SkyBird and can't open the hatch. Is there a trick when it comes to emergencies, or any way to override it?" Beth asked. "Smoke's coming from underneath it."

"Let me put Rocque on. He's better with this part. Before I go, is there a sharp, sort of acerbic smell coming from it?"

Beth sniffed. "No. Just metal and whatever smell this thorny hell of a forest has."

"Good. Here's Rocque."

"Beth. I heard. This is what you do. I'll send you a diagnostic tool so we can find out which bird this is. Once I know that, I can send the signal to your link for you to use your voice command." Rocque spoke tersely.

"Go ahead," Beth said, keeping her eyes on her link, where green and yellow lines began running like a jagged stream of water. Once they stopped, she heard Rocque's voice again. "Beth. I'll try to find you all the help you'll need, but you have to get in there now." He sounded urgent, and behind him, Beth heard Madelon say, "Oh, Creator."

"What is it?" Beth stared at the SkyBird.

"This is LaSierra Delmonte's bird. It not only holds our leader, but also all the most important ways for us to gather our people. Our infrastructure."

"Delmonte's? Damn." Beth stared impatiently at her link. "Am I good to open the hatch?"

"Yes. If it's possible to open it after the crash, it should work now," Rocque said.

"Open hatch," Beth said, and the hatch began to move. At first it looked like it would simply slide all the way up, but halfway, it stopped with a rattling moan. "Rocque, it's half-open. I'm going in. I know Kae and Foster are doubling back to my coordinates, hopefully with help."

"Be careful," Rocque said.

"No problem." Beth shoved the blaster into the harness on her back. Getting on her hands and knees, she began to crawl into the crashed SkyBird, not knowing what she would find.

CHAPTER TWO

The half-opened hatch wasn't hard to push through, but inside the bird, something torn from the bulkhead created a hurdle for Beth as she wriggled inside. Still on a link with the others, she muttered, "It must've been some crash. It's like they've tumbled through the trees."

"Can you see LaSierra?" Madelon asked. "Or any of her team?"

"Hang on. Let me just push this thing aside if I can." Beth braced herself against the hatch frame and shoved the metal object. At first it seemed completely wedged in, but when she changed her angle, a loud, screeching sound pierced the air, and the console moved. As soon as the opening was big enough, she held her breath and stuck her head through first. A few lights were on, which meant the SkyBird wasn't dead. She prayed the passengers were alive also. She adjusted the settings on the visor by testing a few commands. Snorting to herself in the middle of this drama, she figured whoever invented these helmets had made them literally foolproof, considering she wasn't used to anything super high-tech.

The first person she came upon was an unconscious male, though he had a strong, solid pulse. Beth reported this find over the link and moved farther in, making sure she didn't step on anyone. A woman, also in uniform, sat slumped in her harness in a seat. She was facing a blinking console. Pressing two fingers to her carotid, Beth was relieved to find she was also alive. "Hey. Can you look at me?" Beth tried to pry the woman's eyelids up, but she was clearly unconscious. "Second security guard is also alive, but not communicative," Beth said over the link. "Moving on."

"We're half an hour away. Just make sure the ones you find are breathing and not bleeding out," Kae said.

"Affirmative. Although it's hard to know if they're bleeding somewhere I can't see. I can't move them."

"That's all right." Rayne's voice surprised Beth. "Don't move anyone unless their life is in danger. We need to secure their spine and neck."

"Got it. Good to hear that you're awake again, Doc." Beth smiled to herself. "Moving on again."

She pushed two seats that had broken off from the bulkhead to the side. When she rounded them, she had to grip the other seats to keep from sliding down the aisle, since the bird was leaning at a steep angle. After three rows of seats, the aisle widened, and that's when she saw two feet sticking out from under yet another blinking console. One foot wore an elegant shoe, and the other had just a thin stocking. Delmonte.

Beth knelt and pushed debris out of the way before ducking in under the console. The woman whom she recognized as LaSierra Delmonte looked up at her. She was pale, and blood trickled down the right side of her face from her hairline, but her amber eyes were open, and she blinked slowly.

"Hey. Are you okay?" Beth pressed her fingers against her neck. "Heart is racing. At least it's working. Let me see if I can get you out of here, and then we can help your guys."

"Where am I? Who are you? Damn it, who am I?" Delmonte grabbed Beth's arm. She looked panicked, and Beth realized she had to calm her down or she might worsen any potential injuries. She smiled gently and took Delmonte's ice-cold hand.

"I'm not sure I'm the right person to ask about our location, but my name's Beth. You are LaSierra Delmonte and, from this moment on, I suppose, the leader of the free world."

Delmonte stared at her, only to squeeze her eyes closed a moment later. "That doesn't make any sense. I understand that we've crashed. I talked to a person named Carson earlier. He sounded as if he was farther back."

"People are on the way to help us. We'll get everyone out." Beth hoped this Carson was alive too. "Do you remember how many security officers you brought with you?"

Glaring at Beth, Delmonte clenched her teeth. "I can barely remember my name, let alone any other details." She shifted but then cried out and pressed a hand to her side. "Creator…"

"Don't move. We have no way of knowing what kind of injuries you've sustained." Beth took both of Delmonte's hands in hers. "All you have to do is be still and let me know if you think you're bleeding anywhere else." She indicated Delmonte's head injury and tapped her visor. "Locate medical supplies."

Immediately, a grid lit up, and several areas in the SkyBird showed green dots as she looked around. One of them was in the armrest in the row of seats farther in. Beth pried it open and pulled out a flat box. In it, she found field dressings and wands, along with ten different infulizers, which she recognized from when Wes had been hospitalized in the skyscraper.

"Here we go." Beth moved the wand along Delmonte's seeping head wound, making sure she pushed the long hair out of the way first.

Delmonte winced as the wand ran its cleaning cycle. "Have you looked for the rest of my team?"

"A woman is unconscious farther toward the hatch, and I suspect that the others are behind the debris in the aft." Beth looked over in that direction and knew it would be a miracle if any of the security officers back there were still alive. "We'll retrieve them as soon as we can get tools in here. Right now, it's my job to keep you stable, all right?" Beth set the wand to mend and kept running it. "I know this stings, but I'm not a Celestial medic, and I better not administer any drugs."

"Probably smart." Delmonte growled quietly. "Damn!" She fumbled and found Beth's hip. She gripped it hard, and tears leaked down her temples and into her hair. "It's too painful. Please." She waved her free hand at Beth. "Stop."

"I'm almost done, Delmont—eh, LaSierra. Just a minute longer. Can you manage that?"

"No, but keep going." LaSierra didn't let go of Beth's hip. "Just hurry."

Beth focused on closing the gap properly, and when she turned off the wand, she heard a muted whimper from LaSierra.

"There you go." Relieved to be able to pack up the wand again, Beth pushed some debris aside and sat down next to LaSierra. "Have you found your bearings yet? Any more memories floating to the surface?" She wanted to keep LaSierra talking to be sure she was awake and alert until they could properly monitor her condition.

"It's better." Even the distant tone in her voice, almost standoffish, suggested that LaSierra was almost her old self. "I don't know how it happened, but the pain when you used the wand sharpened my senses. Very odd." She groaned softly. "I need to sit up. I'm on something sharp and it's…difficult."

Beth frowned. "I'm not sure that's a good idea. We don't know about any spinal injuries yet."

"Something might pierce me, and I could be bleeding out. It hurts, and I need to sit up. Now."

Beth shook her head. "You're wedged in there. I risk injuring you further if I try to pull you out. I'd never forgive myself if that happened."

"Creator! I can make it an order if that helps." Glaring up at Beth, LaSierra was obviously returning rapidly to her old warm and fuzzy self.

"You can try, but that doesn't move the debris and smooth out the bulkhead." Beth shrugged and engaged her link. "ETA of my backup, please. Our fearless leader is getting restless, and I worry she'll fight her way past me."

"Goodness." Madelon sighed. "Can she hear me?"

"Yes." Beth leaned closer to LaSierra.

"LaSierra. Don't be a fool. Listen to Beth. She's been in the field since she was a child. Use common sense and let us save you in a coordinated way."

LaSierra glared but raised her palm toward Beth. "Fine. Fine! Just get here." More tears welled up in LaSierra's eyes. Beth hated to see the proud, strong leader of the Celestial dissidents this vulnerable. It simply didn't sit well with her.

Sliding in farther under the console, Beth pushed loose wires out of her way. She supported her weight against her left elbow and wiped away LaSierra's overflowing tears with the thumb of her free hand. "There. Better."

LaSierra slowly turned her head toward Beth. "Do I smell smoke?"

Beth hadn't forgotten the smoke she'd seen when she inspected the SkyBird. "Yes, but so far no open flames, as far as I can tell."

"You shouldn't be in here," LaSierra said matter-of-factly. "In case there's an explosion…no need for you to sacrifice your life. You're not even a Celestial citizen, are you?"

"I'm not going anywhere until help arrives. As for my citizenship, it depends on who you ask. Run my chip through a Celestial computer and you'll find I have resided there my entire life. If you were to venture into the tunnels, you'd find the same there. I can play it either way."

"You're stubborn." Raising her chin, LaSierra pressed her finely chiseled lips together. "And illogical."

"I've been called worse, ma'am." Beth grinned and hoped LaSierra didn't realize Beth's motives for challenging her. Even if Delmonte argued with Beth, she didn't do anything stupid like trying to free herself.

A signal from Beth's link made her jump. "Kae to Beth. You still inside? We have located your position. The Celestials rebels brought a device to cut a path to LaSierra's bird."

"Beth here. LaSierra is the same as before. Glad you're here. We need to get some of them in here to move consoles and seats out of the way. Several people are here that I haven't been able to reach."

"Rocque performed a short-range scan, and from what he can tell, everyone in the bird appears to have active circulation and enough oxygen. Rayne says it can change at any time, which means we need to get LaSierra and the one we can see at the door out quickly."

"That'd be great." She placed a hand on LaSierra's. "Help's on the way."

"I heard, but did I hear it correctly—did that woman call my movement 'rebels'?" LaSierra scowled. "We're no such thing. We're dissidents against an oppressive, corrupt regime."

Beth's temper flared at LaSierra's disdainful tone. "Well, that makes us equals, then. The same goes for the Subterraneans. Guess we're all rebels."

LaSierra pressed her lips together, clearly not about to dignify those remarks with a response.

Beth moved around the SkyBird and made sure the ones she could reach were still breathing. The woman she had come across before was showing signs of regaining consciousness, which was good, but also worrisome. If she moved too much, she could make her injuries worse. Running the wand that cleaned and closed the skin along her lower right arm, Beth kept listening for Kae and the rescue party, but she couldn't hear anyone yet.

She returned to LaSierra and realized she shouldn't have left her. To her horror, LaSierra had shifted onto her side and was now panting.

"What did you do?" Beth didn't add "you crazy woman" but knew her tone implied it.

"That thing in my back...it pierced me even worse than before. I had to..." LaSierra gripped Beth with her good hand. "Can you see it?" She trembled now, and her face was even paler than before.

Using the flashlight function on her GemLink, Beth lit up the area behind LaSierra. "Wait. Lie very still." She scanned the area but couldn't see anything sharp. She turned the light onto LaSierra's back and winced. Sticking out of her back, about three inches below her left shoulder blade, was a part of the console support struts.

Beth knew better than to extract the object. "I see what hurts. I can't remove it, or you might bleed. Can you stay in this position? I can't have you lie back down either."

"I won't be able to remain on my side very much longer. It's hurting my arm to try to hold myself up." LaSierra was shaking now. "Maybe onto my stomach?"

"No. Wait!" Beth shifted and moved in front of LaSierra again. "Lean against me, but not fully on your stomach. Let me get into place." Beth slipped in close to LaSierra and wedged her body against hers, taking her weight. "Try relaxing against me."

Long, dark hair fell around Beth as LaSierra let go with a muted cry and ended up half on top of her. Beth pushed the fragrant hair out of her face and placed a steadying hand on LaSierra's hip.

"How is that? Better?" Beth pulled her head back as much as possible and looked down at the pale face half-buried into her shoulder.

"Yes. Better. Oh, Creator…" LaSierra drew shallower breaths. "I admit. Never felt such pain."

No, she wouldn't have. Having access to the best medical expertise known to humankind, all LaSierra and her peers had to do was to get their physician to show up with a battery of infulizers. A stray thought surfaced, making Beth wonder if it was the same for emotional and psychological pain as well.

A clonking sound startled them both, and LaSierra whimpered. "Please. Don't move."

"Sorry. I wasn't prepared." She prayed that it was the rescue team.

"Beth?" Foster's voice echoed inside the SkyBird. "You all right?"

Beth called out and kept her arm around LaSierra. "We're here. We need something to stabilize Ms. Delmonte."

"We're bringing boards. Kae's here. She's coming in, and then I'll try to remove the obstacle. Otherwise, it'll be damn tricky to get you out."

Relief rushed through Beth. Now that help had arrived, Beth recognized the stress of working alone to handle the wounded and keep tabs on the thickening smoke.

"Beth…" LaSierra's cough ended in a groan. "I need to get out of here."

"I know. We all do. They're coming." Beth wasn't sure what she could do to keep LaSierra calm. She felt tremors travel through LaSierra, and it was anybody's guess if it was because of the cool night or pain. Probably both.

Beth used her free arm to stroke LaSierra's upper back in gentle circles. Perhaps she was being too presumptuous and out of line, but she'd be damned if she was going to let LaSierra feel that nobody cared.

Movement to her right made Beth turn her head, and the sight of Kae crawling toward her caused her to grin. "Kae!"

"Hey, you. Oh, damn. That's one way to do it, I suppose. Let me see." Kae moved to LaSierra's other side. "Hi there. Good thing Beth's supporting you, Ms. Delmonte."

"Get me out." LaSierra had clearly had it. She growled loud enough for Beth to feel the noise through her suit.

"We will, but you have a metal bar sticking out of your back, so let's do this in a way that won't paralyze or kill you, okay?" Kae was her usual calm and aplomb self, which Beth knew could change in a second if needed.

Behind Kae, several other people began trying to move the collapsed inner bulkhead to reach the people in the back. Beth held on to LaSierra, praying that everyone was alive.

CHAPTER THREE

LaSierra hid her face against the strong young woman that had entered her SkyBird. She remembered her as one of the Subterranean insurgents that had braved the skyscraper a few days ago. Having remained in the background, Beth had let Kaelyn Dark, the leader of her unit, do most of the talking. Only when Beth had been separated from her unit during an undercover operation had she shown her resilience. She had taken part in a meeting with the top dissidents and handled herself well enough for LaSierra to recognize her strength.

Now Beth held her firmly, as Kae Dark talked to Dr. Rayne Garcia over their GemLinks. This situation reminded her of something vital that couldn't wait.

"Stop," LaSierra said and pinched Beth enough to make her flinch. "Tell Dark to stop."

"What?" Beth looked down at her, clearly confused. "But… okay, okay." She nudged Dark and interrupted the conversation about the best way to handle the object piercing LaSierra.

"Kae. LaSierra needs you," Beth called out.

"All right? What can be more important than saving your life, Ms. Delmonte?" Dark bent over LaSierra and Beth, meeting LaSierra's gaze." She was pale but radiated complete focus.

"Next to the seat behind you is a narrow cabinet. Have Rocque override the code if you must, but you need to open it. Now." Making sure her voice showed force rather than reflected the pain coursing through her, LaSierra glared at Dark.

"All right. Rayne? Did you hear that? Do I need a code for that cabinet?" Dark raised her GemLink to her mouth.

"Father says the entire bird is decoded for now." Rayne's voice was clear over the link, which was reassuring, as she'd been wounded just before the evacuation.

Dark rose and opened the cabinet. Returning with the flat box, she set it down next to LaSierra and Beth.

"Open it," LaSierra said.

Dark followed her order and nodded as if LaSierra's order made sense. "Your GemLink. Wow. The Gem's a lot bigger." Dark held it up and regarded LaSierra's wounded arm. "Where…?"

"Just slap it on. We can figure out the wounds later." LaSierra held her breath as Dark attached the massive GemLink to her arm. The pain still made her whimper, and immediately Beth held her closer and began stroking her again. LaSierra couldn't remember the last time someone had attempted to soothe her, and she wasn't sure she liked it.

Dr. Garcia gave Dark and Beth a list of instructions, and soon, Dark had stabilized the metal bar with bandages enough for them to dare to move her. LaSierra felt her neck was all right, but they still put a collar on her. Beth held her long hair out of the way and smoothed it down afterward.

"There," Beth said. "You look more like yourself this way." She shrugged and gave a lopsided smile that on anyone else would have been tinged with mockery, but on Beth, it was oddly endearing.

Dark pulled out an infulizer from her kit and leaned over LaSierra. "This is a pretty powerful painkiller, ma'am, so do you want a full dosage, or…?"

"I think I have to accept that I need the full dosage," LaSierra said reluctantly. "Go for it."

A cold buzz against her neck and then it took only a few moments until she could finally draw a full breath. She let her head fall back onto Beth's shoulder.

"Damn, that was fast," Beth said and held her steadily against her. "Let's get her on the gurney before it wears off. She's tough, but that thing's got to be excruciating. I remember when the same thing happened to my foot."

"Don't remind me," Dark said. "Thought we'd lose you to that infection."

"Yeah." Beth shifted away from LaSierra.

The next thing she knew, strong, careful hands eased her over onto a gurney, where they placed her on her side. Straps replaced Beth's warm embrace, which she found she missed acutely.

LaSierra engaged her GemLink, which was easier now since they had placed her so she could use both her arms. "Delmonte to Madelon Garcia."

"LaSierra," Madelon said immediately. "Thank the Creator."

"I need a report regarding our SkyBirds," LaSierra said. "I'm heavily medicated but still lucid."

"You sound remarkably collected." Madelon talked to someone in the background and then returned. "All SkyBirds are accounted for. Rocque managed to download the information from your failing computers before they began to break down. Our SkyBird is now also yours, as we have the best equipment."

"Good. Where is the closest medical bird?" LaSierra asked.

"It's airborne again, and ETA is in ten minutes at the plane just north of your position. Rocque is starting our bird and will join it. Several of our other birds will do the same. Circling the wagons, so to speak."

"All according to plan. I'll see you there, then." LaSierra felt dizzy as she disconnected the link. She closed her eyes and didn't open them until she felt the cool night air on her face.

Kae carried the front left side of Delmonte's gurney until they were outside. After engaging the hover support, they simply guided it, and the ones holding Delmonte's security detail members, to the large clearing surrounded by bushes and trees that provided great cover. South of them a large ridge provided more of the same, and she had heard other dissidents talk about setting up sensor scramblers along it to hide them.

Glancing down at the pale profile of LaSierra Delmonte, where she lay on her side, Kae admitted that she was a formidable woman who wasn't giving in to fear or pain. She credited Beth for having found a way to keep LaSierra calm and stable until help arrived.

Beth carried the head of the gurney next to Kae, and she too kept checking on LaSierra.

"You didn't injure anything when you entered Delmonte's SkyBird, did you?" Kae asked quietly. "Lots of sharp, jagged edges in there."

"A few scrapes and bumps, but the suit's pretty good. I managed to rip it on something at the elbow, but somehow that rift closed." Beth smiled at Kae. "Technology."

"Yeah. It's mind-boggling." Kae snorted.

They reached the clearing and watched a SkyBird, at least four times as big as the Garcias', land along the forest line to the east. Four hatches opened on one side, and when people milled out, an awning of sorts extended above the doors and unfolded into three walls and a roof. Kae estimated it to be about 1000 square feet, and the way metal rods shot into the ground and tightened the walls and roof was impressive.

"That's our main medical bird. The crew have trained in secret to set it up in less than fifteen minutes." One of the men helping them with the gurney sounded proud. "We better get Ms. Delmonte inside right away. The theaters are located in the aft."

"All right." Kae wished Rayne were there, but having gone through surgery herself, she had to rest. Kae had only nudged that thought when she heard Rayne's voice.

"I will supervise." Rayne came up to them and walked next to Kae, her father steadying her.

"Oh, no. You need to be careful," Kae said, nearly stopping. "Rayne…"

"I'm fully healed, and I won't be doing the surgery, as I'm still a bit weak. But I will supervise. This would be easy enough to handle back at the skyscraper, but here, away from most of our resources, we have to be careful." Her hair in a simple, low ponytail, Rayne looked impossibly young, despite her pale complexion. Dark circles under her eyes were evidence of all the ordeals she'd come through the last few days.

"You will sit still on that damn stool." Kae growled the order, not bothering with any damn chain of command. "That or I'll carry you back to your SkyBird."

The expression around Rayne's eyes softened. "I will. I promise."

Kae's heart did one of those unusual flips that made her breathless, and it was not only strange that this happened during their evacuation crisis, but seriously bad timing. "Good."

"Aw." Beth winked at Kae as they kept walking to the mobile hospital bird. "Young love." She crinkled her nose.

"Shut up," Kae said, but there was no real force behind her words.

Beth just rolled her eyes and grinned.

Beth refused to leave LaSierra's side. Somehow, she needed to see everything through, and there were enough people outside the hospital bird to help set up their new headquarters. Also, LaSierra had gripped Beth's right wrist hard and didn't seem inclined to let go.

It took Beth a moment, but then she realized the pain relief LaSierra had received was obviously wearing off.

"Rayne." Beth looked over at Rayne, who sat on a tall stool in the inner corner of the operation theater inside the hospital bird. "I think she needs topping up with that good stuff Kae gave her before. She's in pain."

"Do not talk about me as if I'm not here," LaSierra growled.

"Sorry. Or not sorry. I'm still right, aren't I?" Beth crouched next to the operating table, where they'd placed LaSierra after they cut off her clothes. She was covered with a shiny, gray sheet that apparently kept her warm as well.

"Yes." LaSierra trembled.

"We can put you under completely, LaSierra," Rayne said. "That'll be beneficial for the outcome—"

"No. I can't be fully sedated. I demand you perform the surgery with local anesthesia. I do not consent to anything else."

Rayne grimaced. "It'll be difficult for you. I doubt they can fully numb such a large area at that location. We're trying to keep you from becoming paralyzed."

"I know. My orders stand. Pain medication and local anesthesia only." LaSierra looked up at Beth, her eyes hard and unwavering.

"All right," Beth said, even though she knew she had no say in this matter. She glanced at Rayne for support.

Rayne shook her head. "We'll try. You must lie very still. If you so much as flinch after the surgeons begin, it can make the foreign object in your back create more damage, and the medical team might have to fully sedate you."

"I understand, damn it." LaSierra pulled Beth's hand closer and pressed it to her forehead. She was hot, and the sensation of her smooth complexion made Beth's fingertips tingle.

"Here, ma'am," a medic said and pressed an infulizer to LaSierra's neck. Pain relief and electrolytes only."

LaSierra closed her eyes. "Thank you."

The medical crew worked to clean the skin and the injury on LaSierra's lower back. They used a set of wands more advanced than any other medical instruments Beth had seen. Especially in the tunnels under the Eastern Coastal City, they relied on refurbished, quite ancient technology.

"Be careful when you extract the metal piece," Rayne said from her stool. "It may have sharp edges that can cause unnecessary tears. As it's located near vital organs, caution is imperative."

"Wonderful," LaSierra muttered. She turned her head toward Beth and closed her eyes. Tears clung to her lashes, but the proud woman seemed dead-set on not letting them fall. Beth could understand this attitude. LaSierra was their ultimate leader, no matter which way you looked at it, and that meant she was wary of showing any perceived weakness.

"Ready to extract." The physician in charge of the surgery team got ready, firmly gripping the metal bar. "Steady her body and keep her absolutely still." Slowly, with her eyes on a monitor floating above LaSierra's body, which showed a projection of the bar and the surrounding tissues, the physician began to pull.

LaSierra snapped her eyes open, and now the tears fell freely. Beth slid off her stool and crouched next to the operating table, making sure she was at the level of LaSierra's face. "Please let us knock you out," she murmured. "You don't have to go through this—"

"No!" LaSierra's eyes were now narrow slits, and she held Beth's hand so tight, she nearly pulled her off balance. "Don't you dare let them. Just keep…going…" She groaned, and the pain behind the sound was barely human.

"This is insanity," Rayne said, "but we can't go against her wishes. Damn it, LaSierra."

The physician managed to extract the metal bar, which had gone nearly straight through her.

"It's not sharp." A medic took the bar and showed it to Rayne. "Look. Blunt. If we're lucky, it'll have pushed the organs aside rather than sliced right through them."

"Doctor?" Rayne looked over at the physician in charge.

"So far only minor bleeds and contusions." She leaned over to meet LaSierra's eyes. "Your kidney has a small rift, but I can save it. That means a certain convalescence though. After all, a natural kidney is preferable, if possible."

"All right," LaSierra said, her voice husky and barely audible. "Just be quick about it. I have a dissident movement to direct."

Beth gaped. "What part of 'certain convalescence' didn't you understand?" She glanced at Rayne, who merely shook her head.

"I can convalesce while delegating," LaSierra whispered. "Just get me off this table."

Her words were strong and decisive, but her grip on Beth's hand and the way she kept looking at her spoke of immense pain— perhaps even tinged with fear.

"LaSierra." Beth moved closer. "You haven't mentioned any family members that we need to search for. They need to know that you've been found alive—"

LaSierra's scathing glance silenced Beth. "There is no one."
She pressed her lips together and briefly closed her eyes. Beth
wasn't sure what to say to such a stark statement. Sure, she was
an orphan who had grown up in an orphanage and, later, in the
resistance. Why did she find LaSierra's words so heartbreaking?
It was a mystery.

It took the physician an hour to repair the organs and close the
wound. Beth was impressed but not entirely focused, as she hardly
dared take her eyes off LaSierra. When it was over, LaSierra was
grayish pale, and Rayne ordered a new pain-relief cocktail and
spent at least five minutes convincing LaSierra that it was necessary
so they could transport her to her bed in the mobile hospital.

Eventually LaSierra gave in, and Beth could feel in her aching
hand that she had finally relaxed. They walked the hover-supported
gurney to a cordoned-off area. Pulling a semi-transparent wall
around the bed, they prepared to transfer LaSierra, which meant
she had to let go of Beth's hand. Rayne was standing at the head of
the bed and supervised.

"Just let her keep holding on, Beth, if you're not too tired."
Rayne smiled tightly.

"No problem." Beth smiled crookedly. "I hate to state the
obvious, but I'm used to a lot more exercise before I break a sweat,
Rayne."

Rayne chuckled. "My mistake. Just keep her calm during the
transfer. The wand has closed most tissues, but it'll take a while
before they're entirely solidified."

"I'm not dead yet," LaSierra said huskily and then sighed as
they settled her into the bed. The mattress formed around her in a
way Beth had never seen before.

"Good to hear," Beth said and found a sensor she recognized
from the hospital wing of the former dissident headquarters. She
pressed it, a stool appeared from under the bed, and she sat down,
secretly grateful to be off her feet—and, Creator, her knees. "Just
relax. You get all kinds of goodies in the infulizers. And before
you get upset again, it's only nutrition. Even I can read the labels
for that."

"If I hear someone say that I'm supposed to relax one more time, I won't be responsible for their immediate future," LaSierra growled. She paused and appeared to struggle when she drew a deep breath. "You're staying."

Not sure if it was a question or an order, Beth simply nodded. "I'm staying. Try for some sleep at least."

LaSierra gave a low but distinct growl before following Beth's suggestion.

"She's asleep," Rayne said quietly after checking the monitors. "She's exhausted. Straight into REM sleep." She pointed to a jagged pattern that spoke very little to Beth.

Familiar voices filtered through the separating walls. Foster and Kae were outside. "I can't move, but perhaps they need you?" Turning to Rayne, she saw her slide off the stool and fold it back under the bed.

"They can see you from the opening if they're quiet and remain outside." She walked over to the narrow opening and slipped out.

Beth regarded the sleeping LaSierra and saw that her long hair had nearly wrapped around her neck when they transferred her over to the bed. She leaned closer and loosened the long strands carefully. She smoothed them out across the pillow, and now that LaSierra was out of immediate danger, Beth could appreciate the silky masses. She had no idea how anyone could have hair like that—like a chestnut-colored river. She had never seen chestnuts for real, but Kae's library of old entertainment videos had shown such things being roasted over an open fire.

A hand on her shoulder made Beth jump.

"Hey. How are you doing?" Kae showed up next to her and looked down at the sleeping LaSierra. "She's not letting go yet?" She indicated LaSierra's grip of Beth's hand.

"She's starting to," Beth whispered. "She's asleep."

"And you?" Kae asked again.

"How long since we landed? I've lost track of time." Beth rolled her shoulders, and as she did, LaSierra lost the grip on her hand. She caught it gently and put it on the bed under the thermo blanket.

"About four hours. Most of the SkyBirds have maneuvered into place around a, well, I suppose you can call it an Inner Circle." Kae patted Beth's shoulder. "Why don't you join the team outside? We're going to help set up the food stalls. I have to say these cloudheads are efficient."

Beth studied LaSierra for a moment before she stood. "Yeah. Something to eat would be great. I'm running low on energy."

"Coming from you, young thing, means you're starving." Kae smiled wryly. "Follow me. I managed to convince Rayne to join us. She was planning to find her parents first, though."

Walking outside, Beth felt the chill nip at her cheeks and nose. "Creator. This is another type of cold. A mix between the coldest part of the tunnels and the wind howling between the skyscrapers. Except this wind doesn't smell like crap." She inhaled deeply. "It smells of, what *is* that?"

"My best guess is grass, dirt, and fresh air," a voice said from behind them.

Turning, Beth saw Foster approach, accompanied by Rayne and her parents. "Where are the kids?" She frowned.

"In one of the larger tents that are hosting the other kids, until their families have their habitats set up." Madelon walked up to Beth and took her by the shoulders. "We owe you the life of our leader. Thank you." She shocked Beth by kissing her cheeks.

"Eh...you're welcome?" She looked helplessly at Kae, who merely nodded.

"I wasn't thrilled to leave them there, but we have so much to do to camouflage our SkyBirds and set up a perimeter." Rocque made a face. "As soon as our habitat is done, we'll get Tania and Wes. In the meantime, they're safe and cared for, along with the others."

Beth wasn't thrilled to be away from the children again, but she had no reason to doubt the way the Garcias had taken Wes and Tania into their hearts. They had watched over them ever since they took them to the skyscrapers, making sure Wes got the medical help he needed.

"Food stalls are lined up over here." Foster pointed to the east part of the camp.

"We've had plans for how to set this up for decades." Madelon took the lead and began walking toward the food stalls. "The Inner Circle contains the hospital, leadership, and different branches for planning. We will need everything we used to have, albeit on a different scale. "Food, water, schools, maintenance, law enforcement, etc. Everyone has a task, and—"

"And you forget something," Kae said darkly. "The Subterraneans. Our people. If you think your former neighbors won't blame them and go after them, you're kidding yourself."

Madelon stopped. She pressed her hand to her forehead and turned around slowly. "You're right. Of course, you're right. This issue is going to be high up on the agenda. We have to plan on how to retrieve as many as we can, but we have to prepare for them. They need to be transported here in a safe way. We can't risk the Celestial authorities finding our camp, or we'll all perish…and we won't be able to help anyone."

"Stand down, there, Kae," Rayne murmured and took her hand. "It can't happen tonight, as much as I'd want to just whisk them away."

"Yeah, I know. I know." Kae pressed her lips to Rayne's hair before they started walking again.

Beth knew Kae had fallen for Rayne—it was hardly a secret. She and Foster had found it a source of equal parts amusement and concern, but right now, she was glad Kae had Rayne…both because their love was obvious to anyone, but also, it kept them all in the Inner Circle because of Rayne's parents.

They approached the food stalls, long, narrow tents where food storage was set up in long rows, where people could grab a tray or a bag and collect food for their family. Most of the Celestial food was stored in FlatPaks, which weirdly enough seemed to inflate in some sort of oven and turn into regular meals. The first time Beth had tasted something, she had known it would be difficult to settle for the kind of food available in the tunnels.

"Looks like they've managed to erect the first ten units," Rocque said. "Let's grab something to eat, and then we can assist."

Beth fully intended to help, but when she lifted a cabinet that needed to be placed near a power source, she became dizzy and had to put it down. Staggering to the left, she tried to regain her balance but stumbled into Madelon, who flung her arms around her. "Rocque! She's going down."

Rocque, assisted by Foster, who was beside her in an instant, lifted her and carried her to a bench that sat alongside the closest SkyBird.

"Beth. You're exhausted." Foster grabbed a stack of bags and placed it under her head. "You just rest here, and I'll bring you something to eat."

"Chocolate," Beth murmured. "Need something sweet." She had fallen in love with the sweet and smooth treat that was still so new to her.

"I agree, but you're going to have more than that." Madelon bent over her. "You need something nutritious as well."

Feeling ridiculous, Beth eventually sat up when Madelon brought her a tray of food and chocolate. She ate too fast, but she was eager to feel better and get back to work. Madelon and Rocque sat next to her, eating at the same speed. She figured they had important leadership stuff to deal with now that LaSierra was temporarily out of commission.

Kae joined her, carrying two mugs of coffee. "Want some? We have a few more hours of work before the perimeter is as secure as it can be at this point."

"Sure." Beth wasn't trembling any longer and greedily sipped the black coffee. She watched Rayne approach. Beth thought she would sit down next to Kae, but instead she merely ruffled Kae's hair and sat on Beth's other side.

"You got your color back," Rayne said, patting Beth's knee. "You outdid yourself today, keeping our leader alive. If you hadn't been there, I think my mother would agree that LaSierra would have tried to extract that metal bar herself—which would have been bad."

Beth shuddered. "I practically had to restrain her, and she was in so much pain. I felt I was being cruel, even if I didn't have a choice." Sighing, she ran her fingers through her hair, feeling how dirty it had to be. "It was like being back in the tunnels, where we always have a lack of resources and expertise."

"I can understand that," Rayne said and squeezed Beth's leg gently. "But you did it, and unless there are complications, she will recover."

Beth nodded and then let the others talk among themselves until they got up a few minutes later. After knocking back the last of the coffee, Beth rolled her shoulders and walked over to the center of the camp, which she had heard several people call the Inner Circle. There, she checked her weapon that someone had brought back from LaSierra's SkyBird for her. Making sure she had all the extra ammunition possible, she then located her helmet and put it on.

As Foster and Kae moved out, she was right behind them. Hopefully she had a couple of hours left in her.

CHAPTER FOUR

LaSierra woke up, startled out of frantic dreams by a man's loud moaning. She was uncertain of her location, as nothing around her was familiar. Above her, she saw an off-white ceiling apparently made of fabric. It took her a few moments longer to catch up, but then she knew. The mobile-hospital habitat. She had gone through surgery and had the metal bar removed.

Glancing to her left, she half expected to see Beth, the Subterranean young woman who had saved her life, but the stool from under her bed was no longer unfolded. She shifted, eager to get onto her side and relieve some pressure on the area of her lower back that hurt so badly.

The man screamed now, making LaSierra flinch. He sounded agonized. She heard running footfalls, and a stern, loud voice called out, "Sedate him. Now! What are you people waiting for?"

The voice sounded familiar, but LaSierra was too tired to try to identify it. She needed more pain relief but didn't want to disturb the staff that apparently had their hands full with the man outside.

The foldable wall around her shifted, and a woman poked her head in. "Ma'am? I thought you must be awake." A medic came in and checked the infulizers. "I bet you want some more of the good stuff." She smiled gently, and LaSierra forgave her for the irreverent tone.

"I do indeed. But the man—?"

"He's getting all the help he needs. He's going into surgery as we speak." The medic pulled vials from a cabinet attached to the head of the bed. "You can choose between full dose, which will knock you out, pretty much, or half, which will help you enough, but you'll be clearheaded."

"Half, then. I need to get out of here today," LaSierra replied.

The medic inserted a thin vial into the infulizer but then regarded her skeptically. "That's not advisable. Doctor Garcia will come by soon, and I doubt she'll release you."

"Doctor Garcia is recovering from weapons' fire herself." LaSierra wasn't used to anyone contradicting her. "If she can be on her feet after what she went through, so can I."

"Still. Let this medicine take hold and see how you feel. I'm sure you can work around not being able to get up like you're used to, ma'am."

"Hm." LaSierra sighed. "Were you here last night?"

"I was. I'm still here. I'm getting some rack time in an hour." The young medic smiled.

"Beth. A Subterranean, uhm, freedom fighter. Do you know if she's all right? I fell asleep before she left."

"Beth? Is that the tall, wiry, blond girl?" The medic tapped her chin. "You know, she poked her head in for a moment when she came back from patrolling and setting up the perimeter. She was going to bed but wanted to make sure you were all right, ma'am."

This information gave LaSierra pause. It was reassuring that Beth seemed to be all right. She wanted the chance to thank her. Clearing her throat, she asked, "How did she seem? I realize it was a long day for everyone." LaSierra loathed being immobilized in bed.

"Dirty. Exhausted. Hearing that you were in stable condition seemed to help though." The medic shrugged. "I'm sure she'll stop by once she wakes up. She said she would."

"And my team in my SkyBird? I'm so turned around and dazed I can't remember who went with me." LaSierra pinched the bridge of her nose.

The young medic lifted her shoulders and shook her head. "I'm sorry. I'm not privy to that information. We have forty-two patients so far, which isn't too bad, considering how many of us evacuated. I'm off duty soon, but I'm sure you will find out later today. Try to rest some more. I'll come back when it's time for breakfast, and then I'm off to my cot." She smiled briefly. "Just ping us if you need anything."

LaSierra curled up on her side and allowed the pain relief to do its job. If she had been at her apartment in the skyscraper they'd just evacuated, she could merely have the hospital staff tend to her in the comfort of her home, but now, life had changed forever. It wasn't as if she hadn't expected this to happen at some point, but not yet. She had thought she'd have more time.

On the surface, the catalyst was the arrival of the five Subterraneans, accompanied by Doctor Garcia. As it turned out, their arrival was merely happenstance, as different scenarios were playing out in a multitude of places in the Eastern Coastal City. Rumors were brewing about the current administration's lies, corruption, and criminal activities. When Kaelyn Dark and her team arrived with an injured child and thus triggered the drama that later unfolded, LaSierra had seen her chance. Rocque and Madelon Garcia were part of her social circle, and secretly, they had all belonged to the dissident movement trying to expose and overthrow the corrupt government and authorities. When LaSierra met their daughter, Rayne, and the Subterranean freedom fighters, she saw her chance to utilize their status, along with Rayne's connection with the daughter of the former president. The intel they had managed to obtain had nearly cost Rayne her life, and Beth had been stalked through the skyscraper before she escaped back to the dissidents.

LaSierra remembered how reluctantly impressed she had been with the young woman's courage and good-natured personality. It had almost felt like destiny, in a strange way, when Beth entered her crashed SkyBird.

"In the mood for some company, LaSierra?" A familiar male voice sounded from the opening in the wall. Rocque smiled at her, as he poked his head in. "Madelon's taking care of business at the main console. I wanted to update you, if you're up to it."

"Absolutely. Help me raise the head of the bed." LaSierra didn't want to lie flat on her back while Rocque gave his report.

He swiftly pressed the sensor that elevated the bed, effectively creating a backrest. He assisted her gently until she was comfortably reclining, the mattress creating support on all sides.

"There. Better. Now, report," LaSierra said and fixed her gaze on Rocque. He looked tired but didn't seem stressed, which was a good sign.

A movement by the door made LaSierra turn her head, and she glimpsed blond, messy hair before the person withdrew again.

"Beth?" LaSierra raised her voice, which made her cough. Annoyed, she cleared her throat and sipped some liquid from the tube emanating from her side table. Cool water soothed her throat.

Rocque had turned his head and waved at Beth, who hesitated on the threshold. "Come in, Beth."

Beth shouldered through the narrow opening and walked over to the foot of the bed. "Hi, LaSierra. You look so much better." Smiling, Beth patted LaSierra's left foot. "I just wanted to make sure."

LaSierra studied the young woman, who looked refreshed after what could be only a few hours' sleep. That was reassuring. "Unfold a stool and sit in on this report, Beth. I imagine you're privy to most of it anyway."

Rocque gave LaSierra a surprised look, but then he nodded and helped Beth find the sensor for the stool on LaSierra's other side.

"All right. Continue." LaSierra turned back to Rocque, who began to fill her in.

"We've established a perimeter along the ridge and around our camp. All 449 Birds are accounted for and divided into clusters around the Inner Circle."

"The what?" LaSierra blinked.

"It's what the crews call this area. We're in the center of it," Beth said. "Literally the Inner Circle."

"I see. And I suppose the missing bird is mine." LaSierra nodded at Rocque to continue.

"Yes. We've moved as much of the rescued technology to my family's bird as possible. Good thing that it's one of the larger crafts, since it is now also yours, obviously."

"And what about my team?" LaSierra's stomach twitched painfully. "I can't even remember which ones were on duty—oh, Creator, what about Benny...Benny Vance? LaSierra ignored the smarting muscles in her back and sat up unaided. She suddenly remembered young Benny, her computer expert who had saved her and other dissidents so many times, she couldn't count them. "Please?" She hated it, but she heard herself beg.

"He's in the hospital with an injured neck," Rocque said. "I saw him yesterday, and he was awake but, like you, on medication. He was in the aft of your ship, and thank the Creator, he was strapped in properly but apparently suffered severe whiplash. He was mostly upset that his favorite tablet was smashed to pieces. He's banged up but in slightly better shape than you, LaSierra."

Exhaling slowly, trying not to tremble, LaSierra kept staring at him. "And the others? The security teams? And what's our situation when it comes to casualties and wounded overall?"

Beth rose and took LaSierra by the shoulder. "You're reinjuring yourself. Please lean back."

LaSierra glared at Beth but eventually relented, as it seemed Beth wouldn't hesitate to push her against the mattress. A glance at Rocque showed that her old friend wasn't used to someone as forward as Beth either.

"Very well." LaSierra reclined again and then impatiently gestured. "Go on."

Rocque cleared his throat. "Two of your security guards died from the injuries they sustained in the crash. Among the 449 other SkyBirds, we have mostly injuries, some severe, from rough landings. We don't call them crashes, as they were able to hover over to the camp. Those Birds will need extensive repairs later, but that's not at the top of our lists."

"Who?" LaSierra clenched her jaw, and, in a strange way, the pain shooting toward her temples felt like something she deserved. "Among my guards?"

"Carson and Peylon." Rocque sighed. "The rest of them are alive and being treated and, according to my daughter, if there are no complications—"

"I see." On the inside, LaSierra was screaming. She remembered calling out and talking to Carson before Beth pushed her way into her SkyBird. He had answered with his name. And now he was gone. "So, no other fatalities?"

"Not from the rough landings, but there were some acute cases that we simply couldn't reach in time. Four coronaries and eight strokes. Rayne thinks the stress of it all is to blame."

Sitting in silence for a while, LaSierra mulled Rocque's words over. She didn't ask for the names of the deceased. She didn't want to hear if any more of the people she knew and trusted among them had fallen.

"Your team?" LaSierra focused on Beth and nearly regretted it when she saw the sympathy on her face. "All accounted for?"

"If you mean the ones I was with when all hell broke loose, then yes. The kids, Wes and Tania, are with other dissidents' children in a special habitat. Kae is already patrolling the perimeter with Foster. I'm on my way to join them, but I wanted to see you—I mean, check on your condition." Beth shrugged. "I think that's my cue to leave—"

"Stop." LaSierra held up her hand. "Rocque. If I can't sign myself out of here, I need to find a way to run our new headquarters from a place in the…what did they call it?…the Inner Circle? I'm not going to suggest that I have a private nursing staff there, but I'll direct this effort from the bed if I have to. I can't do it here. I need to be in the Primary."

"I know." Rocque rubbed his neck.

"What's the Primary?" Beth frowned.

Rocque looked at Beth with a contemplative expression. "It's the center of the headquarters, where the Inner Circle of the people in charge work, meet, and make their decisions. I just had an idea. I believe we can utilize you better than merely patrolling the perimeter, Beth—at least for now."

"Get to the point." LaSierra felt a new bout of fatigue. "I'd say you have about ten minutes before it's time for my beauty sleep."

"As the Primary is supposed to be a central area, why don't we shift my SkyBird to the center and extend two habitats on either side of it? Each one holds facilities for four people. Walls can be extended to create privacy for each, eh…pairing."

Narrowing her eyes, LaSierra prepared for what Rocque was hinting at.

"Madelon and I will take one, Rayne and Kae seem to get along, and I'm sure Benny and Foster can bunk up. That leaves the last one for you and Beth." He hurried to describe the rest of his plan. "We could use the entire Garcia SkyBird as the Primary. We place it in the dead center of the Inner Circle, and that way, it'll be well protected."

Glancing quickly at Beth, LaSierra noticed her shock. Good. So not just her, then. "We're at war," she said gruffly. "We cannot give in to sensitivities. Beth. I'll need some assistance initially, and you will be my aide-de-camp."

"Do I have a choice?" Beth shook her head in obvious dismay.

"Not really," Rocque said kindly. "You'd be doing more for the dissident cause and, farther down the road, your fellow Subterraneans, than if you carried out a job that anyone can do. Somehow, I doubt LaSierra would accept anyone else available for this task."

"Correct." LaSierra rolled slightly to her right, extending her cold hand. "Look at it this way, Beth. You will have the ear of the highest-ranking member of the dissident government. That will put you in a unique position when it comes to influencing us all regarding how to best help your people. All our people," she added.

Beth sucked her lower lip in between her teeth. She looked impossibly young, and yet so seasoned, a sliver of LaSierra's soul ached for her.

"Fine. All right. Just one thing—if Kae is dead set against it, I won't go against my original commanding officer." Beth folded her arms over her chest.

"You can answer to only one person of authority," LaSierra said, her voice weakening. "I find Kaelyn Dark fairly easy to work with, but if she and I have opposing views, you need to know where your loyalties lie. If you don't, the punishment is severe among the dissidents—almost as strict as the corrupt authorities we just escaped."

"You'd kill me if I sided with Kae?" Beth gaped.

"Of course *not*," Rocque barked, scowling at LaSierra. "But that said, being incarcerated for treason is a harsh punishment."

"Incarceration...you've both lost your minds," Beth said. "If this is how you recruit dissidents, I'm not surprised that there aren't ten times as many of you. I mean, tons of people in the other skyscrapers must have suffered a lot more. Do they also have secret floors and SkyBirds, or are they just sitting idly by while waiting for you lot to show up and save them? I don't get this."

"Beth..." Exhausted, LaSierra held up her hand. "Please."

Beth studied LaSierra closely. "Damn, you look pale. You might need topping up. And here I'm jabbering away. Don't worry. I'll be your babysitter, LaSierra, and I'll be a stern one, don't you worry. You might just regret that you listened to Rocque."

Beth helped LaSierra lower her bed, and then she had the audacity to tuck her in. Stroking LaSierra's long hair from her face, Beth smiled wanly. "Cool hand on hot forehead and so on. You'll hate it and be ready to throw me out in a week."

Rocque and Beth said good-bye, the latter by patting LaSierra's left foot again. "Mark my words, you'll fire me in a week." Beth waved and left with Rocque.

LaSierra closed her eyes and hid her cold hands under the cover. "No," she murmured to herself. "No, I won't."

CHAPTER FIVE

Doctor Garcia?" A man in the same Celestial suit that most of the dissidents wore approached Rayne. His Nova blaster sat in its harness on his back, and he was looking over his shoulder. "It's time to move our leader, Ms. Delmonte, to the new location. Kaelyn Dark asked for you to be part of the crew around her."

"I see." Rayne patted the hand of the woman she'd just derma-fused. "You'll be all right. Keep the support bandage on for a few days, and no heavy lifting during that time, all right?"

The woman nodded and looked relieved as she jumped off the gurney and pulled on the upper part of her suit. It was made from a self-healing material, and the gash that corresponded to her injury had already merged. "Thank you, ma'am."

"You can call me Doctor Garcia." Rayne smiled before returning her focus to the tall man.

"Your name?" She pulled off the disposable safety gloves and shoved a hand through her hair. She normally kept it in a severe ponytail, and now she had to re-tie the elastic band.

"Geller, ma'am…eh, Doctor Garcia."

"All right, Geller. Show me the way." She grabbed one of the canes available and used it for support, as fatigue was setting in after her long working hours, despite not being fully healed. If she reinjured herself, Kae would not be pleased. That, along with being scolded by her parents as if she were a mere child, was ridiculous. After all, she was fifty years old.

Joining the team around Delmonte, she wasn't at all surprised to see Beth standing by the head of the gurney. It hadn't taken Rayne long to think of the young freedom fighter in a maternal way. Beth's irresistibly sunny disposition made her easy to like. Rayne knew that Beth carried the same wounds as many of her Subterranean people did. Orphaned and growing up in the insurrection movement, she was also hardened in many ways. Still, the young woman had a light about her that pulled Rayne in. Kae was immensely protective of Beth, and Rayne could easily see a sibling dynamic between them. Foster, in turn, would go through hell for both of them, and for her as well, Rayne knew, especially after their mission in the skyscraper.

Foster had shown up and was now on the other side of Delmonte, who was half-sitting on the gurney, at least six tablets around her, busy reading. The woman was a force of nature.

"Hi." Kae came up from behind and stealthily wrapped an arm around Rayne's waist. "See. You're smart and using some support. That reassures me. Especially when I can't offer my services."

"Exactly." Rayne wanted to turn and kiss the woman she had fallen for against all odds. Tall and sinewy, Kaelyn Dark was nothing like any of the people she had been introduced to over the years, by her parents or other well-meaning people who wanted to see her settle down. Kae had a dangerous streak but was also immensely loyal. And, miraculously, she had fallen just as hard for Rayne, which even Rayne's parents seemed to accept.

Rayne pressed the back of her head against Kae's shoulder for a few moments, simply needing the connection before she leaped into action as the physician in charge of the transfer. She approached the gurney and didn't hesitate to interrupt Delmonte. "LaSierra. I believe we're ready to proceed. I'm going to have to ask you to lower the head of the bed and accept being restrained as we move. It's a security measure, nothing else."

"Restrained?" LaSierra Delmonte glared at her. She was still extremely pale, and her long chestnut hair was pulled to the side in a braid. Her arms showed signs of recent derma fusing. "That's not going to happen." LaSierra raised her chin. "I can't lie down and take a break from updating myself on the latest progr—what?" She snapped her head to the side and stared up at Beth, who had placed a hand on LaSierra's shoulder.

"LaSierra," Beth said quietly. "We need to secure you to the gurney because we're taking you out into an open area, and if there's trouble, we need to be sure you won't be thrown off. If you're secured, the gurney will protect you."

"Trouble?" LaSierra's amber eyes narrowed to slits. "Are you saying the perimeter isn't secure?"

"It is," Kae said and moved to the foot of the bed. "However, we would be treating our leader recklessly if we didn't do our duty. Be happy that you have this means of protection, Ms. Delmonte. We would have been forced to use an old wooden door, or a former riot fence, if we were in the tunnels."

"Come on," Beth whispered. "Let's just do it."

LaSierra seemed eager to object again but then relented. Tossing the tablet she'd been perusing onto the bed, she flung her hands in the air. "Fine. Fine! Get on with it then."

Rayne and a medic deployed the restraints, and when the last two wrapped around LaSierra's shoulders and then her forehead, she closed her eyes, her lips a thin line.

"We better run," Kae murmured to Rayne. "Move out, people."

Ten people, four on each side, and with Kae at the head and Rayne at the foot of the gurney, engaging the hover support, began to move through the mobile hospital. The rest of the staff quickly jumped out of the way as Kae barked, "Make a hole," in a voice that did not accept any objections.

When they reached the door, eight more armed dissidents lined up on each side of the gurney, most of them keeping an eye on the sky above. Even Rayne understood that the sky was their most vulnerable perimeter. If the scramblers the dissident Celestials had deployed weren't effective enough, a few well-directed missiles would easily take them all out.

Running at a fast jog, the team around LaSierra's gurney raced toward the Garcia SkyBird, located in the center of the Inner Circle. Habitats had been extended around it, and Rayne knew she would share a section of it with Kae. Rayne struggled to keep up, her stamina nowhere near what it used to be before being hit by the high-yield energy pulse.

It was about fifty yards between the surrounding SkyBirds that created the Inner Circle and the Garcia SkyBird, but it felt ten times as long. Rayne held onto the gurney so she wouldn't fall on the uneven field. Keeping her eyes on the monitors, she noticed that LaSierra's vitals were elevated, but not dangerously so. She strongly suspected that LaSierra was mostly angry about what she perceived as an indignity, and perhaps also frightened and in pain.

When they had about five yards left to go, two of the guards ran up and opened the door to the part of the habitat that would house LaSierra, and—*Creator*—Beth. They ducked inside, and Rayne could tell she wasn't the only one exhaling from sheer relief. Gasping to catch her breath, she disregarded her own discomfort and didn't take her eyes off LaSierra and her monitors.

"This habitat has built-in scrambling systems, which is a lot safer for you than in the hospital, even if that's similarly outfitted. However, it's a larger object and thus easier to hit." Kae pushed at the gurney and maneuvered it into the bedroom section. She turned to the others. "Everyone except Beth, Rayne, and Foster are dismissed." Her authority was undeniable, and the guards and assisting medics filed out of the habitat.

"And now you will free me from this fucking contraption," LaSierra growled. "Now."

"Yes, of course, ma'am," Kae said and nodded at Rayne to assist her. With Beth, they pressed the sensors that retracted the restraints.

"Please, LaSierra. Let me check that you're all right," Rayne said and tried not to show she was leaning heavily on her cane.

"You look like you need a workover yourself, Doctor." LaSierra raised the head of the gurney. "Take a seat somewhere while I transfer to my AirFrame."

Rayne still checked LaSierra's vitals. "I want to give you something to lower your blood pressure just a bit. It's not an oral medication, merely a strip that I'll attach to your temporalis artery."

"A strip." LaSierra sighed. "Very well."

Rayne had to ask Kae to administer the strip, as she truly had to sit down. "Beth, can you fetch the AirFrame. I saw it in the far corner in your living area." She saw Beth wince, apparently when she used the words 'your living area,' and who could blame her?

Beth returned with the AirFrame, which seemed to glide on air. Kae and Beth helped LaSierra into the chair, and immediately the frame began to calculate its setting as it scanned every part of LaSierra.

"Just remain still for a minute, please," Rayne said. "Once the chair has scanned you, it'll keep your core temperature stable and also help you visit the facilities, remind you of medication and sustenance, and suggest when you need a rest. If you don't give it a lot of grief, but actually listen to it, you should be able to function independently soon."

"It's like being pushed around in a children's pram." LaSierra grimaced. "That said," she continued, holding her hand up as if she expected Rayne's exasperation to overflow. She wasn't wrong. "*That* said. I'm grateful for your effort. I owe each of you a lot, and I'm not blind to that fact. I will try not to let my, eh, impatience dictate my decisions regarding the AirFrame. It's a wonderful tool, and I'm glad we brought some."

"Some, but not enough. They'll be administered according to medical findings. You will be the only who has your own—until you don't need it, of course."

"I'm well aware of the privilege, thank you." LaSierra had obviously had enough of the discussion and extended a hand to the gurney. "My tablets, Beth." She winced visibly. "Please."

"Sure." Clearly unperturbed, Beth gathered the tablets. "Anything else?"

"I want to enter the SkyBird," LaSierra said.

"I understand." Beth motioned to LaSierra's body. "Don't you want to get dressed, and perhaps lose the braid? I mean, it's cute, but you might want to look the part when you enter headquarters."

Rayne closed her eyes hard and tried to disregard Foster's soft snort. She heard him hastily leave LaSierra's bedroom.

"Creator..." LaSierra growled. "Everything takes ten times as long, and yes, I know I'm bickering, but this is damn frustrating."

Rayne stood and approached LaSierra, holding up a hand. "Please. Calm down. If you go off like this, not only won't it do your system any good, but it won't instill confidence in your crew. I know you're in some pain, since you won't let us administer enough pain relief. You're frustrated, which is completely understandable. Yet, if you want to be able to fulfill your duty, you need to work with the staff, especially Beth, as I heard she's to be your aide-de-camp. If you don't," Rayne hardened her voice, something she did so rarely it usually put the fear of the Creator in people, "I will not declare you fit for duty. No matter if we're dissidents, we still stand on the law."

LaSierra looked up at Rayne. She glanced at the cane and then shifted her gaze to Kae. "I will comply with the law," she said quietly. "I'm well aware of how important it is to stand on ceremony and law, to avoid confusion and anarchy." She turned to Beth. "All right. You're going to assist me, then. Help me into the bathroom area."

Beth nodded. "I'll assist. No problem. It's just that you better maneuver that contraption yourself, or I might just tip you straight into a wall."

To Rayne's surprise, LaSierra smiled briefly, her face softening marginally. "Very well. Let's go then." She pressed a sensor-pad and slid her finger as if she had used an AirFrame before.

"Did you see what I saw?" Kae shook her head as if to clear her mind.

"If you mean that Beth has our leader's ear to some degree, then yes." Rayne leaned heavily against Kae.

"You're exhausted. Time for a rest?" Kae wrapped her arm around Rayne.

"Good thing our habitat is next door. Literally." Rayne pushed her face against Kae's neck. "Just a nap. I need to support a young surgeon later this afternoon."

"All right. An hour? One and a half?" Kae wrapped her arm around Rayne and guided her from LaSierra's and Beth's habitat into their own. It was a mirror image of the one they had left except that someone on the team had removed the partition between the bedroom and inflated the beds flush with each other.

"Subtle," Rayne said and peered at Kae. "Want to move them back to their basic setting?"

Kae ushered Rayne toward the bed. "Not at all. Unless you need your own space after having to put up with my—"

"Shh. I like it this way, Kae. To sleep in your arms, when our schedules allow it, sounds heavenly."

Kae smiled and her face colored, which Rayne found so charming. "I think so too. Now rest up. Set an alarm, because I'm going into headquarters since Rocque and Madelon need to talk to me. I'm not sure how long I'll be."

"I will." Raising her voice, Rayne set the computer to wake her in ninety minutes.

Kae pressed her lips to Rayne's forehead and then her lips. "I hope we'll have more than fifteen minutes together someday soon. It's been crazy, and I've missed you."

"Same here. An entire evening and night together? That's something to strive for, to plan for." Beth raised a tired arm and ran her fingers along Kae's cheek.

"It is. But let's not forget to make the most of our fifteen stolen minutes. We live in dangerous times." Kae bent to kiss Rayne again.

"I know. Yes. You're right." Cupping Kae's neck, Rayne studied every part of her face, imprinting it on her mind. "There's a lot we never seem to find the time to address, isn't there?"

"Yes." Kae pulled Rayne's hand forward and kissed her palm. "Just rest. I'll make time later, and hopefully you can too."

Rayne lay down and watched Kae walk away, trying not to think that their dangerous work might make this the last time she saw her. Too much was unsaid between them, but a lot didn't need saying. Having posed as Kae's partner while on a mission only days ago, it wasn't such a stretch for Rayne to see this situation as reality.

Closing her eyes, she fell asleep with the sounds of a new community forming around her, as a backdrop to her dreams.

CHAPTER SIX

L aSierra studied her reflection in the bathroom mirror. Beth had assisted her with everything that didn't entail being too undressed. LaSierra had limits to what indignity she would put herself—or Beth—through. Now she sat in the AirFrame, dressed in a sleek black suit she had created by using the basic pattern buffer available in her bedroom.

Beth had inspected her part of the habitat and now returned. She looked a bit wide-eyed, and LaSierra tilted her head as she studied her.

"Beth? Something wrong?"

"No. Just the opposite. My room." Beth motioned with her thumb at the doorway behind her. "It's as big as yours."

"Yes?" Not understanding, LaSierra frowned. "And?"

"You're the leader of this entire thing. Operation. Thousands of people. And my room is as big as yours. That doesn't strike you as odd?"

"No? We are all here to do our part for the revolution brewing in the skyscrapers and below ground. We need a place that's just our own. I don't see why my place should be larger than yours. We'll all be risking our lives at some level. That alone should be the great equalizer."

"Well, when you put it like that." Beth still didn't look convinced. "You happy with your appearance?"

"This is as good as it's going to get." LaSierra placed a hand on the controls in the armrest and swiveled her AirFrame. "Let's go find out if they've managed to refit the Garcia SkyBird."

"All right." Beth walked to the door in the habitat leading into the SkyBird. Both doors could be opened, and LaSierra knew both doors could be locked. Clearly Beth had the high-level security clearance she needed to pass through the hatch without any further scans. That made a strange sort of sense, as she had saved LaSierra's life and, subsequently, the others of her detail who had survived.

The Garcia SkyBird had already changed so much, it was hard to see that it had transported people. Around the fuselage sat a multitude of screens displaying the intel that would help keep them safe and had set their plans in motion when Rayne, Kae, Beth, and Foster had obtained the live map over the area just before the evacuation.

Beth whistled quietly. "This is impressive."

"It is," LaSierra murmured and steered her AirFrame to her station on the oval table in the back. "Come here, Beth. I want you to set up a station right next to mine. We have a lot of data to review before I call a senior staff meeting in a few hours."

"Sure." Beth followed her as she navigated behind the operatives sitting in front of the screens. When she couldn't get past a tall, gangly man standing behind one of the operatives, pointing at her screen, LaSierra stopped and cleared her voice. "Coming through."

The man glared behind him, but when he recognized LaSierra, he shifted hastily. "Ma'am. Good to see you're feeling better."

"Well. At least I'm not skewered any longer." LaSierra raised her chin and maneuvered her chair past him. "I trust you have assembled the reports from our department heads?" She tried not to reveal that she had forgotten the familiar man's name. Her brain was clearly still jumbled.

"Certainly, ma'am." The man motioned at her workstation. "It's all ready for you."

After she had adjusted the AirFrame and locked it into place, she pulled up the screens, relieved that this part of her brain was intact. If it hadn't been, she would have had to replace herself, and she wasn't about to give up the position she'd fought to gain, and keep, for the last twenty years.

Pulling up the AirScreens that projected the content seemingly in the air, she heard Beth say, "That's downright eerie."

"What is?" LaSierra asked absentmindedly as she scrolled through the list of topics until she found the map of how the camp was set up and where it was located in reference to the skyscrapers.

"These hovering screens. They give me the creeps." Beth was busy using the physical screens that seemed inlaid in the table. "At least these things have a keyboard and other things I recognize."

"I see." LaSierra was impressed by how the camp was set up, with four "petals" around the Inner Circle and a reinforced perimeter. She expanded the map and entered her security code. Immediately the live map the Subterranean operatives had stolen from the former president of the Eastern Coastal City covered the table. She wanted to stand to get a better overview, but her legs were too weak. "Damn it,"

"LaSierra?" Beth murmured and stood.

"I can't see the movement at the facility. I need to send in a team to survey it, but I can't even estimate the distance from this damn chair."

"All right. Give me a second." Beth moved in behind LaSierra. A moment later, she felt her harness loosen and Beth's arms wrap around her from the right, one around her waist, the other under her legs. "Hold on."

LaSierra gasped and clung to Beth's arm around her waist. Sinewy and muscular, Beth lifted her as if she were weightless.

"Creator," LaSierra muttered but accepted the assistance. Beth approached her duties in an unorthodox way, but, after all, she was a wild child from the tunnels.

"Make it quick. You're not heavy, but the angle's weird." Beth sounded tense, and LaSierra studied the movements in the camp, monitored by one of the ECC authorities.

Just as Beth set LaSierra into her AirFrame again, Rocque and Madelon Garcia joined them. To LaSierra's dismay, Madelon strode over and kissed her cheek.

"So happy to see you back at work, LaSierra," Madelon said. "We've just been at the habitat someone's nicknamed the Orphanage."

"Charming."

"Well, it isn't an orphanage per se, but some of the kids there have parents that didn't get to our headquarters in time for the evacuation, and we have some other children who truly are orphans, so..." Madelon raised her hands. "Hence the name."

"Are they all right? The children?" LaSierra asked stiffly, not adept in talking about, or dealing with, children. She had dedicated her life to this cause, and now she had too much to sort through to keep on top of the operation.

"They are, and the older children, led by Tania, young Wes's big sister from the tunnels, have taken it upon themselves to organize them."

LaSierra blinked. "Into what?"

Madelon chuckled. "Not into child soldiers, if that's what you're thinking. Tania's a lot more mature and self-sufficient at seventeen than any of the Celestial teenagers. Right now, she's busy setting up what she calls a buddy system."

"Tell her I expect a report," LaSierra said curtly, secretly impressed by the initiative of the girl she'd come across when the Subterraneans showed up at the skyscraper headquarters. Tapping the table in front of her, LaSierra nodded briskly at Madelon. "Take a seat. I just got an overview of the area, and we need to start planning how to protect ourselves in the long term. Also, we have to send a team to the structures Kaelyn Stark's team discovered. I just studied the live map—which reminds me, until I can stand up on my own, we have to find a way to project the map vertically. I can't ask Beth to carry me around."

"I don't mind," Beth said laconically. "It's not like you weigh a ton."

LaSierra saw Madelon wince but was starting to find Beth's unfiltered honesty refreshing. "Thank you, I think. But you would be much more useful doing other things, eventually. According to Dr. Garcia, I have to rely on Beth for a while yet, or she'll take me off duty." She grimaced. "And that's not going to happen." She would be damned before she gave up her position, even temporarily.

"As long as you follow my daughter's orders regarding your health, I doubt your position is threatened. You may be feared and able to intimidate people left and right, but we all rely on your skills as our leader. We also need continuity," Madelon said amicably. "Beth, I hope you understand that being LaSierra's aide-de-camp isn't babysitting."

Groaning inwardly at Madelon's wording, LaSierra kept politely smiling as she started going over what she had observed on the live map. "The traffic in and out of that facility is not just frequent—it is punctual to a fault. Every two hours, large ground vehicles leave, only to return four hours later. Before the evacuation, Benny Vance improved the algorithms some, so we now can name, and distinguish, between different vehicles. He was on the verge of making it possible to do the same with individual people." She quieted and thought of the young man who had worked tirelessly by her side to create and oversee the technological inventions they needed to outsmart and outperform the Celestial authorities. She hoped he recovered fast—for his own sake—and for the dissident movement's.

LaSierra was about to continue her thought process when her GemLink began to pulsate, which made her sit up straight. Her back smarted, but she tapped rapidly at her link, as this was an APA, All Person Alert. Everyone with a link, whether it was a simple identifying bracelet or a large piece of technology able to govern a society like hers, needed to take cover and help those who couldn't fend for themselves.

Before she could finish the thought, Beth's arms shot under her legs and around her back, lifting her out of her AirFrame. Moving toward the bulkhead between the stern and the aft of the

Garcias' SkyBird, Beth called out to Madelon. "Get over here. This is the strongest part of the bird."

"How do you know?" LaSierra asked and had to cling to Beth's neck to make it easier for her.

"Simple physics. We had constant cave-ins in the tunnels. The reinforced doorways, walls, and low weight-bearing structures helped keep us from dying. I don't have time to check more, as I was supposed to get you to a safe spot. What's going on?"

LaSierra nodded at Madelon. "Read the message. I didn't have time to finish it." She raised her gaze at Beth, who just smiled.

"Low-soaring exploration Celestial drones are flying in formation on a trajectory that will make them pass right over us. Everyone needs to be indoors or under protection nets. Key members of the different units are meant to do what, well, what Beth has us doing."

LaSierra noticed that all the operatives were crowded in the four different places in the Garcia SkyBird that were reinforced. "Good thinking, Beth," she said. "Now let's hope everyone heeds the warning and that we've put up good-enough cover."

"Kae and Foster have walked the perimeter twice with two engineers, making sure our scramblers are intact." Madelon frowned. "I would like to know where my husband is, though. He was in here earlier, but I think he went over to see Wes."

LaSierra had to think for a few moments before she realized Madelon was talking about the Subterranean boy. "He's fond of the child?"

"He is." Madelon's expression softened. "He's fond of Tania as well. As am I." She shrugged. "They've been through a lot during their young lives, and if we can help provide them, and, of course, other Subterraneans with a better future, we'll do it."

Glancing at Beth, who looked thoughtful, LaSierra nodded slowly. "Unless everyone has justice and freedom, Celestials and Subterraneans can't maintain a lasting peace. It's as simple—and as hard—as that."

They stood near the bulkheads until their GemLinks buzzed again, and only then did LaSierra realize that she'd been counting in her head since they stopped talking. Drawing a deep breath, she patted Beth's shoulder. "You can take me back to my chair now, Beth."

"All right." Beth made her way back to the short end of the table. After placing LaSierra gently in the AirFrame and adjusting LaSierra's hair in the back, Beth took a seat to her left, ready to serve when required.

CHAPTER SEVEN

It is just reconnoitering, Rayne," Kae said, as she pulled on her suit and an extra safety vest on top of it. The Celestial suits worked well in the chilly weather. Her Subterranean gear alone would have left her shivering—and exposed.

"I know. You keep telling me." Rayne stood in the doorway to the room they shared in the habitat, her arms crossed as she leaned against the door post. "I don't like the idea of you and Foster going without Beth and me. I know Beth is on special duty with LaSierra, but I should be with you."

"And you would, if you'd healed enough." Kae hated saying this, but they had been fortifying their new site for five days straight, and even if she hadn't left the camp, Rayne had overexerted herself daily by tending to their sick and wounded. As the senior physician she was always in high demand.

"How many are you taking with you?"

"Three seasoned Celestial soldiers. Apparently, they defected more than five years ago and have been vetted on several occasions due to their background. I talked to the former captain, who said when he noticed how increasingly young the new soldiers were, he began to research the government's methods. Then he ran into two kids from the tunnels, and as he questioned them, he began to get to know them. These two made a lucky escape, and he was demoted from major to captain. He gave me their names, and they were from my tunnel area. I don't know them personally, but I've heard of them. I'm sorry to say, but most people thought they were just making up their story and bragging when they returned home. When I see them, I plan to apologize, even if I wasn't among the ones who doubted them."

"Are you talking about Captain London?" Rayne pushed off the door post and sat down at the foot of the bed.

"Yes. He's the one."

"I talked to him briefly yesterday. He never said he was on your detail."

"I asked all three of the soldiers to keep it to themselves. Apart from the main brass, you're the only one who knows, and that's because you're our chief medical officer, even if it is an implied title—for now. I mean, that's why I told you, not because you're my…uh…I mean that we're…" Feeling her cheeks warm, Kae turned around and busied herself with the rest of her gear.

"Kae?" Rayne wrapped her arms around Kae's waist from behind. "I understand." Kae detected a smile in her voice, but when she turned around, she saw that it was gentle.

"It's just…sometimes, us being caught in this, and then the way I feel for you, when so much hangs in the balance—it makes me feel stupid for not always being able to compartmentalize." Pivoting within Rayne's arms, Kae placed her hands on her shoulders.

"That's not stupid. Compartmentalizing helps us survive emotionally. That means I'm part of sending you out there and must live with the fact that I won't be there to fix you if you're wounded. That's what I compartmentalize. It's not easy for either of us—but you know, I'd rather risk heartbreak when you walk away than to pull back from…this." She motioned between them, tilting her head, a question in her eyes.

"Yes. That." Pressing her forehead against Rayne's, Kae asked herself, and not for the first time, what Rayne saw in a battle-weary freedom fighter raised in the tunnels. "Exactly that."

Rayne stood on her toes and pressed her lips to Kae's. They still moved slowly when it came to the feelings they had barely begun to acknowledge, let alone act on, and the kiss was enough to make Kae's breath catch.

"Come home in one piece," Rayne said quietly. "I'll be cross if you don't."

"I know. And if you can at least pretend that you rest some during the day, that'd be great." Kae deliberately raised her eyebrows.

"Oh, please. I promise to make sure I eat regularly. That's as far as I'll go." Rayne pulled her hair clip out of her hair and redid her austere twist. "I know you've asked Beth to keep an eye on me. Don't even try to deny it."

"No idea what you're talking about." Kae smiled, not feeling even a little guilty, then pulled on her gear and prepared to join her team at the weapons' storage. "This mission must occur with a minimum of conversation via links. When we first arrived here, we had to stay in touch even without protection, but until Benny Vance comes out of the hospital, we have to be careful not to be monitored. I'll be sending you clicks when I can."

"All right. Any particular pattern I should listen for?" Rayne walked out the door with Kae.

"2-1-2-1-1. And if you don't hear from me, don't assume the worst. This is going to be time-sensitive, and communication silence is part of that." Kae put on her helmet, which adjusted to her head instantly. "I feel ridiculous in this thing, but what can you do?"

"You obviously have no idea how good it makes you look." Smiling, Rayne waved at Kae, who started jogging down the newly trampled path over to where the tactical storage was located.

Foster stood ready, together with the three Celestial soldiers. He held her Nova blaster, along with her harness with extra ammunition pods, and had attached two shadow pulse weapons to her left shoulder pad as well.

"Think we need to put anyone to sleep on our way to the grain fields?" Kae glanced at Foster.

"We can't use our weapons if we run into hostile wildlife, but those little shadow pulse weapons will do the trick and not give away our position." Foster nodded at the other three. "We all carry them."

"You never cease to surprise me, Foster. I didn't know you considered them any more useful than throwing yellow peas at a target."

"They're good for stealth. Stealth is my new thing." Foster hoisted a backpack twice as large as anyone else's and looked expectantly at her.

Kae merely shook her head at his sudden bout of humor and motioned for them all to fall in. "Let's go find out what your former bosses are up to in the grain fields."

As soon as they reached the outer perimeter, they engaged their GemLinks to let them pass and then reset it. It had been LaSierra's idea to set the GemLinks every time they passed through the perimeter defense system. If they kept their GemLinks on a continuous passcode setting, it would be disastrous if even one of the GemLinks got into the wrong hands. When Benny Vance was able to work, he would set up something even more secure, but for now, he was recuperating.

It was still morning, the sun coming up, and Kae knew she would never grow tired of seeing a sunrise. She avoided the sunsets, as they highlighted the outline of the skyscrapers in the far distance, which made her think of her people in the tunnels. Hopefully the remaining cloudheads had enough to worry about after discovering the dissidents operating right under their noses. Maybe they wouldn't have time to go after her fellow Subterraneans.

Forcing her mind off the topic of her old life, she focused on the task at hand, refusing to let her emotions take over. She had pushed through enough hardship and heartbreak to allow something she couldn't fix right now mess with her head.

They followed a tree line that set them on a direct trajectory toward their goal. Kae kept her eyes on her GemLink, which was set on stealth mode but could display a map that changed as they progressed.

"I've never smelled air like this before," Foster muttered. "Is something wrong with it?"

Kae smiled. "It's clean. That's why you think it smells funny. It's not like our damp, moldy air in the tunnels, and it's not like the scented, artificially cleaned air in the skyscrapers, and certainly not like the cold, raw, metal-tasting air between them. It's clean air out in real nature."

"I still think it's strange." Foster huffed.

"I never knew such a place existed, even with my former security clearance," Captain London said from behind them. "In theory, I was aware we had facilities inland, but I thought they were part of some wasteland development. Perhaps even terraforming, of sorts."

"Terraforming?" Kae glanced at London. "For uninhabitable places? Is that really a thing?"

"It is. I think we'll all learn a lot during this evacuation, things we didn't know existed." London shrugged. "People at my level back in the day were kept in the dark regarding a lot, so I can only imagine what it's like for civilians. And Subterraneans."

"Ever go into the tunnels when you were a major?" Foster asked darkly.

"Yes. To retrieve wounded soldiers. It was part of my unit's specialties. When we started having to bring back wounded child soldiers, I had second thoughts. They demoted me, and that's when Ms. Delmonte eventually approached me. Well, not personally. One of her closest in command."

"And you shifted loyalties just like that?" Foster sneered, which didn't seem to faze London.

"I was always loyal to the Celestial people. But I shifted my loyalty away from the corrupt leaders that have betrayed them time and time again—and who are ultimately to blame for your situation in the tunnels as well." London sounded matter-of-fact, but when Kae glanced back at him again, she could see his lips thin as he pressed them together.

"We've all gone through that. Even you, Foster," Kae said. "Only weeks ago, we hated everything about cloudheads. We considered them all evil, superior bastards who didn't think twice about killing any Subterranean in their sights."

"True," Foster muttered. "Sometimes I regress. Sorry, man." He slowed his step until London passed him. "I think I need to get to know these guys in the rear."

Kae heard Foster murmur to the younger men behind them and was relieved. He could be a stubborn man, but once he knew the facts, he adjusted his attitude easily.

"Strong guy," London said. "Can't say I blame him for being suspicious. We Celestials have committed such atrocities against your people."

"And we've retaliated with methods that helped create the rumors about our terrorist status. I suppose, when cornered, the tunnel rats fought back," Kae said. "We were lucky to come upon Dr. Garcia."

London brightened for the first time since they'd left the camp. "There's a true hero, if you ask me. She's worked at the Soldiers' Clinic for years, patching up younger and younger soldiers, no charge. I heard that's how you met."

"We did. She saved a Subterranean boy that I helped raise, and then she had to flee with us since your former peers were aiming their weapons at her. We took her to the tunnels."

"And why didn't your people make an example of her? A renowned Celestial in their midst?" London asked as he pushed away some low-hanging branches.

"Oh, they tried, but she kept saving their lives. Then we returned with the boy to the skyscraper after he took a turn for the worse. That's when we all, including Rayne—Dr. Garcia—learned about the dissident movement and the secret floor."

"I can imagine she was shocked to discover her parents were founding members of the movement." London smiled faintly. "But you all had a great impact in just a few days."

"I'm afraid we were why the Celestial authorities launched an attack and eventually discovered the secret floor. I regret that." Uncomfortable at having caused the evacuation, Kae rolled her shoulders under her backpack.

"You're thinking a bit backward." London waved his hand dismissively. "You may have been the catalyst for the evacuation, but you did so after you retrieved the updated live map from the former president's office. You risked your lives for all of us and, ultimately, for your own people. It was just a matter of time before the authorities had either broken one of us in captivity or managed to pinpoint our headquarters." He sighed and adjusted his helmet. "I worry about funneling the rest of the dissidents from other skyscrapers, as well as your people below."

Kae nodded. "That's why we have to find out what this facility is and then take it over and set up another perimeter here. We need somewhere to place everyone." She didn't mention how much she worried about how to transport the Subterraneans to their location. It was too far to walk, even if everyone in the tunnels were that strong and motivated.

"Sir," London said and held up his hand. "Look."

Kae rounded him carefully and raised her fist to stop the other three from advancing. Peering into the tall grass, at first, she didn't see anything. Then her eyes adjusted, and her visor helped sharpen the image.

"Are those...*horses*?" she asked.

"Yes. But how?" London shook his head, sounding equally baffled. "After humanity damn near destroyed the climate, thus killing off their own kind, as well as most of the wildlife, I daresay nobody expected to ever see animals as big as horses in the wild again. Birds. Insects. Of course, rodents, sure. But fucking horses?"

Kae waved the others forward and pointed. "Horses."

Foster gaped. "You're kidding."

"No. Look." Kae waited until he saw them. "Just like in those old movies."

"I'll be damned," Foster whispered.

Kae allowed all of them a few moments to enjoy the sight of the grazing horses—five adults and two smaller ones of undeterminable age. Brown and white, they appeared unafraid even though she knew they had spotted them. They apparently had no reason to fear humans—yet.

Chapter Eight

R ayne knew she was supposed to make sure she took breaks every other hour, to not overdo it, but she had so much to do. She had her interns and sub-level doctors care for the patients, while she made herself available if they needed assistance or advice. Her most frustrating patient was receiving home care but was rarely in her habitat.

Starting to lose her patience with LaSierra, Rayne strode across the hospital to the headquarters. She entered the rebuilt SkyBird and, of course, found LaSierra at her station, reviewing the live maps again.

"Ms. Delmonte," Rayne said sternly. "I just checked your GemLink's medical feature—"

LaSierra snapped her head up, and her amber eyes narrowed as they locked on Rayne. "Excuse me?"

"Your GemLink alerted me. I would like you to join me in your habitat so we can—"

"We will do nothing of the sort." LaSierra waved her hand dismissively. "I feel fine, and I have pressing matters to attend to."

"And as your chief medical officer, I'm the one who determines if you're fit for duty. We've been over that already." Rayne folded her arms across her chest. "I don't want to pull rank, but if it means stopping you from killing yourself, then I will."

Looking annoyed rather than angry, LaSierra pressed a sensor on her computer dais, switching off the map. "Very well, but you'll have to be quick, as I want to follow Kae Dark and her team's progress. We just managed to identify them a moment ago."

Something twitched just below Rayne's breastbone when LaSierra mentioned Kae. "I just have to adjust your medication and make sure you don't present any other symptoms that the GemLink isn't equipped to monitor." Looking around, Rayne frowned. "Where's Beth?"

"Visiting the two Subterranean children. And before you berate me for allowing her to leave, we are on an open GemLink channel with each other. It was the only way I could convince her to go." LaSierra's features softened. "She's refreshingly irreverent when it comes to authority."

Rayne chuckled. "The kids need to see her, no doubt. We can manage on our own. Do you want me to push—? All right. Just asking." Rayne held up her hands, palms toward LaSierra at the sight of her glare.

Inside the living area of LaSierra and Beth's habitat, Rayne worked quickly as she scanned the impatient woman. Her blood pressure was elevated, but as she was annoyed at being interrupted, Rayne wasn't concerned. It wasn't until she scanned one of her arteries that she knew she had been right to intervene. "LaSierra, your white blood count is on the rise. That can signal a developing infection. I won't be sure until I run my findings through the medical mainframe. In the meantime, I want to start you on Omnispectra antibiotics. We can't afford to take any chances."

"It's that bad?" LaSierra leaned in to read the result of the scan. "I don't feel worse. Truly."

"That's probably because of the different strips you're wearing to mitigate symptoms. They're efficient, sometimes too much so, as they can mask symptoms that alert us to sudden deterioration. Good thing I hooked up your GemLink to the medical mainframe. I'd also like for you to grant me permission to place a MedMonitor that sends more detailed data on around your right upper arm."

"Will it hinder me in my work?" LaSierra suddenly looked tired. "I really have to stay on top of things, especially at the beginning of our operations. I'm not being deliberately difficult. Much."

"It should be compatible with the technology in the headquarters. It sends on a special frequency to the Medical Mainframe. You have to wear it around the clock and remove it only when you use the cleaning tube."

"Very well. You've convinced me." Running a hand over her hair, LaSierra sighed. "Believe it or not, I do want to stay alive."

"Of course, you do."

"I'm glad to hear that, considering how I have to strong-arm you to even eat regularly." Beth's voice made Rayne flinch.

"Don't sneak up on people," LaSierra said. "Dr. Garcia could have taken off my arm with a laser scalpel."

"Scalpel?" Beth crossed the floor in two long strides. Glaring at LaSierra, she shoved her fingers through her hair. "Funny. No scalpel."

"You need to inform Beth about the purpose of this MedMonitor cuff." Rayne placed the narrow, thin cuff securely around LaSierra's arm. "There. All done—for now."

"What's wrong?" Beth crouched next to the AirFrame and gazed at LaSierra with sudden seriousness.

"Elevated white blood count. I need to be monitored and will have strong antibiotics to remedy it. Dr. Garcia caught it before I noticed anything at all." LaSierra sent Rayne a glance that forbade her to talk to Beth about any masked symptoms.

"That's it? You can fix this?" Beth stood and looked at Rayne with clear concern.

Though taken aback at how invested Beth seemed to be in LaSierra's wellbeing, Rayne supposed a bond had formed between the two women after Beth had fought to keep LaSierra from deteriorating in the crashed SkyBird.

"Unless something else surprises us, I'm confident the antibiotics will do what they're supposed to within forty-eight hours."

Beth gazed at Rayne for a few more moments but then turned to LaSierra. "Have you had your first dose?"

"Not yet. But I'm sure I'll experience that joyful moment before Dr. Garcia returns to the hospital." She regarded the long, probe-looking instrument in Rayne's hands, and Rayne couldn't blame her.

"I know, this is not very much fun, but at least it's only a matter of four or five seconds. Hold on to Beth and allow her to distract you."

LaSierra gripped Beth's left hand with her right. "I hate invasive treatments."

"Me too," Beth said, "but maybe that's because that's the only type of treatment available in the tunnels. It's that or nothing." She too eyed the long instrument cautiously. "What does that thing do?"

"It is inserted into a vein along her arm. Small nano-carriers will deliver the Omnispectra antibiotics throughout LaSierra's entire system within minutes, then be reabsorbed by the body and rendered harmless."

Rayne waited until she saw LaSierra nod curtly. She slid the long, thin instrument into her lower arm, starting at the crease in it, then pushed it in to the hilt. Pressing the sensor, she launched the nano-carriers. This was the part of the procedure that caused the most pain. LaSierra whimpered through clenched teeth, but then Beth moved closer and pressed her lips against her temple.

Rayne blinked but wasn't about to let on that she had noticed Beth's surprising move. When LaSierra flung her free arm around Beth's neck and pressed her face against her shoulder, Rayne merely surmised she had been correct to assume these two must have formed some sort of bond.

After pulling out the instrument, Rayne closed the tiny hole in the skin with a mini wand. "There. All done. I suggest you take a break before you return to headquarters. Perhaps have some tea and something to eat. It's even more important than before to provide sustenance for your system."

"I will," LaSierra said, her voice husky.

Beth wiped at errant tears of pain under LaSierra's eyes and then stood. "I'll fix us both something. Thanks for keeping an eye on her, Rayne."

"Don't talk about me as if I'm not here." LaSierra frowned, but there was no real force behind her annoyance.

"Sorry," Beth said casually. "I'm still glad Rayne was monitoring you." She walked Rayne to the door. "Have you heard anything from Kae?"

"She's sent me the clicks via the GemLink once. Foster?"

"Nothing." Beth grimaced. "The kids asked about them, and I couldn't tell them anything. Wes is easy to distract, but Tania isn't."

"I hear you." After giving Beth a quick hug, Rayne nodded at LaSierra and left their habitat. Just as she crossed the Inner Circle yard, she felt her GemLink vibrate 2-1-2-1-1. Exhaling, Rayle smiled to herself. Kae was at least safe at this very moment.

Kae looked up at the starlit sky, still not used to the sight of the expanse beyond Earth. On very few occasions, she had been able to see one or two stars glimmering between the skyscrapers, but to gaze at the sky like this, as if someone had tossed diamonds all over a purple-black blanket, was still so new.

"I see it too," Foster said quietly. "It boggles the mind, doesn't it?"

"Sure does." Kae kept walking through the grove of trees. "We have to set up camp soon. I don't know about you, but I need something to eat and a couple of hours of shut-eye."

"I can tell," Foster said and placed one of his huge hands on her shoulder. "You've stumbled a few times too many."

He was right. "Yeah. I tell myself I'm used to operating on scattered hours of sleep, but these last few weeks have been—a lot."

"Agreed."

After another ten minutes, Kae detected a clearing well inside the grove. Her GemLink didn't detect any larger lifeforms, which was encouraging. "In here," she said and motioned for them all to follow. "Pop up two of the habitats, and we'll grab three hours of rest."

"I'll take the first watch." Foster pointed at two of their new comrades in arms. "You take the second hour, and you the third."

Kae frowned. "I can take one hour—"

"No, Kae. You're leading us and need to stay sharp. All right?" Foster gave her a far-too-familiar glance. He wasn't going to budge.

"Fine. All right. Let's get this done." Kae helped Foster pull the compact box from his backpack. After pressing two sensors, she stepped back as it inflated and assumed its dome shape. Meant for three people, it provided inflatable cots and light not visible from outside. The dome's exterior had stealth sensors that scattered sensor sweeps. After a trip into the bushes to relieve herself, Kae nodded to Foster, who sat on a pad, leaning against one of the trees, his Nova blaster across his knees. "See you in three hours. Make the most of your two hours."

"Oh, I will. I'll probably keep you awake with my snoring," Foster said and grinned.

Kae entered the dome and realized it also had a feature that kept the temperature pleasant inside. She took out her whisper-thin emergency blanket and wrapped it around her, not so much for the warmth, but from a life-long habit of needing to hide underneath something.

Kae jerked awake when she felt a hand on her shoulder. She looked up, blinking at the muted light in the dome. A face hovered above her, but it wasn't Foster's. Kae fumbled for her ShadowPulse weapon but saw that Foster had woken up and was aiming his Nova blaster at the intruders.

Sitting up, Kae realized that the person she had thought was bent over her was in fact standing up. It was a child.

"Who are you? Where did you come from?" Kae asked hoarsely. She saw two more figures behind the closest child, both smaller.

"I'm hungry," one of the smaller children said, its voice thin, sounding exhausted.

"We have rations to share," Foster said, still with his weapon trained on the kids.

"Lights on full." Remembering the command, Kae pushed off her security blanket.

When the dome became fully lit, she stared in shock at the intruders. Thin enough to remind her of the children in the tunnels that were never going to make it, and with their clothes in tatters, the two smaller ones stood behind the child that had woken her up.

"Who are you?" Kae asked, modifying her tone. No matter who these children were, they were just kids.

"I'm Zeph," the oldest child said, its voice as hoarse as Kae's. "We need water. Emb won't make it if we don't find clean water."

"Emb?" Kae studied the other two. The smallest one, perhaps three or four years old, nodded. "That you?"

Another nod.

"Here, kids." Foster put down his weapon and pulled a bottle from his backpack. "Don't drink too fast."

Kae studied the children further while the older of them, Zeph, shared the water with the youngest, Emb, and then the middle child, who went by Lux. The two youngest were leaning against Zeph, who was the obvious leader of this little pack. Kae couldn't determine Zeph's gender, and it didn't matter. What struck her was how thin, dirty, and raggedy they looked.

"Foster, check on whoever's on guard. Somehow these three slipped past them."

"I will." Foster hoisted his weapon and disappeared outside.

"Why don't you take a seat?" Kae pointed at her cot. "You look ready to take a tumble."

The children slowly sat down, the youngest flanking Zeph. Kae checked her GemLink and frowned when its sensor registered the kids as "small, indigenous animals, minimal danger." Huh. That showed that even the dissidents' fabulous technology had its limits.

"My name's Kae. I guess you're on the run from one of the facilities a few miles up ahead?"

Zeph frowned. "Faci-lities?" It was obvious they didn't know what the word meant.

"The camps near the crop fields?" Kay gestured in the direction of their goal.

"Slave camps," Zeph said darkly, correcting her. "We dug our trackers out, using our teeth, and then we went on the run. We had no choice. We wouldn't be here if our water hadn't run out. We're on our way to the river, but our map led us wrong." Zeph held up their hand, palm forward, and looked disgusted. "See?"

Kae saw faint blue lines and could only surmise this was the children's "map." She tried for a reassuring smile. "You know, I've been in a similar situation. I once had to trust people I thought were the enemy to help me save a little boy." She regarded Lux. "You're not talking much. Are you all right?"

"My stomach hurts." Lux blinked slowly. "I'm hungry."

Kae's own stomach ached at the sight of the children. "I bet you all are. What do you usually eat—in the, um, slave camps?"

"We get our rations once a day. Two energy bars until we turn thirteen. Then we get three. Sometimes older kids, even grownups, try to take ours as they're in the fields a lot longer and need more energy." Zeph clearly repeated what they'd heard before.

"Are there a lot of grownups there?"

"Yes. A lot. The fields are big. I worked close to the buildings, but in a few months, I would have been sent out with the crafts to work the fields far away from Lux and Emb. They rely on me to protect them. I couldn't abandon them." Fat tears made tracks in the dirty, young face.

"I see." Kae did, only too well. "Do you know anyone who comes from the tunnels, the Subterraneans?" Kae dug in her backpack for ration bars. She knew better than to give them anything they weren't used to. It could make them sick.

"Subterraneans? I only knew the cavers. I'm a caver, but Lux and Emb were born in the slave camps." Zeph held the other two closer.

"Here. Nibble small pieces even if you're hungry." Kae handed over three ration bars. Her mind spun at Zeph's words. "You were taken at some point. Do you know when?"

"I was five. I'd just had a birthday party. That's all I can remember. My party and the cake. Sometimes I see a woman with red hair helping me blow out a candle, but I think that's just from one of my dreams." Zeph bit into their ration bar. "There were a lot on the transport. I remember that. Bigger kids, and smaller kids like me."

Kae covered her mouth to hold back a gasp. She remembered a raid in the northern part of the tunnel system when she was in her early twenties. The cloudhead soldiers had blasted their way into a part of the tunnel system where her fellow Subterraneans had started an ambitious school project. More than eighty children had been taken, and the shocked and traumatized adults had been told that they were going to a reformation camp. So, this was it. A life of servitude in the fields that fed the Celestials in the skyscrapers.

Foster returned, looking both frustrated and angry. "The guy had to pee, damn it." He shook his head. "I let London deal with him. Did you find out something?"

"Zeph here is from the northern tunnels. The school tunnel." Kae bit her lower lip to keep it from trembling. She saw exactly when Foster caught on.

"Ah, fuck," he whispered. "That's…" He shook his head.

"I know. The question is, what do we do with them? We're under communication restrictions, and we can't take them with us. I don't quite trust any of London's people enough to care for caver kids." Kae rubbed her forehead. "And I'm afraid these three will disappear into the wilderness if we try to make them wait here until we get back." If they indeed made it back. Kae shuddered.

"There's only one solution," Foster said. "We have to take them with us but change our mission to not endanger them. Perhaps young Zeph here can provide some intel."

Kae could think of a hundred ways this suggestion could backfire. "It's that or you or I begin to walk back with them and the rest continue. I'd rather not leave any of the two of us alone with the others. I trust London, but I'm not a hundred percent about the others. I mean, I'm hoping they're fine with working with Subterraneans, but I'd never bet your life on it, Foster."

"Or yours. My life would be forfeited when Rayne found out," Foster said and gave a crooked smile.

"True." Kae studied the children. "How would you feel helping the freedom fighters, Zeph? I'm from the tunnels, and so is Foster. The three soldiers outside are Celestials but working against the corrupt authorities there." She was sure Zeph didn't know what 'corrupt authorities' meant, but the child squared their shoulders and stood up. They pushed the younger kids behind them. "And Emb and Lux?"

"We'll carry them with us. They won't have to walk. When we get near the fields, we'll rely on you telling us what you know about the area. Can you do that?"

"And you'll keep Emb and Lux safe?" Zeph looked, not tired exactly, but jaded. They had little reason to put their trust in anyone.

"I would never abandon a child. Ever." Kae placed a gentle hand on Zeph's shoulder. "You have my word."

Zeph looked Kae in the eyes for several moments. "And you'll provide water and food?"

"Absolutely." Foster had begun adjusting his harness. "Who's riding on my back?" he asked and winked at Emb and Lux.

"Me," Emb whispered. Lux merely studied them all quietly. The child hadn't spoken once.

"And you, Lux, will go with Captain London." Kae would have taken the child herself, but she expected to be the one who led the two not carrying children closer to the camps.

Poking her head out, Kae motioned for London to join them. He entered the habitat, and she had to credit him with his kind approach to the children. He adjusted his harness and pulled out his safety blanket before approaching Lux.

"Hey. You'll be fine riding on my back. I'm strong, and I won't let you fall. The harness is maybe a little uncomfortable, but you don't have to walk—" He stared at the child's feet, and for the first time, Kae realized they weren't wearing shoes, not even socks. She bent and held out her hand to Emb. "May I see your feet, Emb?"

Emb didn't answer but extended her small right foot. Kae took it in her hand, stunned at how cold it was, but also feeling how callused the sole was. This child had perhaps never worn any shoes.

"Let's tuck you in under this great silver blanket." Kae swallowed hard but kept the smile going. "It's really a very special, magical blanket that will keep you warm." She didn't add that the blanket also had projectile and energy-pulse protection, in case someone fired on a sleeping soldier. If someone fired at Foster or London from behind, the kids were somewhat protected.

Turning to Zeph, Kae looked at their feet. "You don't have shoes either."

"I had some once. Someone helped me cut the top open when I outgrew them." Zeph shrugged. "I'm used to walking barefoot. We all do, for a reason."

"What reason is that?" Foster asked, and Kae knew he was schooling his features to hide the rage.

Zeph blinked and stared at them as if they doubted their common sense. "Even if we're used to walking barefoot, no matter the season, we could never move fast for very long and would always be wary of cutting our feet on something. The fences are lined with sharp objects, as is the ground just inside them."

"I see. That's good to know." Kae said. "Will you be able to walk with us, as we'll move fairly fast?"

Zeph pulled up their mouth in a lopsided grin. "Since I won't have to make sure Emb and Lux keep up, I'll be faster than all of you." They raised their chin in a clear challenge, as if daring them to laugh or argue.

"I believe you. I've seen kids your age move like the wind." Foster slapped Zeph's back but didn't put a lot of force into his appreciative gesture. The gesture seemed to sit well with the child, as they grinned broadly.

"I think I like you," Zeph said. "Take care of Emb. She's only four, as I said."

"I will," Foster said somberly.

As they exited the habitat and began folding it and the other one by using the sensors in reverse, the children's eyes grew wide, and they watched the process with great interest.

For the second time, Lux opened their mouth and, in a husky small voice said, "Like magic."

CHAPTER NINE

B eth raised her Nova blaster and moved soundlessly, heel-to-toe, around the outer perimeter of the Inner Circle. The alarm had reached everyone soundlessly, and everyone who was not part of the security detail was sheltering in place, which also meant their leader, LaSierra. Beth had made sure she was safe in the center of the SkyBird headquarters before she grabbed her blaster.

At times she missed her gleamer, the remodeled old version of a Nova blaster that she'd carried when she worked with Foster and Kae in the tunnels. She had customized the weapon to fit her perfectly, and even if this state-of-the art weapon had all the features a soldier could think of, it wasn't the same.

Twenty yards away from Beth, she saw one of the dissident soldiers crouching and raising her fist. Beth followed the command and pressed her back against the habitat behind her. Everything was eerily quiet except for the silent intruder alert buzzing from her GemLink. She studied it and used the proximity scanner but couldn't detect anything. She saw only the dots signifying the soldiers around her.

Then—a shadow. Dislodging itself from the wall of a SkyBird ten yards ahead and to her right, a thin figure slipped across to the Inner Circle. Beth used a voice command to engage her GemLink. "All on my position. Intruder at Inner Circle."

"Well, damn it," a voice said over the command, and then Beth could hear soft footfalls as soldiers homed in on her position.

Beth was already running. Carrying her weapon tight against her, she used her talent for dodging and scurrying around people in the narrow tunnels to make her way among the SkyBirds and habitats. As she reached the inner side of the Inner Circle, she scanned the area, rather than using her GemLink sensor. Technology failed at times, and she wasn't about to let the intruder reach the SkyBird headquarters.

She saw several soldiers close in from all directions, which meant the person who had managed to breach their outer perimeter had somehow delayed the alarm system. Beth narrowed her eyes, but the darkness was dense in several places. She flipped down her visor and performed another scan.

At first, she didn't detect anything, but twenty seconds later, her visor lit up the outline of a figure over by Rayne and Kae's habitat. Taking a chance, Beth hoped the intruder wouldn't possess the same advanced technology. She whispered a voice command via her GemLink. "Eyes on the target. Moving in." She didn't wait for a reply.

"No...shit!" It was the soldier somewhere to Beth's right, but she ignored it. The shadowy figure was positioned far too close to the habitats, and she wouldn't risk them reaching LaSierra...or any of the others.

Rushing straight for the intruder, Beth kept her Nova blaster trained on them. When she was about five yards from the person, they seemed to shrink before her. Tapping the visor, Beth made it retract, and when she reached the figure, she saw the person had slumped to the ground. Directing a light beam from her GemLink onto them, she found herself staring at what looked like a young woman dressed in a dirty, but whole, green coverall. Her face was thin, almost emaciated, and she returned Beth's gaze with a venomous stare.

"Don't move. Show me your hands!" Beth said with a growl.

The woman, because she was certain the trembling individual in the green coverall was female, glared up at her. "D-don't fucking shoot," she snarled. "I'm injured."

Beth knew better than to fall for such a ruse. "Perhaps, but you can still carry weapons or something else to hurt me with."

"I'm not going to hurt anyone. I need help!" Curling up on her side, the woman groaned. "Do you think I'd enter a fucking cloudhead camp if I wasn't forced to?" The woman whimpered again. "I'm Max, and I need help. A lot of us do. Please. You can't leave us to die." She howled the last words and fell back into a heap.

Beth had no idea what the woman—or girl, rather—was talking about. "Just stay down."

When three soldiers joined Beth, the leader among them walked closer to the young woman and pressed her Nova blaster against her head.

"Hey. Don't escalate things further." Beth was used to pulling rank when Kae wasn't present, and she placed a strong hand on the weapon. "Keep it trained on her, sir, but at a distance. I'll pat her down."

"She could have explosives on her. You don't know," the female soldier, Beth had forgotten her name, growled.

"I don't think so." Used to trusting her gut, Beth stepped forward after shoving her blaster near the intruder's back. "Are you dangerous?" she asked sternly as she began to run her hands over Max's body.

"Normally, yes, I'd say so. Not now. I'm wounded and it's all your fault." She curled up as shudders spread along her body. "I need help so I can go back and assist the people in my sanct."

"In your what?" Beth had finished patting Max down and turned to the soldiers that stood on each side of her. "She's not armed. Only thing I found in her pockets is some sort of food wrapped in leaves." She held up the strange little package. "It looks like a homemade ration bar. We made similar ones in the tunnels."

"I used to live there," Max said, gasping now. "When I was little."

"We better get her to the hospital habitat." Beth locked her gaze on the reluctant female soldier. "I can go inside headquarters and ask Delmonte or the Garcias, but we all know what they'll say. Besides, how are we going to get some intel out of this woman if she dies on our watch?"

"I just need to know if she's the only one breaking through the perimeter. Well, are you?" The female soldier nudged Max with her weapon.

"Yes. Yes!" Sobbing furiously now, Max clutched her side. A dark stain that could only be blood began to spread and seep into the fabric of her coverall. "You had to shove me right there, you fucking idiot."

Beth had had enough. She bent and pushed her arms under Max's back and legs, lifting her easier than she'd anticipated. "I'm taking her. You can do one more sweep if you think it's necessary." She didn't wait for an answer but hurried toward the hospital, hoping to find Rayne on duty. She worked some evenings, but no nights, as she too was recuperating.

A medic came running with a gurney when Beth entered with Max in her arms. "Who's this, sir?" the medic asked, looking confusedly at the rumpled form before him.

"An intruder. I need you to examine her, and, most important, she's hemorrhaging."

The medic pressed a sensor and then began slicing off the dirty coverall. Beth disinfected her hands and put on a shield apron in case she could help.

"What kind of weapon has done that?" the medic asked, but the question was obviously rhetorical.

"A laser-based one would be my guess. Perhaps even a regular metal blade," Rayne said as she hurried into the examination room. "Hi, Beth. I heard we have a visitor."

"You could say that. This is Max. She breached the perimeter somehow about twenty minutes ago." Beth studied Max's features. She had closed her eyes, and under the dirt, she was very pale.

"That was some feat," Rayne muttered and ran a diagnostic wand over Max's thin body. "She's not wearing any shoes."

Blinking, Beth returned her focus to Max's dirty, callused feet. "Damn. They've got to be cold."

"I'd say so, yes." Rayne turned to the medic. "Close the curtains. I want her to be out of everyone else's view, as we don't know what's happened to her. Let's not take any risks."

"The Celestial soldiers aren't happy. If I hadn't been there, I think she would been incarcerated, whether she needed treatment or not."

"That sounds like something you need to tell LaSierra. We must have strict protocols and regulations for even the most unlikely situations. Granted, there have been enough flybys by drones and sensor pods to fry anyone's nerves ever since Kae and Foster left. Have you heard anything?"

"A few clicks from Foster and once from Kae. You?" Beth looked up at Rayne. Above her transparent mask, the vulnerable skin around her eyes was tense, as were her lips.

"I received the latest clicks about an hour ago. I know it's ridiculous, but I wish that click would come continuously."

"Not ridiculous." Max slurred her words. "You need to take care of your people."

Rayne's eyebrows rose above the eye protectors. "Someone's not as out of it as we thought." She pointed at the tubes behind Max's head and then looked at the medic. "Hook up the usual surveillance equipment and add one sensor for red blood count."

"I don't get it," Max murmured. "This chick said that she was a caver, and now you...I mean, you're here with the enemy. The cloudheads."

"Not a word we use about the Celestials that are part of this camp. They're dissidents, freedom fighters, and so are those of us that are Subterraneans. There's not many of us, but we stand our ground." Beth spoke calmly.

"Idiots. You can't trust 'em. They'll fool you." Max sobbed and turned her head.

Acting without considering the consequences, Beth placed a gloved hand on Max's head. "I know this is scary. When I entered my first skyscraper, I was terrified and certain I'd be captured and placed in a reformation camp."

"Reformation camp. Never heard of that. I've only ever been to work camps, which is a nicer name for slave camps, obviously."

Beth looked up at Rayne, who shook her head in dismay. "Well, you're here now."

"Some—something's wrong." Max had a problem getting her words out. "I think I'm going blind," Max whispered. "It's all dark at the edges."

"You're losing blood, and we're going to replace it. Just hold on, Max. We'll take care of you." Rayne's hands flew across the impromptu operating field. "As soon as I've stopped the bleeding enough, we'll hover her over to the theater. She's not just been fired upon. She has old injuries that I would imagine she's learned to live with, but now they're causing issues that are hard to foresee."

Beth watched Rayne use several wands to repair the bleeding vessels, but the blood was still seeping.

"Damn. She fainted. Old-school methods, then." Reaching for sterile fabrics that were always on hand in the examination rooms, Rayne began to pack the wound.

Beth swallowed hard and held Max's head as Rayne and the medic began moving the gurney. Just as they exited the examination room, a sound that Beth recognized immediately proved that LaSierra had left her shelter-in-place site and was now driving her AirFrame toward them.

Rounding the corner, LaSierra and Rocque were hurrying toward them. "Why is this woman not in custody?" LaSierra asked sharply.

"Because she's been shot with some crude weapon and needs surgery," Rayne didn't raise her voice, and she didn't need to. The confidence was apparent.

"That's not your call—"

"Oh, but it is, LaSierra. As chief medical officer for this camp, what I say goes when there is risk for loss of life," Rayne said decisively.

"That may be, but I'm responsible—"

"For a lot, but not medical procedures. If you want to question this girl once we know she'll live, that's fine. For now, get out of my way." Rayne pulled at the gurney, and Beth saw her glare at her father as she, with Beth's and the medic's help, carried Max into the theater. It had been a while since Beth had seen this side of Rayne, and she hoped it signaled that her friend was regaining her full strength.

Turning her head before she stepped into the theater, Beth looked at LaSierra, who glowered after them. It had been a long time since she had truly experienced LaSierra's solemn and dispassionate leader style. Furious at what she could only see as a callous disrespect for life—anyone's life—she shook her head in dismay before she closed the door to the operating room.

LaSierra moved her AirFrame to the observation window, where she could see what was going on in the operating theater. She made her chair elevate, and that gave her a clear view of the person that Beth and the soldiers had apprehended.

Emaciated, but also wiry, the thin, naked young woman was covered by bruises, which made LaSierra squeeze her eyes closed for a moment. When she opened them, the team had covered the young woman in medical blankets. They had features woven into them that kept her at the optimal temperature and read and recorded her vital signs.

The surgery commenced instantly. Rayne explored the wound on the woman's left side, and even though she was sedated, somehow the pain seemed to penetrate her mind. She frowned and her hands curled. Was she having a seizure? LaSierra switched on the sound system that allowed her to hear what was being said in the theater.

"She's fighting the sedation somehow." Rayne sounded frustrated. "We can only increase the dosage of the sedation two points. Beth, you're gloved up, right?"

"Yes." Beth rounded the table. "Where do you need me?"

"Hold her down. I know, it's harsh, but I need to irrigate and then wand-clean the wound. Whoever did this to her didn't just stab her. They twisted the damn weapon inside her. The laceration of the liver is causing her to hemorrhage uncontrollably."

Beth placed her hands on the woman's shoulders. "Hey, Max, just hold on. Rayne's doing her best." Beth's eyes were dark above her face mask. She glanced toward the window, obvious contempt and disappointment radiating from her gaze.

"Ah. There. There's that annoying little bleeder." Rayne stood with her hands deep in the woman's—Max's?—abdomen. "Vascular wand, size one." She held out her hand, and the medic slapped a small wand against her palm. Rayne stuck it into the wound, and a faint, green light glimmered when she engaged it.

The rest of the surgery took another forty-five minutes, and LaSierra followed it all. When Beth finally could let go of the writhing woman, she straightened and massaged her lower back. She had to be sore after staying in the same position while restraining the girl.

Much like how Beth had immobilized LaSierra in her crashed SkyBird, to avoid further injuries.

After a while, they hovered the gurney out of the theater, and LaSierra moved her AirFrame up to them, following as they took the woman to the ICU. Having been there only recently, she shuddered as she remembered only too vividly the smells and the pain she'd been in.

After they transferred Max to a bed, LaSierra positioned her chair at the foot of it, not wanting to be in the way, but making sure they knew she wasn't leaving either.

"She's stable," Rayne said. "She has bruises on twenty percent of her body, and she had a semi-healed cut on her upper arm that seems to go straight through a tattooed number."

Beth peered at the transparent bandage around Max's arm. "Fuck. I've seen this before. Only once, but I'll never forget it."

"What is it?" LaSierra asked.

"An identity code. I saw one on a young boy that another tunnel resistance crew had rescued after he ran away from a reformation camp. They realized he had a tracker inserted too when cloudheads came to retrieve him. They were unsuccessful, and after that, Boro, our former doctor, removed the chip. I would imagine that Max here did the same—by herself or someone who wasn't a medic."

LaSierra winced at the thought of someone cutting up their arm to rid themselves of a tracker chip.

"Can you estimate when she can be interro—debriefed?" LaSierra asked Rayne.

Rayne sighed and exchanged a glance with Beth. They were obviously not happy with her, but that couldn't be helped. They had their duties to perform, and LaSierra had hers.

"Four or five hours at the earliest. Why don't I put a note in her chart to notify you, or my father, when she's lucid enough?" Rayne tucked a thermo blanket around Max, then waved the medic over. "When she's truly stable, please run a cleansing wand over her. She's filthy enough to cause skin problems or infections just from the dirt. And use some of the derma wands on her feet."

"Yes, sir," the medic said. Her eyes softened. "I would have guessed her to be little more than a kid, but her bone scans show she's twenty-two."

Rayne glowered at her tablet as if technology was to blame. "Malnutrition and lack of medical care have caused some of her general condition. Being subjected to the elements for an extended period of time is another factor."

"Damn." LaSierra clung to the armrests of her AirFrame. "I wonder how long they had her in one of the camps."

"She said she lived in the tunnels when she was little." Beth rubbed Max's foot gently through the blanket. "So, if she remembers that, she could have been in one of those camps, or reformation sites, for up to eighteen years or so." She ran her free hand along her face. "And there are more like her out there, in trouble. That's what she said, and I believe her."

"We can't take what she says at face value," LaSierra said sternly. She watched Beth's cheeks grow an angry red. "Listen to me before you bite my head off again, Beth. Tomorrow morning, I want you to take a team of four with you and trace her way to us in reverse."

"That means I have to find where she entered the perimeter first." Beth was still flustered but had calmed down.

"We can run a diagnostic and see where the incursion took place," a hoarse male voice said from behind a curtain. "Just give me access so I can start earning my keep around here."

"Benny!" LaSierra called out and pivoted in her chair. Beth was already pulling the curtain aside, and there sat Benny, her young tech specialist, on the side of his bed, looking pale but conscious and alert.

"Ms. Delmonte," he said and looked like he was about to stand up.

"Stop, stop," Beth said. "Don't fall on your ass and reinjure your thick skull. I heard that if you didn't have a super-brain, you might not have done so well."

"Beth." Benny smiled wanly. "I'd know that irreverence anywhere." He rubbed the back of his neck, wincing. "I remember that we launched, but the rest is scattered around in my 'super-brain,' and I can only piece together things I hear from the staff."

"Are you sure you're ready to work on a computer, Benny?" LaSierra studied the young man closely. He looked banged up still, but so did she. His eyes were clear and alert, and she knew he had to be going stir-crazy if he was anything like her.

"I am, sir. Even if I have to do it from here, just hook me up to a unit." Benny craned his neck and peered at Max in the bed across from him. "That her? Poor girl. She's had it rough."

"She's tough and fearless." Beth clearly had a vested interest in Max, most likely because she was yet another subterranean.

"Pick your team tomorrow morning, Beth. And pull out as soon as you have the intel you need." LaSierra stretched her abdomen carefully. "If nothing else requires my attention, I'm returning to my bed."

Beth hesitated. "I will assist you," she said coolly.

"Good. Good night, everyone." As soon as Beth had pushed her out and around the corner to exit the hospital habitat, LaSierra slumped against the backrest, moaning as pain seared through her lower back.

"Damn. Did you take your medication the way you were supposed to?" Beth picked up speed and sprinted with the AirFrame toward the entrance to their habitat.

"I'm fine with the Omnispectra antibiotics. I need some of the emergency pain medication though." Speaking through her clenched teeth, LaSierra hated how her body was still failing her. Or perhaps, to be fair, it was she that failed her body. She had placed it in a crashing SkyBird, after all, even if she'd had no idea that would happen, of course.

"I'm on it," Beth said urgently as they got inside. She pushed LaSierra into her bedroom and opened the cabinet that held her medical supplies. "It's this one, right, the one that knocks you out a little."

"I loathe that, but yes. I've been a high-tier harpy enough for one night." LaSierra pressed the sensors that freed her from the harness that kept her in place. She pushed off with her trembling arms, but strong hands pushed them back.

"You're not doing that, LaSierra," Beth said, and her voice no longer harbored contempt and anger. "Put your arms around my neck."

LaSierra was too tired to protest. Holding on to Beth, she pressed her face against her strong neck and closed her eyes. "Beth," she whispered. "I sometimes have to be…this. I can't even apologize for it, as someone must lead…"

"Shh. Just hold on," Beth said and turned around. Carrying LaSierra over to the bed, she lowered her carefully. She took a few extra pillows and placed them around LaSierra, to steady her aching body. "I know all that," Beth said. "I've seen Kae make more than a few decisions during the years I was on her team in the tunnels. It's just…"

"That this girl is one of you and has been through hell." LaSierra watched as Beth placed an ampoule in the infulizer. The cold spray stung her vein as Beth pressed it against the crease of her arm. "This is the part I hate the most. Losing control."

"I'll make sure that doesn't happen," Beth said. "I'll stay here if you like."

"Why would you do that?" LaSierra asked, trying in vain to hang on to her clarity. "You were so angry...or disappointed, in me..."

"I'm not now. I'm just worried about you." Beth bent over LaSierra and pushed a few long tresses from her face. LaSierra didn't know anyone among her fellow dissidents that dared touch her at all, let alone make sure she didn't inhale her hair.

"Then stay," LaSierra whispered, not sure if Beth heard her.

Beth's hand on her cheek warmed her for a while longer, and when she removed it, LaSierra missed it acutely. The bed dipped behind her, and then she felt a familiar, strong hand land on her hip.

"This all right?" Beth asked just before LaSierra let sleep claim her and the pain was a thing of the past.

She wasn't sure, but she thought she heard herself say, "Oh, yes."

CHAPTER TEN

K ae maneuvered through the shrubbery with the small body strapped to her back in mind. She couldn't carelessly let go of thicker twigs or branches and have them hit Emb. She'd taken over carrying the girl while London was heading up the field team. If a branch hit the kid, she might cry out and alert any nearby Celestials to their location. With London's help, they'd managed to synchronize their GemLinks and set them to create a scattering pattern that would keep them close to invisible unless they stumbled upon a sentry.

"Foster," she whispered. "Check on Emb. She's very still."

She felt Foster approach and carefully lift the safety blanket. "She's asleep. I think Lux is awake, but I can't be sure since the kid doesn't make a peep."

"I'll check," Zeph said and rounded Foster. "Lux is asleep too. They're both exhausted," Zeph said. "The rations and water you shared satisfied their hunger enough to allow them to sleep."

"Good. And you, Zeph?"

"I can walk some more. Now that I have protection for my feet, it's easy." A smile flickered along Zeph's face, and Kae was certain this child hadn't had much to smile about in a while. "Just let us know."

Zeph nodded curtly and resumed their place at Kae's side, but one step behind. They had maintained that position throughout their hike and seemed to have no trouble keeping up.

After another hour, she felt Zeph tug at her harness, the skinny little hands frantic.

"Yes?" Kae whispered.

"You need to put the kids down. The first camp is behind that ridge." Whereas Zeph had seemed mature and grownup earlier, now they were wide-eyed with fear and their lips trembled. "We can't risk them being caught."

"Nobody's getting caught, kid," Foster said and unhooked his harness to remove it safely. Kae did the same. They walked farther into a dense grove and placed the children on the ground, wrapped in safety blankets.

"London, I need you to stay with the kids." Kae held up her hand when he opened his mouth, looking like he would object. "I need someone with them I can trust. Your other subordinates are too green. You need to stay alert. I'm taking Foster and your soldiers. Zeph comes with us since they can show us where to go—and where not to. Think of it this way. These children have valuable intel when we return to camp, and we'll go find more."

"Yes, sir," London said, "when you put it like that." He gave her a crooked smile and then gazed down at the two small bundles on the ground. "They're safe with me, Kae."

"I know." She turned and motioned for the rest of her team, including Zeph, to fall in. "Keep Zeph in the middle. We're not risking their safety." Not when the child had gotten their little companions this far.

They moved along the edge of the grain growing on the other side of the narrow path. Kae didn't like how tall the grain was behind them, at least eight feet. A lot of things could hide in there, and she couldn't use their strongest scanners as they might trigger sensors inside the structures.

Zeph pointed at something up ahead, and Kae pushed them behind her. "Stay behind me."

About a hundred yards farther up along the fence, Kae saw a hole that would allow a small body to scurry through, barely avoiding the no-doubt electrically charged barrier.

"Did you dig this?"

"Not all of it. We scooped dirt up every time we passed and spread it somewhere else," Zeph whispered. "We should've made it bigger, but it took too long. We ran out of time."

"I see." Kae waved the two dissident soldiers over. "Do you have any way of marking this for others to find it from the outside and from the air? Something inconspicuous."

Probably eager to redeem himself, the soldier who had let the children sneak past him pulled out a small box from the side of his backpack. "I have the perfect thing, sir." He pulled out an even smaller box from the first one and opened it. Tiny black dots, not unlike the ammunition that went into the ShadowPulse weapons, sat in rows of five, ten rows total. "Place these in the pattern you want. Sensors, or even an Aeroton Map, will pick them up."

"Anyone's sensors?" Kae frowned.

"No, sir. Unless you have the code for them, they won't show up at all, and when placed in the dirt, they won't be visible to the naked eye."

"All right. Put them in a semicircle on this side of the fence and mark where the kids dug through. When soldiers come back to breach the fence at some point, they can use this marker to determine which building this is. When we debrief the children later, this will be a good starting point."

"Yes, sir." The soldier knelt and carefully placed seven small dots in a shallow semicircle around the crawl space.

"Good thing you didn't make it more readily visible, Zeph," Foster murmured. "This way, we just might be able to get inside with a larger force and help the ones inside."

"Mostly children ages four to thirteen are in this barrack." Zeph blinked and then rubbed their eyes.

"How many?" Kae whispered.

"Don't know. Hundreds. It's hard to keep count. Some die. Some in the nursery barracks get old enough and move here. And some here get old enough and move to the grownup barracks."

Kae went rigid at Zeph's words, spoken with such calm. "Did Emb and Lux come from the nursery barrack?"

"Of course," Zeph said in a what-did-you-think? voice.

Kae exchanged a glance with Foster, whose his hands were balled into tight fists. "Good to know, Zeph."

"Can we leave soon?" Zeph's lips were trembling. "I keep worrying they're going to jump us."

"As long as we're using our scattering device, they can't see us, but you're right. We shouldn't linger." Kae motioned with her hand for the others to follow. "Now that we've marked the vulnerable part of the fence, we can return. If you provide us with information back at headquarters, that will save a lot of time—and that would mean saving lives in these barracks too."

Zeph regarded Kae somberly. "I'm prepared to do anything to repay what they did to the young kids."

"And for what they did to you." Foster placed a hand on Zeph's shoulder. "Let's go back to the little ones."

"Yes. Move out." Kae made circular motions in the air and then pointed to where they'd come from. "Step partly into the crop. I want to take a few samples of it. I have a feeling I know how this is used, and I need to have my hunch confirmed."

They walked fast through the crops, and Kae kept an eye on Zeph, who was starting to look fatigued. Digging into her pocket, she pulled up an energy bar and handed it to them. "Here. Eat. You need to boost your strength since we're going to start walking back."

Zeph bit into the bar and then devoured it in three large bites. "So good," they said, humming.

"In other words, what they served you in the camps was little better than cardboard." Foster shook his head. "It's going to get better once we're at headquarters. Guess we need to be careful with what we feed you since your stomachs might rebel."

Kae led the party to where London was watching over the sleeping children. It took them less than five minutes to strap Lux and Emb onto London and Foster. Kae made sure every part of them was covered by the safety blankets. Then she wrapped her own around Zeph's head and torso. If anyone fired at the child, the projectile would bounce off the safety blanket. If they hit Zeph's legs or arms, they could still carry them, and he would hopefully not be lethally injured. It was important to get the children to the camp alive.

❖

Beth jerked awake. She didn't recognize her room, and she wasn't alone in the bed. And why the hell was she fully dressed in her suit, though minus her harness?

Slowly, last night's events crept back into her mind, and she exhaled. She was in LaSierra's room in the habitat, and a glance at the long, dark hair proved that she was Beth's bedmate. LaSierra, the woman who had showed that she could make tough decisions with her focus on the big picture, but who personally suffered in secret afterward.

"LaSierra?" Beth murmured.

LaSierra merely gripped the material of Beth's suit harder and murmured something inaudible. Had last night's incursion by the young woman named Max, and what had transpired between them all, caused LaSierra to have bad dreams—or had she simply been in pain. Neither option was appealing.

"Mm. Beth?" LaSierra rolled onto her back and opened her eyes. As if lit from within, LaSierra's amber eyes seemed to glow as she turned her head toward Beth.

"What…what time is it?" LaSierra asked huskily.

Beth checked her GemLink. "0535 hours. Or, simply put, fucking early." She started to sit up, but LaSierra's slender hand stopped her.

"Wait. Why are you awake? Did you get an alert?" LaSierra turned toward Beth again, keeping her hand on her shoulder.

"No. No alerts. Maybe I woke up because I'm not used to sharing a bed with anyone." Especially no one like this woman. Beth swallowed, her conflicting emotions regarding LaSierra still not resolved. It might take her a while to sort through them, if she ever managed to.

"I thought you were quite crowded in the tunnels." LaSierra studied Beth closely.

"We are. That's why we're so adamant about protecting what little space we have. We don't share things, or spaces, unless we have to—or want to. After I left the orphanage, I swore to never live like we did there if I could help it."

"And then I force you to share my bed." LaSierra sighed and then smiled weakly. "Just your luck."

"You didn't force me to do anything. Nobody can do that. I shared your bed because I knew you might need me. Besides, I admit that I wasn't keen on calling someone else in to do it instead." Beth smiled to show she was joking—for the most part.

"Beth!" Looking scandalized before she began to chuckle, LaSierra patted her shoulder. "I won't keep you here if you were heading back to your room. My pain level is much more stable now."

Beth frowned and raised up on her elbow. "What do you mean, stable? You're not supposed to suffer pain much at all. It's not good for the healing process. Rayne said so."

LaSierra pressed her lips together. "I know she did, but it's not always doable. I can't keep drugging myself silly. I need to stay sharp if I want to keep my position. It's not just my being an ambitious bitch, even if I know I have that reputation. Our people need continuity. If we start changing the leadership they've relied on for years, decades, it'll cause confusion. They can lose faith in our missions, and that in turn can cost lives."

Beth could understand. "I hear you. I just loathe that you're in pain and that it prolongs your recovery."

After a brief silence while LaSierra appeared to mull Beth's words over, she nodded slowly. "You're quite protective. I'm not used to that. Not personally, and certainly not professionally. Being in charge means I must sacrifice a lot to keep things running, and…" LaSierra swallowed hard. "Sometimes I must sacrifice individuals for different reasons. If I have to do this, and it is my firm belief that I do, then perhaps it's only fair that I live with a certain pain."

"That's insane." Beth whispered, because if she didn't, she would be shouting at such a crazy statement. "Are you saying your unnecessary pain is some damn atonement?" Beth leaned over LaSierra and looked her dead in the eyes. "That's crazy. Nobody, I can promise you, that nobody would ever expect that of you. They need their leader to take care of herself, get healthier, and allow them to pick up the slack in the meantime. This whole leadership thing—if it's as symbolic as you say, then fine. Be a fucking symbol. Sit on that pedestal all doped up if that's what it takes. You can still rely on the Garcias, Rayne, Kae, and that guy, Benny, who's on his way back to work. You have a whole team that can do the work you can't—until you can." She grunted from sheer frustration. "And, for what it's worth, you have me."

LaSierra looked up at Beth, her eyes narrowed. "Nobody talks to me like that. Nobody."

"I just did. And if you can't see why I did, then I don't know how to be any blunter." Beth could tell she had crossed yet another line.

"How do you think you can understand what I've accomplished over the years, almost longer than you've been alive? What it has cost me? What I've sacrificed?" LaSierra pushed at Beth, her irises all fire.

Beth shifted, but not too far. It looked like LaSierra was about to bolt from the bed, and that would be disastrous for her healing injuries. "You mean since I lived a life of luxury in the tunnels?" she hissed.

LaSierra opened her mouth but closed it.

"This conversation isn't very productive," Beth said. "If we're going to keep talking like this to each other, we need to do better. I'm protective, so shoot me. I don't agree that you have to sacrifice even more, when it comes to your health, but you're a grown woman. Only you know how much pain you can tolerate. I do reserve the right to ask you about it if I think it's called for."

"Creator, you're trying my patience." LaSierra covered her eyes. "But, as you insisted that I 'have you,' then I want to state very clearly that if I didn't have you, I wouldn't be alive or, at the very least, in a much worse condition. I'm fully aware that you saved me."

Beth pulled LaSierra's hand away as she wanted to meet her gaze. When she saw the damp eyelashes, she immediately felt like the worst person in the world. "Please tell me I didn't actually make you cry." Beth wiped at the errant tears that ran down LaSierra's temples and into her hair.

"I'm not sure why I'm crying. I never do, normally. No time for that." LaSierra drew a trembling breath. "I hate it."

"I'm the same way. I used to cry a lot in the orphanage, but as soon as I was out of there, I—just stopped. There was no room for tears after I joined the resistance. So, I get that part." She lay down and put her arm around LaSierra. "That said, I've never had anything against comforting someone who's crying."

"That makes you stronger than I am. I've been known to panic and leave the room at the sight of someone else's tears." LaSierra pressed her face against Beth's shoulder. "Perhaps because I'm the one who was to blame for them a lot of the time."

"We can always make you do some extra work with the kids in the Orphanage here. There's plenty of wailing and tears in there on occasion," Beth said, hoping the harmless teasing would help LaSierra find her bearings.

LaSierra pushed herself back enough to glare up at Beth. "Not funny. I'm not used to children."

"Thats why an internship would do you a world of good." Beth had to chuckle.

"You—" LaSierra cupped Beth's cheek. "I see what you're doing. Too clever for your own good, I'm sure."

"I've heard that from both Kae and Foster." Beth lost a little of her bravado at the sensations LaSierra's gentle touch created.

"I'm shocked." LaSierra ran her thumb along Beth's cheekbone. "To be honest, I'm sometimes at a loss for how to respond to you."

"What do you mean?" Beth blinked.

"Just when I know, when I believe I've figured you out, it turns out I haven't. It's quite maddening." Despite her words, LaSierra's voice was softer than Beth had ever heard it. "Can you, who always seem to have an opinion, explain that?"

"No," Beth whispered. Something was happening, and she wasn't sure if she should pull back immediately, or just stay where she was and let LaSierra work through her musings. What if she did pull away and that created a chasm between them too wide to bridge? And what was she to do about the heat spreading through her when LaSierra looked at her like this?

"You look...alarmed." LaSierra frowned. "What's wrong?"

"Nothing's wrong. As I said, I'm not used to, uhm, sharing a bed. This closeness is just a little overwhelming." Beth tried for a smile but feared she had missed the mark completely. "I'm not sure I should risk being this close to you."

"What on earth do you think I'm going to do? Use my superior strength and overpower you?" LaSierra spoke angrily but sounded hurt. She removed her hand from Beth's cheek.

"No. Of course not." Beth took a deep breath. "Listen. I've spent my entire adult life in the resistance. That left very little time to socialize outside the group. I have been around the same people ever since then, and that means I haven't had much practice in..." She motioned with her free hand between them. "...how to handle this."

"How to handle—" LaSierra stared at Beth, her lips parting. Her eyes darkened to a bronze color before she closed them. "You mean, physical closeness between two people experiencing unexpected attraction."

"Yes." Beth cleared her throat. "That."

"Are you sure about that last part?" LaSierra's eyes grew opaque.

"Yes. I mean, from my point of view, I am. Not that I ever would assume..." Not knowing how to continue that sentence as LaSierra's gaze made her feel ridiculously awkward, Beth merely shrugged.

"I think we should kiss," LaSierra said calmly.

"What?" Beth flinched.

"I, for one, need to know." LaSierra moved her good arm up and around Beth's neck. "If you'll allow it."

Beth tried to catch the thoughts that lay scattered in droves in her mind. How had they gone from a professional relationship to a budding friendship, to resentment and disappointment, to… whatever this was? It made no sense. And yet, Beth knew, even if she was not very experienced when it came to sex, that LaSierra stirred emotions in her that in turn made her ache in ways she'd rarely felt before.

Beth didn't dare speak, as she was sure her voice would fail her. Instead, she bent and kissed LaSierra's lips gently. Where she had ached before, she now felt a heaviness that made her tremble, which was perhaps what LaSierra meant when she said she needed to know.

LaSierra's eyes grew wide, and then she pulled Beth down again and captured her lips, this time with more force, and for a lot longer. Neither of them deepened the kiss, and Beth was oddly grateful, as she feared she would have forgotten to be careful with LaSierra's healing wounds if they had. Slowly, she raised her head and looked down at LaSierra. "So?" she murmured.

"What?" LaSierra looked dazed.

"Did you find out what you needed to know?" Beth asked, trying to control her tremors.

LaSierra nodded slowly. "I found out two things—neither of them is what I expected."

Beth waited impatiently, as she would rather LaSierra cut her suffering short.

"First, I think I'm going to have to ask you for another kiss when you can see that happening." LaSierra looked shell-shocked rather than elated, which was concerning. "Second, it seems that you are more effective than most of my pain medication." LaSierra looked equally surprised and annoyed.

And all Beth could do was give in to helpless laughter.

Chapter Eleven

Rayne's GemLink clicked five times, then two, then five. Staring at it, she wished Kae could have sent a regular message, but the risk was too great. It was only safe to use the GemLink for messages while inside their camp.

"What's wrong?" Madelon was approaching, studying Rayne's expression with obvious concern.

"I had five-two-five clicks from Kae. We agreed on another set for her to report in that all was well." Rayne rolled her shoulders, still stiff after performing surgery on a little girl who had fallen from quite a height and sustained an open fracture.

"A five-two-five." Madelon blinked. "Send the same back. That's an established click sequence that she must have gotten from Captain London. It means they'll be here soon, but that they have a problem and will need reinforcements when they approach."

Rayne was already returning the series of clicks. "Why would she send them to me since she knows I'm not familiar with all this cloak-and-dagger stuff?" She was frustrated and pushed the surgery mask off with jerky movements.

"She's probably sent it to HQ as well, but the fact that she included you suggests she needs medical attention for someone on her team." Madelon wrapped her arm around Rayne's waist. "Sweetheart, you've been on your feet almost every minute since she left. She'll be here soon, so just hold on. All right?"

Rayne reeled herself in. "Thanks, Mother. I guess I have been pushing it. It's just...I'm responsible, as the senior surgeon on site.

I'll ready my team on duty for casualties." Her stomach rolled at the idea that the injured person might be Kae. "Can you try to find out if someone knows more?"

"Absolutely." Madelon walked next to Rayne as she returned to the main emergency habitat. They had expanded the hospital with two more habitats, as the need for more theater space had become urgent.

Rayne put her team on alert while Madelon talked to Rocque. When Rayne returned to her, Madelon looked confused. "It seems that our team has increased in size during their mission. Captain London added some information, but as brevity was key, all we know is that eight individuals are returning soon."

"Eight?" Rayne's mind whirled. "Can it be a hostage situation? But wouldn't someone in the team alert HQ if that were the case?"

"Yes. Exactly. Rocque has given the command to our units to converge on the field team's entry point." Madelon looked behind Rayne. "Your team's already here. Why don't you bring two medics and join the units at the perimeter? We don't know how much medical expertise they require after they get through."

"All right." Relieved to have a task that didn't entail sitting around waiting in the hospital, Rayne tapped her GemLink and called in two medics. Grabbing her extended trauma case, she hurried toward the site.

Twenty-two dissident soldiers stood, weapons drawn, waiting for Kae's team to return. Rayne wasn't allowed beyond a certain point but had a good view from where she stood behind them. Her medics were setting up gurneys and had taken care of her trauma case and lined up the most vital equipment. They were all ready and could only wait.

"Rayne." Rocque appeared at Rayne's side wearing a uniform and carrying a Nova blaster. "We're prepared for them, and they'll be all right. This is just a precaution."

"It better be," Beth said from behind. She was also in uniform, and her watchful eyes showed an expression far from her usual light-hearted demeanor. She was clearly as worried about the situation as Rayne was.

"Thanks for being here, both of you. I can't help but worry that someone's going to be trigger happy." Rayne rubbed the back of her neck. She hadn't quite healed from her injuries, and this was a hell of a time for this one to act up. "Medic. Mild analgesic."

"Here, Doctor," the medic closest to her said. "Who's the patient?" She looked around them.

"Me. Just place it locally right here." She pointed to the right of her neck vertebrae.

The medic pressed the infulizer against Rayne's skin, and the cold substance hissed through her skin barrier. "There, sir."

"Thanks." Rolling her neck carefully, Rayne could feel the medication take the edge off her pain. Looking at her father, she smiled crookedly. "It's just a mild pain relief that won't affect my performance."

"I wasn't worried about that, Rayne. Just worried why you need it." Rocque had tied his shoulder-length hair back and looked thinner and somewhat jaded. A movement in front of them made him change focus and raise his blaster. "They're here. Stay behind me. That's an order, Rayne."

"All right, all right." Rayne motioned for her medics to do the same. She was wearing a protective vest under her medical suit, but it wasn't as efficient as the soldiers' suits.

The perimeter was faintly lit by red markers, but it was still easy to see when figures appeared just outside it. Rayne's GemLink clicked. 2-1-2-1-1. She could have wept with relief but also understood that the soldiers needed to confirm that the field team wasn't under duress. Someone could be controlling them, even if Rayne knew that Kae would rather go down trying to keep the ones in the camp safe than allow the enemy to cross the perimeter.

"Come through, one at a time!" The soldier in charge kept their weapon trained on the first figure crossing the perimeter. Someone had to have turned off the alarm at this section, as the GemLinks stayed quiet.

"It's Foster." Beth sounded strained. "And…what's that on his back. Surely that's too small to be a person?"

Rayne tapped Rocque on the shoulder. "I need to get over there. I'm no good back here. Foster's carrying someone."

"All right. But I'm going with you." Rocque and Beth walked ahead of Rayne, closing the distance to Foster, who had placed his blaster on the ground. He held his hands visible as he called out.

"Doctor Garcia. Get me Doctor Rayne Garcia!"

"On my way, Foster! Hold on!" Climbing up the embankment toward the plateau where Foster stood, she called, "I'm coming!"

Foster turned toward her and waved as she approached. "Help me unstrap her."

Her? Rayne and Beth rounded Foster and saw a bundle attached to his harness. She knew Rocque and one other soldier had their weapons trained on it.

"Beth, help me." Rayne began untying the cord holding the bundle in place, and as they tugged at the bottom, a little foot dropped into view. "The hell?" Rayne tugged at the safety blanket. A dirty child clung to Foster's harness and looked wide-eyed at them.

"A child…" Beth stared at Rayne. "Foster?"

"Let us through. We're bringing two more children, and the team's intact and uncompromised." Foster turned around after Rayne and Beth had freed the child. "Hey, Emb. We're here among my friends now, like we promised." Foster ran his hand over the child's head while she sat in Beth's arms. "She's dehydrated, even if we've given the kids our water rations."

"On it," Beth said. "Medic? You heard. Water."

"Here, sir." The medic tried to take the child, who wrapped her arms and legs around Beth and burrowed her face into her shoulder. "Okay. Just give me some water then."

Rayne gave the child a quick scan. "Girl. Four years of age. Dehydrated. Emaciated. Vitamin-deficient. She's going to need treatment." She smiled at the girl. "And a bath maybe?"

Foster staggered to the side, having to lean against Rocque. "Sorry, man. I'm exhausted. We didn't dare set up camp. Been on our feet far too long."

"Medic." As the little girl didn't allow Beth to let go, Rayne directed one of her medics to Foster. "Give Foster a Re-Coup. Double dosage." Turning back to the frowning Foster, she rolled her eyes at his suspicious expression. "For the sake of the Creator. It's a boost. It will sharpen you for a few more hours. The only side effect is that when you crash, you go down hard for twenty-four hours, at least."

"That part actually sounds good." Foster accepted the infulizer.

More figures walked toward them, and Rayne kept looking to identify which one was Kae. Of course, she was the last one who crossed the perimeter, which was hardly surprising. As she was clearly ambulatory, Rayne received the second child, this one slightly older than the first and strapped against Captain London. London looked even worse than Foster, and she motioned for the medic to repeat the Re-Coup treatment, then made it a standing order for the rest of the field team.

The second child was a little boy, six years old, who, at first glance, seemed nonverbal. He just stood there between her and London, looking dazedly at her. His eyes were dark blue and oddly vacant. Traumatized, Rayne surmised. "Hi. You're safe here. Captain London and Foster are going to remain with you for now. All right?"

"His name's Lux," a young voice to Rayne's left said. "The little girl is Ember. Emb for short."

Turning, Rayne saw the third newcomer. Equally dirty, and emaciated, a child with big, tired eyes regarded her calmly. "Are you Rayne?"

"I am. And you are?" Rayne began to scan the newcomer.

"Zephyr. Zeph for short."

Zeph turned out to be a girl, with the same symptoms as the smaller children, only worse. She suffered from a vitamin and iron deficiency that was far more developed.

"Hi." Kae's voice was all Rayne needed to feel rejuvenated. She kept a hand on Zeph's shoulder as she turned her head toward Kae and smiled, so relieved to have her back, she was at a loss for words.

Kae returned her smile before handing a bottle of water to Zeph and sipping from one herself. "Rayne," Kae whispered, and even though at least thirty people surrounded them, she bent and kissed Rayne lightly on the lips.

As it turned out, the members of the field team were uninjured and merely fatigued and thirsty. The children were another matter. Rayne admitted them to the small part of the hospital habitats that was designated as the children's ward. The little girl that Rayne had just operated on was almost awake and was placed in the far corner with her own medic watching over her, along with her father. Rayne nodded at them and pulled the privacy curtain to avoid disturbing them.

Emb still clung to Beth, even when she tried to get her to settle on to the bed. Fear radiated off the girl, and only when Zeph stepped up and framed Emb's face did the child calm down.

"Just do as they say, and we'll be all right. Kae and Foster promised us. Same goes for you Lux," Zeph said and turned to the little boy. She glanced over at Rayne. "We'll all be here together, right? Or are you going to place me with adults somewhere?" She stared at them, so defiant and so brave.

"Listen," Rayne said. "I'm the head doctor here, and that means I'm the boss in this hospital. I would never place a child with adults, unless it was a parent. You will stay here in this unit, as this is for kids. You can take the bed next to Lux." She pointed at the bed, but Zeph didn't attempt to climb into it. "Do you need help?"

"I'm…we're all too dirty for this." Zeph indicated the crisp white bedsheets.

"Ah. I see." Rayne studied the smaller children. "Never mind that. This is how we'll do it. You'll all stay on the beds, and my medics will help clean you with a portable instant-cleaning tube. While you're inside it, they'll get your beds all reset."

She could tell that the children didn't know what she was talking about. Smiling as Kae entered the room, she motioned for the beds. "Never mind some dirt. Just get on top of the beds. We'll figure it out."

Kae pulled up a chair and sat down between Emb and Lux. "I'll just put my feet up for a while. I'm really sore after hiking back on the double like this." She sent Zeph a knowing look. "Your feet need attention, Zeph."

Rayne followed Zeph as she reluctantly climbed onto the bed. Zeph's eyes grew impossibly wider, and she pressed her hands to the mattress. "This is so…so soft. Almost like the bales before we wrap them, but even softer."

"Oh, Creator." Madelon sounded shocked as she gasped behind Rayne. "Rocque said you brought children, but…" She gazed around the room.

"Good, you're here," Rayne said, making sure she used her efficient voice. "We're going to have to clean up these children before we can truly examine them. You can help." She studied her mother briefly, relieved to see Madelon already taking off her jacket and putting on a protective apron.

A medic rolled in a portable instant-cleaning tube, and Zeph volunteered to go first, to show the smaller children that it wasn't dangerous. She was about to disrobe in front of all of them when Rayne stopped her. "Zeph," she murmured so only the girl could hear. "I don't know how they've treated you where you come from, but here you are entitled to your privacy when it comes to cleaning your body or using the latrine. We'll show you how everything works when you feel better, but you don't have to remove your clothes in front of people ever again."

Zeph looked dumbfounded. "Everything in the barracks was out in the open. Even for the grownups." Her eyes glazed over, but she didn't cry. "So, I just go inside?"

"I'll pull the special curtain first. If it's all right, I can be here with you. I'm afraid you might feel poorly after your ordeal."

Obviously sizing Rayne up, Zeph then nodded. "Since you asked first."

Rayne smiled. "Good." She pulled the curtain after nodding at Kae first. Taking a bag from a dispenser, she held it out to Zeph. "Toss your clothes into this when you're naked. We'll provide you with new ones."

"That's good news too." Zeph nodded and accepted the bag.

Rayne turned her head and hummed under her breath as she heard Zeph take her clothes off.

"They're in the bag."

"Just step into the tube and I'll start it for you," Rayne said gently.

"I—I don't mind if you turn around. I'd rather you did." Zeph whispered the words.

"Sure." Rayne turned around, and only her years of training made it possible for her not to gasp like her mother had earlier, but she was in complete shock. Despite the dirt, the bruises were still visible, as were old and new cuts, and what looked like a deep gash from a bite on Zeph's shoulder. "Take a few steps back. The tube will close, but you'll still be able to see me. You will feel a sort of tickle, but it won't harm you."

Zeph stepped into the tube, and a transparent aluminum door slid shut. Rayne pressed the sensor for a deep clean, the second highest setting, wanting the girl to get as clean as was humanly possible.

Thirty seconds later, the tube opened automatically, and Zeph stepped out, staring in disbelief at Rayne. "That was strange."

Rayne was even more shocked at Zeph's appearance now that she was pristine and every bruise and wound looked so much worse. "You have lovely auburn hair, Zeph. She wrapped a towel around the girl even if she wasn't wet. "Let's get you into a freshly reset bed."

"I don't think I can sleep. I'm trying to understand what's happening," Zeph said and, ironically, yawned.

"I think you will, once you're comfortable. I just need to make sure I treat what I can when it comes to your injuries." Perhaps she would need to sedate Zeph first. She hoped not.

While she ran a more in-depth scan, she heard some commotion in the doorway, and a glance in that direction showed that LaSierra had just maneuvered her AirFrame through the door, emphatically telling her guards to remain outside.

❖

LaSierra studied the two youngest of their latest additions, not surprised that the youngest, Emb, was clinging to Beth. Who could blame the little girl? The kindness radiating from Beth's eyes was palpable.

"She's afraid to go into the tube," Beth said. "You saw Zeph go in and then come back out. Nothing bad happens in there, honey." Beth stroked the dirty, tear-streaked little cheek.

"She looked all different," Emb whispered. She gazed at LaSierra, who approached her chair. "Why's that grownup floating?"

"She hurt herself a while back. Her name's LaSierra, and she's the boss over here."

"No." Emb shook her head.

"No?" LaSierra had to smile. She wasn't used to children, or especially interested in getting to know any, but the tiny, muddy girl looked at her with such conviction, she couldn't stop herself.

"Doctor Rayne's the boss. All over here." Emb indicated the area with her arm and then clung to Beth's neck again. "But you're pretty."

"Thank you." LaSierra thought fast. "I bet you could go into the cleaning tube if Beth did it with you." She enjoyed Beth's surprise.

"Yes." Emb nodded. "Beth and me."

"I'll get even with you," Beth said under her breath as she passed LaSierra. She entered the tube with Emb, and LaSierra could hear her soothing voice as she told the child what was going to happen. The privacy curtain closed, and after a few moments, LaSierra heard Beth say, "Creator," and as Madelon joined her, LaSierra could tell by how the other woman squeezed her eyes shut for a moment, that she had too. LaSierra moved her AirFrame to sit on the other side of the quiet child in the third bed.

Madelon gave LaSierra a stern look. "Before you suggest I strip down with this poor child, think again. He's a little boy, and he doesn't need further trauma."

"All right." LaSierra glanced over at the older child that was being scanned. "That a girl?"

"Yes. I believe so," Madelon said.

"Kae? Who carried this boy here? Who might he be most comfortable with?" LaSierra asked.

Kae flinched, looking half-asleep by the older girl's bed. "Captain London."

"Medic. Find Captain London and have him report to me here right away."

The medic hurried out through the door. Just as he returned with London, who hadn't yet had time to clean up and change, Beth stepped out from behind the curtain, back in her suit, and with a large towel wrapped around the little girl, who turned out to have a cloud of curly, blond hair.

"No wonder someone named this child Ember," Madelon said.

"Captain London. If you wouldn't mind taking this boy— what's his name, by the way?" LaSierra felt foolish for not asking right away, but London said, "Lux, sir."

"Take Lux and yourself through the tube, so he doesn't have to do it alone. He knows you a little, so I'm told."

"Of course, sir." London walked up to Lux and held out his hands. Nothing happened, but the boy didn't object to being hoisted up on London's arm. "We're going to get clean together, you and I. That will make you feel better, little man."

LaSierra exchanged a look with Beth, and the warmth in her eyes made LaSierra relax some. It took a while, but then the tube began to hum again, and unless she was mistaken, she thought she could hear London start to sing.

Madelon switched to the other side of the bed and deployed a stool, so she was sitting closer to LaSierra. "I've never seen children who've suffered like this. It's heartbreaking."

"Once the field team and the children, at least the oldest one, are debriefed, we can start planning how to stop what's going on in those camps. We also need to debrief the intruder, Max. I know she's not well enough yet to sustain a longer interview, but as soon as as possible."

Beth approached with Emb in her arms. "This one's going to get scanned, and she's worried it may hurt. I told her you had been scanned a lot when you were injured and that you said that part didn't hurt at all." She pleaded visually with LaSierra.

Feeling utterly awkward and out of her depth, LaSierra studied the angelic-looking child. "If you slip into bed like a good girl, I'll come keep you company when the doctor scans you. I promise that scans don't hurt a bit."

"You promise?" Emb's gray eyes didn't waver. "Is that true?"

"It is. I wouldn't lie to you." LaSierra pointed to Emb's bed. "Hop in."

Emb allowed Beth to put her to bed, and LaSierra maneuvered her AirFrame until she was right next to it. "Good girl. We can ask the doctor if you can hold Beth's hand while—"

"No. Your hand. You said it doesn't hurt." Emb's little hand shot out from under the covers.

Taking it in hers, LaSierra's heart broke again when she saw the broken nails, the scratches, a multitude of splinters, and the paleness, as if the girl had never been in the sun. That could well be true.

As Beth sat down next to LaSierra on one of the extendable stools, LaSierra saw London emerge with a clean but equally bruised and emaciated Lux. Madelon took the boy in her arms and tucked him into bed, towel and all, while London hurried off to procure clothes for him.

Listening to Rayne talking to the girl, Zeph, LaSierra held the sleepy Emb's hand in hers, not about to let go.

"Someone bite you, Zeph?" Rayne asked calmly.

"Yes," came the equally somber reply.

"Who did that to you?" Rayne's voice displayed none of her fury, but the hand she had tucked behind her closed into a tight fist.

"Lux." The answer came with no particular inflection.

"Lux? What?" Rayne glanced over at the still boy.

"He did mine. I did his and Emb's. We tried to clean up, but we ran out of water." Zeph sighed. "We had to get the trackers out."

"It hurt," Emb whispered and tugged at LaSierra's hand. "It really hurt, but Zeph had to." The first tears LaSierra had seen on any of the children so far filled Emb's eyes. "Will we get new trackers now?"

"No, dear. No trackers." Swallowing hard, LaSierra peeled back the bedsheet that covered Emb's right shoulder. A deep, jagged gash that looked infected marred the little girl's skin. She put the sheet back and pressed her back against her chair. This was too much for anyone to take, but as the kids had lived under these circumstances for however long, the least she could do was remain by Emb's side as she'd promised.

"You should hug her, Beth." Emb's voice was drowsy.

"What? Why?" Beth leaned closer.

"LaSierra. You should hug her. She's crying." Emb closed her eyes again.

"I'm fine," LaSierra managed. She wiped her lashes with her free hand.

"It's all right. You'd have to be made of stone not to react." Beth didn't hug her, but she placed a warm hand on LaSierra's leg and squeezed gently. "You're doing a lot for her by staying true to your word. It's the start of a new, better life for her." She gazed around the room. "For all of them."

LaSierra knew she had to harness her fury. Always used to being in complete control, she was uncertain what would happen to her, and the rest of the dissidents, if she unleashed the angry dragon that roared in her chest at the sight of the abused children.

She hoped that she, or anyone else, wouldn't have to find out.

CHAPTER TWELVE

B eth sat next to LaSierra, exhausted after tending to the children and then running security around the perimeter with other freedom fighters. Word had spread about the children and the young woman, Max, and as human nature would have it—people talked.

It felt surreal to go from being one of Kae's team in the tunnels to one of the people in LaSierra's Inner Circle, but Beth did her best to handle the situation, one task at a time.

Right now, it was time for a senior staff meeting, and Beth knew almost everyone around the table in the center of headquarters. Not much was left to suggest this was once the Garcias' SkyBird, as the added technology had taken over.

"All right. We all need to hear from Dr. Garcia first." LaSierra had agreed to take some of her pain relief and looked more and more like her old self, which Beth was happy for but also found oddly disconcerting. The more LaSierra recuperated, the less she recognized "her" LaSierra, the vulnerable woman she had been assigned to help. This didn't sit well with Beth, who wanted nothing but to see LaSierra get up and walk on her own and be her steadfast, larger-than-life leader self. That's what they all needed her to be. Yet Beth secretly hoped she'd glimpse the woman under the surface occasionally.

"Zephyr, Zeph for short," Rayne said and smiled, "is doing better. We've managed to get her iron deficiency under control, and I expect that within a week, the vitamin level will be normal. I've healed her bruises and minor cuts. She's on Omnispectra antibiotics—they all are—as they're all infected. Not just the cuts that were exposed to the elements, but the way they bit each other to remove the trackers—well, we all know how much a human or animal bite can fester."

"And Lux?" Madelon asked. "I know a little, as I've visited the children twice this morning...mainly because I made a promise." She interlaced her fingers, and Beth noticed that her hands were trembling. Madelon had a soft spot for children, something Beth had detected when Wes and Tania needed help. Now that they were doing much better and were well cared for, by the Garcias and by Kae's team, these three children clearly tugged at Madelon's maternal feelings. That, or she simply wanted to help the kids.

"Lux is another matter. He's close to catatonic, but it's still encouraging that he utters an occasional word. His deficiencies match Zeph's. His treatment is the same, but he will need counseling." Rayne smiled gently. "And then there's Emb. Not surprisingly, this little girl has stolen everyone's heart. She's resilient in her own way, and she's less affected by deficiencies, but her infection is worse. I have her on the Omnispectra antibiotics, but also painkillers, as she has a bone condition that she most likely was born with. I can't be a hundred percent sure, but I can make an educated guess that her mother wasn't fed well and was forced to do hard labor on top of that. If that's the case for all the pregnant women in those camps, we'll most likely find they've miscarried often."

"From what Zeph's told us, they separate mother and child fairly early," Kae said. She sat next to Rayne, looking somber. "The small children are kept in what sounds like storage, and when they turn four, they're assigned to a new barrack with kids between four and thirteen. As soon as they're thirteen, they're moved to an adult barrack."

"This is...unfathomable," Rocque said starkly. "What the hell's growing in those fields that makes the authorities employ these extreme methods? And damn it, how long has this been going on?"

"I think I can shed some light on that subject," Beth said, then noted LaSierra's surprised look. "I know Zeph was abducted from what we call the 'school tunnel,' a project a while back that our leaders started—especially for orphaned children, but also for kids with one or two parents. I remember Kae and Tania and Wes's mother debated sending her there, as any knowledge in the tunnels would have to be passed down face-to-face, by word of mouth. They decided against it, as it was a little too far for a young girl to travel alone on the tracks. Only a short while after that, the cloudheads attacked, and most of the children were taken. They left word, and pamphlets—can you believe that—stating that the kids were taken to 'rescue camps.' Of course we'd heard of the reformation camps, but it seems that those were only a segue to these...what did Zeph call them? Slave camps. An apt term, as that's free labor."

LaSierra smacked her palm against the armrest of her AirFrame. "It's heart-wrenching, but our objective is clear. We have to establish a defendable position in this part of what used to be the United States. At one time, people lived here in great cities, and they also farmed the land. Obviously, farming is still proceeding on, and with today's technology, it wouldn't be a stretch to wonder why machines and synthetic personnel aren't tending to the crops." She looked at them all, one by one, her gaze darker than usual and flat, like one of the photos of sharks that Beth remembered from Kae's collection of old books.

Rayne raised her hand. "We have one more patient that I'm sure most of the field team know very little about." She regarded Foster, Kae, and London evenly. "Our perimeter was breached, and we now have a young woman, Max, in the hospital. She presents with similar findings as the kids do, and she probably was once a prisoner in one of the barracks. You need to debrief her as soon as possible, as she's awake, alert, and increasingly agitated. She's talking about moving sancts, but she's not making sense enough for me to fully understand her. If she's talking about the barracks, then her feeling toward them is ambivalent. And if she isn't, I can't figure out what a sanct is, let alone where it's located."

Beth thought of Max, who, much like the children, looked almost worse with clean, healed skin. "She might have been talking about refugee camps of some sort. And if they're mobile, that will make them hard to find—for the Celestials, and for us."

LaSierra put a hand on Beth's shoulder. "Aren't we glad we have access to your agile mind, Beth. Good job. I want you, Rayne, and Foster to debrief Max more fully. She might just be more trusting of her own kind, as it were. I'm not a fool. I know that Celestials, albeit freedom fighters, irk anyone who isn't one, especially those whom our former authorities have abused or traumatized."

Beth nodded. "Sure. Sounds likely." She met Foster's glance. The man had gotten three hours sleep and, as always, had bounced back, looking like he'd slept for a week. No doubt a FlatPak of turkey with all the trimmings had helped him recuperate quickly. He winked at her, and Beth knew that with him and Kae by her side, she would do the job her superiors told her to do and do it well. Then, when she was off duty, she hoped she might glimpse the LaSierra who had whispered that, at some point, she might ask for another kiss.

❖

LaSierra looked up from the desk in her habitat as Beth rapped the door frame that led into the center of the HQ. "Yes? Come in. You don't have to knock. It's your habitat too."

"Got it. We've been debriefing Max," Beth said and ran her fingers through her hair. "She's starting to trust us, but she insists on talking to you. Unless she meets the leader of this place, to quote her, she's not going to risk selling out her friends."

Tapping the sensor that closed her AirScreen, the floating projection of the computer content, LaSierra then pinched the bridge of her nose. "Is it strictly necessary, or potentially a power play by this young woman?"

Beth's eyes narrowed. "Excuse me? Did you say power play? Are you crazy?" She stepped closer and pressed both hands against the table. "You're the one who initially wanted to interrogate her rather than debrief her—and before you say anything, there's a fucking difference!" Clearly furious, Beth spat the words. "This woman, and if you haven't received the updated medical report, you'd know, is broken. She's sustained injuries to all her extremities over the years. She shows signs of corporal punishment from a young age, and, according to Rayne, her injuries go back at least ten years, maybe more. That would mean she was Zeph's age when it began. This...*this* is what Zeph was facing if she hadn't taken the other two and run. Max is a victim. She's among the most vulnerable here, and she's certainly not in any position of power." Beth didn't avert her eyes. She glared at LaSierra with such clear disappointment, it seemed to rob the air around them of oxygen.

"Very well. Let's go to the hospital." Wincing at having to ask Beth, LaSierra motioned to her AirFrame. "Will you be pushing me, or should I ask for one of the young people in there?" She pointed toward the HQ.

"Of course I'll take you." Grumbling, Beth moved behind LaSierra. After she adjusted the settings, LaSierra held up her hand, stopping Beth from moving her chair.

"Wait," LaSierra murmured. "Please don't be cross with me, Beth. I apologize for my thoughtlessness. I slip back into old habits far too quickly, don't I?"

After a few moments of silence, Beth placed a hand on LaSierra's shoulder. LaSierra covered it with hers, glad she'd regained so much movability in her arms that she could. Having Beth's strong hand under hers made her feel better than she had all day.

"Let's go then, boss," Beth said, and hearing the change in her tone was all LaSierra needed to be able to breathe freely.

Max sat propped up against several pillows that LaSierra knew firsthand were meant to reduce pressure where necessary.

"Hello, Max," LaSierra said and introduced herself. "It's good to see you doing better, even if you have a bit longer to go before you're on your feet."

Max, who, after thorough cleansing, had turned out to be a pale young woman with short, choppy blue-black hair and dark-brown eyes, returned LaSierra's gaze calmly. Where her skin had been marred with bruises and cuts, new healthy skin was taking over. LaSierra had reviewed the young woman's status on the way over to the hospital habitat and knew that her liver was still affected and causing her a great deal of pain.

"What happened to you?" Max asked huskily. "Since you're not able to walk."

LaSierra moved her AirFrame closer. "I was in a shuttle accident and sustained some bad injuries."

"I was on a shuttle once, when I was eight." Max tilted her head. "The cloudheads pushed a bunch of us kids in there and took us to what they called a rescue camp. I wanted to go home to my mother, but they kept saying she'd signed me over to them. That she was sorry, but she couldn't afford to feed me anymore. It was a lie, of course, but I was a little kid."

LaSierra had aligned her AirFrame with the hospital bed, and now she held out her hand to the one of Max's that seemed less injured. Max regarded her suspiciously but then placed her hand in LaSierra's, very lightly.

"I believe Beth told you that I'm ultimately in charge of this camp. If you can tell us anything to help the people in the barracks, we would appreciate it very much. And if you also could explain what a 'sanct' is, that'd be good."

"I'm afraid to. If you turn out to be just regular cloudheads, I'll have signed my friends' death warrants." Max clung to LaSierra's hand, which hurt, but she didn't move a muscle.

"We have broken with the Celestial authorities, and we've planned this move for decades. We had to do it faster than we planned, as we were found out, but this camp is the most secure place in the sector. Please, Max, help us, as we are in a strange territory. Can you tell us what they're growing in the fields?"

Max stared at LaSierra and then at Beth. "You don't know? But you wouldn't survive more than a few days without it." She shook her head and then seemed to instantly regret it.

"What do you mean? I've never seen this type of crop before, not even in the old park museum area. Neither has anyone else, but our scientists are testing it as we speak."

"It's Fabric Food. It goes into your FlatPak food. Even I've heard of that, as there's talk among the people living in the barracks. Once, someone stole a box of chicken FlatPaks, but of course we didn't have the technology to inflate it. That didn't stop us from eating it. Tasted all right." Max closed her eyes briefly.

LaSierra let Max rest as she looked up at Beth. "This can't be true—can it?"

"Where does it come from, the FlatPak food, as far as you know?" Beth murmured.

"From factories where they bring in harvested vegetables, and from other farms where they've managed to synthesize different types of meat." LaSierra shook her head. "I've seen the scientific reports."

"And how much of a scientist are you?" Beth asked kindly. "I mean, could you determine if they were fake or not, just from looking at them? Remember what you've told me about the Celestial authorities' corruption. Surely a few greased hands among the science department would go a long way."

"Creator. You have a point. It was…it was just never an issue. We trust in our food."

"The crop's fine. It's nutritious. It grows very, very fast." Max sounded exhausted. "Now. You wanted to know about the sancts. Can you give me something to draw on?"

LaSierra handed over her tablet and a stylus. "Here."

Max smiled faintly. "Fancy." She took the stylus in her unsteady right hand. "This is just to try to orient you." She drew a disturbingly accurate, uneven circle that Beth recognized as their perimeter. Then Max marked a few places and wrote a B. "Barracks." She coughed. A few more dots, scattered in an uneven pattern. "Sancts. Short for sanctuaries. Mobile camps where we shelter the ones on the run from the barracks. We dig out the trackers and insert them into rodents, rabbits, even snakes, and relocate them. We try to avoid using too many rabbits, as they're our main source of protein. We do steal grain from the crops, and we have a woman who knows how to process it to make it into the bread that I had with me, wrapped in leaves."

"They're in the lab too," Beth said quickly, as Max was obviously fading fast.

"You will need to give them my ID-code if you approach them, or you'll never find them. That's the thing about the crops. They hide all kinds of sins and signals." Max took the stylus again and drew some clumsy-looking numbers, a twelve-digit code. Then she put it down and closed her eyes. "You have to leave me alone now. Please."

"Sure." Beth stood and fetched a medic, who reviewed Max's vitals.

"She needs at least eight hours' downtime. Please try to leave her be, sirs." She looked pleadingly at LaSierra and Beth.

"Absolutely," LaSierra said and waved for Beth to push her out of the hospital room. "I need to talk to the senior staff again, but it's enough to do so over dinner. She shuddered. "Isn't it an eerie feeling that we've been eating FlatPaks for so many years, and now we learn that children, and young adults, living in slave camps tend to the crops?"

"I had only a few, but I still feel weird about it." Beth swallowed so hard, LaSierra could hear her.

"She claimed the crop is safe, but I bet anything there's more to it. Perhaps something that Max, for all her cleverness and bravery, doesn't know." LaSierra pinched the bridge of her nose again.

"You're due for some meds, according to your chair." Beth tapped a sensor. "Ah, look. There they are. And before you go all huffy on me, these are just regular pills. Nothing that will knock you out or even impair you."

"I'd be glad to take them." LaSierra had found she did work better, and longer, if she used the prescribed medication compliantly, which was something of a revelation.

"Though people often debate whether miracles can happen, I have the proof right here." There was a smile in Beth's voice.

Suddenly feeling elated, LaSierra chuckled. "And I have proof of something else. Who knew?"

"What is that?" Beth still sounded pleased.

"That with you at my side, I feel—not invincible, I wouldn't go that far—but steady and on point." *And not lost and confused.* It was a remarkable revelation, and LaSierra knew that letting Beth know how important she was becoming to her was perhaps the biggest step of all.

CHAPTER THIRTEEN

Kae removed her suit and looked bemusedly at the strange garment as it pooled around her on the floor. She had yet to get used to some of the Celestial technology. She really liked some things, as they were useful and even lifesaving. The helmets with their interactive visors, and the GemLinks, truly made it easier to safeguard the group of people she was with. She felt guilty every time she thought of her people, still in the tunnels and potentially at the mercy of retaliating soldiers.

After she stepped into the small, instant-cleaning tube available in the habitat, she was close to antiseptic in less than thirty seconds. Realizing that she'd forgotten to bring a new set of clothes into the bathroom, she found a towel and wrapped it around her. She padded back into the bedroom she shared with Rayne and up to the machine, the ReCyc. After she punched in the command for her usual attire, she held the too-small towel firmly, since it barely covered her.

As the garments emerged one at a time, she dropped the towel and pulled on her briefs and a tank top. Standing there holding the rest of her fresh clothes, she worried about her people and the children she and her team had just brought back.

"What's going through that mind of yours?" Rayne asked quietly behind her.

Pivoting, Kae stared at the vision before her. Rayne obviously had come straight from the instant-cleaning tube, as her hair shone like gold and was perfectly brushed to fall around her shoulders. And her pale-blue robe set off the green in her eyes. Kae knew Rayne was fifty years old, which was unfathomable, compared to women of the same age in the tunnels.

"Are you angry with me?" Rayne asked quietly. "You're glowering."

"Not at you. I mean, not really." Kae tossed the clothes onto a stool. "It's not your fault that you grew up in opulence. It's just the unfairness of it all."

Rayne folded her arms and gazed at her with the complete calm that Kae had come to recognize as a mask that could hide all kinds of turbulent emotions. Shit.

"I'm sorry." Kae sat down at the foot of the bed. "I'm not making sense, and I really don't mean to take anything out on you. You...you are..." She gestured exasperatedly at Rayne. "perfect."

"What?" Rayne dropped her arms to her sides. "Where did that come from? I'm not, just to be real here." She walked slowly toward Kae and sat down next to her.

"I suppose having the kids find my habitat in the field, and them having gone through hell—for years—and then the comparison with what we have access to here. I mean, we're in a refugee camp of sorts, yet we have all the food we want, medicine, access to health care...well, you know. And I think of the people back home. I mean the tunnels. They're still there, and we don't have any idea what's going on."

"I know." Rayne placed a gentle hand on Kae's thigh. "We'll try to find out. Mother said they're trying to establish contact with the dissidents still living in the skyscrapers. They have to do it in a safe way, or they'll jeopardize us and them, of course. When that's done, we might be able to contact the tunnels, if we can send in a team with a transmitter. That of course can't happen until we have enough boots on the ground, Mother said, but it will happen. We also have to prepare habitats for everyone."

"I understand. I really do." Kae shifted to face Rayne. "But it doesn't make me less frustrated, I'm afraid. I honestly didn't mean to glower at you. It's just...you came in looking so incredibly beautiful…" Kae wrapped an arm around Rayne's shoulder. "You take my breath away."

Rayne's expression softened. A faint smile curled her lips as she cupped Kae's cheek. "I think of the people I met in the tunnels too. Neely, Harlow, Bellamy…Zara. I pray they're all right."

"Yes. I worry about Mama Doc, our herbalist and crop specialist." Kae sighed and pulled Rayne's hand forward, then pressed her lips against her palm. "If there's trouble, she'll be on the barricades right away, and she's not a young woman."

"Bellamy will rally the troops. You put him in charge." Rayne slid closer and rested her head against Kae's shoulder.

Kissing Rayne's hair, Kae closed her eyes. "I refuse to feel guilty for this," she said huskily.

"This?" Rayne moved as if to look up, but Kae held her closer.

"This. Us. What we've found together." Kae pushed a hand under Rayne's robe and cupped her shoulder.

Rayne tipped her head back. "Yes," she said quietly. "This. We can't afford to be careless with it or let anything come between us. We have enough to deal with." She blinked slowly. "It was difficult when you were on your field mission. I buried myself in my work, but it was—a challenge."

"I'm afraid there's going to be a lot more of that. I'll be heading up the liberation force once we've gathered enough intel to commence the mission." Kae bent and kissed Rayne's lips lightly. "I suppose you know that you have to put together a team of field medics."

"Yes. I gathered that as soon as you were back." Rayne slid her hand into Kae's hair and pulled her in for another kiss. Kae held on to Rayne, whose warmth had pierced the emotional armor she took such pride in. Parting her lips, she invited Rayne to deepen the kiss.

"Kae…there hasn't been a proper time for us…well, ever, has there? And yet…" Rayne slid her tongue in to meet Kae's. The kiss lasted for a long time, and when they parted, Rayne's hands were inside Kae's tank top, and her fingers spread out against her back. Kae had her hands on one of Rayne's breasts.

"I don't know how we're supposed to be able to make this work." Kae kissed a path down to Rayne's neck. "I just know that I can't imagine my life without you."

Flinging both her arms around Kae's neck, Rayne muttered, "Darling. Oh, darling." She pushed her robe off her shoulders and let it pool around her waist. "I want you to touch me. I need to feel that you're here, that you truly came back."

Kae lifted Rayne to straddle her thighs. Cupping her breasts, she weighed the fullness in her hands while kissing her neck. "I'm here. Let's make a pact, Rayne. When we're in here, it's just us. Please."

"Yes!" Arching against Kae, Rayne whimpered quietly. "Yes. Just you and me—in here." She rolled her hips against Kae and breathed increasingly faster. "You…you're making me…I need to. I mean, I need you to help me come. Please."

"Damn," Kae whispered as her stomach clenched. She dragged her hand down between them, slipped it inside Rayne's robe, and found only naked skin. "Oh, Creator…"

"Just touch me. Any way you want." Rayne lifted herself a few inches, and when Kae pressed her entire hand in between her legs, she continued to roll her hips, grinding against Kae's palm and fingers.

"This good?" Kae's voice was husky, barely audible. The soft, wet warmth had her teetering on the edge of her own orgasm, and she buried her face between Rayne's breasts.

"Perfect," Rayne whispered. "Just…like this." She began to shake as the tremors grew in intensity. "Now, oh, damn it… now…"

Kae pressed harder against Rayne's folds and created quick circles with the heel of her hand against her. That was what Rayne needed and, ultimately, what sent Kae over the precipice without any direct touch. She'd never seen a woman experience such bliss before, and Kae knew she would always want this only with Rayne, nobody else. This was the woman she wanted to build a new future with, if they were given the chance. She felt Rayne's hands slide to the front of her chest and caress her breasts. Hiding her face against Rayne's neck, she whimpered as her orgasm tore through her, only to finally settle down and flicker like tiny flames between her legs.

Rayne lay slumped against Kae's chest, her breathing still labored.

"I have you," Kae said and kissed her hair. "It's just you and me, like we said. Just you and me in here."

"That's all I want in this moment. Just you. This is pure luxury." Rayne straightened slowly. "Kae. I'm not sure...but I felt this was a long time coming, even if we've known each other only about two weeks. How can that be?"

Kae smiled and pushed Rayne's hair from her face. "I'm not sure, but I feel we're in some sort of time-microcosm, if that makes sense."

Rayne's eyes crinkled at the outer corner as she returned the smile. "You mean, like dog years?"

Kae blinked. "What?" Then she thought back to a few books she'd read from the early 2000s. Seven dog years was one human year. "I see. Yes, something like that."

"Your wording was much more eloquent." Kae kissed Rayne tenderly. "A time-microcosm for just us."

"Yes."

As they settled down for the night, they didn't do as before, a quick kiss and then stuck to their respective side of the bed. Tonight, Rayne lay in Kae's arms, and it was as if this new step, this development, had given her a new outlook on their future. Kae was just as concerned for the fate of her people, and for the Celestials who didn't subscribe to the current Celestial authorities' policy—as in corruption and abuse of their most vulnerable people. Knowing that Rayne's feelings for her hadn't changed made Kae feel no longer alone in her fight for justice and freedom for everyone.

As the wind pushed at the habitat walls, creating faint sounds outside and from the headquarters, Kae reveled in the possibility that as long as nobody sounded the alarm, she would have this night in Rayne's arms.

"You know how I feel about you, don't you?" Kae whispered and tugged Rayne closer.

Next to her, Rayne stilled even more, seeming to hold her breath. Just as Kae feared she wouldn't say anything, Rayne ran gentle fingers down her cheek. "I know now, darling. I know now."

Chapter Fourteen

B eth had never been the reason for verbal crossfire before, and considering the animosity erupting between LaSierra and Kae, she wished she could just fall through a sinkhole in the floor and disappear.

"I need Beth *and* Foster on the liberation mission." Kae stood at the end of the oval table in the HQ. The senior crew sat densely packed around it, and at the other end, LaSierra was glaring at Kae, her expression only too familiar to Beth. Kae seemed unperturbed and said, "What's more, now that we've debriefed Max in the hospital twice, we know we need to find the sanctuary camps. She's given us as much information as her condition allows, but I'm confident we'll be able to reach the ones between here and the work camps."

"And you need Beth for all of that, when you know how much I rely on her?" LaSierra growled.

"I do. Beth's always been instrumental in my unit in the tunnels, and I missed not having her on the mission when we found the kids. Or, rather, they found us. If you want me to head up the team, you can't rob me of my best people. This way we can keep everyone a lot safer, and that includes you, Ms. Delmonte." Beth knew Kae was on a first-name basis with everyone around the table and that she was creating distance between her and LaSierra deliberately.

And obviously LaSierra realized this tactic. "What it *means* is that I'm going to need to allow a perfect stranger to have autonomy regarding my medication, and my—" She stopped talking and pressed her lips into a fine line. Even this incensed, LaSierra was magnificent, and given the way she was recuperating, she would soon be able to lose the AirFrame. Beth longed for that day, for LaSierra's sake, but a selfish part of her, or perhaps only very human, knew she would miss being needed in such a personal way.

Madelon raised her hand. "What about medical?" she asked. "What are your thoughts on that, Kae?" Perhaps she was hoping to redirect the discussion.

"Yes. When it comes to the pre-mission to find the sanctuaries, we'll need one physician, one nurse, and two medics. They should have some military training, if possible." Kae glanced at Rayne. "Because we know very little about what state they're in, and if they're all ambulatory or not, we will need to include those collapsible stretchers that have a limited, but useful, hover function. I want Dr. Garcia to head up the medical team."

Rocque and Madelon exchanged glances, but neither of them objected. Rayne merely nodded. "Unless a case within this camp requires extensive care, I'm ready, Kae."

"Excellent. We move out tomorrow, as I want us to be able to debrief Max and the children one more time. The more intel we have, the better."

"What do you hope to accomplish by bringing people from the sanctuary camps here, where they will no doubt be a drain on already stretched-thin resources?" LaSierra spoke coldly.

"I suppose I look at it from another angle when I estimate the outcome of a chosen course of action." Kae sounded strained, and Beth could tell she was struggling to keep her equilibrium. "Yes, initially, during the recovery-and-recuperation phase, they will cost us. But the intel they'll be able to share will be invaluable. If three ragtag kids and one badly injured young woman can give us this much—you should be able to imagine what a group of seasoned adults can share with us. As we can't use our scanners as much as we'd want to, to avoid revealing our location, we *need* to find out what we're up against by other means."

LaSierra slumped back, and Beth could tell that she was in pain. Reluctant to draw attention to it, Beth stood anyway and circled the table. Then she murmured, leaning close to LaSierra on her left, "I may be overstepping now, but you look like you need some pain relief."

LaSierra grew rigid, but only for a moment. "Not yet." It was not a "no," but it was a "back off." "I'm willing to give you some leeway, a certain amount of autonomy, Kae, but that doesn't mean you can bypass the chain of command."

Kae's eyes darkened, and Beth tried to get her attention. She wanted Kae to ease up a little, or LaSierra would push more of Kae's buttons, and then herself, over the limit of what her still-diminished stamina allowed. Finally, Kae lifted her gaze to meet Beth's, and they knew each other so well, Beth didn't have to gesture, let alone say anything. Kae gave a barely visible nod, and Beth exhaled some of the breath she had been holding.

"Build your team and estimate what gear and resources you need." LaSierra's voice was husky rather than stark now. "I regard this mission as a test, and its outcome will show if you will be the one heading up our main objective regarding the slave camps. You have one more chance to prove yourself." LaSierra backed up her chair and rounded the table. Beth followed her, wincing at Kae's tense expression when LaSierra stopped next to her chair. "And Kae. Don't get anyone killed."

LaSierra pulled off the sling that kept her arm pressed against her torso, mainly for pain relief since all her minor injuries had healed. Only the piercing injury in her back remained, where a persistent infection threatened to take over as soon as she tried to wean herself off the Omnispectra antibiotics.

"That was hardly called for," Beth said from behind, a tense tone revealing her anger.

"I'm sure I have no idea what you mean. Everything I said during the meeting is at my discretion and not something you—or anyone else—can reproach me for." LaSierra tossed the sling onto the table, then maneuvered her AirFrame into her bedroom. Reaching the cabinet that held her array of medication, she grabbed one of the envelopes holding her medium-strong capsules, as she hated the infulizer and didn't think it necessary. She swallowed them dry and made a face. Turning around, she stopped when she saw Beth resting her hip against the door frame, her arms folded over her chest. "What?"

"I know you sometimes lash out at me when you're in pain. Anyone could certainly understand that. But what you said to Kae before you left the HQ—and in front of everyone at that—and what you said to me just now. Neither is all right."

"I—"

"No. You have to hear this, If you keep second-guessing your staff, or your soldiers, and if you do it in public, others will do the same. No matter what, once the decision has been made for a mission to continue, we rally the troops, we go as one, and we'll all act as a unit. If someone, and it takes only one, hesitates or questions an order at the wrong time—we can all die. You can't demand that Kae keep us all safe and then sound as if you seriously doubt her ability at the same time." Beth's eyes were darker than LaSierra had ever seen them. "And as for what you just said to me, it wasn't so much your words as your implication. You know I have your back. You *know* this. So, when I choose to say something, I don't expect you to take it at face value—but I think I've earned the right for you to at least consider that I may have a reason. I might be right. I get it that time is of the essence and the mission has to be planned quickly. I do understand that. I still want to ask another question. Are you angry with Kae for any other reason than her telling you she needs me on the field mission? And is that why you snarled at her in front of her peers and superiors?"

LaSierra was fuming. "You forget yourself. I'm the leader of this advanced group of dissidents. I have been for two decades.

For you to come up from the sewers and take it upon yourself to criticize me is insulting!"

Beth gaped at her. "From the *sewers*?"

"Isn't that where your people built their dwellings? In the subway tunnels and the sewers under what used to be the great city of New York?" Perspiration broke out on LaSierra's forehead, and she had to clasp her hands to stop them from shaking.

"It's entirely true." Beth's voice grew less forceful, but she was frowning. "But what does that have to do with anything?"

"It matters when you criticize someone who has two master's degrees, and more experience in running and planning for a camp such as this." Blinking hard, LaSierra loathed that her body found it prudent to make her feel weak right this instant.

"If that had been what I did—then yes. That would be ridiculous. But I asked if your words were truly called for, considering that I'm about to do what *I* do best—and that you have no experience in—going on a mission, fighting hand-to-hand combat, potentially firing my weapon at a human being, and helping Kae keep everyone safe, including this camp's specialist physician." Beth pushed off the door frame and entered LaSierra's bedroom without asking. "Are your pills helping yet?"

Barely able to keep up with the change of topic, LaSierra merely shook her head. "Uh, no."

"You may need an infulizer." Beth had reverted to her usual, gentle tone. "I realize you're not feeling well, and then you learn that I, who am tasked with being by your side, am being deployed. I'm not trying to minimize you, your experience or knowledge... none of that. I merely ask that you listen. I think I know you a little better than most of the others, on a personal level. You can be damn intimidating at times, I'll give you that, but when you're allowed to be yourself...that's the LaSierra I know and—well, that I know." Beth tucked her hands behind her. "So. Infulizer and then return to HQ to wrap up the meeting?"

LaSierra raised her hand and rubbed her forehead. Her head ached unbearably, and she felt as if someone was poking her in the back with a metal rod, which gave a horrific sense of dèjá vu.

"Fine. Half of an infulizer dose. Just a half. It might interact with the oral medication."

"Got it." Beth began pulling out more medical equipment.

"And yes. We'll go back. I'm not saying you're right, but you may just have a point."

"One more for my collection then." Beth offered LaSierra a smile, and its warmth seemed to wrap around her.

Beth pressed the infulizer against the crease of LaSierra's arm. Forcing herself not to hold her breath, but to breathe evenly the half a minute it took for the medication to take full effect, LaSierra studied Beth as she put the unused vials away.

"I do owe you an apology for my angry words. You didn't deserve that. I can't think of a time when you would, to be honest." LaSierra wished they had time to stretch out on the bed like they had the other night, but that would have to wait—if it ever happened again, the way she'd spoken to Beth earlier.

"Apology accepted," Beth said as she returned to LaSierra's side. She placed both hands against the armrest and leaned closer. "Kiss and make up?" she whispered but didn't wait for a reply. Instead, she closed the distance between them and pressed her lips gently to LaSierra's temple.

"Beth." LaSierra closed her eyes briefly. "You continue to stun me. I just never fully know what to expect."

"Do you want me to promise to never kiss you again?" Beth smiled.

LaSierra had to swallow against a sudden onset of dryness in the back of her throat before she could reply. "No."

"Then I won't promise." Beth pushed her fingers through her short hair.

"Do I need to make you any promises?" LaSierra reached out for her sling and handed it to Beth, who expertly put it back on LaSierra's arm and attached it to her torso.

"Not a thing." Beth let her fingertips slide along the back of LaSierra's hand. "Time to go back into HQ?"

"I suppose we better. I have things I need to say." LaSierra sat back and let Beth push the AirFrame over to the door leading into HQ. Inside, the voices, some agitated, and others sounding marginally calmer, quieted when they returned. As Beth attached the AirFrame to the table at the far end and returned to her chair, LaSierra held up a hand, palm first, toward the gathered senior crew.

"I know I left only minutes ago and none of you have forgotten my impolite and inappropriate words to Kae Dark. No need for the rest of you to weigh in and create more havoc. Leave that part to me, as I seem to have a knack for it." She regarded them coolly. She'd be damned if she would sit here and be all smarmy at her subordinates. "I learned from someone whose opinion I value more than most that I acted in a counterproductive manner, and after first digging my hole deeper by arguing this point, I now realize that she's right more often than she's not." LaSierra turned to Kae, who met her gaze calmly. "Kae. I spoke out of turn. You are the expert here on military missions and rescues. You and your team have proved yourselves several times in a short while. I will not interfere with your plan, unless there is something you couldn't foresee the consequence of."

"Thank you, Ms. Delmonte. I'm glad everything could be resolved before we deploy. Rayne and I will talk some more with Max tonight." Kae studied LaSierra for a moment, and after exchanging a glance with Beth, she said, "Together we'll do our best to save as many as we can."

It took another hour before they had discussed the last topics on the list provided by Madelon and Rocque. As they were all getting up and returning to their habitats or workstations, Madelon came over to LaSierra and Beth. "Rocque and I plan to ask Wes and Tania if they want to join us to visit Zeph, Emb, and Lux. We think it might give the new children some hope to see that we take good care of Subterranean children too."

"Great idea. Tell them all that I'll pop in and say hello before we move out tomorrow," Beth replied.

"We will." Madelon hooked her arm around Rocque's and walked with him out of the HQ.

"And you need food and then more meds and rest." Beth gestured toward the AirFrame's controls. "Want me to help?"

"Yes. Thank you." LaSierra closed her eyes momentarily. She felt her chair move and trusted Beth to push it where it needed to go. She just wished she could trust that Beth wouldn't suffer any harm after going on this first field mission. A thought struck her that made her stomach clench. Of course. If Kae meant that Beth was indispensable for the first mission, she would be even more so for the second.

And if the first mission was dangerous, the second would be disastrously so, but nevertheless necessary.

Chapter Fifteen

Beth stared at the backpack fully stocked with Celestial gear and, not for the first time, thought about her old rebuilt glimmer hidden in a space in a worm alley of a skyscraper. The new blaster was growing on her, and she grudgingly had conceded that it made her feel safer. Along with the blaster, she was also outfitted with a ShadowPulse hidden weapon and the Celestial version of fusionblades. Whereas the Subterranean version of the blades was lethal enough, these upgraded models would slice the throat of an enemy like cutting through cream. Even Foster had looked impressed about that capability.

"You seem thoughtful," Rayne said from where she stood next to Beth, her medics and the nurse lined up behind her. They carried mostly medical equipment but also Nova blasters.

"I can't help but compare this equipment with what we had in the tunnels." Beth sighed and turned her head to look at Rayne. "I try not to go there too much. I worry."

"As do I," Rayne said and briefly touched the back of Beth's hand. "I wish they'd give their last brief and let us get going."

"LaSierra needed a last-minute moment with Kae," Beth said. "Guess they're fine-tuning the tactics. I don't know what for. We keep planning, and then something happens that forces us to improvise like crazy anyway." She smiled faintly. "You saw that happen when we took Wes to the Skyscrapers for the second time."

"Oh, Creator. Don't remind me of those creatures we saw. The tongueless humans. Wraiths." Rayne shuddered. "I can see them in my dreams sometimes. Another crime against humanity perpetrated by the Celestial authorities."

"Yeah." Beth returned Rayne's gesture of support by patting her arm. "But we all know that a lot of different Celestials aren't criminals. I didn't use to think so, it was pretty black-and-white for me, but I know better now."

"That's good. And you operated according to the circumstances that were part of your experience." Rayne adjusted her helmet and tapped her GemLink. "This visor is the medical version. Right now, I can see some of your vitals. Nothing intrusive. Just blood pressure, pulse, and respiration. Good to know that it works." Rayne hesitated, peering up at Beth, who had a few inches on her. "How's it going between you and LaSierra? I don't mean to pry, and just tell me to mind my own business if you don't want to talk about her—well, you and her, I mean." Rayne tilted her head.

Beth thought back to the moments when she'd felt closer to LaSierra than any other person in her life. "She's struggling with some demons," she said quietly. "Being in command takes a toll."

"I'm sure it does. I see the same with Kae. You must too. She was used to running a multitude of resistance teams, and now she's in charge of important field missions where everything hangs in the balance. We try to not talk shop at home." Rayne's fierce blush was visible through her visor.

"Home, eh? I'm glad you two are finally acting properly on what is so readily visible to those of us who know you well." Beth winked, but then she sobered. "I share a habitat with LaSierra, but of course, we have our own space, but she's needed me a lot. It's hard because that factor blurs the lines." Beth weighed back and forth on her feet.

"Does it make you uncomfortable?" Rayne stepped closer and lowered her voice.

"Not in the way you might think, but it means I can't be unbiased, and, I'm afraid, neither can she. She nearly excluded me from the duty roster for this field mission because she feared something could happen to me. She's not just thinking of me as her assistant. That's very personal."

"So, what happened?" Rayne's voice was infinitely kind. It wasn't hard to see why Kae had fallen hard for her.

"We talked it through—and it was a bit messy—but she returned to the meeting, as you saw. She reeled herself in, you could say. I think getting so seriously wounded, and having me save her life, has shaken her out of the comfortable space of being the standoffish, remote leader calling the shots from a certain distance."

Rayne nodded slowly. "Trust you to go straight to the heart of the matter. She's lucky to have you, Beth. When we come back from this mission, she'll see how steadfast and capable you are. And perhaps you can further your relationship. You deserve that." Rayne squeezed Beth's arm. "Don't panic. I doubt a lot of people have seen the sparks that fly between you two, other than Kae and I. We notice only because we were in that exact frame of mind not long ago."

"Okay." Beth returned the squeeze. She saw movement over by the Inner Circle, and then the very women they were talking about approached them, LaSierra guarded by two Celestial soldiers. "Guess it's crunch time."

"Guess so."

Behind LaSierra and Kae, the Garcias and Benny walked toward the assembled field team, all looking serious.

"Now what?" Beth sighed.

Kae stopped in front of them and gazed at them for a few moments. "Good. We're all here. We'll deploy soon, and I want to urge you to give the ones you love a chance to embrace you before we go. We'll do our best to return with everyone in good health, but we all know that this is a mission into a foreign territory. A young woman and small children have provided the intel that informs us of what we may encounter. That's it. We're lucky to have the maps provided by Benny and that they're available to us via GemLink. If you've heard them give a few muted pings, it's because he's uploaded the latest software to them. You'll find the new features useful and intuitive. At least that's what he says." Smiling briefly, Kae nodded. "You have five minutes, people. Then we cross the perimeter and will be under what we in the tunnels call radio silence. The only way to communicate is via clicks, and unlike what we had during our first mission, the clicks will be coded to switch to letters. That means we can send short text messages, but only when it is vital. And by vital, I also mean when we need to connect with a loved one, or a friend, to strengthen morale. But it's not a gossip channel, all right?" Now Kae smiled more broadly, and Beth remembered how she used humor as encouragement when she rallied her troops already in the tunnels.

People dispersed from where they had stood when they listened intently to Kae. Some hugged their spouse or children. Rayne walked over to Kae, and Beth envied them that they could be together, but only for a moment.

She wasn't sure how she dared to approach LaSierra at this point. It was as if Beth's feet simply decided to move in her direction. Sitting in her AirFrame next to Madelon and Rocque, LaSierra appeared to be her usual collected self, but only until she saw Beth approaching. It was only a microsecond, but the first expression on LaSierra's face was bright and held a trace of... longing?

"Ms. Delmonte." Beth was aware of the Garcias, but she had to do something to show LaSierra that she was more than just her boss, and ultimately her leader.

"So formal," LaSierra murmured. She looked up at Beth and probed her gaze with hers. Beth's stomach clenched, and even though she was always alert and rarely foolhardy while on a mission, LaSierra's expression solidified her determination to return to her, no matter what.

"Yes. It's that time." Beth popped off her helmet. Bending, she placed a gentle hand on LaSierra's shoulder. She kissed her cheek—a real kiss, not that polite, stupid air kiss. "I'll come back, and then I'll kiss you again, if you want." She rose and put her helmet back on. "Madelon, Rocque." She shook hands and then gave Madelon a pointed look. "Please."

"Don't worry. I'm prepared." Madelon clearly noticed Beth's wordless plea that someone needed to look out for LaSierra. She held Beth's hand a little longer. "Be safe, Beth."

Foster and Rayne walked up to the Garcias, and Foster shocked Beth by kissing Madelon's cheek and slapping Rocque hard enough on the back for the older man to have to sidestep.

"Now, now," Rayne said lightly. "Don't break my father's shoulder blade." She stepped closer to her parents. "Mom. Dad. Make sure the kids are cared for, okay? All of them."

Beth had heard Rayne address her parents only formally and knew they had a complicated past to deal with, but now when she called them mom and dad, Madelon's eyes glazed over with unshed tears.

"We will, sweetheart." Madelon took her daughter by the shoulder and shook her lightly. "You come back to us, you hear." She swallowed hard and let go.

"Of course I will," Rayne said calmly. "This isn't my first mission." She relented and cupped Madelon's cheek. "I won't take any unnecessary risks. I promise you that."

Rocque seemed at a loss for words and merely hugged his daughter tight.

Their GemLinks beeped, and Beth looked over at Kae, who stood over by the path that led to the perimeter.

It was time.

❖

The first hour was uneventful. Kae had taken up the lead beside Beth, and behind them, four of the dissident core soldiers, armed and ready, were prepared to spring into action if needed. Rayne and her team walked behind them, and four more soldiers made sure nobody surprised them from behind. Foster took up the rear, and that, more than anything, made Beth feel optimistic that nobody could surprise them.

They walked on a path where a forest loomed on their left and crop fields billowed on their right. Beth pushed her visor back into the helmet to breathe fresh air, rather than the recycled, stale-smelling oxygen the helmet and suit provided. It could come in handy if they ran into anyone who had manufactured something toxic.

After another ten miles, Kae gestured toward the forest and turned a quick left. As Beth followed Kae in among the trees, she sharpened her senses, a habit from the tunnels and in the worm alleys—the narrow pathways among the bases of the skyscrapers, where ninety-degree curves were prime spots for an ambush.

She heard that chirping sound that Kae had suggested came from birds. Having seen birds only on film, and as pictures in books, Beth still found it amazing that Earth held flying creatures.

"Time for a fifteen-minute break." Kae pointed at three of the soldiers. "You secure our perimeter. Set it with a ten-yard radius from this location. That might seem over-the-top for a fifteen-minute break, but trust me, a lot can happen within that time span. Stay sharp."

"Yes, sir," the soldiers, two men and one woman, said smartly. It was obvious that they responded well to Kae's life-long commanding persona. Normally, Kae would just roll her eyes when Beth mentioned this trait, but a few times she had actually discussed the entire nature-nurture theory with Beth.

Rayne joined them, and the entire team managed to find seating on fallen logs. "Thank the Creator for these boots," Kae said in a low voice. "Since I lost my best pair in the skyscraper, I'm glad they have these form-fitted ones. One size fits all, as they used to say, according to some of my old catalogs."

"Who used to say that?" Beth stuck her tongue out. "The Neanderthals?"

"Funny." Kae chuckled quietly, then grew serious. "Check your GemLinks for messages, alerts, or possible malfunctions. Then tell the others. Just do it quietly."

They all followed orders, and Beth saw that she'd received a message, without any clicks. "I got a muted kind of message." She examined her GemLink. "From LaSierra."

"I haven't received anything," Rayne said.

Even Kae shook her head. "Me either."

So, it was private. Beth slid her fingertips along the edge of the GemLink and brought up the message. It was a master class in brevity.

Working. Pain manageable. Stay safe.

Beth reread it twice, and then she realized LaSierra was trying to reassure her and not have her worry about how she was doing back at HQ. "I better reply." She used the new feature to enter a short message, which translated into untraceable clicks on its way to LaSierra.

Thanks. Short break. All is well. She thought for a second and then added, *MU.* She hoped LaSierra would understand what it stood for, and if she didn't, no harm done. Surely.

After replenishing their systems with nutri-bars and water, Kae sent a soldier to round up the guards, and they resumed their formation. Beth, who oversaw their progress on the new map system, calculated that they weren't far from the area Max had pointed out as her point of exit from the crop field.

"Two miles," she murmured, after nudging Kae.

"Affirmative." Kae nodded curtly.

Beth glanced behind her. Rayne peered between the soldiers and winked at her. The exchange was nice and resembled normalcy, and Beth winked back.

After they covered one mile of the two, Beth's GemLink buzzed against her wrist. Thinking it might be a response from LaSierra, Beth glanced at it and noticed that Kae did the same with hers, and behind her, so did the soldiers. Reading her screen, she saw the streaming red lines.

"Surveillance drones," Kae said. "Lead us into the crops and plot a new path, Beth."

"Got it." Beth veered into the dense crop, lowering her visor. Soon she saw all the information she needed at forty-percent transparency. Beth felt Kae clutch at her harness and knew she would make sure Beth didn't run into a dangerous object or stumble over something.

"Two hundred yards course eighty degrees. According to Max, that is deep enough into the crop to maintain stealth." Beth let her visor reduce the information at the sides of the visor and move out of her field of vision. She kept only a bright red line that they needed to follow to not veer off course.

It took them only six minutes to reach relative safety. Beth stood still among the tall, fast-growing stems, as thick as her calves. After processing, the large leaves at the top and some of the peeled stems were turned into the basic substance that kept the FlatPak business going in the skyscrapers.

"Did this happen because I clicked back to LaSierra?" Beth shuddered. "I'm sorry. I wanted her to know we were okay this far."

"No. I don't think so. When I asked, Max was adamant that clicks were okay. I think it was simply happenstance," Rayne said. "Stand still, everybody."

Kae nodded. "Considering that we're only a few yards from the area we were supposed to hit, Beth will recalculate, and we'll continue when we don't hear the drones any longer. Good thing they're loud."

For Beth the whirring sound had seemed completely alien at first. In her mind, it sounded like huge approaching insects, or something else from her childhood nightmares. She had heard about insects and envisioned the worst concoction a person could imagine. Shuddering, she kept scanning as they moved forward farther into the crop. She understood more about what Max had tried to describe. If they hadn't had a compass, or access to technology that alerted them if something sinister approached, they'd be lost in this dense maze.

Kae stopped and raised her fist. Behind her, everyone halted immediately. Beth was two steps ahead, her eyes locked on the red line, which had made her veer off to the left at a forty-degree angle.

"Beth," Kae whispered. "What's going on?"

"My Aeroton map has located something. It's unclear, but a faintly trampled path is here." Beth pointed, using the muzzle of her Nova blaster. "See?"

Kae knew Beth was looking at the live mapping system from the satellite Aeroton 6 and stepped up to her, setting her own visor to exploration mode. Where there had been nothing other than a few cracked crop stems, the path was clearly visible. Nearly invisible tracks of naked feet showed that neither soldiers nor guards had created it. Either slaves had made paths when they sowed the crop, or they could lead to one of the sanctuary camps. Max had assured them that the people in the sancts didn't possess weapons, but they still needed to use caution.

"All right. Lead on, Beth. You have the best eye for this situation, obviously." Kae knew her strength was seeing the big picture, which would mean she'd miss the finer details. And sometimes the success of a message lay in puzzling together the details.

Kae let one of the soldiers send the message of their new direction back to the others and hoped their whispered repetition wouldn't change the message before it reached Foster. They had to be as inconspicuous as possible.

Chapter Sixteen

K ae scanned the forest of stems ahead of them. They had made their way through the dense crop for more than an hour but found no sign of any sancts. Beth, who was still heading up the team, seemed tireless as she pushed her way through the rows of stems.

"Kae," Beth said and stopped, raising her fist. "Are you seeing this?" She pointed with her Nova blaster toward the ground.

Kae squeezed past some stems and let her visor scan the ground. "That's…is that a heat signature?" she murmured. Not waiting for Beth to answer, Kae turned to London and motioned for him to join them. "What's that?"

London bent and tapped his visor. "Fresh tracks. Heat signatures. They're nearby." He pointed in a direction forty degrees due west. "That way."

"All right. Good. Fall in." Now that she knew what she was looking for, Kae took the lead again, and Beth gave her a grateful look. Kae understood. It took a lot out of you to be the one in front.

The tracks, made by naked feet, became increasingly clear. Hoping they would come upon one of the sanct camps soon, Kae kept her head down. Their suits had altered color when they entered the field of crops, and one of the soldiers had explained that it was an automatic feature created by something called Cameleo-crystals. He had apologized that no one had briefed them on this, and Kae had assured him they were used to learning on the fly.

Kae's audio gave a muted hum, more of a vibration, alerting her that it had picked up a new sound ahead of them. A quick glance at Beth proved that she had received the same warning.

Now it was Kae's turn to raise her fist. Everybody stopped. Turning around, Kae pointed at Beth, London, Rayne, a young female soldier, and Foster. "With me," she whispered and knew they heard her through the same system that gave the alert. "The rest of you, stay low and vigil. Do not fire unless your life is in jeopardy. We're close."

Kae made sure that Rayne was in the middle of the group, as her knowledge and expertise was the most valuable for this mission. They needed to protect her at all costs, also for the people back at the dissident camp.

They approached with as much stealth as possible. The nearer they came, the more often they detected heat signatures via their scanner.

Beth nudged Kae from behind, and again, Kae's fist went up. Beth pointed to the right, and then Kae saw it, barely visible through the stems, something resembling a tarp, or even kind of habitat, a different color than the crop. Someone had tried to camouflage it, but it was not a Camou-crystal item.

According to Max—and Kae was 90% sure they could trust her—nobody had any weapons other than sticks, branches, stones, or possibly something fashioned into an ancient-looking bow and arrow. Nothing that would penetrate their suits, but if someone slammed a large branch down on them, they could still sustain severe injuries. At least their helmets protected their heads.

"Beth, Rayne, and I will make the initial approach," Kae said. "Foster, London—stick to the plan. And...I forgot your name?" She looked at the female soldier.

"Hunter, sir," the woman whispered, looking impressively calm. After all, the skyscraper resistance had trained her, which meant she'd had a lot of instruction but no real-world experience.

"Hunter. You are in charge of keeping the medical staff safe." She patted Foster's shoulder. "Set the plan in motion. We're off." She exchanged a glance with Foster. "See you in a bit."

Kae motioned for Rayne to stay close behind her. "Hold onto my harness if you have to, but stay protected behind me. If I tell you to pivot, you press your back to me and deploy your weapon, all right?"

Rayne nodded grimly.

Beth gave a thumbs-up, something she'd seen in an ancient film when she was new on Kae's team and occasionally used.

They moved between the stems, now staying to the side of the path where naked feet had recently walked. Beth took up the rear, helping keep Rayne safe.

As they found themselves about fifteen yards from the fabric, or wall, Kae stopped. She tapped her GemLink and sent clicks to HQ that they planned to breach the camp soon, then set her visor to fully transparent, but with increased heat-signature readings. Immediately, it lit up with the outline of at least twenty individuals, perhaps more. Stepping into the camp fully armed didn't exactly send the right signal, but if they were going to be able to help more people, they couldn't risk their lives unnecessarily at the very first camp.

"We move in from this end," she mouthed at Rayne and Beth, who nodded. Rayne was pale but collected. Beth seemed eager to get going. No surprise there.

Kae made a circular motion with her left hand and then pointed forward with two fingers. They didn't hesitate. Keeping low, they moved fast, heel-to-toe, and before the inhabitants of the camp had a chance to react, the three of them stood in the center of the people, their Nova blasters drawn, their aim fluid, as they couldn't know which ones among the people around them were the most dangerous.

Kae gazed along the people who stood, sat, or lay down around them. Tarps, braided thin stems from the crop, and blankets protected the inhabitants.

"Creator…they found us." An emaciated woman covered her face. "After all this time." She began to whimper.

Before the shock of their sudden appearance wore off, Kae raised her voice. "We're not Celestials. We come from a faction of dissidents and freedom fighters. We're not here to take you back to the slave camps. If anyone here knows a young woman named Max, she's the reason we're here. We've come to help—and for information."

"Max?" a youthful voice sounded from one of the small blanket tents. A young woman poked her head out. Thin and dirty, but damn, she was angry. "You took Max? She would never give us up. Not any of the camps. Not if you didn't torture her." She stood on wobbly legs, and Kae spotted a deep gash on her left leg that looked infected.

"Max is being treated for injuries and malnutrition." Rayne spoke calmly. "I'm a doctor. I'm here to start administering medical treatments, if you'll let me." She held her blaster with one hand as she slipped off her sizable backpack with the other. "Please, let me help you." She was talking to the girl. "That looks painful." Rayne indicated the girl's leg.

"Stay away from me," the girl spat.

"You have to leave everything behind," a man said. His arm in a sling, he had a straggly beard and was as thin as the others. He seemed the oldest of them. "Run! Run! Run!" The man threw himself forward, aiming for Beth, probably hoping to create a distraction to let the younger, more ambulatory people get away.

Beth lowered her weapon and caught the man with one arm, gently lowering him to the ground. "Don't, sir. Easy there." She placed him sitting down on the ground and stepped back. "We're not here to hurt anyone."

Some of the younger people had begun to move through the closest stems of the crops, but then headed back up into the camp just as fast when Foster and the rest of the soldiers appeared between the stems and joined Kae and the others. Neither of them had their weapons trained on any of the people, merely deployed as a precaution.

It took them less than ten minutes to round up the inhabitants of the sanct. Twenty-three men and women, some as young as fourteen or fifteen, and some almost thirty. The oldest male inhabitant kept looking at Beth with watery, wide eyes.

"Yes, sir? Do you have a question for me?" Beth asked and hoisted her weapon onto her back, then crouched before him. "First, what's your name?"

The man moved his lips, but it took him a while to answer. "Samuel."

"You thirsty, Samuel?" Beth pulled out one of her ReGen water tubes. "Here. Sip it slowly. It rehydrates you five times faster than regular water."

He stared at the tube and then at Beth, then shook his head. Kae saw fear flicker over his face.

"Ah. Look here." Beth opened the tube and took a sip. "Just water. I promise."

Samuel took the tube with trembling hands and put it to his mouth. He sipped it at first, and then his eyes bugged out, and he began to gulp it down.

"Oh, no. Not that fast, Sam." Beth took his hand and kept it from reaching his mouth, but she didn't take the tube from him. "You can have this tube, but you can't drink too quickly. It'll make you sick. Just very slowly."

"Listen to her, Sam," the young woman with the injured leg said, and now after her bravado had left her, she sounded as tired as Samuel did.

"May I look at your injury?" Rayne said and approached the girl as if she were a wild animal.

"Can I stop you?" the girl asked, shaking her head.

"You can, but it wouldn't be smart, as you desperately need treatment. I have water for you too. Same as Samuel's."

The girl nodded and took the tube after Rayne snapped the lid off it. She drank from it, and tears began to run down her cheeks. "Are you...are you really here to help? Are you from the tunnels?"

"Some of us are. Beth over there is Subterranean. I've been to the tunnels very shortly and tried to help when I was there. We're a mix of former Celestials and Subterraneans, fighting back against the authorities. They're the ones responsible for your situation."

As Rayne opened her bag, she gave medical scanners to Kae, Foster, and Beth. "Get me some vitals. Add names, not numbers. Something tells me these people have been little more than numbers most of their lives."

Kae walked among the people and started with a boy who looked about ten but was most likely older. "Hello, there. I'm just going to run this along your chest, your neck, and your back. It won't hurt. Can you tell me your name?"

The boy blinked slowly. "Sol."

"Hi, Sol. I'm Kae. Just sit still, and I'll be quick." Kae entered the boy's name and ran the scanner over him. It was hardly a surprise that he was in poor condition. If she was reading the scanner right, parasites and malnourishment were his biggest problems. She gave him a tube of ReGen water with instructions, and as she stood, he ran his fingertips along her sleeve.

"Yes, Sol?"

"Are you taking us back?" he whispered.

"You're not going back into slavery. You have my word." Kae swallowed but then patted his shoulder as she moved on to a woman who lay with her head in the lap of a young boy.

"She's my mom." He wiped his runny nose. "She found me, and she got several of us out. Then we ran." As it turned out, the woman's name was Elysia, and her son was Trep. He was in better shape than most in the camp, but Elysia was barely coherent.

"She's been giving him most of her food. She's dying," the girl with the leg injury said quietly. "She saved his life by giving hers."

The nurse arrived and began setting up more elaborate equipment to hook up to Elysia.

Kae walked over to where Rayne was cleaning the deep leg wound. "What's your name?" she asked and wiggled the scanner.

"Mave." The girl grimaced when Rayne pressed what looked like an old-style flashlight into the wound. "Fuck. That hurts, lady."

"I know. I'm ready to close the wound soon." She glanced up at Kae before she continued working. "What's the verdict?"

"Infections, parasites, malnutrition, cuts, bruises, and the ever-present scars or still-open wounds on their shoulders where they got rid of the trackers."

"I see. As I expected." Rayne began to run a different wand to close the wound. In a few minutes, pink skin had covered the wound as it closed from the inside out. Rayne attached a protective bandage. "Don't take this off. The skin is closed but still sensitive." She studied Mave's body. "Give me a second." She ran the same wand at a different setting, and soon the bruises were healed, smaller cuts as well. "There."

Mave gaped and then sipped the ReGen water tube. "Are you one of those magical people?"

"Not sure what those are, but no." Rayne smiled gently. "We're just medical and security, here trying to help."

Kae left Rayne to move on to the next patient, while she circled back to Samuel, who now had some injuries healed by a medic. He seemed marginally more lucid, which meant he might be able to answer a few questions.

"Hi again. I have a few questions so we can help more sancts." She sat down next to the man and took off her helmet. Running her hand through her hair, she studied the man closely. "Are you among the oldest in this part of the camps?"

"Yes." Samuel sipped the water and then took a bite from a special ration bar meant for patients. He swallowed with a grimace, and Kae wondered if he had a sore throat as well. "I've managed to flee the camps twice. The first time, I was only thirteen. The second time was about two years ago. I've gone back, but not inside, to round up more who've fled the fields around the camps this last year."

"How do you stay connected with the rest of the sancts? You have to have a low-tech way to do that, or you would have been rounded up long ago. Max told us that only the leaders of each camp knew—in case people were recaptured."

"People are recaptured all the time," Samuel said and coughed. "But she's right. Max is one of our runners. She's privy to a lot of information, but not all. Are you going to help the other sancts too?"

Kae wasn't sure of how much to tell this man. She needed his intel, but if she gave him too much information, it could backfire and put their camp at risk. "Yes. That's our intention. We need to be able to find them faster than we did today, though. We've been looking for you all day. It's almost night, which means we need to wait until dawn before we start getting you out of here. In the meantime, the more you can tell us, the better."

"What if everything's a ruse?" Samuel spoke quietly. "How can I know?"

"I suppose you have to take a leap of faith," Kae said, placing a gentle hand on his. "Just ask yourself. Have you ever seen anyone in charge at the slave camps dressed like this, treat your wounds and bring you food like this?"

"No. No, of course not." Samuel sighed. "I was born in the tunnels. I was taken when I was eight. It was so long ago, nobody from there would remember me." He closed his eyes. "I'll tell you what you need to know, because the latest news from the other sancts is that people are dying. Some people even chose to go back to the camps."

Kae looked over at Rayne, who worked her way down the row of exhausted former slaves. Rayne nodded. She'd heard.

After the most urgent medical means had been met, some of the people had moved in under their tarps and blankets and settled down on the ground. Beth joined Kae and Foster, who were pulling out rations to replenish themselves.

"Beth. Have you sent a message to LaSierra since we got here?" Kae tapped her chin, busy considering pros and cons.

"No. Haven't had the time." Beth grimaced. "She won't be pleased."

"I'll say. Why don't you use one of the larger screens and hook it up to your GemLink? Get London to help you. Then send a brief account of what we've found today. I'll click a message to the Garcias regarding how to move the sanct camps out of the fields without alerting the authorities."

Beth's eyes lit up. "You have a plan. I can tell."

"I do, but it will require some of Benny's tricky tech. Good thing he's doing so much better." Kae shrugged. "How did we never know just how much worse off some people are, even compared to what some go through in the tunnels? It's a strange feeling."

"Sure is." Beth leaned over and punched Kae lightly on the shoulder. "I'll go set up the screen."

CHAPTER SEVENTEEN

Beth sat in front of the ten-inch screen, which made it easier to use the click feature. She began typing, and instantly the letters turned into clicks that would sound like static to anyone unable to decrypt them.

It took five minutes before a stream of clicks showed that she'd contacted HQ.

HQ: Recipient ID Omega-6939Delta

FT: Field Team here. User ID BetaBeta-889

Beth knew the HQ ID wasn't LaSierra's. She typed again.

FT: Need access to Delmonte.

HQ: Stand by.

Another three minutes passed, and Beth started to worry but pushed her personal feelings aside. She had no choice but to wait.

HQ: EpsilonDelta-0001. Report.

Relieved, Beth exhaled heavily and filled LaSierra in about their mission so far.

HQ: What do you need?

FT: Benny. We have to evacuate all the sanct camps within a certain radius in a single mission. Intel from locals shows us locations.

HQ: While they are in the field? Impossible.

FT: Kae and London have a plan. Benny needs to program something called SkyPods to be able to hover and let down nets. London says it has been done in training.

HQ: To a degree. Stand by.

Beth drummed her fingertips against her bent legs, hoping Benny was nearby and that London hadn't exaggerated his capabilities. Then again, Beth had seen Benny perform all kinds of technological programming magic.

HQ: EpsilonDelta-0001. Benny is here.

Beth explained in greater detail what they needed.

FT: They must be in full stealth mode.

HG: They will be. Hoisted refugees won't. Speed of the essence.

FT: Exactly. Can you make this happen?

HQ: I will work with Rocque.

FT: Estimated time?

After a slight delay, the answer came.

HQ: Two hours, at best.

FT: That gives us time to reach the other sancts.

Another delay, and then LaSierra's clicks said that Benny had left the briefing.

HQ: Are you all right?

FT: Just fine. So is team.

HQ: Refugees?

FT: In bad shape.

HQ: Beth.

Beth stared at her name on the screen. Why did LaSierra risk clicking her name when anyone studying transcripts afterward would see?

FT: We will be back soon.

HQ: I will hold you to that. EpsilonDelta-0001 out.

Beth packed up the gear and headed back to the center of the clearing, where she found Kae holding the young boy, Sol, close as he struggled to breathe. Kae's face was ashen and her eyes as flat and hard as they could be in the tunnels when she found herself helpless. Beth knew the feeling all too well.

"How's he doing?" Beth crouched next to Sol.

"He's going in and out of consciousness. Mave told us he's done this over the last few days. He seems better, then takes a turn for the worse, and the cycle keeps repeating."

Rayne ran one of her multitude of wands over Sol. "His tissues have gathered something toxic, and his toxicity levels keep elevating. He's one of the first to leave when help arrives."

"How did the briefing go?" Kae lowered her voice further.

"Benny said two hours." Beth sighed. "Does this kid have two hours?"

"I hope so. "I'm going to set a filtration pack around his belly. With a little finessing, it might keep the toxicity at the current level for a few hours." She didn't sound certain, but Beth trusted Rayne.

"You can do it, Doc." She squeezed Rayne's shoulder. "I'm going to make the rounds and hand out more ReGen water. You did say one more tube each, right?"

"I did." Rayne nodded slowly. "Except for the youngest boy. He'll be all right with just one."

"Got it." Beth walked among the people, handing out the tubes, until she reached Foster and Samuel. Samuel looked more lucid, his eyes brighter.

"Hi." Beth crouched next to the men. "Any actionable intel, Foster?"

"Yes. We're planning to deploy runners in three directions, which, according to Samuel, will make it possible for us to reach, and map, the closest sancts. Can you believe they're hidden even farther in among these fucking plants?"

"I can, somehow. We live and hide in the tunnels, and they use what's available to hide out here. The irony is, we had no way of knowing this was what we were hiding from, but we were trying not to end up in the camps. These people hide for the same reason, but after coming out on the other side."

"Insane—all of it." Foster got up. "I'll let Kae know that we're starting."

"Wait," Beth said, frowning. "Are you one of the runners?"

Foster grinned. "You're joking, right? With my physique, I'd sound like a stampeding...what are they called again...?"

"Elephant?" Beth suggested.

"That." Foster jogged over to Kae, and Beth watched him talk to her briefly. She nodded, and he gathered three soldiers, London among them, and gave them their assignment. They would be bringing messages from Samuel that held instructions for each sanct leader, and then continue to the next two sancts, thus covering three of them each. The messages were made from braided leaves and thin stems, the intricate patterns are something they'd come up with while in captivity. Beth was impressed.

"Two hours," Samuel said and coughed. "It's not very long. They better be both quiet and fast."

"They will be," Beth said. She knew she sounded certain, but she also knew how much could go wrong. What if Benny couldn't make the SkyPods stealthy enough? Why had no one aboard LaSierra's SkyBird deployed them? And why had she never heard of those pods before? Beth patted Samuel's shoulder and then got up to walk the perimeter. She just couldn't sit still.

LaSierra moved her AirFrame over to Benny's work console. "Tell me you have good news."

"An order I'd be happy to follow, sir, but I've run into a bit of a conundrum." Benny wiped sweat from his forehead. "I've created a subroutine for the operator of the SkyPod's propulsion system to work in complete stealth. I could do that because I had laid the foundation for it not that long ago and was trying to get it approved just before the Subterranean gang showed up in the skyscraper."

"Yet you're still not entirely successful." LaSierra regarded the code on the screen and saw only streaming, colorful lines. "What about you, Rocque? You're not lost behind a console."

"That's true, LaSierra." Rocque smiled weakly. "I'm trying to find a way to encapsulate the bulkhead in a shield of sorts, but it tends to go offline as soon as we open the belly hatch to deploy the nets. The propulsion system will still be invisible, but the body of the SkyPod won't."

"And when the hatch closes again?" LaSierra reached back and pressed two fingers against the base of her skull, where a persistent ache had all but blossomed into a migraine.

"If a certain part of the system has time to reboot, it'll reestablish the entire stealth package." Benny glowered at the floating screen. "But we can't be certain. If we run a dress rehearsal, I'm afraid any signals we might have overlooked will alert the authorities to our general location."

"And if that happens in the field?" LaSierra had to press hard at the back of her neck to keep from screaming in frustration. "We need to evacuate our own people, along with the refugees."

"I know," Rocque said bleakly. "My only child is out there."

Of course. "I realize that, Rocque." She squeezed his arm. "What are our options?"

Benny straightened, and LaSierra noticed his fatigue. "We deploy them in…" He checked his elaborate engineering GemLink. "Twenty minutes. If they're visible for a few minutes when they hoist them, they'll have to be quick to reboot a certain sequence. I can add that to the programming. It'll shave off a few seconds. If the authorities' bots are within range, they might start a search, but with a little luck, the SkyPod operators will be on their way here."

"How many pods do we need to deploy?" LaSierra knew the high-stakes operation would lay the foundation for the bigger one that was vital for their survival, for that of the Celestial people still undercover in the skyscrapers, the Subterraneans, and the ones being kept as slaves in the camps.

"We need to send at least four to each sanctuary camp." Benny slid his fingers along the controls. "I would recommend using four extras as backup just outside our perimeter."

LaSierra had made up her mind. The decision and responsibility were hers. "Rocque, deploy the SkyPods as soon as you receive the coordinates from the field team. I want updates every fifteen minutes once that happens."

"Yes, sir." Rocque nodded grimly. "I'm going to join Madelon at her console. She's monitoring the field team."

"I'll be at my console." LaSierra maneuvered her AirFrame to the far end of the conference table and set her station to maximum. She couldn't afford to miss a thing.

❖

Beth jumped as her GemLink clicked the alert code. "It's them." She slid closer to Kae and opened the screen she had used before when clicking with LaSierra. The soldier who had run southwest sent coordinates, and Beth forwarded them to HQ immediately. Within minutes, the second soldier reported a set of coordinates from due west. After forwarding them as well, Beth shivered from a pure adrenaline surge. "Come on, Hunter," Beth muttered. "Report in."

"She should be at the last sanct." Foster checked his GemLink. "Unless she ran into trouble."

"If she doesn't report in, we'll rescue after these refugees are picked up." Beth looked at Kae for confirmation.

Kae nodded curtly. "Let's hope it doesn't come to that."

Beth sighed. "I sent the coordinates we have so far. They're deploying the SkyPods." She stood and began pacing. "Come on, Hunter. Where are you?"

Foster came over to stand shoulder to shoulder to Beth as she kept checking her GemLink. "Give her some time."

"If she hasn't clicked us when the SkyPods arrive..." Beth shook her head.

"I know." Foster put his arm around her and squeezed her shoulders briefly. "The medics are rounding up the refugees, and Rayne has triaged them. It looks like it's touch-and-go for young Sol, so he'll go up first, along with Rayne."

It took only another fifteen minutes before they saw shadowy figures against the sky just above the tall crops. "They're here." Beth sighed and looked at her GemLink. Still nothing from Hunter. "Should I disregard protocol and click her?"

"No," Kae said sternly. "If she's been captured, any clicks from her GemLink will give this method of communication away. As long as it sounds like odd static and they have nothing to compare it to, we can use it. If they learn to track the clicks, we'll lose our only way of communicating."

"I knew that. I did." Beth wanted to stomp the ground like a frustrated child. "I'm sorry."

"I thought of it too before I caught myself," Kae said. She stared at the now-hovering SkyPods. "Odd vessels."

Beth tipped her head back and stared up at the six SkyPods that hovered above them. Shaped like two large, white balls connected with a narrow tunnel, their matte surface was covered by something resembling a net. The bottom looked like chiseled marble, all asymmetrical angles. "That's what makes them stealthy, especially from the ground. The net and those angles," one of the medics said. "They're opening their cargo hold."

"How the hell did they fit into the SkyBird?" Foster frowned. "They're almost the same size."

"Only when inflated. The round parts look like balls because they're balloons. When you need to escape a SkyBird, your pilot engages the exodus command, and then your chairs fall into the belly of your SkyBird and shoot the crew out and upward. That engages the balloons inside the stealth nets, making them inflate. The pilots' helm codes are transferred at the same time, and they'll keep flying the SkyPods until they find a safe place to land. Pretty basic, really." Catching himself, the medic gestured apologetically. "Ah. Bad word choice. Guess it's only basic when you already know about them."

"Thanks for explaining," Foster said. "Here come the nets. We have to hustle."

Beth began doing her part, steadying the nets while the refugees were put inside. Grownups went up alone, while the young people ascended two at a time. Beth found it impressive how fast the transfers went. The medics had clearly trained for this procedure.

Kae stood watching Rayne go up with Sol. "I'm glad she's going back," she muttered to Beth. "Something tells me we'll have to search for Hunter. She sent coordinates until she had just one sanct left. I don't like that one bit."

"Same here." Beth steadied the net and then watched as the crew in the SkyBot winched his emaciated body up. "Four more to go up, apart from the medics and soldiers. Which of us do you want to rescue Hunter?"

"Just you and Foster. We're better at this part than they are and will be able to move faster. Send clicks to let HQ know. Rayne's going to kill me when we get back, but she's already on her way back with her SkyPod."

Beth thought of LaSierra and didn't even try to envision her reaction. She'd deal with that later. "What do you want me to say to HQ?"

"Same rules apply once the SkyPods have left. No clicks from their end. We check in once every hour with the 2-1-2-1-1 click series to show we're on track. When we find Hunter, we'll double each digit. When we reach the last sanct, we'll send the coordinates, and they can pick all of us up there. We'll bring medical supplies and do our best for the people in that sanct."

"Got it." Beth braced herself and began to click the message via her screen. Her hands shook, but she managed to send the correct message after having Foster read it.

"Good job, kid." Foster punched her shoulder.

"Thanks." Beth ate a double ration bar before putting her helmet back on. They intended to travel through the dense crop at night, and she needed its night-vision capabilities.

As they saw the last of the SkyPods head east, half full, Kae circled her right index finger. "Move out. Beth behind me. And before you say something, we will take turns being up front."

Beth nodded and fell into Kae's step as they made their way out among the stems. They knew exactly what path Hunter had taken until she disappeared, but that didn't mean they wouldn't run into trouble. They kept their voices low, and it felt eerily familiar to be down to their original trio again. Beth missed Rayne as part of their group, and Beth had to keep making a conscious effort to not think about LaSierra.

CHAPTER EIGHTEEN

L aSierra sat in her AirFrame at the landing site her people had hastily prepared for the incoming SkyPods. Medical staff and security personnel were standing by, and LaSierra could tell they were fully focused on triaging and bringing the people who needed their help in under the large canopy that had been erected until they could expand the hospital. Engineers were busy plugging in an outdoor heating system. It was a temporary measure, but LaSierra knew this was a lot more than the refugees had had access to in the crops.

Max had insisted on being present, and after initially balking at the idea, LaSierra had agreed. Now the young woman sat upright on a gurney next to her.

"So, they stuck us in a corner to keep us out of the way. Figures." Max glanced over at LaSierra. "I suppose I should be grateful to sit next to the queen of this place." Her tone was acerbic, but her facial expression showed she was being facetious.

LaSierra cringed. *Queen*? "I'm hardly royalty." She heard herself chuckle.

"Perhaps not, but you sure look the part sitting there on your fancy throne. I bet when kids see you, no matter where they come from, they think you're a real queen. There's something about you, Ms. Delmonte."

LaSierra shook her head. "I disagree. However, your resilience is remarkable, Max."

Shrugging, which made her wince from obvious pain, Max bit her lower lip. "When it's a matter of survival and you have no other option, it's not hard. The people in the sancts have nothing to lose."

This was one of LaSierra's concerns. People who had nothing to lose could allow their desperation to lead them down the wrong path.

"LaSierra." Madelon appeared at LaSierra's other side. "Rocque is monitoring the communication array, but I need to be here." She was wearing a uniform suit, and with her hair in a low ponytail, she looked severe as she stood there. This was a Madelon Garcia that few people had seen—the intense, no-nonsense soldier who had been part of the dissident movement her entire adult life. LaSierra had known Madelon for twenty-five years, ever since they connected within the upper echelons of the skyscraper social circles. It hadn't taken them long to understand that they secretly held the same views of the corrupt Celestial authorities.

"You look like you're ready to hijack one of the SkyPods—I just can't figure out why."

Madelon stood rigid for a moment, but then she relented. "Of course I wouldn't do something rash like that, but...it's the children. I've met five of them during the last few weeks that are caught in the middle of this damn everlasting conflict. I just need to be here, as there will certainly be more among the refugees."

Nodding slowly, LaSierra then glanced at Max. She'd been a kid not long ago. "Max. Are you ready for what you might see as they arrive in..." She checked her GemLink. "Less than a minute?"

"Having been a runner between the sancts, I've seen it all." Max pressed her lips together. "I need to be here to check if anyone's missing."

"All right. Just stay beside me, out of the way, as it were." Turning to Madelon, LaSierra patted her arm. "You'll be our eyes and ears. Turn on your camera, Madelon."

Madelon tapped her GemLink. "Done."

LaSierra checked her AirScreen. "Excellent." She turned to Max. "As you don't have a GemLink yet, you can watch mine." She adjusted her screen to project at a wider angle.

"Look!" Madelon pointed to the sky.

Coming in at a low trajectory, the first SkyPod was about to land.

"Too fast, damn it," Madelon whispered. "They're coming in too fast. Something must be wrong."

The SkyPod had to circle the clearing before it landed at the far end of it. Madelon started running as soon as it powered down its propulsion system. LaSierra kept gazing between the AirScreen and what was happening around the SkyPod. At least the craft seemed intact.

On the screen, she saw everything from Madelon's point of view. She ran to the hatch and slammed her hand against the sensor, clearly not about to wait. When the ramp had almost extended fully, Madelon jumped up and entered the SkyPod.

"Rayne?" Madelon's voice was stark.

"Mother? I'm over here." LaSierra would know Rayne's melodious, calm voice anywhere. "I have two critical patients. Are the gurneys ready?"

"They are. Let me help you unload. Where do you need me?" Madelon's voice had mellowed, probably since she saw that Rayne was unharmed.

"Can you engage the front of this and steer it. It's just a backboard, but they couldn't bring the gurneys because they wouldn't fit." Rayne spoke quickly. "Yes. Like that. Great."

Madelon stood close to the head of the backboard, and when she leaned over the patient, LaSierra saw it was a young boy. "More children."

"That's Sol!" Max gripped the sides of her gurney. "Is he unconscious?" She leaned closer.

"It looks like it. Or sedated. They're carrying him out now. He's going to be in good hands. You know that from experience." LaSierra was aware of the irony that she was trying to cheer up someone. Usually, people needed cheering up after a confrontation with her.

"Yes." Max studied the screen. "They're handing him over to some other people."

LaSierra checked the screen again. "A doctor and a nurse who have trained for this for years. Have faith, Max." She tried to infuse certainty in her voice.

Madelon was now back in the SkyPod and helped unload a man who seemed even worse off than the boy. "Who is that?" LaSierra asked, as she had begun to take notes by recording Max's statements about the people she recognized.

"That's Samuel. He's the leader of this sanct. He sent me on the mission in the first place." Max shuddered. "I was sure I botched it, but here they are—even if it's just the first craft."

As if Max's words reached the other pods, they began to land, one by one. Soon, all of them had filled the clearing, which meant the space between them fit only two people and a gurney. People milled around in controlled chaos, and LaSierra looked for the rest of Rayne's team but couldn't see them.

Madelon was now heading into another SkyPod and helped a young woman down the ramp and onto a gurney. Given their limited supply of gurneys, they had to first unload the patients onto the medical cots set up for them under the canopy.

When LaSierra finally realized that Beth, Kae, and Foster—the latter easily found in any crowd as the giant man towered over everyone else—were missing, she checked her GemLink. No messages. She was starting to get stats regarding the refugees, but other than that—nothing.

"LaSierra." Rocque showed up at her side, dressed in a uniform like Madelon's. "There's been a development."

"Report." LaSierra pressed her back against the chair.

"Hunter, one of our young soldiers, went missing when she had one more sanctuary camp left. After the last of the SkyPods left the crop fields, we had a message from Beth. She, Foster, and Kae have deployed on a rescue mission. They will retrieve Hunter and get the coordinates for the last sanctuary." He rubbed his chin. "I'm not looking forward to telling Rayne."

"They did what?" LaSierra spat. "She promised to return with the SkyPods." Her entire chest cavity threatened to start spasming. Beth had, well, not promised but reassured her enough for LaSierra to trust in her swift return. She should've known better. Beth, Kae, and Foster were made from something other than the highly trained but still inexperienced dissidents were. Even Rayne had more experience, and she was a doctor.

"Who are you talking about?" Rocque looked concerned. "Ah. Of course, I know that you and Beth have become, uhm, good friends. This isn't what we wanted, of course. Still, of all the people we could have sent in to find Hunter, this team is the best— and the most experienced."

"I know," LaSierra said, her voice catching. "But are they properly equipped? They were going on a humanitarian mission, which you tell me is now a rescue mission." Her words came out like lashes from a whip. LaSierra could hear her own tone. Trying to calm herself meant pushing her fear for Beth's safety into the background. "I don't envy you telling Rayne. If she knew, she would've informed Madelon instantly."

"Is Madelon in there?" Rocque motioned toward the throngs of people working to help the refugees.

"She is. Over there to the right." LaSierra pointed. "You better get over there."

"I will. You're needed back in HQ, LaSierra." Rocque looked at Max, who studied the controlled mayhem playing out among the SkyPods. "I know you want to be among your people. I'll have a medic take you to the triage area."

"Thank you," Max said quietly. "I need to keep counting them."

"I started a list. Here's a small tablet where you can continue to record the name of each refugee." Pulling a tablet from the armrest of her AirFrame, she handed it to Max. "Do you know how to use it?"

"I'll figure it out. It looks a bit like the ones we used during sowing season." Max accepted the tablet. "Thank you, Your Majesty." She smiled tiredly.

LaSierra barely resisted rolling her eyes when she noticed Rocque's raised eyebrows. "Don't ask."

"All right." He waved two medics over, then told them where to take LaSierra and Max respectively. "You'll have my report as soon as we have a handle on the situation."

"Good." LaSierra nodded at the medic, who maneuvered her AirFrame along the path that quickly had been formed between the clearing and the Inner Circle. It weaved around the SkyBird, and LaSierra tried to keep track of which path they took to the Inner Circle but lost her way as they kept changing it. She understood that was because of safety precautions, but damn, it was dizzying.

Rayne walked from gurney to gurney, confirming the triage or changing it, depending on the patient's current status. She kept returning to seven of the refugees who were teetering on death's threshold. A few times, she stood in the center of the area covered by the canopy, looking for Kae, but assumed that she was being debriefed by LaSierra and the rest of the brass.

A hundred and seventy-six refugees had been rescued from the sancts. Apart from the seven that were in critical condition, twenty-two were in serious condition, and eighty-nine were stable but needed medical care. The remaining fifty-eight would be transported to a dormitory tent being erected in one of the communal areas. Everyone available was taking care of the former slaves and trying to reassure them.

"Doctor?" a faint female voice said from behind her.

"Yes?" Turning around, Rayne saw a young woman with short-cropped, shaggy blond hair and scars all over her arms and legs. She was wearing too-small pants and a tank top, but at least she had a blanket wrapped around her. "How can I help you?"

"It's not me. I mean, it is, but I think I need assistance." The cryptic answer came just before she pressed her hand to her lower abdomen. "I'm invitroed, and I think perhaps something's wrong? There's blood."

Rayne had to use every ounce of her training not to show her shock and disgust. "Then we better take a look. What's your name?"

"Gillian. Most people call me Gilly." The young woman, not a day over twenty, possibly younger, shrugged. "Either is fine."

"Gillian's a lovely name. Come here, and we'll find you some privacy." Rayne put her arm around the girl and began ushering her past the long rows of medical cots. They stood in eight rows of twenty-five, and medical staff swarmed all around them. "Here. Here's a gurney with a screen."

"What does privacy mean? Is that the screen?" Indicating the extendable screen, Gillian looked confused.

"It is. That way you don't have to undress among strangers." Rayne guessed that nobody in the slave camps gave a damn about anyone's privacy. "If you're comfortable with me examining you, then you can just hop up on the gurney. Pulling a scan rod from her inner pocket, she held it up to Gillian. "It might feel a little warm, but it won't hurt. All right?"

Gillian nodded and lay down on the gurney. "Like this?"

"Yes. If you can unfasten your pants and pull them down a few inches, that'd be great." Rayne set the scanner to the right calibration and waited until Gillian had done as she asked. "Now we'll see if we can find out what's going on."

Soon, Rayne's suspicions were confirmed. Gillian was three months pregnant, and the fetus was not placed optimally in the uterus. The placenta covered her cervix and seemed partially dislodged. She explained this problem to Gillian in easy-to-understand terms. "Do you want to continue the pregnancy, Gillian?" she asked softly. She wanted to ask who had implanted the embryo in Gillian and why, but this wasn't the time, and she could make a reasonably educated guess.

"Continue the pregnancy? I—I don't know what to say. If you had asked me that a month ago when I was still in the fertilization camp, I would have been relieved, as I had started to bleed. But that was because I knew if I carried this child to term, they would have taken it from me after the delivery. Now that I'm here—I'm free, I…I want this child. I don't know if I'll ever get a chance to have another, so yes. I want this child." Large tears ran down Gillian's temples and into her hair.

"Then I'll start the procedure, and you will be on a special medication once a week. If I'm not in the camp, one of my colleagues will know what to do, as I'm starting a chart on you."

Gillian lay very still and so quiet that, a few times, Rayne had to check if she'd fallen asleep. When Rayne ran a few different small rods along her pelvic area, Gillian said, with wonder in her voice, "It really doesn't hurt. It just hums."

"So I'm told," Rayne said and smiled at her. "There we go. That's your first treatment, once you take your pill. I'm going to leave word with one of the medics responsible for the medical producers. They'll make sure you have access to plenty of water. We're going to have to get you used to solid food again soon, but until then, everything you get will be in liquid form, perhaps puddings."

Rayne pulled the curtain aside and saw her parents approach, her mother looking pale, and Rocque…appeared apprehensive.

"Mother," Rayne said before her parents gave her the news they so clearly intended to. "This is Gillian. She's pregnant, and I've started her on a magnesium regiment, as well as mended some small bleeders. If we can manage to shift the placenta to a better spot, that'd be great, but if we can't, we need to monitor her every week until the delivery, which will have to be a caesarean, of course."

"Oh, dear child," her mother said and helped Gillian sit up. "Well, you're in good hands now." She gave Rocque a pointed look. "I'll help Gillian back to her cot, and you can talk to Rayne."

"All right." Rocque pulled Rayne aside, next to a shelving unit holding supplies. "I'll be direct. Kae, Beth, and Foster weren't on any of the SkyPods returning from the crop fields."

Rayne's world stopped. She couldn't hear, and it was hard to breathe. She gripped her father's left upper arm and dug her fingers into it. "What happened?"

"Hunter, one of our soldiers, didn't reach the last sanctuary on her route. They're on a rescue mission for her—and for the refugees in that camp. We can't contact them, but so far, they're using the click system every hour."

"Why can't we click back?" Rayne whispered and glowered at her father in frustration.

Rocque's eyes were flat as he so obviously tried to harness his emotions. "Because if the enemy catch them and discover how we can communicate and make it seem like regular static, we'll lose all of that—and thus the mission. Right now we don't have any other way to reach each other over greater distances. That was why we couldn't answer them on their first mission either."

"I see." Rayne did understand, but she hated the situation. A completely irrational part of her resented Kae's courage and her strong sense of duty and what was right. It had put Kae in harm's way so many times, especially since she'd tried to bring young Wes to a Celestial Soldier's clinic a few weeks ago.

"Hey. Come here." Rocque put his arm around her shoulders and held her close. "It's Kae Dark we're talking about. She'll come back to you, and she'll bring Hunter and her team home—after she's given the coordinates for the refugees. Mark my words."

"Dad." Pressing her face against her father's shoulder for a few moments, Rayne tried to absorb some of his optimism. She straightened and smiled faintly. "She's stubborn enough. And brave."

"She is. They all are. You're the second one who we feared might take off our heads for being the messengers. LaSierra looked ready to implode." Rocque fell into step with Rayne as she made her way along the rows of cots.

"She's relying on Beth for a lot," Rayne said. "I think they're closer than any of us know."

"I agree." Rocque stopped to check his GemLink. "And as if the Creator were listening in...that was their usual series of clicks. All is well in the crop field, but they haven't found Hunter yet."

"If she's been captured—" Alarmed, Rayne pivoted and stared at her father. "That could end up as badly as if they intercepted our clicks. She's young. Has she been trained to be resilient if captured?"

"She has, but I fear not nearly enough. Not like Kae and the others, who have learned on the job, so to speak." Rocque sighed. "Even I would probably give up information, and I've had a lot of preparation. But if they threatened you or your mother—I'd cave."

"Me too." Rayne shuddered. "I have to get back to work. We're moving the ones who are walking wounded to the tent. That means we can bring more equipment here and not inundate the hospital with the refugees. If they happen to have something contagious—which I haven't seen any indications of—it's good to be careful."

"Agreed." Rocque raised his hand and got Madelon's attention. He pointed in the direction of HQ and then himself. "I'm off to HQ for a briefing. Some tactical personnel returned, and their intel should be valuable."

"All right. I might see you when I'm off duty—whenever that'll be. As you can tell, we have plenty to do here. A lot to monitor."

"Then your mother and I will stop by to make sure Wesley and Tania are all right. I'm certain they know something has gone down today, but I'd rather they hear about Kae and the others from us. We've gained their trust, and if we start lying, we'll lose them."

The irony of Rocque's words didn't escape either of them. After having been high-ranking members of the dissident faction in the skyscrapers for many years, he and Madelon had hidden their secret life in the resistance to keep Rayne safe and able to have a life. This situation had unfortunately meant that she had grown up feeling a disconnect between herself and her parents, as she had lived with the impression that they didn't fully trust or approve of her. Even now, she sometimes resented being kept in the dark, even if she could rationalize their motives for wanting to protect her.

"I know." Rocque stroked his face. "We're trying to not make the same mistake again, Rayne."

"I understand that." Intellectually, she did. She was fifty years old and didn't need her parents like Wes and Tania did. Yet, inside, she felt the sting of the realization that her parents had never been as forthcoming and sensitive when she had needed them the most while she was growing up. Rayne put on the polite, broad smile she had perfected during her upbringing. "See you later, Father."

Only when she made her way toward the nurse's station did Rayne realize that Rocque's expression clearly showed that smile didn't fool him any longer.

CHAPTER NINETEEN

Kae pushed her way through the dense crop. Her visor showed recent tracks, and as she saw no others, she surmised they had to be Hunter's. They had already passed the first evacuated sanctuary camp that had been on Hunter's list, and now they were nearing the second.

How had Rayne taken the news that she, Beth, and Foster had stayed back to locate Hunter? Rayne could slam on her professional mask hard when required, but Kae knew that this didn't pertain to her. They had both had cause to worry for each other on several occasions, and when Kae thought about when Rayne was shot in the skyscraper, icicles tingled along her back. She had once and for all let Rayne into her heart, even after promising herself early on in her life that love wasn't for her because it would keep her from functioning properly as a resistance fighter. She first broke that vow when she became a guardian of sorts for Wes and Tania. She loved those kids as if she'd given birth to them herself, and it had pained her that she'd been able to visit them only very sporadically since they escaped from the skyscraper. As soon as she found Hunter and brought her back to the camp, she would ask Rayne if they could have the kids visit their habitat, perhaps for a proper sleepover with Beth and Foster as well. It was perhaps a silly idea, but the kids needed to know they were still a priority.

A whirring sound made Kae stop and raise her fist. Trained to perfection, Beth and Foster immediately halted behind her.

"Surveillance pods?" Kae mouthed to Beth, who tapped her visor and tilted her head back.

"Six of them," she whispered. "They're flying low."

"Fuck." Kae pressed her lips together. "Hit the ground."

They all dropped onto their stomachs, and Kae hoped their low-emitting helmets, which could receive a lot of information via the visor, didn't emit too much interference in the surveillance bots' scans.

"They're circling. And hovering." Foster looked tense as he pressed his imposing body to the ground. "I remember when they sent a few of these through one of the outer tunnels some years ago. We shot them down."

"We can't do that now. That would just alert them to our presence." Kae made a face. "Wish we could."

"Playing possum it is, then," Beth said and shrugged. "In this case it's a good thing the crop is fifteen feet tall. The top part is luscious enough to cover us."

Kae agreed. The meaty leaves at the top were apparently what went into the FlatPak food, before it was treated in a way that made it look and taste like what was on the box. According to Max, the stems were used to create fuel for the massive cooling system, the Phyto-Chambers, that surrounded the Bio-Nexus, the heating/cooling system that made it possible to reside in the skyscrapers. This wasn't news to LaSierra or the Garcias, but it was obvious that not even they knew the exact machinations behind the slave camps until now.

After another ten minutes, the soft whirring sound had stopped, and Kae turned to Beth, who, unlike her and Foster, had been on her back to scan through the foliage fifteen feet up.

"Anything?"

"Just an occasional small, flying Aves. I mean, birds." Beth rolled over. "I think it's safe to get up."

"Good. We need to keep going. I want to reach the third camp as soon as possible, preferably before dark." With a little luck, Hunter would turn out to be there but incommunicado for some reason.

She kept that hope up for another hour. They didn't speak much as they made their way through the crop. Kae had to be careful not to let go of the stems she pushed out of her way too fast, or they would smack Beth in the face. Clearly, Beth wasn't as careful, judging from an occasional "oof" from Foster.

Kae was turning forty-five degrees northwest, when her visor lit up with warnings.

She tried to read everything as the information ran like water along her visor.

<BIO MATTER>
<UNSAFE NOVA BLASTER>
<INCOMPLETE SUIT UNIFORM>
<UNAUTHORIZED USER HANDLING>
<ENEMY COMBATANT—TIMESTAMP>

Kae stopped her team again and only had to look at them to see that they were getting the same disturbing alerts.

"What the hell does half of that even mean?" Foster asked. "Enemy combatant?"

"Hang on." Beth was using her screen. "Good thing I can still find information on this without alerting anyone." She then stared at the small screen for a moment, only to flip up her visor to read again. "Damn."

"What's going on?" Kae used her visor to scan among the stems.

"We have either a wounded person, a corpse, or a, well, crime scene about twenty yards ahead. Someone's blaster and helmet are in the vicinity, and we have to assume it's Hunter's, right? And someone else must have pawed her gear, as the visors alert us to 'unauthorized handling.' Those would be the enemy combatants." Beth puffed her cheeks and then sighed forcefully.

"Stay close to me. I wouldn't be surprised if this is a trap, but we have to see if it's her. Damn it, she's, what, twenty-two?"

"Something like that. A lot of the soldiers are very young. Remember the ones at the street-level entrance to the skyscraper?" Beth shrugged, but her eyes were darker than normal.

"I know. All right." Kae readied her blaster and then gestured for them to continue. "360 vision." She spun her hand twice and then signaled for them to move forward.

Beth and Foster were already in position behind her. They wouldn't let anyone surprise them from behind.

Twenty yards farther up, Kae gestured for Beth and Foster to flank her. Ahead, she didn't need to use the visor to see the blood staining the ground. She clenched her jaws but kept going. As she walked closer, her visor picked up more information, forwarding it to her GemLink. Pressing the sensor for the small AirScreen, she read the information.

"Good news and bad news," she murmured to Beth, who had returned, carrying a helmet like theirs. "Some of this blood is Hunter's, but not all of it. In fact, sixty percent belongs to a male individual. If this is all she's lost, her blood loss shouldn't be threatening." She eyed the dirty helmet. "The visor is broken. I assume it's hers?"

"If she called herself 'The Huntress,' then yes." Beth shook her head. "I've heard that the younger among the soldiers have unofficial call-signs. I think it's a way to cope, to feel camaraderie."

"Got it. It fits." Kae watched Foster return with a blaster. The weapon looked untouched.

"Someone other than Hunter has tried to use it. It's locked because of that attempt, but I'm still taking it with us." Foster attached the weapon to his back. "I wasn't aware the blasters are personal."

"Yours isn't. I used it once, when I mistook it for mine." Kae frowned.

"I think that's protocol for the younger soldiers. If they lose a weapon, the enemy can't use it. I'm sure there's a way for us to unlock it if we have to." Beth scanned the area again with her visor. "The camp's supposed to be about four clicks northwest of us."

"We'll move out soon, but I want to scan this site and save our findings. After we're done, I want you to report this incident to HQ, Beth."

"Will do." Beth looked worn and as if she'd aged in the last few days. This didn't stop her from carrying out her duties, and Kae knew her friend and teammate would go until her legs gave out, and when that happened, she'd crawl. The same went for Foster, though he'd do all that carrying Beth on his back if he had to.

❖

LaSierra was working at her console in HQ and had studiously ignored Rayne's attempt to persuade her to retire for the day. She was so tired she saw double, but she wanted to hear from the team and know that they were making camp for the night before she did the same. Looking up, she saw Rayne sitting to her left, working on her tablet. She was clearly not going to rest before she heard from the team either.

Soft footfalls made both of them turn their heads. Madelon walked toward them carrying a tray containing three mugs. "Tea. Decaffeinated. You both need it. I added two Nutri-drops in each. No soothing stuff. Sheer fatigue will render both of you unconscious as soon as you're smart enough to go to bed." She bent and kissed the top of Rayne's head. "Here you go, sweetheart." Madelon placed a mug next to Rayne's tablet.

"Thanks, Mom," Rayne said and smiled up at her mother. Madelon blinked.

Rayne usually addressed her parents formally, but the casual "mom" seemed significant to Madelon.

Madelon rounded the table and gave LaSierra a mug. She frowned slightly as she studied LaSierra's face.

"You don't have to worry. I don't require any kisses." LaSierra raised an eyebrow.

Madelon blinked but then chuckled. "Oh, I wouldn't say that. From the right person one can work wonders. But until she's back, I can act as her proxy." She bent and kissed LaSierra's cheek lightly.

Charmed against her will by Madelon's forwardness, LaSierra returned her focus to the screen before her. Only a minute later, when she was still sipping the fragrant tea, a series of clicks traveled across the top of the screen and then translated instantly into words.

"It's them." Rayne came over, and she too clung to her mug. "Mom. Come see."

Soon Rayne and Madelon stood on each side of LaSierra as they read Beth's update.

We are safe. Found tracks and items suggesting attack against Hunter. Retrieved blaster and helmet. Bio-matter found from Hunter and unknown male individual. Moving on to the last sanct. ETA approx. 1t40h. Terrain dense. Expect the next report then. Have at least 4 SkyPods ready to deploy. Need orders for Hunter's rescue.

LaSierra sat up straight in her AirFrame. "They want to go after whoever took Hunter."

"Let's get them to the last sanct first," Madelon said. "I'll make sure they return here first. It's protocol to assess their status. And no, we're not abandoning the girl, Rayne. That's a promise." Madelon leaned against the table, palms to the surface, and her eyes held an uncompromising glare as she continued. "I will be part of the unit that goes out with the SkyPods when we get the coordinates."

"Mother?" Rayne frowned.

LaSierra blinked. "You're going on a field mission, Madelon?"

"I am. I've kept all my licenses intact. Physical training, weapons, and tactical. I have a perfect score, and my rank allows me to deploy myself." She raised her chin, and LaSierra was reminded of the first time she met Madelon Garcia. Formidable even then in her passion for the truth and against the corruption more than twenty years ago. At seventy-five, Madelon didn't look her age, and her stamina kept her going long after the younger dissidents had given up for the day.

"Very well," LaSierra said and nodded. "Rayne, I want you on that SkyPod as well. There are bound to be as many patients as there were in the other sancts."

"Of course." Rayne turned to her mother. "You're sure about this?"

"Couldn't be more certain. I need to see the truth for myself, even if the reports have been detailed enough. If we're going to convince those who are too complacent in their comfortable lives in the skyscrapers, we need to be able to put weight behind our words. If I merely repeat what others have described to me, I won't be able to reach people the same way."

"If that's the case, then I should go to." LaSierra flicked her hand in the air. "I'm not serious. Don't look at me like that. But if I was able to stand more than a few minutes at a time, I should be the one on the SkyPod."

"We know," Rayne said. "And, with time, you'll be back on your feet completely. You'll get your chance, LaSierra. In the meantime, Mother and I will get ready to save the last of the sancts in this crop area. It truly bothers me how many sancts there are throughout the entire stretch of farmland."

"That's for later. We have to be systematic. If we spread ourselves too thin, we'll lose control." LaSierra studied her nails for a moment, a habit that was one of her tells, she knew. "Please bring back Beth in one piece. For some reason, she's become important to me."

Rayne's expression softened. "Trust me. We'll return with all three of them, as they're our friends, and they're instrumental in future operations. And if Kae has gotten herself injured, trust me, she and I'll have words."

LaSierra had to smile. "I hear you."

As Madelon and Rayne went to prepare for departure, LaSierra and Benny sat by the communications array. LaSierra knew he could have done the work without her, but she needed to know the second Beth sent the clicks.

After half an hour, one of the HQ officers, a young woman, stood at attention next to LaSierra. "Sir?"

"Yes?" LaSierra glanced up from the live maps they'd downloaded off the satellite.

"Max, the woman who breached the perimeter, is outside. She's adamant about seeing you, sir."

"Max?" LaSierra turned to Benny. "I can't let her inside HQ, but I can see her in my habitat. Ping my GemLink the second you start receiving clicks."

"Yes, Ms. Delmonte." Benny nodded where he sat in a special armchair by his console. "Eh. You're not going to see her alone, are you? I mean, you're still…vulnerable."

LaSierra smiled at his attempt to be diplomatic. "Weak as a kitten is another colorful description. No. I won't see her alone." She glanced over at the young operative. "My apologies. I can't remember your name."

"Piper Baiardo, sir. I'm one of your ops engineers." She stood straight with her hands on her back.

"Piper, with me. You will be my bodyguard. I doubt Max is well enough to attack anyone, but Benny has a point. I'm in a vulnerable state for the moment."

"I have your back, sir." Piper nodded calmly.

"If you know how, you may push my AirFrame to the door to my habitat. Then assist Max there. Don't trust anything she says or does."

"Yes, sir."

When Piper brought Max, who was in a smaller, less elaborate AirFrame, LaSierra raised her eyebrows deliberately. "Well, if you're an assassin, the criteria for such a position have been watered down."

Max smirked. "Funny. Ma'am—"

"Ms. Delmonte, or sir." LaSierra made sure she was ramrod straight. She didn't have an official title yet. In fact, hardly anyone did. People referred to her as "our leader," or "the commander," and even "the boss lady." Those who hated her called her "fucking bitch" and variations on that theme.

"Sir. I heard that one of the soldiers was abducted enroute to the last sanct."

LaSierra scowled. The rumor mill always won. It was as if a dozen people had crouched under the tables inside HQ and then immediately ran to spread what they'd just heard. Ridiculous. "And if this happened to be true—and I'm not saying that it is—then what?"

"She's in major trouble if it is. I can't do shit about it since I'm confined to this contraption of a chair, but someone has to. They must've taken her to one of two or three areas in the closest facility. They have rooms there—"

"What does that mean?" A cold sensation of dread erupted deep into LaSierra's stomach. "What kind of rooms?"

"Rooms for interrogation with all kinds of persuasion techniques. She won't be used to that, which means she won't be able to fight it. Given enough time, they'll break her."

"She's a dissident soldier," LaSierra said slowly.

"She's no more able to resist them than if she were a baby alone in the woods. The ones in charge of these rooms have gone through extensive training."

"How do you know about these rooms?" LaSierra asked slowly.

"We all know of them. I've actually been to one of them, twice. I was accused of stealing, and after a mock trial, they sentenced me to—we can leave out the details. I still have the scars to prove it. I'm sure you saw some of them when you studied me that first night." Nothing in Max's tone sounded accusing, but LaSierra still felt guilty. Watching someone else's pain was always complicated.

"I did." LaSierra motioned for Max to continue.

"They're easy to distinguish from any other scar that I got while working in the fields. They're neat, straight, and perfectly done. They make sure to place them where our nerve endings are especially sensitive, for maximum effect."

LaSierra tried to hide a shudder. This wasn't just bad news. This was disastrous. "Max, Piper here will take you back to the hospital. I will make sure to relay this information to the people who need to know. Thank you for your courage and for coming forward."

"It might already be too late. I wish I'd known about the missing soldier." Max rubbed her forehead. "And I wish I weren't totally trashed so I could join the ones going after her."

The girl was truly brave. "Piper," LaSierra said. "Make sure Max is taken care of." Moving her AirFrame into the bedroom for privacy, LaSierra used her GemLink to reach Madelon and Rayne. They had to know what they were up against. It might not be possible to bring the field team in before they had rescued—or neutralized—the threat Hunter had become when in the hands of the enemy.

CHAPTER TWENTY

B eth stood in the center of the last of the sanctuaries, which was even worse than the first one. Sick, emaciated refugees sat or lay in a circle of dwellings made from braided stems or tattered blankets. However, the number of children in this camp was greater. Two were infants that must have been born in the crop field. Their mothers looked gaunt and stared at Kae's team with something that would have been horror if they'd had enough strength left.

"Send the coordinates and start handing out ReGen water." Kae pushed her Nova blaster onto her back and began pulling tubes from her side pockets. Beth and Foster did the same, and they made the rounds, trying to reassure the former slaves that they would soon be transported to a safe place. It broke Beth's heart to see their doubt or, even in some cases, their certainty that this was all a dangerous ruse.

"Who is your leader?" Kae asked a woman of undeterminable age. "You, perhaps?"

"In a manner of speaking," the woman said slowly. She had long, black hair, tied back into a whip-hard ponytail, and her clothes were skillfully cropped and tied firmly to her thin body. She seemed to notice Kae's attention to her garments and smiled weakly. "My name's Finlay Nash."

"Finlay, call me Kae. I'm with the Celestial resistance movement. We truly are here to help. My team and I are

Subterraneans who have formed an alliance with the dissidents from the skyscrapers."

"I wish I could believe that," Finlay said, obviously exhausted and apprehensive.

"You will, in time. We have already rescued eight other sanctuary camps, and they're in our facility getting medical aid and sustenance." Beth joined the conversation. "I'm Beth, and this is Foster. Please drink some of this." She handed Finlay a tube of ReGen water. "I'll have a sip of it if you're wary of our intentions."

"Please do," Finlay said sternly.

Beth opened the tube and held it an inch from her mouth, then squirted some of the water into her open mouth. Swallowing, she then handed the tube to Finlay. "Here you go. It's not as cold as I'd like it, as we carry it in our pockets, but it still rehydrates like magic."

Finlay studied the tube and then sipped it carefully. "Thank you."

"We have intravenous electrolytes with us if someone is truly bad off." Kae indicated her backpack.

"I'll make my rounds in a few moments. If Beth accompanies me, we can ascertain the situation." Finlay ducked into the shadow under her braided screen. "I'll just get my stuff."

Kae nodded at Beth. "Send the clicks with our coordinates. Estimate the number of patients."

Beth walked out of reach and turned her back while she added the coordinates to her message, also including that they needed four SkyPods with medical staff. There wouldn't be any reply, but her GemLink would at least let her know that someone had read her message back at HQ.

Finlay reappeared carrying a long rod, which Beth recognized as a walking stick, but considering the stains on it, it had been used for defense or attacks.

"Do I need to be concerned about your weapon?" Beth eyed the rod, raising her eyebrows.

"Not at all. Unless you get trigger happy and turn out to be the enemy after all." Finlay smiled crookedly.

"All right." Beth gave Kae a glance that she knew Kae would understand. *Keep an eye out.*

They made the rounds among the withering inhabitants of the sanct. Several of them looked like death could come for them within moments, and Beth was getting a headache as she had to clench her jaws to not get emotional. Her tears wouldn't help anyone. They pointed out the ones in dire need of intravenous fluids, and Kae and Foster walked in their wake, administering the infulizers.

One by one, they moved the ones unable to walk to a better spot under the large crop leaves. Babies whimpered, sounding too fatigued to wail. One mother, rocking her baby, kept falling over from exhaustion. Beth hurried over and crouched next to her. "Hello, there. I'm Beth, and I'm Subterranean. May I hold your little one? You need to lie down, I can tell, and your baby is a little unhappy."

"You can't take her," the young woman said, trembling. "She's mine."

"Of course she is. I'm not taking her away. Just sitting here next to you. What's your name, by the way?" Beth sat down next to the woman on the ground.

"Veronia. This is Hope." She slowly handed her little girl over to Beth. "I can't lie down. It hurts my hips too much." She drew a deep, raspy breath.

"Then lean against me. I'm not going anywhere." Beth shifted and moved little Hope—and what a heartbreaking name that was for a child born to a former slave—over to her other arm. She made sure Veronia leaned against her in a way that didn't cause her unnecessary pain and watched Kae and Foster walk among the ones needing treatment and assistance, together with Finlay.

"She risked everything for us." Veronia spoke huskily.

"Who did? Finlay?" Beth asked.

"Yes. She saw what they did to us and kept protecting us, and eventually, she got us out of there. She kept going back to help more poor souls that made it out, over and over, knowing full well that they would kill her if they ever caught her."

"It's amazing that one someone living under such conditions could be this resilient and brave for so long," Beth said.

Veronia turned her head and looked up at Beth. "She wasn't living among the slaves. She was well off and put in charge of the night shift for two barracks. Finlay used to be one of them. A Celestial guard."

"What?" Beth's voice, louder than was advisable, made Kae snap her head around and walk over to her and Veronia.

"What's up, Beth?" Kae asked, her eyes sharp.

"I think I know." Finlay appeared from the other direction after having lifted two small children over to the shade. "We need to be honest from the beginning here, or we won't be able to work together. I was one of the guards, until I realized what the facilities were really doing."

Kae placed her hand on the butt of her Nova blaster. "Is that so?" she asked in what Beth recognized as a deceptively mild tone.

"Yes. As soon as I learned the truth of the living conditions of the workers—which is what they call people held as slaves—I began to plan how to get the most vulnerable out, a few at a time. The pregnant women were among them. Also small children and those who had been worked to a pulp."

Beth swallowed hard when she heard Finlay's list.

Kae and Foster studied Finlay closely. "Debriefing you will be just what the resistance needs when you've been taken back to our camp."

"And incarcerated, no doubt." Finlay looked wary. "I could stay out here in the crops. Get more people out before it's too late."

"Not an option. Your knowledge of the barracks, the operation, and the routines is far more useful when shared with our leaders." Kae studied Finlay. "And you need treatment as well. I think you've been running on empty for quite a while."

Finlay raised her chin, but Beth saw she was struggling to keep her proud stance.

A whirring sound made them all flinch, but it took Beth only a moment to figure out it was the SkyPods. Compared to Celestial vessels, SkyPods only hummed.

"Already?" Kae frowned. "Until we're sure it's them, take a defensive position."

Beth handed over baby Hope to her mother and deployed her blaster. Together with Kae, Foster, and Finlay, holding her rod, she made sure to stay between the sick and injured and the approaching SkyPods.

As soon as the first one hovered about two feet above ground level, the hatches opened, and Rayne, hoisting her by-now familiar medical bag, stepped out first. She hurried over to them and hugged Kae, Nova blaster and all, before scowling at her. "We are going to have a few words when we get back to camp."

"All right," Kae said evenly, probably having anticipated Rayne's reaction to her remaining behind to search for Hunter.

More medics appeared and began working among their new patients.

"Damn," Foster said and straightened. "Is that Madelon?"

"It is," Rayne said calmly. "She's here as the senior field-mission leader, on behalf of LaSierra. There have been some developments, and we couldn't risk clicking the message to you, as you know. Hence, Mother."

Kae frowned. "Field-mission leader, as in outranking me." She wasn't asking.

"Yes." Rayne focused on her small patient as she examined Hope. "This little girl needs sustenance and her mother's warmth. All women with infants go in the first SkyPod. I have two pediatric medics for them."

Madelon had made a round of her own and now approached them, her gaze firm and looking much younger than her actual age. "Who do I talk to?" She didn't elaborate, and Kae pointed to Finlay.

"This is Finlay Nash. Former Celestial guard who has been instrumental in bringing a lot of these people and others out from the barracks. An unexpected asset when it comes to our next move."

"I see." Madelon extended a hand to Finlay. "I'm Madelon Garcia. You'll be leaving in my SkyPod, and when we get to the camp, I know it might seem frightening, but we'll have to keep you secluded and debrief you before we can allow you out in the general population."

"I doubt it will be as frightening as living in the barracks, no matter if you're a reluctant guard or one of the slaves." Finlay regarded Madelon evenly. "I'm at your disposal if you can guarantee you'll save the rest of these young men, women, and children."

"Guarantee?" Madelon pursed her lips.

"It's that, or I won't talk. I'm not giving away my only leverage. If you can't make guarantees, I will remain in the crop fields and rescue those I can, one at a time, if I must." Finlay coughed and shook her head in obvious dismay. "Although this damn cough is bound to give away my position."

"Then I suggest you scrap the idea of trying to rescue one at a time and help us rescue all of them." Kae placed a hand on Finlay's shoulder. "And if Madelon here says you can trust her—then you can."

Beth regarded Madelon with increasing concern. Not that she didn't trust Rayne's mother—she did—but she thought she saw something new in her eyes and in the way she kept looking at Kae.

It took them forty minutes to load the refugees, and Beth had begun to pull her gear together, when Madelon stepped up to them with Rayne by her side.

"Time for you to board the last SkyPod." Madelon motioned with her hand toward the last hovering vessel.

"What? No. Our mission isn't over," Kae said, but then she looked between Madelon and Rayne. "What aren't you telling me?"

"We need to move you closer to the barracks. You have one more mission, and it's time sensitive." Madelon's tone was cool, and she seemed more like the woman Rayne had described when Beth first got to know her. All business and keeping her distance. No trace remained of the woman who had taken Wes and Tania to her heart.

"The only mission is to retrieve Hunter, right?" Foster grumbled. "I don't know how you operated in the skyscrapers, but in the tunnels, we don't leave a missing team member behind."

"I know." Madelon looked at a pale Rayne, who ran a hand over her face. "And the mission concerns Hunter."

"We have new intel from Max." Rayne met Kae's gaze. "Apparently there are rooms in the barracks where interrogations happen. Max described torture, and we've all seen her scars. Some of those are from being interrogated in those rooms, long before she managed to escape. She let us know that if Hunter is subjected to this ordeal, and we unfortunately must suppose that she is, not even a trained dissident from the skyscrapers can be expected to remain stoic."

"We must operate under the assumption that they will know where our camp is, how many of us there are, and who we are, soon." Madelon sighed, and Beth glimpsed some of the woman she'd begun to know. "I hope Rocque has managed to find information about how much intel Hunter is privy to. As she's a low-ranking officer, I doubt her clearance involves tactical information, but until we know, we have to prepare for the worst." She pinched the bridge of her nose.

"What else?" Kae asked starkly.

"One of the outcomes of enhanced interrogation, which is just a fancy word for torture, is that it can be used to turn a person quite quickly, when used a certain way. And once she's turned, the process of undoing the change would be hard on her—and take quite some time." Madelon shrugged. "It really can't get any worse than this, for Hunter—and for us all."

"I realize why we have to hurry," Kae said and glanced at Beth and Foster in a determined manner.

"Just hold on." Beth knew there was more. "They've only had her for a couple of hours."

"I'm afraid that can be enough, depending on Hunter's resilience, according to Max. I listened to her recount their methods, and I agree." Madelon shook her head, and a pained expression flickered over her face. "This is why we reached you so fast. We were already in the air, circling the last known coordinates. We need you to perform what we call a surgical incursion. Go in, do what you need to, and then get out. Fast. Good thing Finlay Nash is in this SkyPod. She might prove invaluable. We do have the intel Max provided for us, but perhaps Finlay can add to it as she used to be a guard." Madelon looked at them firmly, one at a time. "Remember this. Hunter is your only goal. You can't remove any of the slaves this time. The decision has been made. Depending on her condition, you either retrieve Hunter or neutralize her."

"What do you mean?" Beth asked. She could see from Foster's stricken look and how Kae and Rayne both pressed their lips together that she wouldn't like the answer.

"Hunter might be too injured, physically, or mentally." Madelon folded her arms across her chest. "If Rayne determines that nothing can be done for her, it is the most humane thing to—"

"What the hell are you talking about? Kill her in cold blood? Rayne's a doctor, not a damn executioner." Beth growled. "Who made that decision?"

Madelon stepped closer to Beth and gripped her upper arms firmly. "It comes from the highest authority, Beth. Do you understand?"

Beth's mouth instantly became dry. She knew all too well. Only one person had the power to make this call.

LaSierra.

CHAPTER TWENTY-ONE

Kae disembarked the SkyPod with Rayne, Foster, and Beth. They stood still as the strangely shaped vessel disappeared along the edge of the crop fields. Keeping low, the SkyPod seemed to sniff along the ground, merely six feet above it. As its engine was equipped with a low-noise propulsion system, it made only a whispering sound that reminded Kae of how the wind sounded out in the crop fields when it sieved through the stems and leaves.

"How far until we reach the barracks?" Rayne asked. She was the only one among them who hadn't been anywhere near the slave camps.

"Less than an hour, but it's still a long time from Hunter's point of view," Kae said. "We have to keep up the pace." She tried to disregard that they had been on their feet all day, working in the sancts and taking care of the refugees.

"Before we do," Rayne said, "I have something that'll help us. She pulled a small pen-like instrument from her breast pocket. "This is a mini infulizer, designed to carry on field missions. I prepped it with twelve dosages of *LiveWire*. It's a synaptic stimulant that's harmless when used sparingly. We have three dosages for each of us."

"I'm good. Thanks." Foster looked ill at ease. "Synaptic stimulant. No, thanks, Doc."

Normally Kae would have sided with Foster, but she was running on empty. Besides, she trusted Rayne to never administer anything harmful. "Sure. Go for it. What are the side effects?"

"Some jitters initially. They'll pass in about ten minutes. And it's not advisable when you're pregnant." Rayne smirked briefly. "Beth?"

"I better, even if I'm wary of stimulants as a whole." Beth, who seemed subdued—and Kae didn't think it was only because of emerging fatigue—pulled up her sleeve. "Arm?"

"Sure." Rayne placed the infulizer pen against the crease of Beth's arm. She repeated the maneuver with Kae and then herself. Glancing at Foster, she said, "I'll have it ready for you when you change your mind, Foster."

"I notice you said 'when.'" Foster's scowl had no force behind it. He rubbed his chin. "Thanks, Doc. I'll keep it in mind."

They made sure their backpacks were firmly attached, visors down, and their GemLinks set to find each other, should they become separated. They were ordered to use transmissions via clickers sparingly, as nobody knew if Hunter had broken under pressure.

Keeping a steady jog along the edge of the crop field, Kae thought back to when they had moved in the opposite direction with children strapped to their backs. Now they were on this—what did Madelon call it?—surgical incursion, to retrieve, or may the Creator prevent it, eliminate Hunter. She envisioned the compact, strong woman who wasn't very tall and, much like most of the Celestial soldiers, was far too young. Before she had put on her helmet back at the camp, she had displayed curly, blond hair, freckled pale skin, and bright, blue eyes. Kae had thought she didn't look a day over sixteen. A young girl like her couldn't possibly withstand "enhanced interrogation" for very long. Kae often trusted her instinct, and right now, her gut told her they would be too late. But that didn't mean she wouldn't give it her all.

❖

Rayne jogged next to Beth while Foster took up the rear. In front of them, Kae kept a steady pace, and soon she and Foster would change places. A quick glance at Beth concerned Rayne. Beth looked strong and alert, thanks to the LiveWire medication, but she seemed off—and had done so since they left the last sanctuary camp.

"Hey," Rayne murmured through the inter-helmet communication system and closed the distance between them, making them rub elbows. "What's the matter? Is it the harshness of our orders?" She knew Beth, the youngest on Kae's team, must be shocked by the callousness of it all—no matter what she'd seen as a freedom fighter in the tunnels.

"Harshness?" Beth spat the word quietly. "Harsh is what the matron of the orphanage I grew up in was when we stole food or sneaked out at night. This…this is euthanasia." Clearly Beth didn't let their conversation distract her from scanning the area around them.

"Beth. It might not come to that. We might reach Hunter in time, or at least early enough to be able to take her back for treatment and deprogramming. And that's not as bad as it sounds. It's mostly a medical procedure." Rayne wasn't sure she was reaching Beth. "But there's more, isn't there?"

"I don't know what you mean." Beth pressed her lips together.

"Sure, you do. I think it's also about who had to give the order. I'm not blind, sweetheart. You're head over heels when it comes to LaSierra." Rayne had lowered her voice to a mere whisper. "And if Kae had given the same order, which might well happen one day, we know that I'd be worried about her too."

"Worried about *her*?" Beth snarled the words under her breath. "It's not LaSierra who risks being killed off by her own people."

"No. But it's her immortal soul that you worry about. Don't think I haven't noticed how you've looked up at the sky over and over, muttering something. Prayers." Rayne placed a hand on Beth's shoulder. "I'm not prying—"

"Ha. You are definitely prying." Beth shook her head. "But I don't mind that. I need to talk about it, and this seems to be my only chance."

"You talked to the Creator. You prayed for LaSierra's soul because even through your upset and your concern about young Hunter, you're heartbroken for the decisions forced upon someone in command, such as LaSierra. I can relate to some degree."

"How so?" Beth extended a hand and steadied Rayne as they stopped where the path turned around a sharp bend.

"Glad you're processing, but let's make sure we don't have a welcome party behind this curve." Kae nodded at them. "Foster, take the lead. Use the mirror."

Foster produced a speck of a mirror that Rayne recognized from when they had reached corners in the worm-alleys between the skyscrapers. Foster let the mirror slide out a few inches, squeezed between his index and middle finger. Studying it for a good minute or more, he tucked it back into his jacket and stepped around the corner, his Nova blaster raised and ready.

Waving at them to follow, Kae took up the rear, and they continued forward. "Normally I'd swat both of you over the head for talking while on the move, but as this conversation needs to happen for Beth to keep her head clear—I'll allow it."

"Thanks. I know it's not how it's done." Rayne nodded, glad Kae understood.

"So?" Beth said. "Go on. How can you relate?"

"You have to remember that both my parents' ranks are just below LaSierra's. Yes, every decision-making ends with her, but she would rarely go against my parents. She would ask for their counsel, and that means they all have the same opinion. Retrieve or eliminate. No other options exist, as Hunter's abduction puts all of us at the camp at risk. The children, everyone."

"Fuck." Beth bared her teeth behind the visor. "Talk about being squeezed. I mean, the brass. No matter what they do, they sacrifice their peace of mind. How can you live with a decision like this—or several decisions like it?"

"Kae has, many times, I would imagine," Rayne said. "It comes with command. You, Foster, and I are in different mid-level positions, but don't forget that we're all senior officers. The time will come when we'll have to back up LaSierra, my parents, or Kae, when they have to act with what might appear to be callousness."

"I worry for her. LaSierra. I'm not sure there is an 'us,' not really, but that doesn't matter, Rayne. I worry what these decisions will do to her overall. And I hate that she will have to make them in the long run." Beth growled quietly. "What do I do? When we get back, I mean. Whether we rescue Hunter or not."

"From what I've observed between you two—and I think I've witnessed the ambiance between you two the most, when treating LaSierra—I know she'll need you. Without accusations, or questions, or perhaps without speaking at all."

Beth mulled this concern over. She moved lithely next to Rayne, her young physique making the most of LiveWire. "I'll try to be that person for her—if she'll let me."

"She will. Eventually," Kae said from behind, surprising Rayne.

"I hope so." Beth seemed to be done with the conversation, and Rayne hoped her words had had some effect.

❖

LaSierra sat rigidly in her AirFrame, regarding the influx of new patients. Madelon had given her a cursory report, and it had not mentioned anything about how the field mission members had received her orders. She knew only that the "original four," as Madelon had put it, were on their way to carry them out.

"This looks like mayhem, but I suppose the medics are used to it by now and have their routines down." Rocque joined LaSierra. He looked tired, but his hawklike gaze was as sharp as always. "I heard my daughter and her Subterranean friends are on their way to get Hunter—or not."

"Exactly." LaSierra pushed the worst-case scenario to the back of her mind. "We don't expect to hear from them until they've achieved some sort of result."

"That's a heartbreaking message to wait for, LaSierra." Thankfully, Rocque didn't put a supportive hand on her shoulder, or LaSierra would have had to maneuver her AirFrame into a dark corner and medicate.

"It is," she merely said.

Madelon joined them, wearing a dark-gray coverall. More people in their camp had begun using the basic clothing available, mostly to save energy regarding the clothes dispensers. LaSierra knew this wasn't an option for her. To make it easy for their people to spot the one in command, she had to remain as stylish and elegant as always. It was perhaps a shallow way to think about it, but so far it had worked. Between the AirFrame and her mauve suit, she was easily recognizable.

"How many, all in all?" LaSierra asked, nodding toward the large tents holding the hospital beds.

"Counting Max too," Rocque said, "one hundred and eighty-one. They are putting together a list of ages, genders, health situations, and, if possible, origin. I don't know when we'll have time for in-depth interviews, as everything has to happen so quickly at this point."

"Understood. Good." LaSierra remained for half an hour longer to observe, but it was dark, and she was starting to get cold.

"This won't do." Madelon plucked a blanket from the back of the AirFrame and wrapped it around LaSierra. "If you get sick again, Beth's going to string us up. Let's go back to the HQ. I'm satisfied that the medics and the ones in charge of medical planning have this situation under control."

LaSierra allowed Madelon to maneuver her AirFrame back to HQ, while she considered Madelon's words. Perhaps people had caught on to how close she and Beth had become. How attached. She didn't comment on Madelon's words, merely huddled under the blanket, thankful for the warmth it provided. Knowing it was time to start wearing drab, gray coveralls and thus blend into the surrounding crowd made LaSierra purse her lips. She'd heard that advice ever since she resumed her duties. *Don't stand out. Snipers could be anywhere.* At least the coveralls seemed a lot warmer than her Shantung silk skirt suit.

Back at HQ, LaSierra parked her AirFrame at her desk and pulled up the AirScreen computer. She read the reports that came in one after another, in real time. Most of them were about the refugees, and she found out that they'd lost two since they were evacuated from the crop fields. Both were among the oldest, which heartbreakingly only meant that they were in their early thirties. Another report from the science lab in the upper eastern circles had broken down what the field crops consisted of. At first glance, she saw a list of minerals, vitamins, fibers, and fluids, which seemed harmless enough. At the bottom of the list, a chemist had flagged two lines where an unknown substance was simply named *XYZ123*.

LaSierra made a note of the chemist's signature and paged him on her GemLink.

"Ms. Delmonte." Looking dazed, and clearly in bed, Morton Timble blinked repeatedly. "I, uhm, assume you read my report."

"I did. What more can you tell me regarding *XYZ123*?" LaSierra tapped the document on her larger AirScreen, but as before, the ridiculous name the man had given this substance wasn't linked to anything.

"Nothing," Timble said and yawned discreetly behind his hand. "I need to work with a few other people and cross-reference our findings. I'm thinking especially of the Feldt sisters. They're botanists."

"You're a chemist…are you saying that this substance is a mix between something chemical and botanical?" LaSierra had never heard of anything like that, but it was hardly her field of expertise.

"It's rare, and hard to pull off in a stable way. It also depends on what it is meant to do. All the nutrients are already present in the Food Fabric plants. Nothing else is required. As soon as you use this formula to synthesize the FlatPaks, the food doesn't need anything else to enhance the process." Timble rubbed his eyes.

"I'll let you go back to sleep, Mr. Timble. Once you've collaborated with the botanists and reached a theory you can all get behind, bring it to me instantly."

"Yes, sir." Timble nodded, and LaSierra disconnected the call.

When she turned to scroll through more information on her screen, her back muscles began to twitch incessantly. She had ignored her symptoms too long, and checking the time, she winced. Even longer than she thought. Rayne and Beth wouldn't forgive her for being this careless, if they found out. Summoning the medic who was to replace Beth, she hoped the person wouldn't be completely incapable. Beth had let her try her limits when it came to her nightly ablutions, helping only if LaSierra was entirely unable to do it or simply too fatigued. Tonight, she was both and loathed having a stranger help her with deeply personal functions.

She pulled out her medication from the pocket in her right armrest and swallowed the capsules dry. Then she pressed the thin, pen-sized infulizer with extra pain relief against the inside of her arm and closed her eyes in relief about fifteen seconds later. She would be able to sleep for only about four hours, but with the extra medication, she had a decent chance of not tossing and turning because of pain.

As the young male medic helped her reach her habitat, she wondered how great the risk was that she might toss and turn while worrying about Beth.

CHAPTER TWENTY-TWO

Beth sat in the small dug-out opening in the fence around the barracks that Zeph, Lux, and Emb had escaped through. The scrambled trackers they'd placed to be able to find the exact spot again were still transmitting on a nano level.

"We'll leave this here. If they haven't found it yet, they won't do so in the near future." Kae mouthed rather than whispered the order. "According to Finlay Nash's sketched recollection of the layout of the buildings, they're all the same, pretty much. Large dorms on six levels. Food stations. Office areas. Staff accommodation. And, most important, the 'enhanced interrogation' rooms. Most of the barracks have two of them—one that holds tables and chairs and another outfitted with...tools."

"Gross." Beth swallowed back a sudden onset of bile. "It's our kids in there."

"Subterranean kids for the most part, yes, but also Celestial children that've been orphaned or possessed 'undesirable' traits." Kae shook her head as if to clear her mind. "Are we all set to go in? Rayne, once we find Hunter, you have to work fast. It doesn't matter what state she's in when we reach her. We're retrieving her, and once we're reasonably safe, we'll ascertain her mental status as a first measure. If she's been outfitted with a tracker, we'll remove it. Everything clear?"

"Clear as soot." Foster strapped his blaster onto his back and pulled out a ShadowPulse weapon that fit into his palm.

"Moving in." Kae nodded at Beth, and she hit the ground and began worming her way under the fence. They couldn't touch it. It could perhaps kill them and most certainly alert the barrack guards to their presence and location.

Foster wiggled through after Beth and barely made it. Beth held her breath when his blaster came less than half an inch from the bottom wire of the fence.

"Damn it, Foster," she whispered after he was finally through and got up. "That was too close."

"I don't want to know," he said, his eyes darkening. "Too many variables where we might screw up, if you ask me."

"True." Beth kept an eye on Rayne, who pushed her sizable backpack containing her medical kit in front of her through the opening. Rayne was more full-figured than Beth and Kae but managed to arch her way through the opening a lot easier than Foster had.

Kae, unsurprisingly, slipped through the opening as if it were twice as big. "Good. That went quickly." She pulled her hand-held weapon in her right hand and left her blaster in its harness on her back. "ShadowPulse weapons only for now. Too many kids around for the blasters, unless we're backed into a corner." The S-shaped ShadowPulse weapons were small and fit in the palm of one's hand. They didn't possess lethal force—merely small needle darts that tranquilized people. The closer to the head you hit someone, the faster they went down. If you hit their carotid, they might need artificial life support until they started breathing on their own. Usually, the soldier would aim for the chest area, or the upper back, for maximum effect.

They nodded, and even Rayne pulled out her ShadowPulse after she secured her backpack.

Kae led them along the rugged wood, concrete, and windowless wall. She glanced at Beth a few times, and Beth gave her the old thumbs-up sign every time, keeping an eye on her GemLink, where a faint map glistened in the last of the daylight, now that dusk was chasing them from the north. She held up her hand and showed three fingers. A few more seconds and then they would be just outside the room where the worst of the interrogations took place.

Beth watched Kae count down the last two fingers until she came to a halt. Placing her hand gently on the wall, Beth couldn't decipher her feelings. Kids were behind this wall. Small ones, but also older ones who had been taken and placed here—in what the Celestials called "rescue camps." It was fucking ironic. These internment camps, slave camps, whatever you chose to call them, were nothing but humanity going crazy and acting from their worst perspective. Beth couldn't imagine what lies the Celestial authorities told themselves, and their people, which made it all right to keep people in servitude until they perished from exhaustion and malnutrition. There were more from where they got the others. Or they could simply breed some when the girls were old enough. Beth thought of Zeph, Max, and Nash—three women of different ages who had suffered each in her own way, at the hands of the Celestials. And little Emb, who was blissfully unaware of most of it, but still battled a basic, instinctual anxiety.

"Beth. You're on." Kae stepped back and scanned the area with her visor deployed.

Beth had received a quick class in how she was supposed to attach the slimy content in her jar. It was a stable compound until she hit it hard with the mini hammer-looking object attached to the bottom of the jar.

Kae pointed to the outline of the fence she wanted gone, and Beth began slathering on the yellow-tinted, slimy gel, working as fast as she could without missing a spot. Foster kept an eye on where they had come from, and Rayne stood next to Beth, ready to assist.

"There. I've used half of the jar." Beth held the small hammer in her hand. "You need to stand back. According to Madelon, this will work soundlessly, but it sprays dust and splinters. Protection visors down. The suits will cover us." She swallowed hard, as whispering made her throat dry. "Here goes." Beth made sure the others stood at a distance and realized that Kae was right behind her. "You ready, Kae?"

"Hit it." Kae gripped Beth's waist hard, obviously ready to yank her out of harm's way if need be.

Beth raised the hammer and then gave the left part of the opening they were creating a good smack. At first, nothing happened. It barely made a sound. Then a faint whistling sound emanated from the wall, and Kae pulled Beth back two steps, while pointing her ShadowPulse weapon toward the wall.

The opening pulverized within less than five seconds. But that still felt like far too long, and Beth blinked at the acrid smell that managed to faintly permeate her suit, though it could be her imagination.

"Moving in," Kae said quietly and waved two fingers forward.

Beth hurried after her, followed by Rayne and Foster.

❖

Rayne stood in a room where the sparse furniture was covered by a fine, slightly glittery dust. The room was empty, and so far, they couldn't hear any running footfalls. Their proximity readers were on, but the many levels in the structure made for confusing reading. Kae shook her head and closed the small AirScreen on her arm. She set the GemLink to enhanced sound instead and showed the others.

Rayne pressed the sensors for the elevated sound and added another scanner for her medical visor. If there was an excess of bodily fluids somewhere, her built-in scanner would find it.

Kae waved them closer. "The other interrogation room is next door. I don't want to give them a chance to kill Hunter if she's in there, so we're doing this the old-fashioned way. Beth, you go high, I go low, and Foster—"

"I go center and grab Hunter." Foster nodded solemnly.

"Exactly. And Rayne, you stick to Foster's side and don't deviate. I mean that." Kae looked into Rayne's eyes, her own entirely opaque.

"Got it," Rayne murmured.

"Moving out." Kae walked over to the door, which was a simple analogue contraption on hinges. Pushing the sensor, Kae opened the door a crack and peered outside. She pointed to the left and held up two fingers. Then one. Then just her fist. Rayne's heart hammered, and she wanted to just rush into the other interrogation room and tear the young Celestial dissident out of the guards' cruel hands.

"Now." Kae bent and was out the door in a fluid movement, walking heel-to-toe. Rayne had mastered how to move fast and soundlessly. She ducked out after Beth, and when Foster had joined them and closed the door, Kae pressed her GemLink against the next door. This wasn't simple like the other one. Here, sensors suggested they needed another method to break in.

Kae shook her head and looked back at Beth and Rayne. "Still locked," she whispered.

"We better hurry. Surveillance on a swivel over our heads." Foster's deep voice made Rayne jump even if he was also whispering.

Rayne thought fast. She grabbed Kae's left arm where she carried the GemLink and pressed their two devices together. They both had top clearance at their camp, but Rayne knew she was grasping at straws when she turned their wrists and held them against the door sensor. It began to blink, and for a moment, Rayne could barely breathe as she fully expected it to set off the alarm klaxons. When it instead silently shifted the sensor from blue to light gray, she nodded quickly. "It's open, but I'd guess not for long."

Kae raised her hand holding the ShadowPulse weapon, and Beth and Foster did the same. Rayne made sure her safety feature on the small weapon was off, and then Kae opened the door.

❖

In the back of her mind, where Kae stored visions and experiences that never should've come to pass, she knew she had never witnessed another scene as the one they saw as they barged through the door.

It wasn't hard to differentiate between Hunter and the three Celestial guards, as she was restrained and they were surrounding her, all holding elaborate devices in their hands. Not hesitating, Kae fired her ShadowPulse weapon at the closest guard, a middle-aged woman who had just turned her head and gaped at them. Before she shifted her aim, someone else had fired upon the tall man standing near Hunter's head, and then the young man on Hunter's right side.

When the guards went down, Kae used her weapon to double-tap them. This might have an adverse effect on their breathing, but she didn't care.

"Foster," Kae said, "secure the door.

Foster knelt next to the sensor and began working on his GemLink. Though he had been completely suspicious of Celestial technology only a month ago, he had come a long way.

Rayne was already at Hunter's side, and Kae joined her. "Beth, look around for proof, intel, and anything else that we might use later. Use your best judgment."

"On it." Beth said and hurried over to a desk at the far wall.

"She's barely lucid, Kae," Rayne murmured. She scanned the naked, trembling body before them. "She's going to need clothes or something to cover her with."

Kae looked around but didn't see any garments at all. Spotting something resembling thin blankets, she grabbed several and began tying them around Hunter.

"What…?" Hunter's eyes opened fully, and she stared up into the ceiling. "Please…stop. I don't…know anything."

"Hunter. It's Kae Dark and Doctor Garcia. Foster and Beth are here too. Can you hear me?" Kae bent over the young woman as Rayne slid her scanners in a crisscross fashion along her body. "We're getting you out of here. We just have to make sure you don't have a tracker."

"T-tracker?" Hunter's eyes rolled back for a moment, but then she seemed awake again. "Think…maybe my hip? Hurts." She whimpered, and large tears ran into her hair. "I smashed m-my GemLink…when I knew I'd be…taken…the fuckers. Ah!" Hunter attempted to move against the wires immobilizing her.

"Let me see." Rayne pulled back the blanket and scanned the area on the left hip, then the right. "Are you sure, Hunter? Anywhere else?"

"They pushed it deep. All the way…into…groin…" Hunter's eyes closed. She was bruised, and wires dug into her flesh along her arms and legs.

"Will we be able to cut her loose?" Foster asked quietly.

"We have to. Or…" Kae plucked one of the guards' devices from the floor. "They're still logged in on these. We should be able to—"

"Allow me." Rayne held out her hand. "I'm a Celestial, after all." Her lips were pale and tense.

Kae handed over all the devices, and Rayne gave the scanner to Kae. "Use this. My visor will show me if you happen upon something."

Kae scanned both of Hunter's hips, and then over her groin and pubic area.

"Stop. Back up, half an inch." Rayne was busy tapping in commands on one of the devices. "Yes. There. Any sign of a scar? It'll be very small."

Kae looked at the area just below the curve of the hipbone. A very faint white line, which she recognized was like the scar that a derma wand would leave behind. "Found it." She hoped she was right.

"Dig it out. If she wakes up and screams, anyone overhearing it will just assume the torture is ongoing." Cold and flat, Rayne's voice sent chills through Kae. Holding out a small laser cutter, another instrument Kae was vaguely familiar with, Rayne glanced at her. "Hurry."

Kae nodded at Foster to hold Hunter down. Before she started, Kae turned to Beth, who was just finishing off the last drawer in the desk. "Create another opening toward the field. Save enough of the substance to open the fence too."

Beth hurried to the outer wall, and Kae returned her focus to the smooth, caramel skin before her. "Here goes." When Kae pierced Hunter's skin and heard her whimper and then begin to wail, she knew she would have to compartmentalize this part of the mission as well.

"Here. I can't stand it." Rayne's usual tone of voice was back, and she pressed a small wand in Foster's hand. "Run it every few seconds. It can't take away all the pain—but some…"

Hunter's wails were reduced to soft whimpers immediately, and Kae worked faster. Hearing a clicking sound at the tip of the laser cutter, she knew she had found it. Blood was oozing around the wound, but that couldn't be helped. At least she hadn't hit an artery. She engaged the magnetic feature of the laser cutter and heard the clicking sound again.

"Done," Beth said, and Kae saw Hunter's short curls move as the wind came in via the opening Beth had created.

A knock on the door made them all jump.

"Eddie? Your shift is over, but I can't open the door," a female voice said, sounding muffled through the door. "What's wrong with the sensor? My scanner says that it's in preventative lockdown. Oh, damn. We need to initiate the 'all stations lockdown' sequence, don't we? But I've never done that before. Eddie? Fuck it, Eddie? Denise? Hello—can't you hear me?"

A device on the wall began to hum, and then its sound turned shrill.

"We need to leave now. Get this blanket around her. Foster, remove your blaster. You're carrying her, and as soon as we're outside, we run farther west along the building. When we reach the corner, Beth opens the fence, never mind any alarms. They'll already be going off by then." Kae rattled off her orders.

Rayne had managed to loosen the wires enough for them to slide Hunter free, even if it meant scraping her skin in several places. Fortunately, she was a diminutive woman, and Foster would barely feel her on his back.

Louder bangs came from the door leading into the barracks, and a hissing sound suggested the guards outside were busy cutting their way in.

When they had secured the unconscious Hunter to Foster's harness, Kae ushered them to the opening. Then they were all on the outside, where she pulled a flat package from behind her backpack. "Here. Cameleo-blankets. They'll protect you in a pinch." She handed them out, and then they all did as she ordered.

They ran.

Chapter Twenty-three

K ae and Rayne kept vigil while Beth used the last of the substance in the small jar. It singed through the fence as if it were made of paper. Kae scanned the broken-off piece of fence and found that it was harmless.

"All right, people. We need to stay low and move fast. Move out!" Kae motioned for Foster to push through the opening first as he carried the unconscious Hunter on his back. Around the corner, where they had broken out of the barrack's interrogation room, she heard raised voices. They sounded young, and Kae nourished a faint hope that the guards at this facility were young and inexperienced, as well as not used to being challenged.

Rayne and Beth slipped through the opening, and Kae glanced toward the corner of the building. So far, no one had rounded it. Perhaps the guards thought they had made a run for it through the hole under the fence where they entered. She could only hope. She pushed through the opening, feeling the edges of it singe her suit, but they didn't break the resilient material.

Catching up to Foster and allowing Beth to take up the rear, Kae shoved the stems of a dense area among the crops out of the way, then found a barely visible path. She intended to keep them on that route at first, making it easier to move faster.

She heard the voices call out back at the fence and knew they'd made it out just before they had company.

"Send up drones!" a male voice on the verge of breaking called out. He did sound very young, indeed.

They shouldered their way through the crop field, and Kae made them change directions, trying to not break off too many of the younger stems. They had to conceal their route but keep a steady pace.

"Got to stop," Foster said after half an hour. "She's slipping."

Kae raised her fist, even if she figured Beth and Rayne had heard him. "Check her vitals, Rayne. We don't know what substances they shot into her system."

"On it." Rayne helped Beth pull Hunter free from the harness. The knots holding her legs in place had become loose, and soon she lay on a rescue blanket. Rayne scanned her with her medical GemLink, and Kae tensed when she saw a growing frown on her face.

"Rayne?"

"She's not in critical condition, but her coma concerns me, as her brain waves suggest she's not only wide awake, but hyperactive. Look." She pushed up Hunter's left eyelid.

Kae shuddered. Hunter's eyes moved in all directions, suggesting she was looking at something. Her fingers fluttered and seemed to search for something—or someone.

"Hunter?" Rayne rubbed her knuckles hard against Hunter's sternum.

Hunter moaned but appeared to dream, or hallucinate. "Hunter," she said, making her voice full of command. "Calm yourself, Hunter. We're taking you home."

"S-sir," Hunter managed through clattering teeth. "So cold."

"Here. She needs it more than I do." Beth had jerked off her backpack, opened her suit, and removed a thermo sweater. She dragged it over Hunter's head, and as Beth was tall, it covered Hunter to just above her knees. "There. Better." Beth pulled on her suit again and hoisted her backpack in place.

A whirring sound made them all freeze. It sounded far too familiar, and Kae peered up through the foliage. "Use your Cameleo-blankets. The leaves aren't dense enough to cover us!" She pulled out her blanket and sat down next to the trembling Hunter, making sure she was covered as well. The drones hovered right on top of them, and Kae could feel the downdraft, as it made the blankets flutter.

"Hold on to the blankets," Foster hissed. "They might blow right off us."

Kae squinted down at Hunter, who looked up at her with bulging, frightened eyes. "Hey, kid, you'll be fine. We're getting you home."

"Why? Why did you risk...coming after me?" Hunter whispered the words just under her breath.

"We leave no one behind if we can help it." Kae squeezed Hunter's shoulder lightly.

"Are those drones? I think they inserted...a tracker..." Hunter drew a labored breath. "You have to leave me and continue, sir. It's not safe—"

"We removed the tracker. You don't remember?" Beth asked from Hunter's other side. "They can't scan for you."

Hunter gave a soft sob. "Okay." She paused and then continued, "Thank you...the sweater."

"Hey, no problem." Beth patted Hunter from the outside of the blanket and managed to touch Hunter's face. To Kae's astonishment, Hunter gave a sound that was something between a hiccup and a giggle. It lasted only a few moments, but it gave her hope that the bastards that had interrogated her hadn't yet broken her. The experts at the camp would make sure, but Kae trusted her instincts.

The drones hovered a few minutes longer and then moved back toward the barracks. When the air was quiet for a minute longer, Kae decided it was safe to move. Getting out from under the Cameleo blanket, she was overwhelmed by the residual fumes that hit her respiratory tract before she slammed down her visor. "Visors down. Mask on Hunter."

They worked together in silence after that, strapping Hunter to Foster's chest instead this time, as he claimed he could move easier and protect her better that way. With Hunter's knees tucked in under his right arm and her head leaning against his shoulder, they covered her with double blankets.

"Better?" Kae murmured, looking over the edge of the blanket at Hunter.

"Warmer. Better." She hid her face against Foster's neck, and he nodded solemnly. "I'll get this girl home."

Surprisingly, Kae had to swallow against an unwelcome lump in her throat. "Good."

Rayne came up to her and asked Foster to crouch some so she could see Hunter. When she was pleased, she quickly took Kae's hand and squeezed it. She let go after a mere moment, but the touch was still reassuring.

Kae made sure they weren't leaving anything behind before they moved out. The more they could keep the Celestial guards and, by extension, the corrupt authorities guessing, the better.

Kae set a new course, and she knew she wasn't the only one listening intently for that special sound that the hovering drones made. Beth and Rayne took turns heading up the team next to Kae, and she appreciated it. It was exhausting work, and by now they had been on their feet for more than eighteen hours. When it was Rayne's turn again, Kae didn't care if Foster or Beth saw. She took Rayne's hand and knew she would always find it mind-boggling just how rejuvenated she felt by merely touching Rayne.

They didn't speak, as they needed to be on the lookout for the enemy. Checking the time on her GemLink, Kae frowned. They might not be able to make the long hike back to the camp tonight. She began a list in her head of what to consider if they needed to deploy an emergency habitat—and, if so, where.

"I can hear your mind turn over, repeatedly," Rayne whispered.

"Just trying to come up with contingency plans. Damn. It actually was easier in the tunnels in some ways, as I knew those places so well." Kae sighed. "I'm going to do my best to get us all back to camp. I don't want to stay out all night, but it may come to that. How's Foster doing?"

"Him?" Rayne chuckled almost soundlessly. "He's like a mother hen on speed."

Kae had to smile. "Don't tell him that."

"I heard," Foster whispered from behind, being much closer than Kae realized. "I will plot my revenge, Rayne."

They kept walking, and just as Rayne began to stumble every tenth step or so, Kae finally relented. "We're parallel to the path home. I suggest we move onto it and then into the woods. We'll set up the habitat—"

Faint footfalls made Kae go quiet instantly. At the same time, her GemLink, and the others, sent a silent proximity alert to their visors. It was unmistakable. They had company, and it was approaching from the direction Kae had meant to take them just now.

Kae swiveled, hissing, "Cameleo blankets. Now!"

Beth pulled the blanket over her and curled up. She kept it an inch off the ground in front of her eyes, to have some chance to see who was approaching. Looking upward in Kae's direction, she met her gaze parallel to the ground.

Unlike the guards back at the barracks, the ones approaching them were a lot stealthier. If they hadn't been using the GemLinks' proximity alerts, whoever was moving toward them would have been on them before they had a chance to hide.

Beth prayed Hunter wouldn't suddenly come to or be in excruciating pain. If she moaned or screamed, they might as well wave a flag to show where they were. Beth thought she heard something and couldn't tell at first if it was her pounding heart or actual footfalls. She took the chance to move her hand in the opening, gesturing to Kae. She pointed in the direction of the sound and made a questioning sign with her hand. They were used to hand signals in the tunnels, and Kae nodded grimly and held up three fingers. Kae had distinguished three sets of footfalls.

The approaching individuals appeared to come from the path they had walked along the crop fields. That didn't make a lot of sense. Why would the guards in the barracks take such a detour? And if the guards had summoned the Celestial authorities to hunt them down, why were they on foot? The crop field was a large area to cover, even when using the drones. On foot, it was impossible. Yet some people, probably three, were walking right toward them. If they didn't change course even a little bit, they would step on them.

"London to field team." A crackling voice spoke in Beth's ear. "Come in."

London? What about the radio silence? And why did London's voice sound like a crackling old radio from centuries ago?

Beth peered over at Kae again and met her widening eyes in the gap between her blanket and the ground. She saw Kae raise her GemLink to her lips, and then she heard a faint whisper.

"Field team leader to London. Are you approaching?" Kae's signal was crystal clear, but her whisper was barely audible.

"Affirmative." London's voice crackled and gave out in the middle of the word.

"Send ID code," Kae hissed.

Beth's GemLink showed London's code as confirmed. Kae motioned for Beth to get up before pushing off her Cameleo blanket and doing the same. Beth stood quickly and held out a hand toward Rayne, who looked ready to copy their actions. She shook her head as a warning and readied her Nova blaster. If it wasn't London and a couple of other dissident soldiers approaching them, she was ready to fire to kill.

The footfalls were close enough now that they should be able to see who was approaching. Beth and Kae stood five yards apart, their blasters trained on the same spot up ahead.

Something white and gray glimmered between the stems, and it looked like one of their suits, but they didn't lower their weapons until the individual heading the small group was in sight. They stopped and held up their hands after holstering a handheld weapon. When they removed their helmets, Beth could have wept when she saw London's mussed hair and familiar face. The two coming into view behind him did the same, and Beth recognized them as the two that had been on the first field mission when they found the kids. Or vice versa, as it were.

London came up to them, smiling, but then looked around. "The others?" His face fell.

"Here." Rayne stood and turned to assist Foster. "And here."

"Fuck. Hunter!" London made his way to Foster and peered around the blanket that covered the young woman. "Is she—how is she?"

"She's alive. She seems to have fought them every step of the way during interrogation," Foster said, his face dark. "We'll know more when we reach the camp."

"That's what we can help you with. We've stashed an AirPod in the woods across the path. We had to deflate it so it wouldn't be seen from the sky, which means we get only one chance to inflate it and take off. We'll be vulnerable until we're above the treetops. The pilot and two soldiers are guarding it."

"The best news ever." Beth grinned despite her increasing fatigue. "We better hurry, as we don't know when the drones will be back, or if someone has picked up on your presence."

"What she said." Kae gathered her Cameleo blanket and folded it. Tucking it between her and her backpack, she nodded at London. "You came right when we needed you most. We'd just decided to find a place to erect a habitat."

"Let us carry some of your backpacks, sir. We're traveling lightly." London pointed at his subordinates. "Take Foster's and Dr. Garcia's backpacks. I'll take—"

"Beth's," Kae said. "I'm fine."

Beth wanted to argue, but in all honesty, she was so close to running out of energy, she might slow everyone down. When London took her backpack, she felt she might be able to make the last stretch to the AirPod.

❖

Rayne climbed into the AirPod as soon as it had inflated enough. She assisted Foster as he entered behind her, still carrying Hunter strapped to his chest. Beth was next, and together, she and Rayne unhooked the harness that kept Hunter in place. They lowered her onto a gurney and used padded straps to secure her. Opening a box on the floor, Rayne pulled out heated blankets and wrapped them around Hunter.

"Grab one for each of you. We're all cold, despite the suits." Rayne pulled out a few rods and ran them over Hunter. "She's in shock, and I don't like where her blood pressure is heading." Using a standard set of infulizers, she administered the appropriate medication. The floor hummed and vibrated around her, and she saw the pilot in the front punching in one command after another.

A loud hum made Rayne's GemLink vibrate. She glanced at it. "Another proximity alarm!"

"I have it too," Kae said just as she climbed on board. "We need to get this pod in the sky, and if we need to deploy the camouflage feature, we have to risk it. We're no good to anyone if drones or guards shoot us down."

London and his subordinates threw themselves through the hatch, and they pulled in the short ramp and closed it. "Strap yourselves in!" London hurried over to take the seat next to the pilot.

Rayne reached below the gurney and found the special harness that would strap her to it. She needed to remain by Hunter's side, if they were going to have a chance of saving her. When someone repeated her movements on the other side of the gurney, Rayne didn't have to look up to know it was Kae.

"I'm staying with you," Kae said huskily. "This'll be a close call for all of us. Hold on."

Rayne kept one hand on Hunter's chest and one holding Kae's hand. "We'll be all right. We couldn't have gotten this far, only to fail just before the finish line. I refuse to accept that possibility."

"Good," Beth said behind her. "I refuse it too. I need to get back to the camp. There's someone I need to…talk to."

Rayne pulled Kae closer. "I wouldn't want to be LaSierra," she whispered.

Kae raised her eyebrows and then nodded slowly. "I see. I think you're right."

"I can hear you, you know," Beth said darkly. "Mind your own business."

Rayne wasn't perturbed by Beth's stark tone.

In fact, she found it healthier than Beth's usual role as the happy-go-lucky individual within their little group. Among the four of them, they obviously fell into archetypes. Kae, somber, strong, and a bit aloof. Foster, strong, slightly volatile, and loyal. Beth, upbeat, kind, and cheerful. What was her own role? The nerdy doctor, perhaps. Rayne snorted softly at her own musing in the middle of pending combat, which made Kae look at her with slight concern.

"Don't worry. I'm not losing it." Rayne leaned over Hunter, glad she had managed to attach a few scanning patches to her chest, temple, and the inside of her wrist. "Her vitals aren't brilliant, but at least they're stable for now."

"Good." Kae winced as her and the others' GemLink gave a muted beep when the enemy was nearly upon them. "London!" she called out. "How far away are they?"

London punched in commands on the console next to the pilot. "Less than seven minutes out. We need to get farther up from the trees before we can deploy the camo protection. It's going to be close!"

"As fast as you can. And if you can ask the pilot to engage the propulsion system at the same time, that'd be great."

"It'll cost us a lot of energy." London stared back at them. Rayne could see how pale he was.

"If we can get away from them before the pilot sets a course for home, then we have to take that chance. If we need to go on foot the last few miles, so be it. We have to go camo and go fast."

"Got it, sir!" Looking reenergized, he discussed tactics with the pilot. "All right. Secure harnesses."

Gripping the edge of the gurney, Rayne pushed her feet into loops in the floor, meant for this purpose. "The loop!" She raised her voice over the whining propulsion system. "For your feet!"

Kae looked down and nodded. "Got it!"

The AirPod shot up from the ground so fast, Rayne was certain her stomach had been left behind. When it banked at a nearly ninety-degree angle and scraped along the top of the trees, one of the younger soldiers gasped and put his hands in front of his face. Rayne didn't blame him. She tugged at the gurney and prayed to the creator that it was attached well enough.

Looking over at the seats located just inside the hatch, Rayne saw how Beth clung to the edge of the seat when the AirPod shifted and banked in the opposite direction. Beth grimaced and closed her eyes, and Rayne tried to see if she was injured somehow.

"One more time," the pilot called out. "They're almost on us." He threw the AirPod into a nearly vertical climb, something Rayne doubted it was designed for.

Kae let go with her left hand and studied her GemLink. "Thirty seconds! They're within sight of us in five—four—three—two—"

"Camo deployed. Level out!" London sounded more excited than Rayne had heard him before. "Damn, you're a hell of a pilot, Jensen."

As the AirPod leveled out, Kae unhooked her harness and made her way to the pilot and London, after quickly stroking Rayne's cheek.

Rayne focused on Hunter, relieved to see that her vitals were stable, if not stellar. She listened absentmindedly to the conversation in the front, which now also included Beth. Apparently, the stunt the pilot had to pull had used too much of their energy reserve. If they were lucky, they might reach the camp, but they could also lose power miles from it.

Kae returned to Rayne and studied Hunter closely. "That's one damn resilient young woman," she said quietly. "I know they're going to put her through some pretty harsh debriefings when she's well enough, but my gut says we got to her in time."

"However, you wouldn't bet the lives of everyone in the camp on a gut feeling." Rayne looked at Kae's pale face and noticed the tension around her eyes.

"No, I wouldn't." Kae rubbed the back of her neck. "I have to admit that I can't wait to get home to our habitat. I'm exhausted, but I suppose we need to debrief first. I hope that's quick at least, or I'll fall asleep with my head on the table."

"I'm going to insist it be quick, from a medical perspective. We've been running on empty for a while. Beth was barely coherent earlier. Only the fact that London took her bag made it possible for her to make it to the AirPod."

"I thought as much." Kae rolled her shoulders. "Let's hope we don't run out of energy until we're home."

Rayne lowered her voice to barely above a whisper. "I love that you call the camp and our habitat home. I know your heart's still in the tunnels, and so is mine. I was there for just a few days, but I truly took the situation of the Subterraneans to heart. I know we'll get back to them—since we promised—when we've established our presence more firmly here."

"Of course it's home. Anywhere you are, Rayne, is home to me. You know that, right?" Kae smiled faintly. "But you're still correct, of course. I can never fully settle down until I know that those from the tunnels who yearn for freedom will have the chance for a life out here."

"Or in the Skyscrapers?" Rayne studied Kae closely.

Surprise written across her face, Kae shrugged. "Now there's a thought. If the corrupt government and the authorities are dealt with, perhaps that would be an option for some." She blinked and locked her gaze on Rayne. "Would you consider that option? Go back to the skyscraper and resume your work at the hospital?" There was no judgment in Kae's voice, but perhaps apprehension in her eyes.

"No." Rayne took one of Kae's hands in hers. "I seem to thrive on being a frontier kind of woman. I want to be where you are, work toward the same goal, as saving people is why I became a doctor. A lot of Celestial physicians can do what I did at the hospitals in Eastern Coastal City. I've learned special lifesaving and life-affirming skills here. I've had to think in a completely different way, and yes, the challenge is rewarding, but it's all about sharing my ability to heal and support the injured and sick. I want to do that wherever you're sent to do your duty. Something tells me, Kaelyn Dark will always be placed at the front and sent on the missions whose results help carve out our future."

Applause came from behind them, and Rayne flinched and snapped her head back over her shoulder to look at Beth, London, and the others, who had clearly heard everything she said.

"Best thing I've heard in ages," Beth said and came up to Rayne and Kae. "And if it's okay, I hope to steal some of it one day. Unless I strangle her first."

Rayne gaped but then closed her mouth quickly. "I suggest you mix it up with your own sentiments. I can see how being infatuated with LaSierra can fit with some of what I said though. Just don't bite her head off, Beth. We do our work, and she's got her part to play."

"I know," Beth grumbled. "I know that. It's just...some of what she's asked to do, and what people expect her to do, she does far too easily, far too willingly, from my point of view. I have to hear her out about that. After I've tried strangulation."

"That's a capital offence," Kae said lightly. "I suggest a metaphorical approach."

"All right." Looking close to pouting, Beth rolled her shoulders and then stomped a few times. "I hear you."

"Energy level down to thirty percent," the pilot called out. "We're four miles from the camp."

"I've turned off everything but what's keeping Hunter alive. We have camo going, and we're using the most cost-effective propulsion setting. If you believe in the Creator, say your prayers."

Rayne watched Kae and Beth lower their heads. Foster, Rayne, and one soldier did not. The others closed their eyes, and she saw their lips moving soundlessly. She turned to Kae. "I thought you believed in the Creator."

"I do. I prayed earlier. Right now, you and I need to focus on Hunter." Kae cupped Rayne's cheek. "And I know you're not indifferent to the Creator either. You're like me, or at least that's what it looks like."

"You're right. I pray quietly, on the inside, and usually just for a moment. Some days when I feel I haven't helped people as much as I set out to, I only have energy for a simple 'Please help.'"

"I understand." Kae looked down at Hunter. "She's paler than before. She's not bleeding somewhere, is she?"

"Not last time I—" The pinging alarm from the scanning patches made her jump into action. "Damn it." She scanned with a proper wand and tried to find what was happening inside Hunter. The answer appeared quickly, and she didn't like it. "She's hemorrhaging around the left frontal lobe. I need to absorb the blood and stop the swelling of the brain. Beth! Foster! I need more help. Sterilize your hands quickly." She looked up at Kae. "We need to perform an emergency craniotomy. If she were in better shape before this happened, we could give her some time and infulizer medication. Now we have to open her skull and use a special infulizer to douse the brain in deswelling medication. She's losing pressure as we speak, so no debate, people." Rayne raised her voice. "Jensen! Increase speed as much as you dare."

Foster and Beth approached, keeping their gloved hands away from everyone. Kae and Rayne had used a quick sterilizer unit attached to the gurney. They were ready.

CHAPTER TWENTY-FOUR

L aSierra!" Madelon came running into LaSierra's habitat
without asking permission, her face pale. "They've set
down the AirPod half a mile to the west of us. They need help."

"Is the AirPod's fuel depleted?" LaSierra tugged a blanket
over her legs as she anticipated going outside at some point.
"Deploy soldiers with chargers. No matter what, the AirPod can't
end up in enemy hands." She wanted to ask about Beth, yearned to
do so, but restrained herself. "And the field crew?"

"I didn't have time to do a headcount, but they're on their
way on foot, as Hunter is in critical condition. That's all I know."
Madelon wasn't the handwringing type, but now she crossed her
arms and gripped her elbows hard. Of course, she had a lot to lose
if something happened to her daughter. LaSierra fought to slap the
mask of command into place.

"Push me back into HQ for now, Madelon. I can do it, but if
you push, it'll go faster." She saw that her stark tone made Madelon
straighten, and her gaze sharpened.

"Of course." She walked behind LaSierra and changed the
setting of the AirFrame. Pushing LaSierra to her station at the end
of the large, oval table took only a minute.

LaSierra pulled up the AirScreen and began deciphering the
intel that streamed from the operatives sitting at their consoles
along the headquarter bulkhead. She could pinpoint exactly where
the field team had landed the AirPod, and it seemed as if it were in

the middle of a field, which wasn't ideal. If the Celestial drones or airborne forces found it before her troops reached it with a charger, they could lose their tactical advantage.

"Is the team underway to secure the AirPod? Does the field team need reinforcement?"

"Yes, to the first. No, to the second," Madelon said from her smaller console. "They're moving quickly toward us, and I've deployed a team to the perimeter. Ops have calculated a probable trajectory for them. Unless they need to hide, and I pray to the Creator that they don't, for Hunter's sake, they should arrive west of us at these coordinates."

LaSierra's computer received the coordinates instantly, and she pulled them up and superimposed them on her map. "I see. That's reasonably close to the hospital. Let's hope Hunter can hang on. And let's hope none of the others are injured." The team had been gone for a long time with little or no rest. LaSierra clenched her hands, the one on her injured side smarting, but she welcomed the pain. It kept her sharp, and it kept her annoyed—both vital when she needed to focus.

After ten minutes, the large, central GemLink station alerted LaSierra and Madelon that the team of soldiers had reached the abandoned AirPod. They were super-charging it and estimated it to take half an hour. They had covered as much as they could with Cameleo blankets, but LaSierra knew it was just a stopgap measure.

Madelon slammed her palm against the table, making LaSierra flinch, which also added to her pain.

"The perimeter guards report that their proximity alarm has gone off for eight contacts. They're two minutes out. Permission to have two guards meet them."

"Granted." LaSierra maneuvered her AirFrame away from her console. As she looked up, she saw Rocque enter HQ.

"Did you hear?" He had his long hair tied back with a piece of cloth and was clearly as flustered as Madelon was pale. "I'm meeting them at the perimeter. Why don't you go over to the hospital, Maddie? That's where they'll be heading. I took the liberty of telling the head medic to prep the OR."

"Let's go, both of us," LaSierra said and tucked the blanket more firmly around her. It was the middle of the night, and the temperature had dropped to 40 degrees F, so having lived her entire life in perfectly calibrated temperatures, 40 F was excruciatingly cold. Not even the suit fully insulated her.

With Rocque engaging the propulsion system in her AirFrame, LaSierra clenched the armrests when he ran across the Inner Circle to the hospital. Behind Rocque, Madelon hurried after them, and LaSierra could only imagine what went through her and Rocque's mind. Madelon took over pushing LaSierra's chair, and it was a blessing to get inside. LaSierra wasn't sure if she was trembling because of the tense situation or the cold weather...perhaps both. Inside, she managed to relax a bit as special heaters kept the hospital comfortably warm.

"They'll be here soon." Madelon smiled weakly. "I admit that I'm worried. I know Kae would rather die than let anything happen to Rayne."

"They're an unlikely couple," LaSierra said gently, her thoughts locked on Beth and the more than unlikely feelings that were brewing between them. "But I'm not blind to it."

"Not more unlikely than you and Beth, if something comes from you two sparring the way you do." Raising her eyebrows at LaSierra, Madelon seemed relieved to shift her focus.

LaSierra closed her eyes briefly. Peering over at Madelon, she sighed. "Am I that obvious?"

"No, not entirely. But Beth has no filters around you. That young woman looks at you like she would kill for you. Actually, knowing Kae and her team, she probably would, if you were in danger. And come to think of it, she's already saved you once."

"She has." LaSierra could easily feel Beth's strong, protective arms around her when she couldn't move aboard her crashed SkyBird. She had been experiencing the worst agony of her life but also known instinctively that Beth wouldn't let go—never abandon her. "As you said, she's a very young woman. Far too young for me, naturally."

"Rayne's fifty and Kae's thirty-nine, I believe. Age is irrelevant, especially in our situation. We have all our plans and strategies, but we know very little about what's going to happen. It's a terrible waste to disregard personal happiness." Madelon rubbed the back of her neck. "Trust me, LaSierra. I made that mistake with Rayne. I kept everything from her for fifty damn years. I wanted her to grow up without putting this burden of our struggle on her shoulders, but I was wrong. Plain and simple. She sensed the distance between us that was necessary to not drag her into it all, and she resented us for it. Rightfully so." Madelon sighed and wiped her eyes. "I think she's almost forgiven us, though at times she looks at me with that old bitterness shining through."

"Are you saying I should pursue Beth while we're in the middle of a crisis?" Had Madelon lost all her common sense? "The age difference is larger between us. I'm forty-six, and she's… twenty-six, I believe. Besides, she has enough to think about when she's on field missions instead of what could or couldn't happen between us."

Madelon tilted her head, and her still very beautiful face displayed sympathy. "Do you honestly think Beth doesn't give you a second thought when she's out there, doing her duty? Surely you realize you're part of her motivation for succeeding, and for fighting to stay alive. She wants, no, *needs* to come home to you!"

LaSierra took in Madelon's words. She hadn't thought of her personal situation before, and it made a strange sort of sense. "Perhaps. I just wish they were safely inside the perimeter!"

"As do I." Madelon shifted to sit close to LaSierra. "Don't you find all this surrealistic, considering how many decades we've worked toward this scenario? One day we're conducting our stealth operations as usual in the skyscrapers, and the next day, my daughter brings a team from the so-called enemy, and a couple of children at that, and all hell breaks loose."

"It has dawned on me." LaSierra had to smile faintly.

"And once we left the skyscraper behind, we burned our bridges because of the Subterranean team. Their undercover job didn't exactly go as planned, but the outcome happened to be part of one of our exit plans. It's truly strange," Madelon said, then froze and looked over LaSierra's shoulder. "They're here!"

LaSierra made her chair pivot and saw a group of people hurrying in with a gurney. They were all in uniform and wore helmets, which made it hard to distinguish between them. Medics were quick to take over the gurney, where a figure that had to be Hunter lay motionless. One of the field team appeared to have their hands inside Hunter's stomach, which had to be wrong, surely. Driving her AirFrame closer, LaSierra confirmed that her initial thought was correct. Therefore, the person walking next to the gurney, wrist-deep into Hunter's stomach, had to be Rayne.

"Creator...Rayne..." Madelon hurried after the gurney, but LaSierra remained in the area outside the OR. They had to be going into the theater, which was no place for civilians—unless you were the surgeon's mother.

"LaSierra," a female voice said, but it wasn't Beth's. "We all made it back." Kae stood to her left and held her helmet under her arm. "I understand you've powered up that inflatable monstrosity?"

Blinking, LaSierra had to reset her brain to understand the question. "Right." She checked the time. "The SkyPod. Yes. It should be on its way back by now." She was just about to ask about Beth, when she heard a male voice call out.

"She's going down. We need a medic here!"

LaSierra snapped her head to the right and saw Captain London holding onto a slumped Beth, who seemed to be sagging to the floor. LaSierra acted without hesitation. Driving the chair over to Beth, she slammed on the brakes and then pushed free of the harness and stood on wobbly legs. She heard people gasp around her, and she knew she would pay for this stunt later, but she could think only that Beth had fainted and needed her.

Foster helped LaSierra sit down on the floor next to Beth. "Grab my blanket. She's cold." When someone brought the blanket, LaSierra tugged gently at Beth, thankful someone helped her wrap Beth in it. "She's so pale." Stroking Beth's unruly hair from her face, LaSierra spoke to her. "Beth. It's LaSierra. Try to open your eyes. You're back at the camp, and you're safe."

Beth didn't move, and LaSierra stared at Foster. "What happened?"

"Beth's been running on empty for a long time. We took Hunter back from her to lighten her load, but she's simply exhausted. She, Kae, and I have helped Rayne with Hunter, and the last stretch when we had to walk, it was honestly excruciating, since we all had to move forward with our bodies turned toward the stretcher. Rayne said we should all get muscle relaxants, glucose infulizers… and, fuck, I can't remember the last…" He rubbed his head and mussed his black hair.

"Clean us up and then sleep." Kae looked at LaSierra, her eyes red around the rims. "I volunteered to leave a first report. It'll be the bare bones of one, but it's something."

Rocque came over from the direction of the OR and stopped in mid step at the sight of LaSierra and Beth on the floor. An approaching medic, holding a medical kit, rounded him.

"Rocque. I need you to debrief Kae. I'm…occupied." LaSierra knew she was pleading but didn't care.

"Certainly." He took Kae aside, and they sat down on one of the built-in benches.

Beth stirred a little when the medic, a young woman, LaSierra noted absentmindedly, ran her wand and two smaller rods across her abdomen. "She's dehydrated and suffering from extreme exhaustion and pre-hypothermia. I'm adding concentrated glucose, and once she comes to, she needs to drink. If she can't, I'll attach an infusion." The medic looked up at LaSierra, obviously assuming she was responsible for Beth.

"I'll make sure of it," LaSierra said. "I'll need help to get her home. I don't think she'll want to take up a hospital bed unnecessarily. Foster? Do you have any energy left?"

Foster held up a large can. "I had a few infulizers too," he said and motioned to the left of him, where a young man was busy administering the same as Beth was getting.

"But what's in the can?" LaSierra frowned.

"Beer! Someone brought me a FlatPak beer, and I'm not saying no." He downed the last of it. "There. Better." He walked over to Beth, who was looking up at them now, her gaze unsteady.

"What the fu—? LaSierra?" She fumbled with her hands in the air between her and LaSierra. "Too far away."

LaSierra leaned in and captured Beth's hand. "I'm here."

"Hey, Beth. I'm going to pick you up and take you to your habitat. All right?" Foster looked remarkably rejuvenated, and LaSierra knew he would credit the beer for helping him bounce back so fast. "Hold on, girl." He hoisted Beth, who had to be at least 5'8", as if she were a child. "Someone needs to help Ms. Delmonte into her chair. I'll start walking."

London came closer. "May I help, Ms. Delmonte?" He clearly wasn't as worn as the field team, and she nodded.

"Please."

After she was safely back in her AirFrame, she set it to hover and didn't ask for help. Taking off through the corridor, she caught up with Foster at the doors. She slowed down and followed him, as she found it difficult to maneuver in the dark. Relieved when they reached her and Beth's habitat, she showed the way into her bedroom.

"I thought Beth's room was—never mind." Foster placed Beth on the bed and helped her get out of her suit. "I think I'll leave the rest to you two." He bumped Beth on the shoulder and then nodded briskly at LaSierra. "Take good care of her."

"I will." LaSierra parked the chair close to the bed and disconnected her safety harness. Sliding over to the bed, she sat next to Beth, smoothing her blond hair from her forehead. "You're exhausted, but I have to ask. Do you need to use the facility?"

"Yes. I'm usually not so self-conscious about it, but I didn't want to ask Foster." Beth sounded more lucid, which was encouraging.

"Why don't you use my chair, if you feel unsteady? I'll wait here." LaSierra saw relief on Beth's face as she spoke.

"Thanks. That'd be great. Good thing I'm used to that thing. I might have pushed a hole in the wall to HQ otherwise."

"Probably." Moving down the bed to allow Beth to sit up, LaSierra watched as she rolled out of bed and into the chair.

"Hey. Not bad." Beth drove the chair into the ensuite facility, and the door closed behind her. When she'd been gone a lot longer than LaSierra thought she would, she began to worry.

"Beth? Are you all right?" she called out, debating whether to attempt the few steps she knew she could manage.

"I'm almost done. Had to do a cleaning cycle." After another minute, Beth appeared, but this time, she was pushing the chair, even though she walked slowly. "I'm feeling better. I know I have to drink, so I managed to fill a bottle without getting your chair all wet. I intended to figure out some nightwear, but my brain won't allow me to remember how to do it." Beth was wearing only a towel that she'd tied just above her breasts.

"Oh. I can fix that for you." LaSierra moved to grab the armrest of the airframe.

"No, no. Don't get up. I'm just going to slip into bed, drink a lot of water, and then sleep. I didn't know you could have lucid dreams about sleep."

"You must've been completely worn out." LaSierra watched Beth pull the covers back and climb into bed. Once she was completely covered, she pulled the towel off and let it fall to the floor.

"I promise to fix that tomorrow. Honest." She held the covers to her chest as she flipped the water bottle open and drank greedily, a few drops slipping down her chin and neck, then between her breasts.

LaSierra closed her eyes. This was too much. And it was completely inappropriate. Beth was, if not wounded, then in a weakened state. And although she clearly wasn't as cold as she had been initially, she was still trembling.

Beth put the bottle on the floor next to the bed and curled up under the covers. LaSierra took a blanket from the foot of the bed and tucked it around her. If they'd been in her home in the Skyscraper, her bed would have been set to the perfect temperature, but this was merely a simple habitat—even if she understood that a Subterranean would consider it a lot less simple than she did.

"I'm going to take my medication, and then I'll join you," LaSierra said and hoped she sounded matter-of-fact, though she feared she only appeared breathless, which was ridiculous.

"Don't take too long. I—I like that you're here." Beth spoke from under the covers.

"I won't."

LaSierra moved over to her chair and drove it into the bathroom. After taking her oral medication, hoping she wouldn't need the infulizer pen with the extra-strong pain relief, she used a cleansing wand quickly. Programming a simple sleep shirt that reached to her knees, she managed to stand for ten full seconds without experiencing vertigo. Then she made her way back to the bed and hoped Beth had fallen asleep, but instead she had turned over in bed and lay closer to the middle of the mattress.

LaSierra slipped into bed, feeling cold now. She had no idea where the thermostat was in the habitat and instead tugged another blanket from the foot of the bed and laid it on top of the covers.

"Are you still cold, Beth?" LaSierra murmured, in case Beth was asleep after all.

"A little, yes." Beth poked her head up, her eyes huge and her eyelashes glued together. Had she been crying?

"I can't lie on my right side very long, but if I turn my back, you're welcome to slide closer," LaSierra said, not even attempting to filter her words.

"You sure? I'm naked." Beth's voice was husky and filled with emotion.

"I know you are. I'm not." LaSierra turned and sighed in relief when she relaxed as the fast-working capsules took effect.

Behind her, Beth moved closer, and then a strong, wiry arm wrapped around LaSierra's stomach and pulled her close.

"This okay?" Beth asked, her breath moving LaSierra's hair and creating goosebumps down her back.

"Yes. Try to relax. We'll both be warm soon." LaSierra had tensed but now willed herself to allow Beth to mold against her. Even if Beth's skin was cool to the touch, she could still feel how their proximity to each other generated increasing warmth.

"I'm so glad to be home. That you were there, at the hospital," Beth whispered. "We have so much to talk about. I have questions, but they can wait...must wait. Too tired."

She had questions? LaSierra placed her arm on top of Beth's. "I'm so relieved you made it back. I was worried." That was an understatement. She'd been frantic at times and worked too long at a time through the day. Stroking Beth's arm, she was amazed at how smooth her skin was. "You're safe here." Compared to outside the perimeter, they were safe in the camp, but truthfully, their camouflage techniques and scrambling technology could be challenged—or destroyed—and then they'd be far too easy to locate. They needed to get inside the barracks and set up a proper base with access to food and a defense system that consisted of more than habitats and SkyBirds.

Beth pulled LaSierra even closer and hid her face against her hair. She pushed their joined hands farther up and stopped just below LaSierra's breasts. LaSierra doubted Beth was awake, as she merely hummed and settled in. Slowly LaSierra gave in to the intimacy of their sleeping arrangement, and she'd be a horrible liar if she couldn't at least confess to herself that she hadn't felt this safe and cherished in a very long time—if ever.

Closing her eyes, she allowed herself to slump back against Beth. How someone as tall, lanky, and muscular could feel so soft and inviting, she had no idea. Beth's small, firm breasts pressed against LaSierra's back and stirred something inside her that wasn't appropriate right now.

Beth moved her legs, seeming a little restless until she managed to press one leg halfway in between LaSierra's. More shivers raced through LaSierra, and she forced herself to breathe evenly. She had to go to sleep quickly, or her physical reaction to Beth's presence would become a problem. Her emotional reactions were already off the chart and seemed impossible to harness. Certain that falling asleep would be impossible, in fact, LaSierra did so in only a few minutes.

CHAPTER TWENTY-FIVE

R ayne stumbled out of the theater after she finished her part of the surgery. Pressing her body against the wall, she tried to keep her balance, but she had tunnel vision and was starting to tremble after suppressing her fatigue for the two hours she had been operating.

"I have you." Kae's voice came from outside Rayne's field of vision, and she fumbled for her. Blissfully warm, strong hands caught Rayne. "It's just me here. I insisted that your parents get some rest."

"Good. Mother waited for a while before we realized the surgery would drag on." Rayne leaned her forehead against Kae's collarbone. Before she realized Kae's intention, she found herself scooped up and carried.

"Oh, Creator, no, Kae, no. I'm too heavy." Rayne clung to Kae's shoulders.

"No, you're not. Think of it this way. It's this, or I get you a gurney, which will freak out your underlings, and they'll insist on admitting you for the night."

Cringing at that possibility, Rayne shook her head. "Then by all means." She pressed her face against Kae's neck and realized that she'd taken the time to clean up and change clothes after whatever briefings that had taken place. "I'm sorry if I smell bad." Rayne sighed.

"You don't. So, you're a little sweaty—you're allowed." Kae chuckled. "Remember when we had our first bath together? Well, our only bath, come to think of it."

"Of course. It was a few weeks ago. I'm not mentally impaired." Rayne had to smile. "And that place was something else. I wasn't ready to get naked with you and jump into a tub after coming with you all to the tunnels. But it was lovely, even if I'm sure I didn't show the proper appreciation."

"I was responding to you already then," Kae murmured against Rayne's hair. "I tried to act casual—with limited results."

"You weren't the only one. I'd never met anyone like you. And here you go sweeping me off my feet again—literally."

Kae shouldered the door open and crossed the Inner Circle. Around them, it was mostly dark in the surrounding SkyBirds, but lights showed the paths to the HQ and their habitats that surrounded it. Kae hurried toward their area, and the door slid open as they neared it.

Rayne held onto Kae's arms as she placed her on the ensuite bathroom floor. It was just large enough that they didn't step on each other, but Rayne didn't mind. She didn't take for granted having their own place, where they could feel reasonably safe.

Kae helped Rayne pull off her clothes, and when Rayne came out of the cleansing tube, she had recycled her clothes, except the uniform. It had to go through another cleansing process at one of the SkyBirds, where especially trained staff would take care of that.

"Here." Kae tugged a nightshirt over Rayne's head. "You look a little better, but you need something more substantial to eat than the rations the nurse gave you during surgery."

"You saw that?" Rayne walked out into their living area. "I agree with you, as I'm dying for something hot but not too rich. Chicken soup, perhaps."

"Let's see if I've developed a new and less testy relationship with the FlatPak machine. Kae pulled out a FlatPak box and browsed through it. "You're in luck. Chicken soup with vegetables." She placed it in a small piece of technology that inflated the food and rehydrated it. "To answer your question, Foster, London, and I were in an hour-long debriefing with Rocque. He grilled us rather extensively, but I think he relented when Foster started to doze off. We were dismissed, we all ate, and then we hit the cleaning tubes. When I got back to the hospital, you had just stopped yet another bleeder, I believe. How many were there?"

The FlatPak machine pinged, and Kae pulled out the box and poured the contents into a bowl. "Here you go."

"Thanks." Rayne downed a few spoons of soup before she answered Kae's question. "We were quite successful holding the larger bleeders at bay while we carried Hunter here. Especially the one in her frontal lobe. There was one more big one in her abdomen that burst just as we got her on the table. That wasn't the biggest problem, though. She had a multitude of small nicks in her liver. I won't be surprised if her toxicology report notes something that made that happen. I can't see any other reason. The bigger bleeds were from blunt-force trauma to the abdomen."

"Damn them." Kae pressed her lips together. "We have a lot of work to do. Perhaps it's because I'm starting to fade here, but I'm having a hard time sorting in which order I believe we must proceed."

Rayne had finished eating while Kae was talking, and now she extended a hand. "I have a suggestion. I want to clean my teeth and then go to bed. With you. I want to fall asleep in your arms."

"You have the best ideas, Doc." Kae smiled crookedly. "I'll make sure we're secure, and then I'll join you."

After drinking a large glass of water, Rayne stepped into the ensuite to use the dental cleanser. Returning to the bedroom, she found Kae pulling down the covers for them, already dressed in a sleepshirt. As they crawled into bed, Rayne found she could draw her first easy breath since she had joined Kae in the sanct to help rescue the refugees and then look for Hunter.

Kae pulled Rayne onto her shoulder and hummed something inaudible.

"What?" Rayne tipped her head back and looked up at Kae.

"I said, 'Thank the Creator.' A few times today I worried that one of us might not make it back—or even both of us."

"I was concerned, but I knew you never give up, so I found all I had to do was keep going and do what I was there for, and you would get us back." Rayne kissed Kae's jawline. "You, Foster, and Beth…you're all family. And you…I know I'm perhaps being presumptuous, but you're mine." Rayne trembled at her own words. She was rarely audacious when it came to personal relationships.

Kae got up on her elbow and looked down at Rayne, her eyes wider than normal. "Yes," she whispered. "Yes. I am. And that means you're mine, right?"

"It does. I've been yours since that time in the aqua tub, I think. Or perhaps when you made me ride that strange contraption hanging from the ceiling. Perhaps it was when you let me sleep with my head in your lap." Rayne smiled through tears. "So many choices."

Kae wiped at Rayne's cheeks. "You're tired, but I want you to know that learning that you see us this way, I suppose… committed? It makes me very happy, and I haven't been truly happy in a long time."

Rayne studied Kae's stunning face. Her eyes glowed, and her smile transformed her into the woman she so rarely got to be because of her duties. She surmised that the same went for herself. "I have never been so scared as I was just before London reached us. I thought they would take us. And now, I've never been happier learning that you feel like I do. " She hesitated. "I've never felt like this for anyone."

"That makes two of us," Kae said and lay down again. "Now come closer and try to get some sleep. Tomorrow's going to be hectic, I imagine. We'll have to stand up for Hunter, for one thing."

"Agreed." Rayne curled up closer and yawned. "Sleep well, darling."

Kae kissed the top of her head. "I will. You too."

Rayne sighed contentedly, and just before she fell asleep, she thought she heard Kae whisper, "Mine."

❖

LaSierra sat in her AirFrame and tried to understand how *this* Beth was the same Beth that had held her in her arms all night. This Beth was furious, to say the least, and her wrath was directed at LaSierra.

"Let me get this straight," LaSierra said, modulating her voice into the one she used when addressing the troops. "You are under the impression that you have any say about the command decisions we take among the senior staff."

"I'm not a Celestial, and I'm not of Garcia or Delmonte pedigree, but the last I checked, I was part of the senior staff. Yet this has nothing to do with that—it has to do with human decency!" Beth stood over by the dining table, her hands in tight fists. She was formidable, and when she took a step closer, LaSierra realized she could be intimidating.

"Human decency." LaSierra smiled joylessly. "I had no idea you found me lacking in that department as well."

"I don't." Beth shoved her fingers through her hair. "But the decision you made, with Madelon's and Rocque's approval, is inhumane. To have us go on a rescue mission for one of us and then expect us to fucking euthanize her if we suspected she'd talked. It's insanity."

"And so is endangering the people here at the camp, back at the tunnels, and the dissidents still trapped in the skyscrapers all along the coastline." LaSierra knew she should end this fruitless argument and drive her chair into the HQ, but it was impossible to leave Beth when this rancor hung between them.

"I would never endanger anyone other than myself, and I don't do that unless the stakes are high and all other ideas have been exhausted. I'm not suicidal, but damn it, I'm not an executioner either."

"And if you had found Hunter in a state where she was beyond help and any prolonging of her life would be cruel?" LaSierra held her hands lightly folded on her lap, even if she wanted to slam her fists against the armrest.

"Then Rayne would have sedated her, we would have strapped her to Foster, and we would have brought her back—which is exactly what we did." Beth coughed, and it seemed as if her anger was close to choking her.

"Beth. Please." LaSierra wasn't sure what to say. How could she make Beth realize that her job was not to look at the individuals but at what had to be done for the entire dissident movement. Perhaps this issue was unsolvable. To LaSierra's utter embarrassment, she felt tears fill her eyes. She didn't dare blink, or they would run down her cheeks, and she had no *time* for tears. Still raw on the inside from worrying about Beth, she had been completely blindsided by Beth's accusations. They had literally gone from waking up in each other's arms to being at war with each other.

"LaSierra?" Beth looked alarmed. "Are you...are you crying?"

"No," LaSierra lied. She wiped quickly at her eyelashes. "I'm obviously fine. Never better." She looked down at her hands. They were indeed curled into tight fists now. She was losing her grip on her feelings, and she wasn't sure how to get it back. The meetings were scheduled to start in half an hour, and she couldn't enter with tears in her eyes, flushed, and angry...and upset.

Beth shocked her by crouching next to the AirFrame and taking one of her aching fists between her hands. "I'm not well versed in how you Celestials do things, or plan things, but I hate...I *hate* that it is up to you to enforce such rules. How can one single person have all this power, and all this responsibility, to decide something like you did about Hunter? It's soul crushing..."

"I'm sure you found it that way—"

"...for you. Each of these decisions that you must make, like with Max—and yes, I know I went off on you then too—it eats away at you. It has to." Beth reached over and stroked LaSierra's cheeks with her thumb. "It breaks my heart," she whispered.

LaSierra felt all the anger and defensiveness seep out of her system. Perhaps she had, if not misunderstood Beth's viewpoint, then perhaps not understood all the facets of it. Beth loathed the order regarding Hunter, which was obvious—and understandable.

But she'd also worried so much for LaSierra that she'd looked ready to throttle her just a moment ago.

"Are you saying you're worried for my immortal soul, Beth?" LaSierra saw tears on Beth's cheeks too and guessed they were of the same origin as hers. Anger and distress. She pushed them away with gentle fingertips.

"I have no idea of what to do about anyone's soul—immortal or not—but it tears me up that it appears to be up to you to make these kinds of decisions, ultimately." Beth shook her head slowly.

"And for someone like you to carry them out." For the first time, LaSierra disregarded her principle to never allow anything to become personal. Of course, a young woman like Beth could be scarred for life for carrying out—what had Beth called it— euthanasia? Were they perhaps different sides of the same coin? One who makes the heart-wrenching decision, and the other one the person meant to perform the act. It was a horrible affair either way.

"I'm relieved that it seems that Private Nikki Hunter showed exceptional fortitude and didn't succumb to the enemy's enhanced interrogation techniques. She has a long way to go, when it comes to her recovery, but she has you and the others to thank for that." LaSierra tried to keep the thoughts about what this newest fight meant for her, well, relationship with Beth. Was last night the last time she would be allowed to hold this stunning creature and feel like even she, who had lived in solitude for so many years, could belong with her?

"I'm relieved too." Beth studied LaSierra closely, and a new frown appeared between her eyebrows. "What are you thinking about?"

Don't bring it up now. LaSierra pushed and shoved at the insistent voice inside her that wanted her to beg Beth to not abandon her completely. "Only that it's time to head into HQ. I have preparations to make before the first meeting." Raising her chin, LaSierra saw Beth's eyes go opaque. Of course. It was to be expected.

"Let me help you." Beth rose and rounded the AirFrame.

LaSierra ignored her hemorrhaging heart and held up a hand. "That's all right. You should get something to eat. You're still trembling from yesterday, I think." She turned the chair around and drove toward the door that led into the HQ. "I'll be all right on my own."

Wasn't she always?

CHAPTER TWENTY-SIX

Beth sat by her computer console at the oval table, and since they each had their own units, she couldn't switch places with anyone else. That meant she sat next to LaSierra, who had her enormous AirScreen up.

It was of course ridiculous to try to soothe her own aching heart when lives were on the line and they had so many dangerous missions ahead. They needed cool and clear heads to plan how to reach their goal with minimal casualties. The latter was probably wishful thinking, as Beth had seen too many well-planned missions go wrong, as unforeseen variables always existed.

"Beth?" Rayne sat between Beth and Kae, and now she leaned in and nudged Beth's shoulder. "You are not being subtle. Just so you know," Rayne whispered gently.

"What?" Beth winced. "I don't know what you're talking about."

"You're actually leaning away from LaSierra. I don't think adding a few more inches to the distance between you two is going to help."

"Damn." Beth gave in. "All right. Thanks. I'm trying to focus on what really matters, but..." She shrugged and ignored the burning sensation behind her eyelids. She had stopped crying, well, with a few exceptions, perhaps, when she left the tunnel orphanage.

"It's all right." Rayne kept her gaze on LaSierra as she continued whispering. "We feel what we feel—no matter what goes on around us. These are our lives going on. Just because we carry a lot on our shoulders doesn't mean we stop loving, aching, dreaming…you know?"

Beth had never thought of her life that way. Raised at the orphanage until she was sixteen, she had spent her mid-teens working with the small children, but when the orphanage burned down, she was approached by Foster, who wanted her to join Kae's team. Just as she had been around the kids at the orphanage, she had assumed the role of the enthusiast and the cheerful member of the team. Right now, she couldn't find a happy cell in her entire body.

"If everyone's ready, we have some hard decisions to make this morning," LaSierra said. She let her even gaze travel from one senior member to the next. When she reached Beth, she showed no emotion, merely continued to Rayne and kept going. Beth had to find a way to ignore the stabs of pain that working alongside LaSierra would induce. This was not the woman who had aligned her body with Beth's all night, to keep them both warm. This LaSierra was a stranger.

"Rocque, please list the most pressing matters, and by that, I mean regarding the big picture." LaSierra leaned back into her AirFrame and pressed her hands against the armrests. "The details will have to come later."

Beth knew LaSierra wasn't as relaxed as she looked. Definite tension showed around her eyes and in her lips. A small, nearly dormant part of Beth wanted to reassure LaSierra that they would find a way to reach each other, but at the same time, she didn't flatter herself that LaSierra's tense expression had anything to do with her. The burden of command that chipped away at her while she was trying to regain her health was the main cause. Beth was a blip, at most.

"All right," Rocque said. "In no particular order, the list is as short as it's important and overwhelming. We need to help the Subterraneans who want to leave the tunnels to do so. We have to do the same with the Celestial dissidents trapped in the skyscrapers. And, we need to find better housing, even if our SkyBirds and habitats are providing sufficient shelter right now."

"'Right now' being the operative words," LaSierra said. "Madelon, you have a tactical mindset. Where do we start? Do we take one at a time, or do we create teams and do it all simultaneously?"

"No to the latter, LaSierra." Madelon rose and placed both hands against the table. "We can't bring any more people here. We're stretched thin as it is. We have to secure better living arrangements, and that means taking over not just one or two barracks, but the entire compound. Not only that, but we also have to be prepared to take the guards and Celestial-friendly staff prisoners and secure the border around the area. Benny is working on a rudimentary forcefield to fit such a large structure. If we can keep energy weapons from penetrating, we will gain time to continue our mission."

"All right. And then?" LaSierra nodded and glanced at a young operative taking notes.

Rocque spoke again. "We need to get the Subterraneans out of harm's way after we take the compound." He nodded at Kae. "We are all guilty of allowing a quarter of all the human beings residing in the Easter Coastal City to live under sometimes deplorable, inhumane conditions. If we're going to succeed with the next phase, this is how it needs to happen."

Beth covered her mouth, but her gasp was still audible. Nothing could stop her tears now, and she had to suffer the humiliation of having them run down her cheeks and between her fingers.

"Hey." Rayne put a hand on Beth's shoulder, but she couldn't accept any consolation right now. She felt like slapping Rayne's hand away, and only the fact that Rayne was her friend and only meant to show her sympathy kept her from following through.

LaSierra's eyes grew large as she stared at Beth. "What's going on?"

Kae stood. "LaSierra...and Rocque. Beth, like Foster and I, have been waiting for those words from someone in an official position, in a setting like this. Not just said in passing...like an afterthought," Kae said somberly. "You know the truth more than the rest of the Celestials, merely from listening to us. Not to mention the important testimonies from Rayne, who is the bravest among you for throwing herself down a laundry chute and coming back to the tunnels with us after saving a little caver boy."

Kae didn't try to console Beth, but her gaze appeared apologetic as she continued. "One life-experience you have not heard of is when a girl of sixteen worked at one of our orphanages. Raiders, as in disguised Celestial soldiers, or operatives, set explosives that caused a fire. The girl saved as many as she could, but the kids were lost, and so were several of the other adults working there. She sustained burns too, but when she'd healed, she joined the freedom fighters in the hope she could make a difference." Kae turned to Beth. "And from the day you joined our unit, you have been the bravest, strongest one of us all. You are kind to everyone, but you hide the heart of that girl who saved so many children, as you must be strong to cope with everything we go through in the tunnels. Yet you save lives over and over. It's your mission in life. That and nothing else. You don't care if it is a kid in the tunnels or a resistance leader in a crashed SkyBird."

"Or a young woman entering unknown territory to help her people—or a young female soldier in enemy hands," LaSierra said slowly. She was so white now, her hair and eyes looked black in comparison.

Beth snapped her head up and looked at LaSierra. Those were the first words she had said to Beth after she left the habitat this morning. "LaSierra." Her vocal cords felt thick and uncooperative.

"Right after this meeting, Beth, if you'll allow it," LaSierra said, her jaw looking so tense, Beth feared she might chip her teeth. "The habitat."

"All right." Beth nodded, not sure what to think.

"The ultimate goal, of bringing down the corrupt government, coincides with freeing the dissidents among the Celestials," Madelon said, after offering Beth a look of empathy. "It's going to need a completely different type of plan, as we have to find ways to deploy people to reach the dissidents we have on our roster that hold influential positions. If they're following protocol, they're laying low and going about their day as if nothing is amiss."

"I know it's our last mission on the list," LaSierra said, and she looked more collected now. "But we have to send in some undercover agents to begin transmitting and receiving intel instantly. Benny is working on how that could happen without the current authorities intercepting anything."

"Damn. This makes my head spin," Foster said. "I'm glad we're moving toward the tunnels first, as they were in a worse condition than normal after the attack that happened the day before. They lost their only proper physician in the explosion, and even if Rayne did all she could before we had to leave, a lot can have happened since then."

Beth had waited until there was a lull in the discussion. "Have any of you given more thought to your initial idea of deploying someone to the tunnels to set up communications to and from there in the same way you plan to do at the skyscrapers?"

LaSierra exchanged glances with the Garcias, and then they all looked at Beth with something close to embarrassment. "No," LaSierra said softly. "I'm ashamed to say that this is one of the plans that has fallen by the wayside. You're correct, of course. It was part of our initial objectives."

"We had so much to do, even we lost track of that plan," Kae said, bitterness present in her voice. "Hardly surprising that you'd be the one to remind us, Beth. Good thinking."

"Is it? How do we know if it's even possible?" Beth shrugged. Her tears drying, she tried to ignore an unwelcome sense of awkwardness at being the center of attention, which normally never fazed her.

"We don't know if it is entirely possible in the skyscrapers, and we're still ready to go forward with that plan. Of course we need to do that with the Subterraneans too." Rocque smiled at Beth. "I'm starting to believe we have underutilized you by sticking you on guard duty at the perimeter. We need to do better there too."

LaSierra nodded briskly. "And we will."

The meeting continued, but Beth found it hard to focus. The dip into old memories rattled her, some that she hadn't, if not blocked out exactly, then at least tucked away for times when she was alone or in a strong and safe frame of mind. Now, given the stress they were under, the memories were flooding her brain, drenching it in guilt, a sense of failure and wasted opportunities. She thought of Boro, the beloved doctor who had helped keep the people in the tunnels alive. Not thriving, but at least not terminally ill.

After another hour, Rayne had to return to the hospital, and LaSierra decided that it was time for a break. She looked ashen, and Beth couldn't help but worry. She was still aware of the woman she cared about more than was good for her, and she loathed to see LaSierra overdo and possibly prolong her recovery.

"Beth?" LaSierra tilted her head. "Are you still interested in clearing the air?" She maneuvered her AirFrame and faced Beth head-on.

Beth tried to decipher the soft glow in LaSierra's amber eyes. "Why not? It's going to be a pain sharing quarters and working together if we're going to be all awkward." Rigidly, she shrugged, and it didn't escape her that LaSierra flinched at her flippant words.

"Right." LaSierra moved ahead of Beth and steered her chair to the door leading to their habitat.

As soon as Beth closed the door behind them, LaSierra pivoted and said, "Lock it," in a stark tone.

Beth started but then locked the door. "There. Whatever secrets you intend to share are safe." She meant to make a joke, but obviously LaSierra had missed that point.

"If you're going to mock everything I say, or insinuate that my intentions are only self-serving, then I might as well go back to work."

Beth winced. "I'll cut it out. I tend to crack so-called jokes when I'm nervous or awkward." Or when she was afraid. Afraid that LaSierra was going to say something more about Beth's duties as damn executor, Beth clasped her hands behind her back and stood almost at attention.

"Beth…" LaSierra spoke Beth's name like a sigh. "I'm not military, and even if you are by now, sort of, you don't have to damn near salute me." With hasty, sharp movements, LaSierra pulled at some offending hair pins and moaned when her long, chestnut hair fell around her shoulders. "Ah. Finally." She rubbed the back of her head.

"You have a headache?" Beth lost her rigid stance. "Where are you on your medication schedule today?"

"Stop, please. Beth...I don't need medication. Not now. I...I...Fuck. I don't know what I need." She pulled her hair away from her neck and let it fall forward over her left shoulder.

"Want to get out of the chair and sit on the couch a bit?" Beth couldn't stop herself from offering help. She cared about LaSierra, no matter what was going on between them. She had gotten under her skin from the moment Beth found her in the downed SkyBird, and she couldn't stand to see her uncomfortable and in pain.

"I'd like that." Glancing at her massive leader GemLink, LaSierra calculated quickly in her head. "I have a little more than an hour before I'm due in the hospital."

"Hospital?" Beth had neared LaSierra and now stopped and narrowed her eyes. "What's wrong? Or is it just a checkup?"

"Neither." LaSierra shook her head. "I'm there to see some of the new arrivals and, of course, Hunter." She hesitated and plucked the hem of her blue tunic. "I would like for you to join me. I agree with Rocque when he says that we've underutilized you. You possess traits that can be very useful for my decision making."

"I do?" Was something amiss with LaSierra? She seemed to be talking about some alternative reality. "I mean, I'm not well versed in anything that you need to know to figure out half the shit that you do."

"I used to think you were audacious, irreverent, and the worst person to take orders I've met in a long time."

"Wow. Please. Don't hold back when it comes to my shortcomings." Where was this going? LaSierra wasn't making much sense. Still, not about to let her sit in that chair and suffer, Beth lifted LaSierra and placed her cautiously on the couch. "There. Better?"

LaSierra actually pressed her right palm to her chest. "I...yes. But a heads-up wouldn't be wrong next time." She drew a deep breath.

"Noted." So, there might be a next time. Or an imagined next time. Beth sat down next to LaSierra and turned sideways to face her.

❖

LaSierra studied Beth for a moment, while she gathered and sorted her fragmented thoughts. Would something good come out of this meeting—one that Beth could get up and leave at any moment, as LaSierra could tell Beth wasn't especially relaxed.

"I'm sorry." LaSierra hadn't expected those exact words to pass her lips until she had explained herself further.

Beth didn't say anything at first, and she didn't even blink for at least half a minute. Eventually, she opened her mouth and said, "Go on."

Obviously, Beth didn't intend to offer her the easy way out or give away her own standpoint. That said, it wasn't very hard for LaSierra to determine Beth's point of view, as she had stated it clearly on multiple occasions.

"I wish I had been better at asking questions this morning, to discuss and learn more of your past." LaSierra tried to remain clear and consistent. "If I had known more about your persona, no, your soul, I would've understood your reaction in the field and, later, to the orders I gave." LaSierra's hands shook so badly, she pushed them between her knees to keep them still and out of sight.

Beth followed the trajectory of LaSierra's hands and then quickly looked away when they reached their goal. "You mean, when you knew of my tragic, orphan past, all was forgiven?" Beth's words were all the more cutting when spoken in such a soft, pensive tone.

"No. I meant that the way I *do* know you, or *feel you*, rather, should have been explanation enough. If I'd only... If..." LaSierra took a deep breath. "Your passion for saving lives, no matter whose life—I already sensed that. When I gave myself time to think...of course I understood."

Beth's blue eyes slowly lost some of their tension. "You really seem to want to understand," she murmured.

"I do. I know that my duties will not always mesh well with your pathos, and I'm willing to try to work through that problem, if you are." LaSierra's heart pounded so hard, she trembled.

"You mean, I shouldn't automatically think of you as someone ready to terminate another individual. Don't forget that I'm not some damn bleeding heart who hasn't made a single hard call in her life." Beth's matter-of-fact tone made her words almost unbearable. "Don't underestimate me." Beth's voice mellowed marginally. "Just see me, please, LaSierra. If that's what you want."

"It is." Nearly choking on her response, LaSierra dug her nails into the back of the couch. "It's exactly what I want," she said throatily. "If it's at all possible. If you'll allow it." LaSierra made herself stop talking. It was up to Beth now.

"I want to focus on how well you took care of me last night," Beth said slowly. "You were exhausted and cold, yet you put me first when I had nothing left to give."

"Because you had given it your all," LaSierra murmured. She carefully extended her hand and placed it on Beth's shoulder.

"I suppose." Beth put her hand on LaSierra's, where it lay on her shoulder, and for a shattering moment, LaSierra thought Beth meant to push it off. Instead, she took it in hers, raised it to her lips, and kissed it softly. "And you had pushed yourself beyond your limits, worrying us."

"For all of you, of course, but heartbreakingly so for you, Beth. I won't pretend there's not a difference."

"LaSierra," Beth whispered, and then she acted so quickly that LaSierra found herself half on Beth's lap, not sure how it happened. "You can always back off if this closeness is too much." Beth cupped LaSierra's cheeks.

"Not...not close enough..." LaSierra's heart was slamming painfully against her ribs. "I don't want to be anywhere else."

Beth pulled her closer and wrapped her arms around LaSierra's waist. "I know that so much is going on, and we simply don't have any time to talk about personal matters. And don't think that I believe that you suddenly had a gap in your schedule. You made time for me—us."

LaSierra was torn between feeling caught and relieved. "You're not wrong." She resisted for a few seconds but then buried her face into Beth's neck. "Can we just be like this for a little while?"

"Yes." Beth hummed under her breath, moving her hands in gentle circles against LaSierra's back. "I have an uncooperative mind, though. You might as well know that about me too. When you're around, and even when you aren't, my mind thinks up, eh, scenarios."

LaSierra chuckled quietly, and an entire new type of heat erupted in the lower part of her abdomen. "I want to know more about this subject. What kind of scenarios?"

"Creator. You know. Things." Beth trembled. "I'm not very experienced when it comes to—things—but I've read about some stuff."

"What 'stuff,' exactly?" LaSierra didn't know if she should ask, as it was like putting Beth on the spot—again—but she was uncharacteristically dying to know. Perhaps this was merely part of her truly wanting to know everything about Beth.

"Kae collects old books. You know, written on paper and glued together. There were quite a few about people falling in love and having a lot of sex. It was strange, though. They fought throughout the book but kept growing closer and closer, and finally they tore it up in bed together. Isn't that kind of strange—" Beth stopped talking, and then she said, "Oh."

LaSierra wanted to meet Beth's eyes, but she could feel how hot her cheeks were, and she was also torn between hysterical laughter and arousal. Then she realized what Beth's "oh" was in reference to. "Oh."

"Right? Isn't that a kick in the gut?" Beth gasped and combed through LaSierra's hair with her fingers. "It could have been us in one of those old books—minus the sex—yet."

"That's one way of putting it." LaSierra had to sit up, as she needed to see Beth's expression. She pushed against the couch, rather than Beth, and pulled back enough to study her face. "Are you making comparisons?"

"I would never be so presumptuous, but I suppose the authors of such books must have seen that kind of, well, scenario happen. Even lived it?" Beth ran gentle fingertips along LaSierra's check. "It made me wish for something more than what I was offered in the tunnels, though. Something, I don't know. Deeper? Not necessarily lasting, as we do live in dangerous times, but something worth risking it all for." She pressed her lips together.

"Like how you risk your life on a daily basis for your people?" LaSierra felt her lips grow fuller, as if need in itself could have this effect on her physically. She was probably a lot more experienced than Beth, but she hadn't indulged in years.

"Maybe. But not quite." Beth didn't take her eyes off LaSierra. "I was talking about risking one's heart and soul, which I imagine is the same as risking one's life."

"You're right. Of course." LaSierra wanted to stop Beth before she took the conversation about hearts and souls too far. She knew she wouldn't be able to keep the last shred of distance from Beth then. Considering their circumstances, perhaps it was already too late. Weren't their strong reactions, their almost over-the-top pain this morning just another side of the heart-and-soul coin? LaSierra detested feeling confused and unfocused. She meant to withdraw and return the conversation to a more constructive way of addressing each other. Instead, she asked, "Please. May I kiss you?"

Beth framed LaSierra's face with her warm, trembling hands. She leaned in and brushed her lips across LaSierra's, over and over. Again, she hummed, and eventually, she parted her lips but didn't go beyond that.

The next move was clearly up to LaSierra. Pushing her tongue into Beth's mouth, LaSierra deepened the kiss and reveled in the taste and feel of Beth's lips and mouth. She changed angles, and it was her turn to push her fingers into Beth's hair. Keeping her in place, LaSierra whimpered as she felt herself run out of oxygen—breathing through her nose was no longer enough. She pulled back but kept the caresses going and brushed Beth's now-swollen lips with her own, making the kisses gentle.

"Damn it, woman..." Beth moaned. "That—nobody's kissed me like that. Ever."

"Nobody has ever been as responsive as you. And I freely admit I have been on my own in every sense of the word, for a very long time." LaSierra ran her thumb along Beth's lower lip. "You are truly an anomaly in my life. A beautiful, amazing anomaly that I find impossible to stay away from. Physically, and emotionally. Like you said—heart and soul?"

Beth rolled her eyes. "I did say that, didn't I?" She kissed a path between LaSierra's lips, along her jawline, and down to her neck. "Please overlook my weird sense of romance."

"Is that what you're doing?" LaSierra asked. "Are you romancing me, Beth?"

Beth blushed. "I...do you mind?" She didn't let go of LaSierra, but she appeared guarded.

There could be only one answer. "Not at all, Beth. Not for a moment." She kissed Beth again, murmuring something even she found incoherent against Beth's lips.

And then both their GemLinks gave an alert neither of them had heard before. LaSierra still held onto Beth as she looked at her arm. "We have unknown individuals at the eastern part of the perimeter. I have to be in HQ, and you have your duties, darling."

Beth nodded and stood with LaSierra in her arms. She helped her over to her AirFrame. "Will you be all right? I have to run."

"Of course." LaSierra put her hand on Beth's arms. "Be safe."

Beth pressed her lips hard to LaSierra's in lieu of an answer.

And then she hurried into her bedroom, where she kept her gear. LaSierra turned to reenter the HQ—and before her mind was completely focused on the matter at hand, she wondered if it was right that she just called Beth "darling."

Chapter Twenty-seven

Kae had put on her safety vest and helmet but didn't feel she had time to pull on her suit all the way, merely stuck her legs in and tied the sleeves around her waist. She wore her weapons' harness slung over her shoulder and held her Nova blaster in her right hand as she ran toward the east perimeter. Civilians had already begun to gather in the other parts of the camp, to be as far from potential battle as possible.

She spotted Benny by her side, and while she carried several weapons, he had his computer console and scanner attached to his back.

"Why didn't these fools show up on our proximity scanner, and how the fuck did they find us?" Kae snarled. "This location has been foolproof against drones and shuttles for weeks."

"I have a theory, but there's no point in telling you until I know for sure. Until I do, keep yourself safe, Kae." Benny was joined by two women with computers strapped to them as well. "Good. I'm going to need all the power available to find out what's going on."

"Kae!" Beth caught up with her. "Are we being attacked?"

"Not yet, but it's probably just a matter of time. LaSierra back in HQ?" Kae rounded a large tree and then began to climb the ridge that circled the camp on three sides.

"She is. I saw the Garcias there with her, along with a few of the other older senior members. The operatives were punching in commands so fast, it was a blur."

"Good. We're going to need all the intel they can bring us."

"Hi, Benny. Glad you're doing so much better." Beth punched Benny in the shoulder and nearly knocked him off course. "Sorry!"

"I'm all right." Benny had his eyes on the transparent, hovering AirScreen. "Better not trip me though."

Kae was the first to reach the top, followed by Beth, London, and, a few seconds later, Foster and Benny.

"Stay low," Kae hissed as she finally had time to put on her suit properly and adjust her harness. "Benny. Run your scans."

"I can't see...wait...over there?" Beth pointed to the left, slightly northeast. "Are those...surely it can't be. Rows of people?" She gaped.

"It looks like it." Kae engaged her helmet and deployed the radar feature. "I'm getting a lot of disturbance from the sensors along the perimeter. Wait." She adjusted the settings like Rocque taught her and winced when she suddenly saw an image that reminded her of ancient X-ray plates. "Damn. There are so many of them. I see only pale outlines, but I would estimate at least two hundred souls are out there. Where the hell did they come from, and how could they get so close without the alerts going off until they're practically at our doorstep?"

"Kae, I'll have it soon. Just wait." Benny sighed.

"Are you crazy? Wait until they attack?" Kae smacked her palm onto the ground.

"LaSierra to Kae. Report." LaSierra's voice held its usual stern and dispassionate undertone.

"Kae here. We're at the perimeter, and scans show at least two hundred individuals among the shrubs and trees. They're staying still and not making a sound." Kae forced herself to breathe evenly. "What can you see from the HQ?"

"About what you see, but I think you may be able to observe the scene in greater detail." LaSierra paused. "Is Benny there yet?"

"He's keeping up with us and running his scans with two of his subordinates."

"Ms. Delmonte," Benny said, standing closer to Kae. "I'm transmitting to your main screen. You will see what we see."

"Thank you. Use your best judgment, Kae. I want you and London to head this up. If you disagree about something vital, page me."

"Yes, sir." Kae used her visor to zoom in among the trees and shrubs, even if the procedure made the image blurrier. "There. Can they be more runaway refugees? Too many of them to be guards from the compound. This isn't them."

"Hang on. Getting signals with identity signatures." Benny tapped so fast on his own computer, Kae couldn't keep up.

"Signatures?" London asked as he joined them. He stood on Kae's other side. He nodded at Foster and Beth. "Only Celestials have signatures around here."

"So, it's either Celestial soldiers or law enforcement?" Kae frowned. "But why are they standing still in the middle of the woods? Why aren't they calling in an air strike and plowing through the perimeter?" She couldn't figure it out.

London shook his head. "I can't tell you, but I—" He stopped and swiveled toward Benny. "Hey. Signatures."

"What kind of signatures?"

Benny smiled. "Old ones. *Really* old ones. At least ten or twelve years old." He nodded rapidly. "Yes, sir. I think they're in a holding pattern, so to speak, waiting for us to figure it out—or not."

London turned to Kae. "If this is what Benny and I think—what we hope—we need to send a field team to find out."

"A field team into a two-hundred-strong potential enemy force?" Kae stared at London. The man had lost his mind.

"Benny, you explain. You do it better." London began to close his suit, clearly preparing to go.

"The fact that they carry signatures that are more than a decade old shows that none of them is a current Celestial soldier. If they are who I think, these are part of the rogue company that left the northern part of Eastern Seaboard City almost twelve years ago."

"You mean, like deserters?" Kae frowned and exchanged a glance with Foster and Beth.

"I suppose, technically. They were called the Ghost Pack, and they defected. Of course, from the Celestial authorities' point of view, they were indeed deserters. I can only say that if they hadn't, the mission they were meant to carry out would have decimated the northern tunnel system by more than fifty percent. Thousands of Subterraneans would have died—or wished they had." Benny shuddered. "In the dissident movement, the Ghost Pack is stuff legends are made of."

Kae studied London and Benny. "Well, if this doesn't qualify as a reason to call the boss, then I don't know what does." She held up her hand. "And before you get too excited, I'll do it. I need to hear this story corroborated by LaSierra and the Garcias, without the two of you acting as if you'd met your favorite celebrity." She engaged her GemLink with a privacy setting that would transmit to her helmet only. "Kae to Delmonte and Garcia."

"LaSierra here. That was fast, Kae."

"We have an interesting development. What can you tell me about the Ghost Pack?"

"What—?" LaSierra's stunned tone told Kae that she had taken their leader by surprise. "The Ghost Pack. The military unit that disappeared off the face of the Earth to avoid carrying out a massacre of thousands?"

"Are they...why are you asking us this, Kae?" Madelon also sounded stunned. "Are these people outside the perimeter—is it them?"

"We haven't confirmed it." But at least Kae knew now that the Ghost Pack had been real, and even if the story of their bravery had become a legend blown out of proportions, obviously everyone in charge seemed to know about them. "Benny will send his intel now."

"We have it. Stand by." LaSierra spoke fast.

Kae tapped her foot as they waited. She could only imagine the frenzy that had broken out at the HQ at the idea that potential allies might be at their doorstep.

❖

As soon as Kae turned to her, Beth knew that she and Foster would be going. She also knew why Kae, as the leader of the military unit—at least so far—intended to stay back just inside the perimeter. London was joining her and Foster, as was one of the soldiers that had accompanied them on their very first field mission.

Kae stood fuming next to them. "I should go. Beth, you've been through the wringer worse than Foster and I have."

"But you can't." Beth patted Kae's shoulder. "Calm down. Foster and I have Benny's and each other's back, and London's... and what is your name again? Grass? Or Glass?" She looked at the younger dissident soldier.

"Brass, sir," the young man said. "And it goes both ways. If the people on the other side are not who we think they are, or if something else goes south, we have *your* back." He was obviously not being flippant.

"See?" Beth smiled. "What might get tricky after we get back...LaSierra won't be thrilled. She thinks I'm fragile."

Kae studied Beth. "Not per se, but when it comes to her, perhaps there's some truth to it."

"Creator, save me from all this lovey-dovey stuff going on." Foster groaned, but Beth could tell he was only half serious.

"Captain London is in charge, but if *any* of you sound the alarm, we'll all cross the perimeter and come to your aid." Kae looked at them pointedly. "Keep an open channel to me."

As they crossed the perimeter, London took up the rear. Walking next to Benny, Beth saw how he kept working and was impressed with his multitasking abilities. He had calculated that the dense group of people was located three hundred and forty yards into the wooded area.

"Any signs of sentries or stragglers?" Beth leaned in as if she knew how to read his tablet where data ran like water along it.

"Not yet, but that's not to say that there aren't any. They could be masking their signatures. If I know how to do it, they could have some tech savvy person who does too." Benny kept closer to Beth. "Don't let me stumble. I'm used to doing this working-and-walking thing on smooth floors."

"I'll keep an eye on you," Beth said. "You're too valuable in all kinds of ways to walk straight into a tree."

When they had followed the tree line for about fifty yards, London took a sharp right, and they began pushing through the dense, low vegetation. Beth used every feature on her visor that she could think of, but she still saw only the initial figures. "I'm reading the first contacts at the two-hundred-and-fifty-yard mark," she said. "What do you have, Benny?"

"Two hundred and forty-seven. So that's accurate enough."

They pushed twigs and branches aside, and Beth was grateful for the helmet when London accidentally let go of a branch that hit her in the head.

"Hey, Captain. None of that," Beth muttered.

"Sorry, Beth. It slipped out of my hand." London turned and made an apologetic gesture.

"Hm. All right." Beth was about to tease him about retaliation, when she saw a shadow to her left. "Contact!" She ducked and pushed Benny behind her. "Ten o'clock, London."

Behind them, Brass and Foster were pressing their backs to the nearest trees. "Get behind something, Beth," Foster said.

A large boulder, big enough to hide behind, was located two yards to their right, but that would mean stepping toward the figure she'd seen.

"You sure, Beth? I'm not reading anything," London said, but then a tall, dark figure showed up from behind one of the trees Beth had been eyeing. Of course. If it provided protection for them, it would perform double duty for the sentry on guard.

Dressed in a black, tattered uniform, the person aimed at Beth with an older type of Nova blaster. In fact, it resembled Beth's old Glimmer rather than a high-end Nova.

London, Foster, and Brass had their weapons trained on the uniformed individual. Beth had never seen a uniform like that among the Celestials. As she was the only one who wasn't aiming a weapon at the soldier, Beth decided it was up to her to open her mouth.

"We're here to reconnoiter and also to greet you." She spoke slowly, succinctly. "My name's Beth. I'm Subterranean. Who are you?"

The person facing off with them must have realized that they were temporarily outnumbered. Pulling off their helmet, they turned out to be a woman, perhaps in her forties.

"My name's Anya Quinn, Sergeant Major of the North Command. The Ghost Pack."

Benny breathed twice as fast as normal. "I knew it!" he whispered.

"I'm Captain London, Celestial Dissident Corps." London lowered his weapon, but like Foster's and Brass's, the safety was still off. Beth was sure the same went for Sergeant Major Quinn's weapon.

"We saw your unit on our sensors," Beth said. "Why have you come?"

"That should be obvious." Anya made a dismissive gesture with her free hand. "We have come to join your military and take down the criminally corrupt government."

"Join us? How do you even know about us?" Beth asked, exchanging a glance with London.

"We have eyes and ears all over the Eastern Coastal City. We get reports frequently." Sergeant Major Quinn pushed her fingers through her short-cropped, dark-red hair. "Just point to where we can set up camp within the perimeters. The sooner the better. Our signals can be dampened, but eventually the enemy will find us, as we're a sizable party. Two hundred and eighteen, to be exact."

"As you didn't make yourself known and identify yourself," London said, "I'm going to assume that you are aware about the virtue of radio silence outside of the perimeter."

"For a long time. When we learned that a vast group of traitors, as in dissidents, had escaped from one of the largest towers, I figured Delmonte had pulled the plug."

"You know Ms. Delmonte?" Foster asked, his voice harsh. He didn't give any other information away but merely studied Sergeant Major Quinn closely.

"Never met the woman, but my contacts within the resistance let me know that Delmonte is in charge. Is this still the case?"

Beth exchanged a glance with London. He nodded slowly.

"We want to bring you into the fold, but this is a dangerous undertaking, Sergeant Major," Beth said. "To allow two hundred-some people, all armed, I imagine, into our camp could easily backfire as we know nothing about your intentions."

"Beth's right," London said somberly. "We can take, let's say, ten or fifteen of you back with us for debriefing. In the meantime, our people will help extend the perimeter and provide you with the same shelter. That would give you a space of your own, until Delmonte and the senior officers have finished debriefing you."

Quinn looked hesitant. "A space with a perimeter such as yours," she said slowly. "Why does my mind immediately think 'internment'?"

"You wouldn't be able to enter the main camp, per se, and you would be under the command of Ms. Delmonte and the Dissident Core. You would have access to food, healthcare, etc. I assume you've brought some sort of tents or habitats with you?" London didn't take his eyes off the weathered woman before him.

"We have."

"Great. Until we can provide you with the better equipped habitats, that would have to suffice." London motioned in the direction of Quinn's people. "Why don't you pick the ten people you want to bring? Time is of the essence."

Quinn merely nodded. "Understood, sir."

Beth figured that London outranked her and her followers since he held the rank of captain. "I also want to point out that

Foster and I outrank you too." If Quinn hid a desire to be in complete command, she was in for a surprise. "Just to clarify things before we continue."

"Really? Well, then, thank you for bringing that fact to my attention, sir. I'll be right back with some of my subordinates." She motioned at her people to follow her, and they disappeared into the dense vegetation.

Beth watched them leave. "I think she's the real deal when it comes to being in the military, but I'm not convinced—yet—that her loyalty lies with the dissidents. She may have saved lives when she refused to commit mass murder, but she could have stood on principle, rather than caring about Subterraneans specifically. I don't envy the ones ultimately in charge of this balancing act."

"Me either," London said. "I think you need to warn Kae that we're heading back soon and about who we're bringing."

"Oh, I will. Nobody's going to blindside us if we can help it, London." Beth gave him her version of a friendly shoulder punch.

"So, you can punch, but I can't? Completely unfair." Foster huffed.

"There's a difference," Beth said as she pulled out her communication device that translated letters into clicks, and vice versa. "When *I* do it, people generally don't need an artificial shoulder inserted." She smiled angelically at him. A glance back at London made her smile as he stealthily rolled his shoulder. "Ah, don't mind us. We have a habit of joking around at the most inappropriate moments. You know. Safety valves."

Half listening to Foster explaining what a safety valve was, Beth typed the first field team note to Kae.

FT: Made contact. Sergeant Major Anya Quinn in command.
KD: Friend? Foe?
FT: Remains to be seen. Seems legit at first sight.
KD: Strategy?
FT: Bringing AQ to camp with 9 subordinates. Rest of unit still stationary. London suggests they get their own camp and share resources.

KD: Reaction?
FT: Talked about "internment" but not uninterested.
KD: Proceed. Use caution. Watch your back. Brass is here at a safe distance.

Beth groaned. Anya Quinn was a hardened soldier who, much like Kae, Beth, and Foster, didn't have much good to say about high-ranking civilians, and particularly not politicians. LaSierra and the Garcias could be considered both. The fact that they were brave and did their best to free anyone oppressed by the criminally corrupt Celestials might get lost in translation. Beth typed an affirmative answer to Kae and then shut down the piece of technology just as Anya returned with five men and four women, all looking as battle hardened as she did.

"Before you ask, let me assure you that we come unarmed," Quinn said calmly. "Trust me, it violates everything I've ever learned or taught, but I realize it's how it has to be—for now."

Reluctantly impressed, Beth thought back to when she and her team entered the skyscraper clinic with a dying Wes and held everyone at gunpoint. That would not have been the right time to trust someone. Perhaps this encounter was truly different that way.

"All right," London said quickly. "I'm taking the lead. Beth, you and Sergeant Major Quinn walk behind me, and Foster and Brass flank the rest. Let's move out."

Beth motioned with her chin for Quinn to join her. "It's not far, as I'm sure you know."

"We have some idea, but we didn't want to risk sending scouts to reconnoiter, as we figured you have access to sensors that are twelve years more advanced than what we are used to."

"Clever." Beth nodded. She carried her Nova blaster in a deceptively relaxed position, but the safety was off, and she was ready to engage if things went south. Quinn's glance at the blaster didn't escape her. It felt like a weird sort of "I know that you know that I know" situation.

As soon as they were within sight of the dissident soldiers at the perimeter around the camp, at least twenty of them filed out and flanked the team and the newcomers. Kae stood just inside the perimeter, her Nova blaster ready but not directed right at them.

"Quite the turnout," Quinn said under her breath. "I feel so welcome."

"If you are who you say you are, and if you're ready to fight beside us, you will be." Beth motioned for Quinn to move in behind London. "Go ahead." Behind them, Foster and Brass walked through with the nine Ghost Pack soldiers between them.

"Welcome to our camp," Kae said. She hoisted her blaster and extended her hand to Quinn. "My name's Kae Dark."

"Sergeant Major Anya Quinn, commanding officer of the Ghost Pack." Quinn hesitated for a moment but then shook hands. "These are some of my subordinates. My next-in-command is back in the woods with the troops."

"You are safe and will be well cared for during your stay. Our leaders are waiting to talk to you. We realize there's a time crunch when it comes to making a decision." Kae started walking, and Beth followed. She, together with London, had the group's first impression of Quinn, and they needed to share that.

They didn't end up in the HQ, and Beth realized that LaSierra and the Garcias were reluctant to bring someone able to read the screens and understand the data only too well into the heart of the camp. Instead, they used part of the large tent where the refugees had first been placed. Some of them were in the hospital, others in newly erected habitats, and the rest occupied about twenty-five percent of the tent. Cordoning them off provided space for a makeshift conference table.

"Please, have a seat," Kae said and motioned toward the chairs.

Quinn sat down, and her people did the same on chairs right behind her. Beth, Kae, Foster, and London also pulled out chairs, and Beth admitted it was nice to sit down. She hadn't recuperated entirely after rescuing Hunter. Three dissident soldiers served as security inside the tent, and Beth knew ten times as many did the same outside.

A tent flap opened, and LaSierra came in. Beth gaped. She was not in her chair but walking with a cane. Her head held high, she looked regal, even if she limped. Rocque walked to her right and Madelon on her left. Behind them, four other senior officers joined them.

"This is an interesting development," LaSierra said after sitting down. "I'm LaSierra—"

"Delmonte. I'm familiar with you. Even before we left, we heard of a woman who had taken over the entire dissident movement." Quinn crossed her legs and leaned back. "I believe you are flanked by the quite-famous Garcias?"

LaSierra's expression went from reasonably polite to cold in a fraction of a second.

"You have me at an advantage…" She narrowed her eyes as she let her gaze probe Quinn. "Sergeant Major."

"Anya Quinn."

"Ah. Yes." Turning to Madelon, LaSierra tilted her head. "We have quite the file on Quinn, don't we, Madelon?"

"That's correct, Ms. Delmonte," Madelon said, addressing LaSierra formally. "All her old army records, up till the desertion."

"We did not desert!" Quinn sat up straight and uncrossed her legs. "We refused to commit mass murder on the orders of the fucking authorities, and then it was up to me to save lives!"

"You'll get your chance to explain, Quinn," LaSierra said softly. "I'm sure there is more to your story than the official records tell. I have the statements made to my people by allies to our movement. Carry on." She flicked her hand and had the expression of casual disdain that had driven Beth crazy in the beginning. Now she knew it was LaSierra's go-to way of keeping the person in her searchlight slightly off their axis.

"You have heard of us in great detail. Seems your…uhm… allies are very loyal to you. That fits." Quinn seemed only marginally rattled. "Then you know of the order I received. My corporal was dead, and I obviously had no time to find us so much as a second lieutenant. I was placed in command and given the order to place barrels containing a substance that was supposedly incendiary and poisonous in every major hub in the northern tunnel system. Each barrel was equipped with explosives. I wasn't going to be the one pressing the sensor to set them all off. That was someone else's duty."

"What happened to the barrels?" Foster asked darkly.

For the first time, Quinn's shoulders slumped. It took her only a couple of seconds to regroup, but her entire demeanor spoke of something horrible as she gazed around the table.

"I gave the orders to gather the barrels and place them on one of the flatbeds on the tracks in the tunnels. I, along with some of the people behind me, managed to start the propulsion of the flatbed and drove it farther north. We weren't sure how long we had, minutes, hours?" She shrugged. "We pushed that flatbed to the limits. Once we were out of range of the tunnels—or at least we thought we were—we knew there were old mines in that area. Some of the others in my company had been there and blasted through from the tunnel system and into the bedrock where the mines stretched far. We hoped it would be enough." Quinn quieted, and everyone sat in silence, giving her time.

LaSierra exchanged a glance with Beth, an obvious question in her eyes. 'Do you believe her?' Beth nodded slowly, mouthing, 'So far.'

"We got out of there. Most of us. I lost twenty-six of my soldiers that day. If my next in command, Corporal Zhang, hadn't dragged me out of there, I wouldn't be here today. I was determined to be the last out, but Zhang had other ideas." Quinn looked behind her at a woman of Asian origins, who calmly returned her gaze under raised eyebrows. "I estimate that this area around the mines is still unhabitable and don't recommend a visit. The explosion was one for the ages."

"I received reports about that explosion," Rocque said. "The authorities claimed a massive sinkhole had suddenly opened up in the northern part of the Eastern Coastal City, and that the area wasn't safe and could collapse at any time. The timing fits."

"I'm sorry for your loss." Madelon had been working on a portable AirScreen computer. "How have you stayed alive—and away from the authorities for this long?"

"We crossed the old border." Quinn seemed to hesitate. "I can't share exactly where we went, but we found ways to build a new community. We have made a good life for ourselves. It took us a while to settle into it, as we all left family and friends behind. You must be able to relate. You're protective of this new camp full of dissidents…" Quinn turned and glanced over at Kae, Beth, and Foster. "…and Subterraneans."

"And yet you all came here?" LaSierra frowned, more in confusion, Beth guessed, than annoyance.

Quinn looked surprised. "This isn't all of us. This is what is left of my company, after twelve years. They all voted to come to help in your fight against the oppressors. The rest of our community are back home."

This piece of news took the senior staff completely by surprise. "You mean," Madelon said slowly, "that you your community, wherever it is, has grown that much since you, eh, defected?"

"We are a thriving democracy, so yes. That's what I mean." Quinn's eyes narrowed. "My community is not why we're here. We're here to help right a long, ongoing wrong. If you can't accept that offer and meet us halfway, then my company and I risked our lives and came in vain."

LaSierra nodded slowly. "I see."

Beth watched LaSierra as she appeared lost in thought for so long that the others began looking at each other in confusion. Eventually Madelon touched LaSierra's shoulder lightly.

"Ms. Delmonte?"

Blinking slowly, LaSierra appeared to return to the present. "I think you've given us more than enough to earn the benefit of the doubt. We will erect a perimeter with the same security settings to cover your presence as we enjoy here. You may rest until tomorrow—I expect you'll need it. We can offer food and also medical attention if anyone needs it." LaSierra shifted her gaze to the ones behind Quinn. "You in the back, Corporal Zhang and those next to you. Do you have anything to add?"

Corporal Zhang rose, and even if she wasn't very tall, her compact form appeared strong. "Ms. Delmonte. We second everything Sergeant Major Quinn has told you. We all voted unanimously to return to help fight corruption and attempts at genocide."

Beth drew a deep, tormented breath. Genocide. Against her people. Against the Subterraneans.

"I have a question." Kae sounded casual, but Beth knew this was her friend at her most dangerous. "Why? You have your lovely new community where you seem to thrive and be away from all the hardships of being asked to do horrible things, and you don't have to live in the tunnels either. So why?"

Zhang looked at a young woman at the far end of the row of Ghost Pack soldiers. "Why don't you introduce yourself and answer Ms. Dark."

The woman stood. Her blond hair was pulled into a firm braid. If Zhang was short and compact, this woman was short and slender. "My name's Private Bree Guthier. I'm twenty-six years old. I was brand new in the company, with only six weeks in, when the orders came." She stood straight and looked right at Kae. "Together with thirty new recruits, I hoped that by joining the military, I would find a way to earn my right to attend college. I wanted to become a doctor. I'm an orphan, and my prospects were the army or perhaps even one of the rescue camps. Anyway, when the order came to place the barrels in the important junctions in the tunnels, Seargent Major Quinn gathered us all in the barrack floor and informed us. She gave us a choice. Everyone but five agreed that the time had come to pull out. It was an easy choice for me, even if I lost the path to higher studies, but I had no family that would miss me. Those who balked at the idea were all young, like me, and did have living parents." She swallowed hard. "I heard from the older soldiers in the company that they had participated in a lot of things that went against their grain, but mass murder, bordering on genocide such as this, would spread throughout the tunnel system and keep killing even if it were at a slower rate... they just couldn't do it."

"Go on," Kae said softly.

"So, we did just what Sarge…I mean, Sergeant Major Quinn said. "We shoved them into the old mines and hoped they'd be contained. I think six of the new recruits, like me, died."

"All right. Thank you." Kae turned to Quinn. "And yet, my question remains. You already did your heroic part. Why are you here now?"

Quinn stood and moved to stand next to Private Guthier. "Because before the day we defected, we had been part of too many missions that 'went against the grain.' Look at it as atonement. Or a bid for all of our future. We've been managing to remain safe for twelve years, but that doesn't mean that the Celestial authorities can't find us in a week, a month, or a year from now. But mostly we're here because it's the right thing to do."

Kae looked at Beth and then Foster. "All right," she said. "That's a good-enough answer for me."

"For me as well. Let's get your people over here, Sergeant Major. Near our camp on the west side, where it's easier to hide among the vegetation. My people will have started the perimeter once you get back here. Until it's finished, I suggest you place sentries to safeguard your soldiers while they make camp. I also suggest you make a list of the bare necessities you might require, and we'll do our best to accommodate you." LaSierra stared around the room, and Beth recognized the look in her eyes. She was plotting new solutions and tactical approaches. LaSierra wouldn't let this golden opportunity slip through her fingers. "Very well. We all have work to do. Dismissed." LaSierra stood and leaned heavily on her cane. Rocque offered her his arm, and she took it after a brief hesitation.

Beth turned to Kae. "Guess we're going back to the woods with Quinn?"

"We are, but not you. I want you to be LaSierra's aide-de-camp the rest of the day. She overdid right now, to not show any signs of weakness, but that means she can crash at any time—and now I just realized I don't have to persuade you." She smiled crookedly. "Go find your lady and make sure she's all right. I know Rayne will want to scan the newcomers—at least the ones that gain access to our camp, which means she's going to be busy and won't be able to help harness LaSierra."

"Got it. It's not that she needs anyone to tell her what to do, but she might require a subtle nudge to remember her medication." Beth smiled and felt her cheeks warm.

"Slight nudge, my ass." Kae snorted. "The way I see it, either you shove the pill down her throat, or you bribe her with a kiss... either of those two."

Gasping at Kae's words, Beth then had to laugh. "You spend too much time with...well, with me. That's something I would say."

"I know. Scary." Exaggerating a shudder, Kae bumped her fist against Beth's shoulder and then moved over to Quinn and her people.

Beth went to find LaSierra.

CHAPTER TWENTY-EIGHT

LaSierra sat in the center of her habitat living area, clinging to the armrests of her AirFrame. Beth was over at the hospital fetching more of her medication, and LaSierra was sure that she was bringing some of the strong infulizer vials with her back. Granted, it was perhaps not the worst idea in the world.

Checking the time, LaSierra was shocked to find that it was midnight. She had been active for twelve hours straight, which she would have considered a normal workday in the skyscraper, but out here, with her healing injuries, it was a lot.

She was still proud of how she had walked into the meeting earlier in the day. Having been able to display her unbending persona in the meeting had been vital—at least in the beginning. The statements by Quinn and her subordinates had not failed to move anyone present, including her.

"I'm back," Beth said as she hurried through the door. She locked it behind her and then placed a case full of medication on the table.

"Are you going to sedate me for a month?" LaSierra moved her chair forward and peered into the case. "Infulizers, medical kits, capsules, and, what's that? An assortment of wands?"

"Yes. One of the nurses wanted you to have access to this without having to replenish your meds so often. Especially now that we have more people to tend to. The replication of some of your stuff is a lengthy procedure, and we can't have our intrepid leader—"

"Your what? Intrepid leader? People actually say that?" Groaning, LaSierra covered her eyes.

"Well. Not *people*, exactly. More the Garcias, Kae, Foster, and I. And some of the kids that have picked up on it." Beth smiled angelically. "So—not people."

"Dear Creator. Anyway, so this is just in case I need it? Rayne hasn't suddenly gone mad and thrown everything available in the medicine cabinet at me?"

Beth snorted. "Of course not. Speaking of Rayne, she's still in the new camp, and Kae went to find her. I think she plans to drag her home even if she's not done scanning people."

"I can understand that she needs to be thorough. They can have illnesses or injuries that we have to know about immediately." LaSierra reached into the case and pulled out her usual capsules. "I'll have two of these. That's enough—" She caught Beth's frown. "What?"

"You promised Rayne you'd have half an infulizer of the good stuff since you were walking today. I mean, I'm so proud of you for doing that, but it takes a toll."

"You heard her, I take it." Caught, LaSierra waved her hand at the case. "Be my guest."

"You sound like you think I enjoy drugging you." Beth shook her head. "And here I am, biding my time."

LaSierra had pulled out a tube of water from her armrest but now stopped moving. "Biding your time?" She frowned. What was Beth talking about?

Beth's fair complexion grew pink. "Eh. You know. Waiting. Reasonably patiently." She fiddled with the infulizer. "For you to get better."

"I understand that. But what are you biding your time for, exactly?" LaSierra wasn't a fool, but she needed to hear it from Beth. Perhaps it was the wrong time, as it was midnight, and they were both tired, but could they dare to postpone *anything* at all? Could she afford to let Beth go on her next field mission without having told her at least some of how she felt?

Beth had loaded the infulizer and wiggled it in front of LaSierra. "Take this, and I'll tell you." She winked.

LaSierra had to smile. "Bribes. I don't mind them as much as I should." She extended her arm, and Beth pressed the narrow nozzle against the crease of it. The medication stung, but she simply kept her eyes on Beth, wondering how she could have endured so many years without those blue eyes in her life. "Darling?" LaSierra heard the word leave her lips and didn't mind it.

"Yes?" Beth whispered. She looked uncharacteristically vulnerable, as if she weren't sure what to expect from LaSierra.

"Do you realize how much you mean to me?" LaSierra unfastened her harness that kept her safe in the chair.

"No. I mean, perhaps. Or I hoped you'd see how much you mean to me." Beth meticulously put away the infulizer and closed the medical case. Then she startled LaSierra by swiveling and falling to her knees next to the AirFrame. "Are you saying you... you might care for me—I mean, truly care?" She placed her hands on LaSierra's lower right arm, looking up at her.

"Beth. Get up from the floor, and if you're not too tired, carry me into our room." LaSierra tilted her head. "If you want." She had to stop sounding as if she was giving orders. At least in their habitat. The only space that was just theirs.

"I'm never too tired for that." Beth stood in one fluid movement. She lifted LaSierra and carried her into the bedroom, but when she was just inside the doorway, she stopped.

"What's wrong?" LaSierra asked.

"Nothing. It's just...you said *our* bedroom. Not yours. Ours." Beth began to move again and placed LaSierra on her side of the bed.

Her side. Their bedroom. The terms clearly had moved stealthily into her mind. LaSierra pulled Beth down to sit beside her. "Yes. Our bedroom. You've slept in here most nights lately. It's been both a blessing and a curse."

"A curse?" Beth frowned. "Do I snore or something?"

"No." LaSierra raised her hand and pushed the wild blond hair from Beth's forehead. "What's Beth short for?"

"Elizabeth. My full name is Elizabeth Kelly." Beth took LaSierra's wandering hand and kissed her palm. "Curse?" she reminded LaSierra softly.

"Because for the same reason that you have been biding your time—I have been biding mine. To have you so close and not be able to ask permission to make love to you. That's like a curse. But a sweet one."

Beth drew a trembling breath. "Yes. Exactly like that. I've been awake too, my mind racing with all these thoughts—and some of them have been really stressful."

"Explain." Alarmed, LaSierra leaned against Beth, who automatically put an arm around her.

"As I told you, I'm not very, you know, skilled at this sex thing. I'm no virgin, but I'm just not used to it being connected to…Fuck. To all these feelings!"

LaSierra pressed her face against Beth's neck. "You don't have to be any certain way, Beth. Don't you see? It's the fact that it's you…you who I've fallen for in a way that's never happened to me before. That's what matters. The way we've felt when we've kissed—that alone has done more for me than anything or anyone else."

"LaSierra…" Beth tipped LaSierra's head up with gentle fingers under her chin and kissed her. She didn't deepen the kiss, but the way she explored LaSierra's lips, pulling her close with hands that showed LaSierra such tenderness, made it easy to distinguish how Beth felt. The sweetness combined with restrained desire made it obvious.

"I'm grateful for your patience with my infuriatingly slow healing," LaSierra said huskily. "I'm an impatient type of woman, and all I want is to undress you right now. I want to show you in every way possible just how much I care…how much you mean to me. I know I've said and done things you don't agree with—"

"And I've hated what being in charge does to you when you have to make those decisions." Beth cupped LaSierra's cheeks. "I will always stand by you and have your back, even if we'll argue about some things until our neighbors start banging on the walls.

I don't care—I want to be with you. I want to come home to you after every field mission."

LaSierra pressed her lips to Beth's, a hard, emphatic kiss. "And you *will* come back to me after every single field mission. I don't want to hear about something happening to you."

"I will do my best to not get injured," Beth said, her eyes widening.

"I said I don't want to hear about that!" LaSierra tugged at Beth's shoulder, wanting her closer still.

"Hey. I'm here. You're here." Beth held her close and rocked her gently. "Why don't we hit the cleaning tube and then go to bed. I can be persuaded to sleep naked."

LaSierra pulled back enough to meet Beth's eyes. "You didn't just say that." She wasn't sure if Beth was joking or not.

"You think I'm not being serious?" Beth smiled broadly. "I dare you to reciprocate."

"Sleep in the nude. Next to you, the woman I dream of every night?" LaSierra groaned. "You're relentless."

"And you love it." Beth looked so pleased, LaSierra had to kiss her again.

"Yes," she said, caressing Beth's cheek. "I do love…it."

When Rayne turned around after scanning the last of Quinn's subordinates, she pressed a hand to the small of her back as she reached for her tablet. Making sure the wand had uploaded the information to the right individual, she said, "So, that leaves you, Sergeant Major." Quinn had insisted on going last.

"Thank you for doing this yourself, Dr. Garcia," Quinn said and stepped closer. "I would imagine that any one of your medics or junior doctors could have scanned us."

"That's what I tried to tell her," Kae said and stepped into the large tent. "At least brought some of them along to speed up the process."

"Hi." Rayne's entire body ached, but seeing Kae made her shoulders relax and her heart race for all the good reasons. "And I told you that I wanted to do this to get an overview—which would make it easier, and quicker, for me to draw conclusions about possible contagions, etc."

"And did you find any?" Kae asked.

"Let me scan the sergeant—"

"Please. Call me Quinn when we're not in an official setting," Quinn said and grimaced. "All these titles being thrown around— it's been a while since I lived in that world. We have a command structure, obviously, but off duty, we're just neighbors and friends." She sighed and rolled her shoulders. "I think you'll see some arthrosis in some of my joints, Doctor."

"Rayne. And this is Kae, as you know." Rayne ran the wand along Quinn, where she stood dressed in just her briefs and tank top. "Is it all right that Kae's here? I sometimes forget to ask as we're all over each other's business in the camp."

"It's fine." Quinn nodded.

"You're right about the arthrosis. I can't stop it from happening, but I can help heal it once it exacerbates. You won't have to suffer so much pain and discomfort. I can give you an infulizer with medication that you can easily administer yourself once a day. One infulizer vial should last you two weeks."

"You—you're not joking." Quinn looked stunned, which was unexpected, but perhaps not, when Rayne thought about it. For all she knew, the woman could have suffered in silence for years. She doubted Quinn was the type that told anyone about some health issue she suspected they could do nothing about. To hear from Rayne that something could be done to keep the pain and stiffness at bay had to be shocking.

"I—I was certain this was something I'd have to reconcile myself to. It's been this bad only the last two years." Quinn ran a hand along her face. "Damn."

"Damn indeed. I'm glad Rayne can help you. I know all your subordinates will get the same offer, should they need it." Kae turned to Rayne again. "So—contagions?"

"Just a few cases of the common cold, some upset stomachs, and one case of conjunctivitis. That was it. I gave all of them the first dose of three to deal with it. I'll send over a medic to administer the second dose tomorrow evening."

"Thank you," Quinn said and pulled on her dark uniform again. It was patched in places but was obviously Celestial. "Anything else than my sore joints?"

"You have a lot of scar tissue on your back. I can help you with that, if it hinders your full range of movement." She began closing her bags.

"Not yet, as I don't doubt that there'd be some rehabilitation required after that. But if the opportunity comes after we've done what we came here to do, we can discuss what it entails," Quinn said.

"You're right," Rayne said. "I'd have to perform some surgery, and even if the healing should be quick—physiotherapy is involved during the upcoming month."

Quinn grimaced. "I thought as much." After a brief pause, she continued. "I better go supervise the last of the perimeter going up. I admit I'm impressed how far technology has come in the last twelve years."

Rayne smiled. "This isn't the run-of-the-mill technology available in the skyscrapers. The dissident movement has come even further with a lot of new inventions, thanks to our tech-savvy young people. My mother tells me it has been one of their goals—outdoing the authorities in every way possible. They are superior in numbers, obviously, and in the way they've indoctrinated or intimidated most of the people."

Nodding slowly, Quinn seemed to agree. "We too have had an in-depth conversation about what could be done to move in on that part of Celestial warfare. Because that's what this has always been about. Declaring war against their own people to remain in power. Most Celestials just don't realize it."

"You usually don't, until the consequences hit you personally." Kae lifted Rayne's bags off the table.

"Like it did with me," Rayne said. "For me it started little by little in the Soldiers Clinic and ended when I chased Kae down a laundry chute."

Quinn's eyebrows went up. "A laundry chute?"

"It's true." Rayne chuckled. "It's quite the story. I might just tell you about it one day. Now, back to business, as it was. If you or your subordinates need medical assistance, guards will be on duty where your inner perimeter coincides with ours. They'll contact us. I'm not sure when GemLinks will be available for you. That's the Garcias' decision to make."

"Another piece of technology that I've never heard of." Quinn sighed but then shrugged. "I suppose I'll see at least one of you tomorrow. Good night."

Kae and Rayne said good night and then passed the gateway between the two camps.

"I can take one of the cases," Rayne offered, but then relented when Kae merely shook her head. "Or not."

They walked among the habitats and SkyBirds, listening to the dissidents talk among themselves over a meal or a beer—some even using electric fire pits, as real fire was prohibited for safety reasons. Not only could smoke not be contained and was clearly visible, but it was also hazardous, as they had "circled the wagons" densely. A fire could spread rapidly among them.

After a brief detour to the hospital, they went back to their habitat.

"I should have popped in to see my parents, but I'm too tired," Rayne said and stretched. Her hair fell down her back, and Kae realized it had grown at least an inch since the first time she saw her.

"We'll see them in the morning. I bet they're busy plotting and planning. Your mother's mind has been going at record speed these last few days. I think she's counseled LaSierra as well."

"Oh?" Rayne came out of her safety vest and then her scrubs. "How do you mean?"

"Well, LaSierra doesn't need much help when it comes to her duties as our leader, more regarding private matters. I think she's letting Beth in more, allowing for them to be, you know, closer." Feeling foolish for stumbling a little over her words, Kae pushed her hands into her pockets.

"Good thing we didn't need Mother's advice for letting each other in. That would've been awkward as hell." Rayne shuddered.

"I hear you." Able to free her hands now, Kae pulled Rayne into her arms, the fact that she stood there in only her white underwear making her irresistible. "How about a joint session in the cleansing tube? I bet we would fit."

"Hm. It'll be a tight squeeze," Rayne said, looking serious. "I wonder whether you want my back or my front pressed against you." She tilted her head, making her hair fall like golden silk over her left shoulder. "What do you say, Kaelyn Dark?"

Kae's mind stalled for a moment, and she couldn't take her eyes off Rayne. "I say…what I've wanted to say for a while now. I love you." Her abdomen trembled, but she wasn't truly nervous—not that way.

Rayne was a study in how many different expressions could pass over a person's face in a few seconds. Surprise, shock, happiness, tears.

"Rayne?"

"Oh, Kae. I love you very much." Rayne melted against Kae, who hadn't realized she'd forgotten to breathe and gasped for air.

They held each other, and Kae was content to stand like that for a long time, until she realized Rayne was shivering. "Time to get into the tube and then to bed." She eyed Rayne's serene expression and then lifted her in her arms. "Allow me, Doctor Garcia."

"Kae!" Smiling broadly, Rayne clung to Kae. "You have an unexpected romantic side that you hide very well."

"It must remain a secret. Foster would never let me live it down." Kae put Rayne down in the ensuite and helped her undress completely. She tore off her own clothes, and together they squeezed into the cleansing tube. As they stood there, in their own little world, watching the light change toward the completion of the cycle, Kae knew that no matter how the rest of their dangerous mission played out—they had this perfect moment. Nothing could take it away from them. Kae had always yearned to fight for the survival of her people. It had been, and still was, her top priority—her reason for living.

But now, with her arms around the woman she loved, Kae knew this too was her top priority, and also something deeply personal. They belonged together, and they would fight as one. A small voice added that she would take lives, and Rayne would keep saving them, but she silenced it. All she had to know was that her love was reciprocated, and judging from how Rayne clung to her, it seemed she was reluctant to let Kae go.

It was all right. They could always run a second cleaning cycle.

EPILOGUE

Max stood on wobbly legs. She truly had had enough of the hospital, no matter how kind the staff were and how much she appreciated them healing her so quickly. She had been admitted for a week now, and in her own opinion, she had never felt better. Not counting before she had left for the market with the pretty dolls her mother had made for them to sell.

That's when strangers, Celestials, came and snatched her and several other children that were walking just behind her, for the same reason. It had happened so fast, and when she thought of it, so had her rescue once she'd made her way into the dissident camp. Her action had also helped save the people hiding in the crop sancts, according to Beth.

But now, Max was ready to regain her strength and go find her people. She knew that all but two had survived the rescue operation, which was both impressive and yet so heartbreaking.

Tiptoeing out of the hospital, she knew that someone would eventually see traces in some computer log or other that she had left the hospital during the evening, but she didn't care. She hurried over the Inner Circle and then disappeared among the vessels the dissidents called SkyBirds. She was going to find where they kept her friends.

❖

Sergeant Major Anya Quinn stood by the perimeter, still, after two days, trying to fathom that they'd managed to locate the dissident Celestials and a few Subterraneans so far from home. She hadn't shared where exactly her own community was located, but it had been a two-week march through what could only be described as wasteland. They had walked twelve to fourteen hours a day and cooked and slept the rest of the time. Quinn calculated that they'd covered around 330 miles.

It was late in the evening, nearly midnight, but the plans hatched at today's meeting were still brewing in her mind, making it impossible to sleep. She gazed over the tents, far fewer of them now, and habitats, which had increased in numbers. Her people were slightly less wary of the welcome that was still tentatively warm. She could only pray to the Creator that the former Celestials would not let them down.

A sound to her left made her pivot and squint across the perimeter. It wasn't entirely invisible, this state-of-the-art protective barrier around them and between the dissident camps and her company, the Ghost Pack.

"It can't be you, but I think it is," a disembodied voice said.

Quinn thought it came from the dissident camp.

"Hello? Who's there? Are you talking to me?" She pulled her side arm even though she knew there was hardly any chance of it penetrating the perimeter shield.

"You wouldn't know, even if I said my name." The voice sounded young, but it wasn't that of a child. "I remember you though, whatever your name is. "I remember how you dragged me across the marketplace, making me drop all the dolls my mom made, and then everything went black. When I came to, I was in the back of a vehicle, and even though I never saw you again, I still remember."

Something icy encased Quinn's heart, and she pressed her hand against her sternum. She knew exactly what this person—a woman?—was talking about. The last of the roundups she had ever taken part in. She had belonged to another unit then, fourteen years ago, and had asked for a transfer to the northern part of the

Eastern Coastal City. She had heard they rarely had to round up children for "rescue camps," but as it turned out, they ended up being tasked with something a thousand times worse.

"I saw you. That red hair. Those eyes." A young woman entered the small clearing next to the joint perimeter. "You were a lot younger then, and I was a child. I was eight."

"How can you possibly remember me?" Quinn hated how frail her voice sounded. "You say you were a child."

"I was, but even if all the other fucking cloudheads are just a blur, you stood out." The young woman walked up to the perimeter but kept enough distance between them to not be zapped by the shields. "Red hair. Bright green eyes. Even your striking features could have become just another thing of the past that I can't remember, if it weren't for one thing." The woman paused, and Quinn's heart pounded so hard, it should have shattered against her ribs.

"What?" Quinn asked thickly, against her will.

The woman tilted her head, and her short, shaggy hair moved slightly in the wind. "You," she said, "were the only one that was crying."

About the Author

Gun Brooke, author of thirty-four novels, writes her stories surrounded by a loving family and two affectionate dogs. When she isn't writing her novels, she works on her arts and crafts, whenever possible—certain that practice pays off. She loves being creative, whether using conventional materials or digital art software.

Books Available from Bold Strokes Books

An Extraordinary Passion by Kit Meredith. An autistic podcaster must decide whether to take a chance on her polyamorous guest and indulge their shared passion, despite her history. (978-1-63679-679-6)

That's Amore! by Georgia Beers. The romantic city of Rome should inspire Lily's passion for writing, if she can look away from Marina Troiani, her witty, smart, and unassumingly beautiful Italian tour guide. (978-1-63679-841-7)

The Unexpected Heiress by Cassidy Crane. When a cynical opportunist meets a shy but spirited heiress, the last thing she plans is for her heart to get involved. (978-1-63679-833-2)

Through Sky and Stars by Tessa Croft. Can Val and Nicole's love cross space and time to change the fate of humanity? (978-1-63679-862-2)

Uncomplicate It by Kel McCord. When an office attraction threatens her career, Hollis Reed's carefully laid plans demand revision. (978-1-63679-864-6)

Vanguard by Gun Brooke. Beth Kelly, Subterranean freedom fighter, is in the crosshairs when she fights for her people and risks her heart for loving the exacting Celestial dissident leader, LaSierra Delmonte. (978-1-63679-818-9)

Wild Night Rising by Barbara Ann Wright. Riding Harleys instead of horses, the Wild Hunt of myth is once again unleashed upon the world. Their ousted leader and a fey cop must join forces to rein in the ride of terror. (978-1-63679-749-6)

Heart's Appraisal by Jo Hemmingwood. Andy and Hazel can't deny their attraction, but they'll never agree on the place they call home. (978-1-63679-856-1)

Behold My Heart by Ronica Black. Alora Anders is a highly successful artist who's losing her vision. Devastated, she hires Bodie Banks, a young struggling sculptor as a live-in assistant. Can Alora open her mind and her heart to accept Bodie into her life? (978-1-63679-810-3)

Fearless Hearts by Radclyffe. One wounded woman, one determined to protect her—and a summertime of risk, danger, and desire. (978-1-63679-837-0)

Forever Family by L.M. Rose. Two friends come together after tragedy to raise a baby, finding love along the way. (978-1-63679-868-4)

Stranger in the Sand by Renee Roman. Grace Langley is haunted by guilt. Fagan Shaw wishes she could remember her past. Will finding each other bring the closure they're looking for in order to have a brighter future? (978-1-63679-802-8)

The Nursing Home Hoax by Shelley Thrasher and Ann Faulkner. In this fresh take for grown-ups on the classic Nancy Drew series, crime-solving duo Taylor and Marilee investigate suspicious activity at a small East Texas nursing home. (978-1-63679-806-6)

The Rise and Fall of Conner Cody by Chelsey Lynford. A successful yet lonely Hollywood starlet must decide if she can let go of old wounds and accept a chance at family, friendship, and the love of a lifetime. (978-1-63679-739-7)

A Conflict of Interest by Morgan Adams. Tensions rise when a one-night stand becomes a major conflict of interest between an up-and-coming senior associate and a dedicated cardiac surgeon. (978-1-63679-870-7)

A Magnificent Disturbance by Lee Lynch. These everyday dykes and their friends will stop at nothing to see the women's clinic thrive and, in the process, their ideals, their wounds, and a steadfast allegiance to one another make them heroes. (978-1-63679-031-2)

A Marvelous Murder by David S. Pederson. When a hated director is found dead in his locked study, movie star Victor Marvel, his boyfriend Griff, and friend Eve seek to uncover what really happened to Orland Orcott. (978-1-63679-798-4)

Big Corpse on Campus by Karis Walsh. When University Police Officer Cappy Flannery investigates what looks like a clear-cut suicide, she discovers that the case—and her feelings for librarian Jazz—are more complicated than she expected. (978-1-63679-852-3)

Charity Case by Jean Copeland. Bad girl Lindsay Chase came home to Connecticut for a fresh start, but an old, risky habit provides the chance to save the day for her new love, Ellie. (978-1-63679-593-5)

Moments to Treasure by Ali Vali. Levi Montbard and Yasmine Hassani have found a vast Templar treasure, but there is much more to the story—and what is left to be found. (978-1-63679-473-0)

The Stolen Girl by Cari Hunter. Detective Inspector Jo Shaw is determined to prove she's fit for work after an injury that almost killed her, but a new case brings her up against people who will do anything to preserve their own interests, putting Jo—and those closest to her—directly in the line of fire. (978-1-63679-822-6)

Discovering Gold by Sam Ledel. In 1920s Colorado, a single mother and a rowdy cowgirl must set aside their fears and initial reservations about one another if they want to find love in the mining town each of them calls home. (978-1-63679-786-1)

Dream a Little Dream by Melissa Brayden. Savanna can't believe it when Dr. Kyle Remington, the woman who left her feeling like a fool, shows up in Dreamer's Bay. Life is too complicated for second chances. Or is it? (978-1-63679-839-4)

Emma by the Sea by Sarah G. Levine. A delightful modern-day romance inspired by Emma, one of Jane Austen's most beloved novels. (978-1-63679-879-0)

Goodbye, Hello by Heather K O'Malley. With so much time apart and the challenges of a long-distance relationship, Kelly and Teresa's second chance at love may end just as awkwardly as the first. (978-1-63679-790-8)

One Measure of Love by Annie McDonald. Vancouver's hit competitive cooking show Recipe for Success has begun filming its second season and two talented young chefs are desperate for more than a winning dish. (978-1-63679-827-1)

The Smallest Day by J.M. Redmann. The first bullet missed— can Micky Knight stop the second bullet from finding its target? (978-1-63679-854-7)

To Please Her by Elena Abbott. A spilled coffee leads Sabrina into a world of erotic BDSM that may just land her the love of her life. (978-1-63679-849-3)

Two Weddings and a Funeral by Claudia Parr. Stella and Theo have spent the last thirteen years pretending they can be just friends, but surely "just friends" don't make out every chance they get. (978-1-63679-820-2)

www.ingramcontent.com/pod-product-compliance
Lightning Source LLC
Chambersburg PA
CBHW021951010726
47494CB00003B/681